HER ARMS ROUNDED COLERAINE'S BROAD shoulders, one hand gripping his neck while the other sank into his gleaming black hair. He, in turn, crushed her against the length of his body so that their hips were joined and Lindsay's full, firm breasts seemed to scorch his chest through the thin fabric of their shirts.

She found herself loving the taste of Ryan's mouth, the texture of the curls at the nape of his neck, the pressure of his hard male body against her own, the warmth and the scent of his skin, and the sure touch of his fingers. For an instant, Lindsay reveled in Ryan Coleraine before it dawned on her that this was not the way she was supposed to feel. Panic struck like a slap in the face.

Ryan felt her stiffen and tremble simultaneously and, guessing the reason, released her. "Had enough?" he whispered hoarsely. . . .

Also by Cynthia Wright
Published by Ballantine Books:

A BATTLE FOR LOVE

CAROLINE

SILVER STORM

SPRING FIRES

TOUCH THE SUN

YOU, AND NO OTHER

SURRENDER
THE STARS

Cynthia Challed Wright

BALLANTINE BOOKS • NEW YORK

All rights reserved under International and Pan-American
Copyright Conventions. Published in the United States by
Ballantine Books, a division of Random House, Inc., New
York, and simultaneously in Canada by Random House of
Canada Limited, Toronto.

Library of Congress Catalog Card Number: 87-91477

ISBN 0-345-33484-1

Manufactured in the United States of America

First Edition: September 1987

FOR MARK CESA,
with my love

PROLOGUE

Philadelphia, Pennsylvania

April 7, 1814

A LUMINOUS FULL MOON SPILLED SILVERY LIGHT OVER the Georgian façade of Hampshire House and its vast lawns that were lavishly studded with beds of daffodils and hyacinths. Because Senator Lion Hampshire and his wife Meagan were in residence at their country estate south of Philadelphia, the villa was also lit from within, aglow with candlelight and convivial laughter.

Only one upstairs window still shone with light. Inside, Devon Raveneau sat at a pretty Queen Anne dressing table. After inserting an emerald comb into her strawberry-blond curls, which were swept up into a fashionable Grecian knot atop her head, she absently appraised her reflection.

"Are you ready to venture forth?" inquired her husband. Coming up behind her, he bent to kiss the curve of her neck.

"Yes, I suppose so. André, why do I have the feeling that there is more afoot here tonight than a simple supper among friends? It shouldn't seem odd that Caro and

1

Alec Beauvisage would write to us in Connecticut and
invite us to visit them in Philadelphia, or that Lion and
Meagan would travel up from Washington to see us and
arrange this lovely party, but it does. It's as if there's
something in the air, waiting to be said. Did you sense it
when you were around Alec and Lion today?''

Raveneau was loath to fuel his wife's uneasiness, even
though he, too, was aware of the undercurrents now that
the six of them were together at Hampshire House.
"*Chérie,* we should join the others. They've already
gone downstairs. If there's something that's waiting to
be said, perhaps we'll learn what it is this evening.''

She stood up and smoothed back his silvery hair.
"You're right, of course.''

In the hallway, they parted. André Raveneau went
down to join the two men he had known since the
Revolutionary War, before any of them had met their
wives. Devon walked toward the back stairway, where
she was met by tantalizing aromas of soup, salmon,
lamb, and tarts.

"Devon, is that you?'' Meagan Hampshire called up
to her. "I'm just checking to see that Bramble doesn't
overexert. Come and join us!''

She found Meagan and Caro at the bottom of the
stairs, and compliments were exchanged all around. All
three women were in their forties but retained a fresh,
intelligent vitality that made them seem more beautiful
with age. They remained petite and slim in the flattering
high-waisted fashions of the day, the soft tendrils that
brushed their creamy cheeks lending them a girlish charm.
Meagan's hair was ebony, Caro's honey-hued, and Devon's a rosy-gold; all three shades mixed with strands of
silver that gleamed in the lamplight.

The kitchen was huge, whitewashed, and dominated
by a scrubbed oaken table. Firelight not only bathed the
room but danced around a kettle of fragrant soup that
hung in the hearth. Bramble, a bent, sour-faced old

woman clad all in gray, was tasting her creation when the trio of females emerged from the stairway.

"Good evening, Bramble!" Meagan called.

The long wooden spoon clattered to the floor as the cook jumped, one hand pressed to her sinewy breast. "Have ye no thought for the heart of an old woman?" she scolded. "In future, don't be creeping up on me!"

"I'm sorry, Bramble, but—"

"I suppose ye mean to remind me that ye are mistress of this house and may come and go where ye like, but I don't mind repeating that I have a few rules of my own and if ye cannot abide by them, I vow I'll work elsewhere!"

"So you've been telling me for twenty-five years, dearest Bramble." Meagan's emerald eyes twinkled affectionately as she remembered the long-ago days when she, at seventeen, posed as a maid and had answered to Bramble. Later, Meagan had been appointed housekeeper, eventually becoming Lion's wife, but through it all and over these many years, Bramble had never quite forgotten the original arrangement between herself and her mistress. It amused Meagan to allow a measure of power to this dour old woman, knowing how much she enjoyed it. "Truly, I am contrite. Forgive me—and then tell me how our supper progresses."

"That's a foolish question! Ye should know well enough that my meals are always served at the scheduled hour!"

Devon and Caro exchanged glances as their younger friend crossed to the hearth and whispered, "Bramble, *you* should know well enough who is mistress in this house. Curb your tongue."

Seeking distraction, the two women across the kitchen exchanged news about their children. Caro told Devon that her son, Etienne, now thirty, was a major who was away in the war. He and his wife had a new baby daughter. Natalya, her elder daughter, was living in France with the family of Alec's brother, Nicholai, and had written her first novel. Kristin, the youngest, had been

engaged twice but now was in love with yet another
young man.

"Natalya is very independent and claims she doesn't
need a man to take care of her"—Caro sighed, smiling—
"while Kristin adores men but can't seem to make up
her mind. I've given up worrying about them. I'm certain that love will come to each of them when the time is
right. What of your children?"

Devon wore a rather bemused expression. "Mouette
has been married for several years and has given us two
grandsons, but they live in London so the war has kept
us apart these past few years. Nathan is captain of one
of André's ships and is away in the West Indies now.
Lindsay, our baby, is nearly twenty. She's the one I
worry about. . . ."

"Is she fickle, like Kristin?"

Devon smiled. "No. Lindsay is . . . an original. She is
teaching school in Pettipauge, since the traditional male
schoolmaster is off in the war. She claims that she's in
her element, spending all her time with books and lessons. She longs to be different from the rest of the
Raveneaus, who, as you know, are adventurous to an
extreme. Lindsay came along late, when Nathan was
seven and we didn't really plan to have more children.
There are moments when I think she actually is different
from the rest of the family, but more often I suspect that
she decided, at some point, what sort of person she
wanted to be and has been trying ever since to fit herself
into that mold."

"Take heart. She's still young, and no doubt time and
experience will help Lindsay to grow."

"I hope, with all my heart, that you're right. She's a
lovely young woman and I would hate to think that she's
missing out on life because of some stubborn course she
has set for herself."

Meagan returned to join them, laughing. "Talking about
Lindsay, hmm? Well, if she's stubborn, it's no more
than you should expect, given her parentage! Weren't

you the young lady who had to be chased down by a privateer before you'd yield to André's charms?''

Devon had to smile. ''Something like that . . .''

The two kitchen servants returned from setting the table and Bramble cleared her throat.

''I perceive that we are in the way,'' Meagan remarked. ''Let's roust the men from the study and think about supper.''

The meal was splendid. Pea soup was followed by crimped salmon with sauce and butter, accompanied by a fine white Bordeaux wine.

Animated conversation swirled around Devon. It centered on Lion Hampshire and his knowledge of the war's progress, but, as the entrée of fricandeau of veal was served, she found her attention wandering.

Twists of fate had brought each of these three couples together. Gazing around the dining room, Devon thought of the tale she'd heard Meagan tell about how she had helped Lion decorate this house when another woman had been meant to come here as his wife. Like the rest of Hampshire House, it had changed little over the years, as if in memory of Lion and Meagan's beginning. Lion had been a sea captain who had made many voyages to China when trade had just opened up there. This dining room was lined with wallpaper that featured bamboo, tree peonies, and butterflies against a soft green background. The Ch'ien Lung rug was in jade tones, and the Chinese Chippendale furniture was laced with delicate fretwork and latticework. Porcelains and treasures from the Orient lined the breakfront shelves. Candles on the table and in sconces along the walls accentuated not only the room's elegant warmth, but also the love between Lion and Meagan Hampshire as their eyes met in a shared moment of pleasure.

Devon sighed inwardly, wondering if her daughter Lindsay would ever know the kind of love enjoyed by

the couples in this room. The selection of eligible men in
Pettipauge, Connecticut, was most discouraging. True,
nearly every male near Lindsay's age was off in the war,
but the memory of them, and the possibility that the
conflict might end soon, returning them to Pettipauge,
did little to cheer Devon. There wasn't a man in their
large circle of acquaintances whom she considered worthy of her daughter—and Lindsay herself didn't seem to
care one way or the other.

Over a magnificent roast forequarter of lamb with
baby carrots and new potatoes, Devon made an effort to
enter into the conversation. André had already given her
a questioning look from his place across the table, and
as usual she felt that he could read her mind. "Stop
worrying about Lindsay and enjoy yourself!" his steely
eyes seemed to say. The force of his love never failed to
lighten her heart, and now she turned to Meagan, inquiring about the Hampshire triplets.

Meagan was happy to relate the news about her twenty-
year-old offspring. Benjamin had left Georgetown University to join the navy, while Michael had been exploring
the frontier in Michigan before the war broke out. A
wound suffered at Niagara kept him safe for the time
being. "Only a war could prompt a mother to feel relief
over her child's injury," she reflected dryly, then smiled.
"Susan, on the other hand, is both safe and healthy! She
would be with us tonight if not for a previous engagement in Philadelphia."

Lion laughed and ran a hand through his gold-and-
silver hair. "Daughters! Susie will be the death of me
yet! It seems that every swain in both Washington and
Philadelphia is in pursuit of her, and yet she refuses to
fall in love. I have welcomed at least fifty ardent, drool-
ing young pups into the house and suffered their company through interminable meals, only to have Susie
invariably remark a few days later, 'Oh, Martin? Percival?
Archibald? Don't be silly, Daddy. Did you really think
he suited me?' " Hampshire laughed, feigning aggrava-

tion, and Alec and André entered into the good-natured discussion with their own horror stories about daughters and their suitors.

Rhubarb tarts and pretty meringues were served as the conversation turned to André's exploits as a privateer captain, the many ships he currently owned, and the crimp put in his livelihood by the British blockade of Long Island Sound.

"Are your ships able to get out at all?" Alec asked casually.

Raveneau smiled, arching a brow as he finished his tart. "*Bien sûr, mon ami!* My son, Nathan, is in the West Indies as we speak, and I have one other captain who can elude any blockade. The war hasn't hampered Ryan Coleraine!"

"Captain Coleraine reminds me of you thirty-five years ago," Devon remarked.

Beauvisage and Hampshire exchanged meaningful glances while, as if on cue, Meagan said, "Lion, why don't you take the men into the library for brandy?"

When they were gone, she rang for sherry and told the maid to leave the bottle. Lifting her glass, Meagan's green eyes met those of her friends. "I've never been one to encourage the idea of men leaving the women so that they can engage in 'serious' conversation. However" —she sighed, looking at Devon—"this evening may be an exception."

Firelight played off the brandy swirling in the snifter that Lion Hampshire turned unconsciously with agile fingers. Across from him, André and Alec sat in wing chairs, sipping their brandy while contemplating the fire and, from time to time, each other. Finally, Raveneau drew a slim cigar from his breast pocket. Standing, he lit it with a candle that guttered low on Lion's desk, then directed a stare at his host.

"Senator, is there something on your mind?"

Lion smiled and cleared his throat. "I've been rude. Accept my apologies. I've been searching for the right words, but I suppose that the best thing to do is just get on with it. The fact is, Raveneau, President Madison has asked me to speak to you. Perhaps you'd better sit down."

"Shall I leave you two?" Alec asked.

"No, no, that's not necessary. In fact, the president may be interested in your point of view, Beauvisage, if this discussion turns into an argument. He trusts your judgment."

Raveneau lowered his tall body into the chair and rubbed his jaw. "*Eh bien,* senator. Having aroused my curiosity, I beg you to proceed!"

"All right. Hear me out while I outline President Madison's proposal. At that point, I'll answer your questions and provide further details." Lion took a long sip of brandy, then began, "As you are doubtless aware, the United States has no ambassador in residence in London because of the war. Furthermore, the peace commission that is convening in Ghent, in the Austrian Netherlands, commands the attention of prominent Americans in Europe who might otherwise lend their eyes and ears to England's affairs. President Madison has made the peace negotiations a priority by appointing John Quincy Adams, James Bayard, Jonathan Russell, and Albert Gallatin to the commission. And, of course, Henry Clay sailed from America three months ago to join them."

"It does look promising," Raveneau agreed, "what with Admiral Lord Gambier, Henry Goldbrun, and William Adams representing Great Britain. All able and, hopefully, wise men."

Alec Beauvisage nodded. "Goldbrun has been parliamentary under-secretary of state for war and the colonies, hasn't he? At least Castlereagh's chosen delegates for their knowledge rather than their rank."

"The president tells me that this Peace Commission was masterminded by Lord Castlereagh," Lion said.

"He maintained that maritime rights were too important to be negotiated by neutral third parties."

"And where do I fit into all of this?" inquired André, his gray eyes deceptively lazy.

The golden-haired senator glanced at the fire, then met Raveneau's gaze. "President Madison wants an American whom we know and trust to live in London until the war is over. Someone who would also be trusted by the British, accepted in the highest social circles—"

"Are you asking me to *spy*?"

"Well, that's putting a rather sharp edge on it, Raveneau! It's simply that we don't know what's being thought and said among the powers that be in London because there's no embassy. Some of the British military maneuvers are cause for deep concern on the part of our government. Believe me, I *know*! I'm part of that government. Admiral Cockburn's vicious raids up and down the coast, for example. Who's behind those decisions and what mental climate fostered them? It's quite possible that someone in London is passing American secrets; information that may not even be accurate! President Madison wants to know the truth, especially as worry mounts that the British may launch an all-out attack against Washington, D.C. It's certainly not the sort of thing they've done before, but lately we've come to realize that we can't expect them to conform to past rules of military etiquette. With their full troops freed now that the war with Napoleon is ending in Europe, it's frightening to contemplate what could happen next." Lion paused to sip his brandy while silence saturated the air. "It's hard to say just how effective you might be in London until you are actually there and able to take stock. The president is very hopeful, though. And it's not as if your ships can't spare you, Raveneau. You said yourself that only two of your captains have been able to penetrate the blockades."

Beauvisage couldn't resist joining the discussion. "I can certainly understand why President Madison thought

of you, André. You're French born, and even though
you fought during the Revolution, you did it as a renegade
privateer captain rather than as a member of the United
States Navy. You and Devon have kept a home in
London for over twenty-five years and are welcome
even at the Prince Regent's Carlton House. Your daughter, Mouette, is married to an Englishman and lives in
London. I suspect that the British, hearing your French
accent yet knowing you have homes in both America
and England, think of you as neutral.''

Lion nodded. ''That's exactly right, Alec.'' He looked
to Reveneau then, his blue gaze unwavering. ''There's
also the matter of your character, André. You're perceived as being dispassionately fair.''

''You mean that the English wouldn't take me for a
spy?'' Raveneau retorted sarcastically.

''I'd appreciate it if you would refrain from using that
word. We're not even certain whether there is anything
to spy *on* yet! The president simply wants you to evalu-
ate the situation in London, keep your eyes and ears
open, and report to him from time to time.'' Lion smiled
soothingly. ''Perhaps nothing is amiss after all. Why not
think of yourself as an ambassador of goodwill! I understand that Devon is extremely popular with the London
ton, and we're counting on her and the rest of your
family to remind the English that Americans do have
redeeming qualities.''

''I see. You want my wife and children to spy, too!''
Raveneau arched a silvery brow at his host. ''You'd
have been wise to present this scheme to Devon rather
than me, senator. She'd find the notion of spying for her
country quite thrilling!''

Lion shifted uneasily in his chair, resisting the impulse
to flinch each time Raveneau said ''spy.''

''I must say,'' André went on, ''I'm impressed with
the careful consideration you and President Madison
have given this plan, but I'm wondering why it never
occurred to you that I am a trifle *old* to gain the confi-

dence of every influential man in London. Many of them are young enough to be my sons and would be unlikely to socialize with an aging French-born American—let alone take me into their confidence."

Hampshire smiled reluctantly. "You anticipate me, my friend. The president desires that you include your son Nathan when your family travels to England. Those of us who have met him are well aware that he is intelligent, charming, and handsome enough to quickly win a place in London society."

Raveneau drew on his cigar, then slowly exhaled. "As much as it pains me to thwart your plans, I must remind you that Nathan is in the West Indies. He isn't due back until summer."

Lion realized that Raveneau would have been delighted to *completely* thwart the plans that were being forced on him so systematically. He wasn't the sort of man who took orders well, especially at his age, and Lion empathized with him. However, he also knew that André Raveneau was reasonable, brave, and patriotic. He felt certain that his friend, if left alone to consider, would come around and do the president's bidding wholeheartedly.

"I'm sorry that Nathan isn't available," Lion said quietly. "It's imperative that you have a socially active son while you are there." He paused. "What about the other captain you mentioned? Coleraine? Didn't Devon say that he's much like you?"

This was too much for Raveneau. He laughed acidly and cried, "*Mon dieu,* are you crazed, first asking me to spy and then telling me that I should ask someone to masquerade as my only son? What makes you think that I would consider such lunacy?"

Senator Hampshire glanced helplessly at Beauvisage, then met the stormy gray eyes of André Raveneau. "There's no one else the president will consider for this mission."

"That's ridiculous! There are plenty of Americans

who are at home in London society. Choose some other family!''

''I'm afraid that's out of the question,'' Lion said with a sigh. ''It's true, there are other men who might be able to play the role I've described in London, but none of them could get there! We haven't forgotten the spectacular success you enjoyed as a privateer captain during the Revolution, André. You are the only eligible candidate who can slip past the British blockades along America's coastline!''

Raveneau sighed. ''I'll have to think about it. There's so much to consider! Ryan Coleraine is at sea now, and though he's due back any day, there's no telling whether he'll return safely. Besides, he might laugh in my face if I present this insane plan to him. The man was raised in Ireland and may still be loyal to Great Britain under the surface. I don't even know him that well. He's scarcely ever in port!'' His sigh deepened as his thoughts turned to Lindsay. ''And my daughter . . . Lindsay is a schoolmistress who prefers books to society. I cannot begin to imagine her among the ton at London's assemblies and routs. She's very stubborn about living by her own rules.''

''Wouldn't Lindsay want to help her country if she could?'' Lion wondered softly.

Raveneau opened his mouth, waiting for his brain to furnish a rebuttal, but sighed again instead. ''I'll make no promises tonight. Give me a few days to consider.''

''There's very little time . . .''

''I said I'll *think* about it! Now, is there any more of that brandy?''

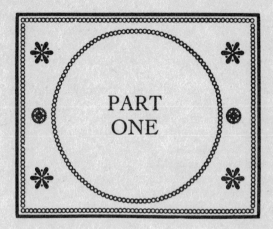

PART
ONE

Take heed of loving me.

—JOHN DONNE (1572–1631)

CHAPTER
1

Pettipauge, Connecticut
April 7–8, 1814

Descending the *Chimera*'s gangplank, Ryan Coleraine set foot on American soil for the first time in one hundred days and smiled. Behind him, the privateer he commanded swayed at anchor alongside other proud ships lining the Point. Painted pale yellow, with a blue stripe between the wales, the sleek brigantine basked in the spring sunlight as sailors scurried over her decks and up the ratlines, unloading cargo and securing the lines.

"Are you off to the Griswold Inn for a drink, Captain?" inquired Drew, the *Chimera*'s first mate, as he set a crate of rum on the wharf.

Coleraine gazed distractedly out over the glittering Connecticut River. "Not just yet. I have to report to Captain Raveneau first on the success of our voyage." He gave the young man a smile then. "When you and the others are finished here, come along to the Gris and I'll buy you all a round."

"Thank you, sir! I can taste it already!"

Ryan's progress up Main Street was slow as various

15

residents of Pettipauge stopped to welcome him home. The greeting jarred a bit, for Coleraine was there so little that he'd never felt that this was his home. He was more at ease on board the *Chimera,* surrounded by a sweep of ocean, than here on this street lined with clean white houses and shops, budding oaks and rows of sunny daffodils.

Young women turned to stare as the privateer captain passed by, but he was too preoccupied to notice. At thirty-one, Ryan Coleraine was shockingly attractive. Tall, lean, and strong, he was blessed with shining, crisp black hair that curled against the back of his neck, brilliant blue eyes, chiseled features that were somehow accentuated by his trim beard, and a devastating smile. Today he wore a white shirt, a simple, snowy cravat, a blue-gray waistcoat with a thin charcoal stripe, gray breeches that skimmed his long, hard thighs, and black knee boots. In his left hand, he casually held a midnight-blue coat.

Approaching the Raveneau house, he considered what he wished to say to the man who had been his mentor since his arrival in Pettipauge nine years ago. Ryan had worked long and hard, earning Raveneau's trust and saving his money. Now he was ready to strike out on his own. He wanted to buy the *Chimera,* which he had designed and christened himself. How would Raveneau react?

The large Georgian house owned by the Raveneau family had been built on the right side of Main Street within sight of the ship-lined Point. Painted a warm, light yellow, in contrast to its white neighbors, the home seemed to exude contentment. Square boxwood hedges marked the boundaries of the corner yard, while budding elms arched before beds of jewellike crocus and narcissus. Ryan thought that the house's windows made the inviting picture complete: green shutters framed open sashes and clean, fluttering curtains. It was hard for him to believe that when Raveneau was Coleraine's age, he, too, had called the sea his home and had been a confirmed rogue and womanizer.

Able Barker, the family's tall, rawboned butler, answered Ryan's knock at the door and informed him that the Raveneaus were away in Philadelphia and that he wasn't certain when they'd return. Then, seeing the younger man's disappointment, he added, "I'll wager that Miss Lindsay would know. Why don't you stop by the schoolhouse and ask her?"

"Miss Lindsay?"

"Captain Raveneau's daughter. She's been the schoolmistress since Ethan Painter went off to war. Doing a fine job of it, too. The schoolhouse is up on Pound Hill. Think you can find it?"

"I'll manage. Thank you, Able."

"Captain, how did you fare at sea?"

Coleraine's grin flashed white. "I'd say we did rather well. We took eleven prizes and our hold is well packed with rum, sugar, brandy, wine, dry goods, iron, fish, and fruit. Best of all, we lost not one man."

"Congratulations, sir! Just the sort of news Pettipauge needs to hear."

Back on Main Street, Ryan searched his memory. He couldn't recall ever meeting this mysterious daughter, but then he usually saw André Raveneau in the latter's office on the Point. Ryan vaguely remembered hearing that the attractive, adventurous Raveneaus had somehow produced a serious, bookish daughter, but he'd laughed at the time, dismissing the idea.

The handsome, three-story, green-shuttered Griswold Inn loomed up to his right, its open doors beckoning him to enter. Ryan longed to relax inside with his friends, to prop his booted feet on a scarred table and drink a tankard of ale, but first he had to pay a tiresome visit to Pettipauge's schoolhouse.

"I wish you would let me finish this tonight," complained Betsy Urquhart. She sat alone, surrounded by empty desks, and gazed mournfully at the figure sorting papers at the front of the schoolroom.

"If you had written your theme last night, as instructed, you wouldn't be here now," her teacher replied without looking up.

"*King Lear* is so tedious." She pouted. "Besides, I thought you were my friend, Lindsay!"

"When we are in this room, I am your teacher and you must address me accordingly. Now, finish your theme so that we may both go home!"

Betsy wrote laboriously for several minutes, then said, "One would never guess that you are just two years older than I am—or that you come from such a dashing, adventurous family. I don't understand how you can be so dull—"

"I am not dull!" Lindsay answered sharply. "Simply because my relatives are afflicted with wanderlust, that does not make me dull. I choose to remain on land and pursue more serious endeavors. I enjoy teaching. Imparting knowledge to others is a great source of satisfaction to me."

"Do you never long for even a bit of adventure?" Betsy eyed her speculatively. "Or . . . romance? Mary Pratt told me that the *Chimera* is supposed to dock today. She's practically the only ship that has been able to elude that blockade of the sound, but considering her captain, it's no surprise." She paused to sigh dreamily. "I was planning to walk to the Point after school in hopes of seeing him. Surely even *you* must grow weak at the thought of Ryan Coleraine! I've never seen a handsomer man. . . ."

"Don't be absurd. In the first place, the *Chimera* is not the first privateer to achieve such feats. My father was just as successful during the Revolution, and, as you know, Papa had the *Chimera* built, so your precious Ryan Coleraine is in his employ!"

Betsy tossed her shining brown curls impatiently. "You

haven't answered my question! Don't you find Captain Coleraine attractive?''

"We've never met, but from what I've seen, the answer is no." Lindsay shuffled her papers nervously. "His looks don't appeal to me. I prefer fair men. Aside from that, Captain Coleraine's character is, in my opinion, repugnant."

"Repugnant?" Betsy was unfamiliar with the word but sensed its meaning. "How can you say such a thing?"

"He's an uneducated, cocky, ill-mannered rogue," Lindsay stated with finality. "Take my advice and stay away from men of his ilk. They lack scruples and take pleasure in ruining the reputations of gullible females like you."

From the doorway, a male voice spoke. "Am I to infer that you don't approve of me, Miss Raveneau?"

Startled, Lindsay spun around to find Ryan Coleraine leaning against the door frame, one eyebrow arched. A smile of cynical amusement played over his mouth.

"I—I—" she stammered. Hearing Betsy's muffled giggle, she looked in her direction. "You may go now, Elizabeth."

"But what about my theme? I'm not finished yet!"

"You may finish it tonight."

As the teacher and pupil continued to argue, Coleraine's dark blue eyes wandered over Lindsay Raveneau. He was surprised to discover that she was beautiful, perhaps even more beautiful than her mother. She was about twenty and taller than Devon Raveneau. Even though Lindsay wore a demure, cream-colored chemise frock and a cashmere shawl, Ryan's practiced eyes detected a lithe, long-legged body with a narrow waist and high, perfect breasts. Lindsay's hair was the same amazing color as her mother's, a rosy-gold shade of strawberry blond, and she wore it in a fashionable Grecian knot high atop her head, with a profusion of soft curls escaping to frame her lovely, intelligent countenance.

"Good-bye, Captain Coleraine," Betsy said as she passed him in the doorway.

Ryan looked at Lindsay. "Dare I enter? I can assure you that I have come not to ruin your reputation but to inquire after your father."

"Please, come in. I apologize for the things you heard me say about you, but you should have made your presence known instead of eavesdropping."

Ryan approached her desk, thinking that he had never met a young lady with so cool and confident a gaze. Lindsay's eyes were striking: thick-lashed and the color of smoke. Her complexion was creamy, with smudges of pink accentuating her cheekbones, and below a delicate nose reposed a lush mouth with a frankly sensual lower lip. Perhaps there was hope for this bluestocking after all, he thought as his eyes lingered there, then rose to meet her questioning gaze.

"My father is in Philadelphia, Captain Coleraine."

"So I heard. It's a pleasure to meet you at last, Miss Raveneau." Ryan extended a strong, tanned hand and gently clasped her slim fingers. "I'm sorry that you're unable to say the same."

Sensing his amusement, Lindsay drew her hand away and strove to retain her composure. What a humiliating situation this was! "It's been a long day, Captain Coleraine, and I may have spoken rashly. Again, I beg your pardon. Now, if you don't mind, I would like to finish my work here. What can I do for you?"

Her coolness was contagious. "I am anxious to see your father. Able Barker thought that you might know when he's returning to Pettipauge."

"Within the week. I'm sorry that I can't give you an exact date."

Coleraine shrugged, frustration further darkening his mood. "Well, then, I suppose I'll just have to wait. I appreciate your speaking to me, Miss Raveneau. I know it can't have been easy." He gave her a remote, polite smile and turned toward the schoolhouse doorway. "Good afternoon."

When his hand touched the latch, Lindsay called, "Wait! There's something I've always wanted to know. Will you tell me how you chose the *Chimera*'s name? I was surprised when Papa told me that you had christened her."

He glanced back over one broad shoulder. "I liked the image of a she-monster with a serpent's tail, a goat's body, and a lion's head spitting flames. I think of my ship like the chimera from Greek mythology: a magical creature with the ability to overcome all obstacles."

Lindsay lifted her chin slightly. "I wouldn't have expected you to be a student of Greek mythology, Captain Coleraine."

He laughed shortly. "Believe it or not, Miss Raveneau, I don't spend *every* spare moment seducing unsuspecting young females!"

The door closed behind him and Lindsay found herself alone in the schoolroom, muttering rude rejoinders that she was certain she'd never have an opportunity to employ.

Misty clouds veiled the luminous, perfect crescent moon that hung suspended in a black sky. Lindsay knew that midnight had passed, yet she continued to sit at her window, gazing down at Main Street. At one end, ships, including the imposing *Chimera,* swayed at anchor along the Point, while at the other end, Main Street was bordered with clean white houses that shaded upward into Pound Hill.

The village was quiet now except for an occasional sailor or two emerging from the Griswold Inn. Lindsay guessed they must be from the *Chimera,* still celebrating their sea triumphs. Able Barker had said earlier in the evening that rumor had it the *Chimera* would head a fleet of men-of-war from Pettipauge that would slip into the sound in an effort to break the British blockade near New London. Able had marveled, "What an honor for Captain Coleraine! Your father certainly knew what he was doing when he gave that Irishman command of the *Chimera!*"

Able's wife, Cassie, was the family's housekeeper. Still pretty and buxom at fifty, she never missed an opportunity to tease her earnest husband. Lindsay sighed now, remembering how Cassie's eyes had twinkled as she rejoined, "I think the women of Pettipauge have benefited most! Ah, but it's pure pleasure to behold Ryan Coleraine! How I hope that Lindsay's parents invite him to supper when they return from Philadelphia!"

It was certainly a strong possibility, Lindsay thought, propping an elbow on the windowsill and resting her chin on her hand. She was unnerved to realize how much time she had spent this evening reviewing her meeting with Ryan Coleraine—and unconsciously spinning fantasies for the visit he would doubtless pay to her home after her parents returned. She tried to give herself the same lecture she'd delivered to Elizabeth Urquhart about the foolishness of mooning over a rake like Coleraine. Still . . . when he'd smiled at her with those dazzling blue eyes, female instincts Lindsay hadn't known she possessed had kindled deep inside of her. The mere thought of him sent a current of inexplicable exhilaration through her heart, while her mind shouted, "Danger! Beware! Keep Away!"

I have to get some sleep, Lindsay thought. She was just about to turn from the window when she caught sight of a tall, broad-shouldered, lean-hipped figure silhouetted in moonlight on the street below. Lindsay didn't need to see the man's face to know that it was Ryan Coleraine. Perhaps it was the way he cocked his head ever so slightly to the right before bending to kiss the woman he held in his arms. Lindsay couldn't identify her and realized that she didn't want to. The embrace was continuing as Lindsay drew her curtains closed and turned toward the bed, her cheeks burning.

In bed, she stared at the snowy curve of the canopy and thought, I was right the first time. The man's a *tomcat*. He'd turn his charm on for anything that moves and wears skirts. Thank God I came to my senses and took his measure before I did something incredibly foolish!

Yanking off his boots in total darkness, Ryan Coleraine supposed that the hour of three must be at hand. Certainly it was the middle of the night and he was a fool to be awake. Harvey, his literate steward, would be shaking him at dawn, waving coffee under his nose and urging him to eat the plate of scones, kippers, and eggs he specially prepared for his Irish master.

With a moan, Ryan threw himself down on his moonlit bunk. Muscles flexed over his hard, tapering chest as he crossed both arms over his eyes, too tired even to remove the ever-present books that poked his side and the sole of his left foot.

The woman's scent lingered on his skin. Frowning, Coleraine removed his arms from the vicinity of his face. He wasn't proud of what he'd done tonight; he wasn't even certain of the woman's name. Kathryn? Kathleen? They'd just met that evening. Her husband had been killed at Fort Erie and she'd been alone ever since. Ryan supposed that Kathryn (Kathleen?) and he had come together out of mutual need, and the woman was certainly an adult, but he'd seen the familiar softening in her eyes when she looked at him, heard the note of joy in her voice, and, as always, he felt unsettling twinges of guilt. Now it would be necessary to avoid her, for Ryan certainly had no intention of using the woman on a regular basis. If his mother were still alive, she'd label him a sinner, but that wasn't quite true. At least he told himself so late at night when sleep wouldn't come. Ryan never took a woman who wasn't willing, and he backed away instantly if he sensed that she hoped for love. He hadn't been raised to break women's hearts, but at the same time he had no wish to marry and believed celibacy a sacrifice for saints. Nights with women like Kathryn (Kathleen?) were inevitable.

Sighing, Ryan ran long fingers through his hair and flipped onto his stomach. When he closed his eyes again, he saw Lindsay Raveneau: a shaft of sunlight on her strawberry-blond curls, color suffusing her fair cheeks, a glint of fire in her rare, smoky eyes. He wondered what her smile would be like, then decided it was better that he didn't know. Miss Raveneau would be a female to avoid even if her father weren't the owner of Ryan's ship.

A sudden instinct caused him to end his fantasy abruptly, then rise to look through the transom at the far end of the cabin. Ryan couldn't see anything, but the slight shifting of the *Chimera* told him that there were boats on the river.

"Captain!" Harvey burst in, his eyes blazing in the moonlight. With his usual flair for the dramatic, he cried, "The British have arrived under the cover of darkness to deal a fatal blow to all Pettipauge's ships!"

Coleraine pulled on his boots, then followed his bounding steward up through the hatch onto the gun deck. Not far in the distance, chill winds whipped whitecaps on the dark waters around several double-banked, eight-oared boats that were crowded with red-uniformed soldiers. Obviously, the British had left their larger ships in the sound and rowed the five miles to Pettipauge, but Ryan saw that they had come prepared. His sharp eyes discerned nine- and twelve-pound cannonades, boarding pikes, bayonets, and other sundry equipment necessary for naval attack. Plus, there were torches, already being lit.

"My God, they mean to burn us all out of the water!" he whispered hoarsely.

"So it would seem, sir," Harvey agreed in mournful tones.

The rest of the crew was struggling up on deck, bleary-eyed from the night's celebrations. Coleraine's heart thudded as he realized how many were absent. It was his own fault. He'd been hard on them at sea and they'd performed beautifully. Today, when the officers and crew had come together in the Griswold Inn's taproom, hoisting frothy mugs of ale, their benevolent Captain Coleraine had granted a night's leave to anyone who wished it. It seemed that more than half the crew had accepted the offer, including his first lieutenant.

Chaos seemed to erupt around the *Chimera*. Men were barreling down Main Street and lining up along the Point, muskets in hand. Ryan felt as if he were having a bizarre dream as he watched the villagers load their one viable weapon, a four-pound cannon.

Meanwhile, flames shot up from the vessel that was under construction next to the *Chimera*. The British were returning Pettipauge's attack with their own cannonades, and British marines lined up along the barges to deliver a volley of musket fire.

"Captain, what shall we do?" cried Drew, the *Chimera*'s first mate.

Ryan leaned against the main mast and smiled crookedly. "There isn't a thing anyone can do. We're at anchor; we can't position ourselves to return fire, and you know it. They're prepared and we aren't." It galled him to admit defeat without a struggle, but he was a pragmatist. He'd never attacked without knowing that the odds were in his favor and thus had never lost. Ryan knew every member of his crew and he wasn't prepared to see even one killed for a futile point of pride.

The cannon fire had come to a stop on the Point. The men, realizing that it was hopeless, laid down their muskets to indicate that they would offer no further resistance. Even from a distance, Ryan could see the burning frustration in their eyes.

"Captain, look!" Drew exclaimed at his shoulder.

Coleraine glanced back, then followed his first mate's

pointing finger to the flames that were spreading over the deck of the nearly completed ship next to the *Chimera*. It had promised to be André Raveneau's finest accomplishment, a privateer that Ryan had been forced to admit would surpass even his own sleek and beautiful vessel.

"I know, Drew, it's a damned shame, but you may as well brace yourself. I fear we're destined to lose the *Chimera* as well—and every other ship at anchor in Pettipauge."

"That's not what I mean! Look, near the stern! There's a boy trying to douse the fires!"

Ryan surveyed the neighboring craft through his brass telescope. Drew was right. A boy was crouching on the quarterdeck, heaving a wooden bucket of water into the flames on the gun deck below. He wore a sailor's knit cap pulled low, but coppery curls escaped from the sides, and there was something about the profile of the boy's face and the shape of his legs and hips that made Ryan's insides knot with foreboding.

Turning to the first mate, he said, "I'm going to remove that boy from the ship. I ought to be all right alone but stand by to assist me."

There was a momentary lull in other activity as the British organized for the row to shore. Grimly, Ryan sprinted down the *Chimera*'s gangplank and boarded the adjoining vessel. Through the billowing smoke and leaping flames, he discerned the slight figure of the ship's would-be savior coming toward him.

"Come on! Are you trying to kill yourself?"

The boy was choking on the smoke and had one arm over his eyes as he staggered forward with the cumbersome bucket. "Can't let it burn!" he croaked.

Ryan grasped the thin arm. "You're coming with me!" His own eyes burned from the smoke and he could barely make out the boy's face.

"Let *go*!" Fiercely, the boy wrenched free and, pulling off his coat, began batting the spreading flames. The coat caught fire, sending orange flames licking toward the boy's pale, sooty face. Just then a steely arm came around his midsection, hoisting him into the air. "Let me be!" he shrieked.

"I have no intention of watching you burn to death, you little fool," Coleraine ground out, hoisting the slim form over his shoulder and fighting his way through the flames and smoke toward the gangplank. His struggle was complicated by the flailing legs of his captive and the fists that rained ineffectual blows against his back. "Stop that, you hellion, before I toss you in the river and let the British fish you out!"

"They couldn't be worse villains than you!" came the furious reply.

Getting back to the *Chimera* was an ordeal, but finally Ryan was back on his own quarterdeck. Harvey and Drew stepped forward to relieve him of his burden. The boy continued to struggle wildly against the restraining grips on each arm while Ryan rubbed his eyes and sighed. Finally, with slow deliberation, he reached out and removed the knit cap, freeing cascades of luxuriant golden-rose curls.

"I feared as much," he murmured, arching a brow. "Miss Raveneau, do you really think it safe to venture out of the house so late at night? I doubt that your parents would approve."

CHAPTER
2

April 8, 1814

"**K**INDLY TELL YOUR HENCHMEN TO LOOSE ME!" LIND-
say cried angrily. Drew and Harvey were already back-
ing away from her, staring in consternation. When their
captain cocked his head slightly to one side, they were
glad to remove themselves from the confrontation.

"I would like a word with you in private," Ryan told
her coolly, his eyes sweeping Lindsay's male garb, which
did little to conceal the feminine curves of her body.

"You have no right!" she protested, even as his fingers closed around her elbow and he masterfully steered
her toward the hatch.

"I think your father would disagree, Miss Raveneau."

Realizing that she had little choice, Lindsay saved her
tirade for the privacy of the captain's cabin. Ryan said
nothing as he guided her along the narrow gangway,
pausing only once to pluck from the bulkhead a lantern
that provided weak, flickering light once they reached
his darkened cabin.

"I would offer you a glass of sherry, but somehow

this occasion doesn't seem to call for a display of manners," he remarked sardonically, setting the lantern on the table next to them.

"I seriously doubt that you have manners to display, Captain Coleraine!" Lindsay shot back. "However, I did not allow myself to be dragged down here to discuss your lack of breeding. How dare you interfere in my efforts to save Papa's ship?"

Ryan's Irish temper flared brighter, but he clenched his teeth in an effort to hold it in check. "My dear Miss Raveneau, I have neither the time nor the inclination to engage in an argument with you. Let me say simply that I feel certain your father would be the first person to thank me for removing his daughter from a situation that was not only life-threatening but incredibly foolhardy and—"

"And *what*?"

"Forget it."

"I see. You are not only ill-mannered but also too cowardly to say what you think."

"Oh, Miss Raveneau, believe me, it is an exercise of will for me *not* to say *exactly* what I think of your stupid behavior!"

Lindsay knew a powerful urge to slap his bearded face. "Stupid! *Stupid?* How dare you? I was only trying to protect my father's property, and if you were half the man you pretend to be, you'd have saved me the trouble instead of standing by like a half-wit while those redcoats maneuvered to destroy every Raveneau ship in the harbor!"

His hand caught her forearm, and blue eyes blazed down at Lindsay. "What do you suppose would have happened if I trotted over to join you in throwing buckets of water on that fire? If, between us, we had even succeeded in putting it out? Would the British have thrown up their hands and given up?" Ryan laughed harshly. "Ridiculous. They'd have simply removed us from the ship, quite possibly by killing us, and torched it all over again. The unfortunate truth is that there isn't a single defense anyone can wage tonight. The British have planned and executed a successful sneak attack, the aim of which is to destroy every ship at the Point. A girl dressed in breeches with a few buckets of water could not deter them.''

"You had no right to interfere!" Lindsay cried in frustration. "I refuse to play the coward and surrender! At least we could fight back!"

"I can see that you're in no mood to listen to reason.'' Ryan started to turn away, then paused to stare down at her, his eyes softening. "It's certainly hard to believe that the proper schoolmistress I met this afternoon could have been transformed within hours into a raving, bloodthirsty rebel clad in dirty breeches!''

His amusement made Lindsay burn with hatred. "I'm not raving—and these breeches were clean! They're my brother's. And—where are you going?"

"I'd love to continue this riveting conversation, Miss Raveneau, but duty calls.'' He was walking toward the door.

"But what about me?"

"I think you'd better stay down here until we're ready to leave the ship. For your own safety, of course.''

Rushing forward, Lindsay caught his arm. "You can't do this! My father will be furious!"

Ryan shook her off as if she were a kitten. "I doubt that. And if I were you, Miss Raveneau, I'd use this time to compose myself. Strive to behave like an adult rather than one of your eight-year-old students.''

He went out then and Lindsay heard a key turn in the polished brass lock. Loathing boiled up inside her. She nearly gave vent to a wild scream but held it in when she realized it would probably amuse that uncouth Irishman to hear her lose the last vestige of control.

Lindsay suddenly realized that, until this morning, she hadn't known what hatred was. Never in her life had anyone dared to treat her so rudely, and never had she felt such raw, hot anger. If she were male, Lindsay decided, she would challenge Ryan Coleraine to a duel and aim straight for his heart.

"I might do it, anyway," she muttered, pacing in the lantern-lit cabin like a caged tiger. "Odious, high-handed, arrogant, vain, uncivilized *man!*"

Dawn lent an incongruous beauty to the sight of the British landing at the foot of Main Street. Under the cover of darkness, Ryan Coleraine had overseen efforts to remove everything of value from the *Chimera*. The warehouse André Raveneau had built to store his ships' goods was located farther around the Point than the others, and Ryan held out hope that it would escape any pillaging the British might do. Ryan surmised that the townspeople's awareness of the attack meant that an alarm had been raised, and the British would have little time to waste if they intended to get safely back to their ships in the sound.

Now as the landing craft disgorged what appeared to be nearly three hundred redcoats onto Main Street, it was clear to Ryan that his time on the *Chimera* was ending. Anger burned in his gut like a fiery coal, but reason told him that resistance would only endanger the lives of his crew and the townspeople as well.

The sun, bright and juicy as a freshly cut orange, rose over the Lyme hills across the Connecticut River. Ryan was oblivious to its beauty, though, as he motioned Drew to join him on the quarterdeck.

"The men should leave the ship now. Why don't you see to it, Drew."

"Yes, sir." The slim young man looked pale and lost. He wanted to cry: What happens to us now? Is it over? Will there be another ship? Have we lost our home, our trade, our lives? Will we have to find a new port and sign on with a new captain? Drew felt sick at the thought. The *Chimera* had been home and family to them, and

Ryan Coleraine was the fairest, smartest, and most successfully daring captain alive. At least his crew thought so.

"For the moment, we should just deal with today," Ryan said softly.

Drew blinked, astonished that he had taken the time to discern his thoughts. "Yes, sir."

"After Captain Raveneau returns and I speak to him, I'll call you and Harvey together for a drink. The prospects aren't good, but we can at least toast past exploits, eh?"

Tears crowded Drew's throat. Coleraine was staring down the river, toward the sound rather than at the red columns flowing up Main Street. A chilly dawn breeze ruffled his black hair, and Drew thought that the captain's rakishly handsome profile was accentuated by an air of sorrow.

"I'll see to the crew, sir. And, sir?"

Ryan glanced down at the young man's earnest face and flinched inwardly. "Yes, Drew?"

"I'll look forward to making those toasts with you."

Rather than suffer eye contact with each departing member of the crew, Ryan decided to subject himself to what would doubtless be an even more bitter dose of Lindsay Raveneau's temper. When he lowered himself through the hatch and jumped lightly down to the gangway, ignoring the ladder as usual, tears stung Ryan's eyes as he realized that soon all this lovingly polished wood would be ashes. He was counting on Lindsay to distract him from the sharp pangs of grief that were becoming more painful by the moment.

Entering the cabin, he found her sitting in the bow-backed chair in front of his desk, asleep. Though her back remained straight, her breasts thrusting against the white fabric of her brother's shirt, Lindsay's head had dropped to one side. Looking at the silken spill of curls that fell over her right arm, Ryan decided that her hair was nearly the same color as the leaves of the sugar maple in autumn. Quite amazing, even to an Irishman who had grown up with red-haired girls. Lindsay's was different, it seemed . . . or perhaps it was *she* who was different.

Ryan shook his head and rubbed his eyes. Would he ever sleep again? Sighing, he looked around the cabin. Harvey had come down and packed most of his things, removing them from the *Chimera* along with everything else of value. The bottle of Irish whiskey still nestled in its bulkhead niche, however, and now Ryan reached for it, drew out the cork, and indulged in a long, fiery swallow.

His gaze returned to Lindsay. Her guarded, upright sleep posture made him smile. He allowed himself the luxury of admiring the provocative curve of her lower lip and the sweep of her lashes against creamy, soot-smudged cheeks.

Ryan's smile took a cynical twist as he thought, It's damned lucky we don't get along. This woman could be dangerous.

After replacing the whiskey, he touched Lindsay's arm. Her eyes flew open instantly, her head came up, and she stiffened.

"Time to go," Ryan said shortly.

Lindsay adopted an air of frosty reserve. "Would you do me the courtesy of telling me what has been happening in the world above this cell you locked me in?"

In spite of his exhaustion and despair, Coleraine was amused by the sight of Lindsay, smudged and disheveled in her boy's garb, lifting her nose and addressing him in queenly tones. However, he knew that if he smiled now it would be like lighting a keg of gunpowder, so Ryan strove for an air of solemnity.

"It's dawn. The British have landed in an orderly fashion and are marching into the village. It's my understanding that they will not harm anyone unless provoked. I suppose that their commanding officer will speak to the townspeople and then see to it that the ships are burned."

Lindsay bit back a fresh tirade. She wanted to see and hear for herself what was happening in town but realized that Coleraine would never allow it if he suspected that she might make a scene. Lifting her chin, she said coolly, "I'm ready to go, then, if you are."

Ryan put out a hand to help her up, but she ignored it. Gingerly, Lindsay rose and stretched, looking around. "I don't suppose you have any water? I'm awfully thirsty."

"Sorry, no. Just some whiskey." He inclined his dark head toward the bottle.

It seemed a suitable outlet for her rebelliousness. Uncorking the bottle, she observed, "For a ship's captain, you certainly have barren quarters!" Her eyes were fixed on the empty bookshelves as she decided that here was final proof that the man was a boor.

"I would offer you a glass, Miss Raveneau, but my steward packed all my things less than an hour ago. Didn't you hear him? We were fortunate enough to remove everything on board of value to your father's warehouse. I hope that the constraints of time and space will force the British to confine their crimes to the ships, leaving the warehouses untouched."

Lindsay flushed, embarrassed to realize that she had slept so soundly she hadn't been aware of the steward's activities in the cabin. She had slept right through a perfect opportunity for escape! Ryan was watching her, one black brow arched slightly, so she lifted the bottle and swallowed bravely. The whiskey was like liquid fire coursing down her throat, and the next thing Lindsay knew she was coughing and then choking, tears gathering in her eyes.

Ryan patted her on the back with mock solicitude and relieved her of the bottle.

"This is poison!" she accused, gasping for breath.

"I beg to differ, Miss Raveneau," he countered mildly. "You have just tasted the very finest Irish whiskey."

"Irish! No wonder it isn't fit for proper human beings!"

"Careful now, Lindsay. You know that we barbaric Irish are famous for our ungovernable tempers. You and I are all alone on the ship and I doubt that you want to discover what I'm capable of when aroused." He couldn't help the twinkle that danced in his dark blue eyes. "Or do you?"

Lindsay's cheeks flamed. "I will not dignify such a base, lascivious speech with a response." She swept past him to the door, then turned back to deliver another icy setdown only to discover that Ryan was chuckling silently to himself. Trying to ignore the appealing sight of white teeth against his trim black beard and the way his eyes crinkled at the corners, Lindsay declared, "You are the rudest man alive! *And*"—she drew herself up to her full height—"I have not given you permission to address me by my Christian name."

Ryan laughed aloud at that. "Well, it's plain that my sins are so myriad that there's no hope of redemption." He gestured toward the gangway with an ironic flourish. "Shall we go, Miss Raveneau?"

Standing on the Point, Lindsay placed delicate hands on her hips and glared at the British seamen who remained behind with the landing craft. They stared back, obviously curious about this beautiful girl got up as a scruffy boy. Her hair was the color of the sunrise, a glorious mane of tangled curls framing a pale, fine-boned face that featured great gray eyes and smudges of ash. She wore a loose linen shirt haphazardly tucked into ill-fitting breeches. The redcoats' eyes roamed the girl's body as they wondered how such masculine attire could successfully emphasize the female shape. There was something provocative about the way that loose shirt blew this way and that against her breasts and narrow waist, and it was exciting to see such long, shapely legs displayed in breeches rather than being hidden under a gown.

"What are you savages staring at?" Lindsay demanded.
"If I had a musket, I'd shoot you all!"

This prompted the Englishmen to look at each other in
astonishment, then engage in a great deal of whispering.

Ryan Coleraine took in the drama on shore as he
descended the gangplank to join his charge. One side of
his mouth quirked upward; in a strange way, he was
thankful for all the trouble Lindsay had caused since the
appearance of the British three hours earlier. She had
been relentless in her unconscious efforts to distract him
from the tragedy, which he was powerless to stop, being
played out.

Striding up behind her, Ryan lightly took her arm.
"Either the whiskey or those breeches have gone to
your head, Miss Raveneau," he murmured ironically.
"Your behavior is that of a hot-headed fifteen-year-old
boy, and you believe you can get by with it because it's
obvious that you are *not* a boy. However, before the
story begins to spread that Schoolmistress Raveneau has
gone mad, I think we should take you home. No doubt a
hot bath, some sleep and a maidenly frock will work
wonders."

Lindsay jerked her arm away. "I'm going to the Griswold Inn to see for myself what's going on."

"I think not."

"Think whatever you like, but leave me alone." She
pivoted away and started up Main Street. Striding along,
Lindsay decided that she liked walking in breeches.

Only the memory of André Raveneau and all he'd
done for him over the years kept Ryan from leaving
Lindsay to fend for herself. Regarding the sway of her
hips as she strode away from him, he told himself that
she was upset and exhausted, that she must imagine
she's defending the Raveneau honor in the absence of its
men. Lindsay had seemed poised and mature during
their meeting the previous afternoon, but in fact she was
probably a dozen years his junior. It was a situation that
called for patience.

Drawing alongside, Ryan attempted to appeal to her pride. "Lindsay, the whole town will be outside the inn. Do you want them to see you like that?"

"It's none of your concern," she replied coldly, staring straight ahead. The fact that she could not walk faster than he made her furious.

Ryan rubbed his eyes with his right thumb and forefinger, thinking, The hell with it! I'll stay close, in case the little hellion goes berserk, but no more. It's Raveneau's own fault for not hiring a keeper for his daughter when he left town.

An almost macabre feeling of excitement hung over Main Street's budding trees, handsome houses, and neat shops. People were everywhere, their voices high-pitched in the dawn sunlight. Grumbling men, whispering women, and shouting children crowded near the Griswold Inn where ranks of British marines stood in silent contrast to the conquered Americans.

Ryan followed Lindsay as she sought a place as close to the inn as possible. He was relieved to see that no one seemed to recognize her, or if they did, they were too preoccupied to care.

"Captain Coleraine!" a shopkeeper exclaimed in his ear. "What's happened? What do these cursed redcoats mean to do?"

The sound of Ryan's name prompted other people to crane their necks in the crush. In the absence of André Raveneau, they all hoped his celebrated protégé might perform a miracle and dispose of the British or at least reassure them that this was some kind of mistake.

"I know little more than any of you," Ryan said grimly. "That's why I'm here. We'll just have to see what—" He broke off in relief at the sight of a British officer mounting the steps of the Griswold Inn.

Above the crowd, the young officer cleared his throat and unfurled a sheet of parchment. "I am Lieutenant Lloyd and I am here to read a message from Captain Coote, the officer in command of this expedition." The

stilted proclamation announced that the British intended
only to destroy shipping. No harm would befall the local
residents unless there was resistance, in which case the
torch would be put to the entire town. Seagoing ships
would be warped out into the river to be burned, while
vessels under construction would be torched in the yards.
Marines who were not employed in the destruction of
the ships would seize supplies from the naval stores to
be loaded on two ships that the British intended to spare
and take with them when they left Pettipauge. Captain
Coote had chosen the *Young Anaconda,* a 300-ton brig,
and *The Eagle,* a 250-ton schooner, both of which were
privateers. "We mean you no harm and appreciate your
cooperation in ending this episode as speedily as possible," Lieutenant Lloyd declared in closing.

Murmurs swept through the crowd. Lindsay exclaimed,
"I don't believe it! Isn't anyone going to stand up for
our rights?"

"What rights?" Ryan said tersely. "This is a war.
We're the enemy. Haven't you heard accounts of the
raids on towns farther down the coastline? Our fate
could be much worse."

Lindsay fell silent at that, remembering the stories her
mother had told of the British attack on New London
during the Revolutionary War. It had been a nightmare.
Still, Lindsay was in no mood to thank these redcoats
for only burning her father's ships and refraining from
destroying the town and raping its women. She couldn't
believe her eyes when she spied Charles Jones approaching the British soldiers with a tray laden with glasses and
rum. Was this going to turn into some sort of celebration?

"Fool," Coleraine muttered.

Even as he spoke, a red-coated officer swung his
musket across the tray, smashing the bottle and glasses.
"Do not think that you can tempt us with liquor!" he
declared.

Lindsay jumped off the ground, her eyes flashing.
"Brute!" she managed to scream before a strong hand

covered her mouth and its mate clenched her waist. For the second time in four hours, she found herself being forcibly hauled away by the detestable Ryan Coleraine.

Much later, Lindsay would see the humor in a small incident that occurred as Ryan was dragging her out of the crowd. Lindsay was too busy trying to twist around and pummel Ryan's face to notice Able and Cassie Barker standing on the edge of the throng, but Cassie recognized her in spite of the breeches and the fact that half her face was obscured by a large, sun-bronzed hand.

"Why, Lindsay!" Cassie exclaimed. "*There* you are! I thought you must have gone in to school early to grade examinations! Goodness, why are you wearing Nathan's old breeches?" Eliciting no response except some wild flailing of Lindsay's arms and a boyish you-know-how-women-are shrug from Ryan, Cassie tried another tack. "You didn't tell me that you and Captain Coleraine were acquainted!"

Ryan laughed out loud at that, nearly losing his cargo in the process, but he recovered neatly. "Miss Raveneau is upset by the morning's events," he called as they drew farther away. "I thought it best to take her home."

In the distance, Able stared while Cassie bobbed her head. "It's kind of you to look after her, Captain!"

Lindsay sank her teeth into his palm.

"You little wildcat!" They were nearing the Raveneau house now, and Ryan risked removing his hand from her mouth.

"Let *go* of me!" she warned in murderous tones. His arms were like iron, his chest like sculpted marble against her slim back, and Lindsay was incensed by her powerlessness against him. When she twisted wildly, she only succeeded in jamming her left breast against his hand.

"Why, Lindsay," he murmured, "I'm surprised at you. Couldn't you wait until we're inside?" Then, for good measure, Ryan covered her breast with his hand and squeezed gently.

Her cheeks burning, Lindsay managed to catch him

off guard and turn just enough to bring her knee up between his legs. Ryan's jaw clenched with pain and fury, his eyes blazing in a way that sent a current of fear through her.

"I ought to—" He bit off the threat, then, in one swift motion, swung Lindsay's slim body over his shoulder and reached up to deliver a sharp *whack!* to her derrière.

"Ouch!" she yelled.

"Behave, you little hellion!"

"You'll have to kill me first!"

"That idea is not without merit. . . ."

"I hate you!"

Throwing open the front door, Ryan deposited her in the entry hall. Lindsay immediately drew her hand back to slap him, but his fingers caught her wrist.

"What's wrong with you? All I've done is protect you these past hours and you behave as if I've been torturing you."

"You have!" Lindsay accused, breathing hard. "I'm a grown woman. I didn't ask for your protection; you forced it on me!"

"Good Lord, child, do you never stop? If you want to prove you're a woman, why not try behaving like one?"

"What would that accomplish with a beast like you?"

Exhaustion and exasperation combined to snap Ryan's patience. He gripped Lindsay's slim shoulders through the fabric of her shirt and when she opened her mouth, he knew that more insult would be unendurable. His own mouth swooped down to silence Lindsay with stunning efficiency. The hot, angry joining of their lips scarcely qualified as a kiss, and although Lindsay's knees buckled in reaction, she would not surrender. It didn't occur to her to fight back by resisting; instead she joined in the battle with a counterattack.

Her arms rounded Coleraine's broad shoulders, one hand gripping his neck while the other sank into his gleaming black hair. He, in turn, crushed her against the length of his body so that their hips were joined and

Lindsay's full, firm breasts seemed to scorch his chest through the thin fabric of their shirts.

Ryan bent her backward as he deepened the kiss, expecting her to yield and melt, but instead Lindsay made the embrace a battle of wills. He never would have believed that she had only been kissed twice before or that she hadn't realized that men and women opened their mouths to kiss with such intimacy. Now, when Ryan's tongue plundered the softness of Lindsay's mouth, her own tongue fenced with his, alternately taunting then vying for control. For long moments, a primitive fury governed this skirmish between their bodies, but nature won in the end. Lindsay's naïveté was such that she was scarcely aware of the gradual change in her physical response. Slowly, pleasure replaced anger as the source of her passion, and Lindsay experienced arousal for the first time.

She found herself loving the taste of Ryan's mouth, the texture of the curls at the nape of his neck, the pressure of his hard male body against her own, the warmth and the scent of his skin, and the sure touch of his fingers. For an instant, Lindsay reveled in Ryan Coleraine before it dawned on her that this was not the way she was supposed to feel. Panic struck like a slap in the face.

Ryan felt her stiffen and tremble simultaneously and, guessing the reason, released her. "Had enough?" he whispered hoarsely.

She had to grip the edge of the Pembroke hall table for support. Surrounded by her tangled mane of curls, Lindsay's face looked poignantly stricken and pale, but then sparks kindled in her smoky eyes. "You are an animal. I despise you!"

Ryan laughed outright, looking wickedly piratical as one brow arched upward and white teeth flashed in contrast to his beard. "So you keep telling me, Miss Raveneau! Would it be rude of me to wonder what favors you bestow on the men you *like*?"

Narrowing her eyes, Lindsay said, "You forced yourself on me."

"Oh." He nodded with painstaking sobriety, as if he were slow-witted. "How thoughtless of me. No doubt an apology is in order. I must have been overwhelmed by your extraordinary charm and beauty."

"I see that it was wrong of me to call you an animal, Captain Coleraine. Your rudeness prevents you from winning a place among those innocent creatures." Lindsay was pleased to hear how dispassionate she sounded. "Now please leave my house. I pray never to have to suffer your company again."

Opening the door, Ryan remarked, "For once we are in wholehearted agreement, Miss Raveneau." Then he sketched a mocking bow and was gone.

CHAPTER
3

April 15–16, 1814

DEVON PAUSED ON THE THRESHOLD OF THE KITCHEN TO demand, "What is that heavenly smell?"

"Hotchpotch of mutton," Cassie replied, beaming and stirring. She watched her mistress lean over the stew pot to inhale the fragrance of mutton simmering with onions, carrots, savoy cabbage, turnips, and thyme. "Captain Raveneau asked me to make it this morning. He said he'd had his fill of rich food in Philadelphia and craved something plain."

"It *is* good to be home. It felt as if we were away three months rather than three weeks—especially in light of all that happened in our absence."

"Such a shock for both of you," Cassie commiserated. "Those ships were Pettipauge's lifeblood and now they're just gone! I still can't believe it. And I don't mind telling you that Able and I were sick with dread, waiting for you and the captain to arrive home evening before last. Able knew that he'd have to break the news to Captain Raveneau and we had no idea how he might react! I suppose, though, that we worried needlessly. We've certainly known him long enough to have expected him to bear this tragedy with fortitude.''

Devon poured herself a cup of tea and took a Windsor chair near the hearth. ''Well,'' she said with a sigh, mustering a weak smile, ''all we lost were ships—''

''The four finest craft on the Eastern seaboard!'' Cassie amended proudly.

''But replaceable, unlike human lives. And André is consoled by the fact that our two favorite ships, the *Black Eagle* and *La Mouette,* are anchored safely at Stonington. Also, at this stage in our lives, we have a greater fortune than we ever dreamed of when we married. When the war is over, we can afford to rebuild the ships that were burned—and help some of Pettipauge's less financially secure shipowners to do the same.'' Her clear blue gaze held Cassie's. ''You lived in New London during the battle in 1781, didn't you? I've been reminding myself these past two days just how much worse this British raid could have been. None of our townspeople were killed or hurt, and none of our homes were destroyed.''

Wiping her hands on her apron, Cassie sat down opposite her mistress. ''Ma'am, ever since you confided yesterday that you and Captain Raveneau may sail to London, I've thought of little else.'' She spoke in a whisper, glancing over her shoulder as if worried that a redcoat might be lurking at the garden window. ''You said that he hadn't made up his mind completely, and he told that senator in Philadelphia he wanted to think it over, but hasn't this catastrophe with the ships decided the matter? There's nothing to keep the captain here now, and it's occurred to me that the Lord may *want* you to go to England. I believe He has plans for this family!''

''Might your enthusiasm be influenced by my wish that you and Able accompany us?'' Devon teased.

Eyes twinkling, Cassie allowed, ''I won't deny that

I'd love to see England, ma'am. I have relations in Cornwall that I've never met, and as you know, Able was raised in Kent and his family live there still. I can spy with the best of them, too!'' She glanced suspiciously under the table.

Devon laughed fondly. ''I don't doubt that for a moment!''

''Still and all, I meant what I said before. I'd call that senator's request to Captain Raveneau a blessing in disguise.''

''I hope you're right, Cassie, because André has decided to agree to Senator Hampshire's plans. Not that he really had a choice since the request came from President Madison himself, but my husband has a mind of his own. Like you, he realized that he isn't really needed here now that the ships are gone, and in any case, I think that the scent of new adventure attracts him more than he was willing to admit when the senator first broached this subject.''

Cassie beamed with satisfaction. ''I wish I could've seen Miss Lindsay's face when you told her the news! Gracious, but London will do her a world of good. I don't mind telling you that I've been concerned about that young lady. She sorely needs some excitement—parties, gowns, dancing—and beaux! Now more than ever. This past week, she's kept even more to herself than usual, behaving as if she's seventy-five instead of twenty!'' The housekeeper shook her head, then brightened. ''What did Miss Lindsay say when you told her she's going to London?''

Devon sipped her tea. ''Well, I haven't broken the news to Lindsay yet. In fact, I am planning to tell her when she arrives home from school and, to be honest, I'm a bit worried about her reaction. She's so unlike me and everyone else in the family that I often despair of ever understanding her! Cassie, you mentioned Lindsay's behavior this past week. We've noticed that she's been unusually quiet since we returned, but then the entire town seems subdued. How did Lindsay react to the British attack? Was she terribly frightened? Naturally, André and I feel sick that we weren't here with her. Thank God the British didn't raid private homes and that you and Able were here so that Lindsay didn't feel abandoned and defenseless!''

Rising, Cassie stirred the stew and wondered how to respond. She hadn't said anything to her employers about their daughter's behavior the morning of the British attack because it wasn't clear to Cassie exactly what Lindsay had been doing. She'd tried to talk to her since, but all the girl would say was "When the alarm was sounded, I put on Nathan's breeches to go down to the Point to see if anything could be done to save Papa's ships. Captain Coleraine brought me on board the *Chimera* and kept me safe after that. There's nothing else to tell.'' Cassie had pressed, "But when we saw the two of you in front of the Griswold Inn—'' Lindsay cut her off. "I was upset, and Captain Coleraine was afraid I would make a scene. It was a horrible day, one I'd like to forget. Please, don't ask me about it again.''

It occurred to Cassie that Devon might welcome the tale of her daughter's apparent bravery in the face of an enemy attack, but she decided to opt for discretion. Lindsay had never been impulsive or headstrong in the past, so Cassie found cause for worry in the girl's adventure on the Point. The memory of Ryan Coleraine hauling a flailing, breeches-clad figure barely recognizable as Lindsay away from the gathering on Main Street never failed to strike bemused concern in Cassie's considerable breast. She might have deduced that the British attack on Pettipauge's ships had caused Lindsay to go mad, but the very next morning the girl had risen at dawn to teach school, just as she always had. Lindsay had appeared in the kitchen to make her own tea, clad in a demure gown of pink-and-white-striped muslin. Freshly scrubbed, every hair neatly arranged atop her head, she had been the embodiment of restrained gentility. It was an image that hadn't even wavered during the following days; if anything, Lindsay's usual tendency toward proper reserve had only intensified during the past week.

"Cassie, did you hear me? How did Lindsay respond to the British attack? Perhaps it was more traumatic for her than she lets on?"

"She was quite upset that those redcoats just sailed into our harbor and burned the ships—particularly those built by Captain Raveneau. After the British warped the ships out into the river and set fire to them, I saw Miss Lindsay walk out the front door and stand in the middle of Main Street to watch that tragic spectacle. Tears were running down her face, and I'm not sure she even realized it." Cassie took a breath, searching for the right words. "She seemed frustrated that nothing could be done to stop the redcoats and that the townspeople weren't fighting back. But once it was over and the damage was done, Miss Lindsay seemed quick to recover and to go on with her life as usual."

Devon listened thoughtfully. It was hard to imagine her daughter weeping in the middle of Main Street or wishing violence on anyone, even red-coated enemies. Perhaps Lindsay was pluckier than her parents had ever realized. Devon could only hope that this was the case and that the adventure of moving to London would release some of that pent-up liveliness.

From the front of the house came the sound of the door opening and closing, then Lindsay calling, "I'm home!"

"We're in the kitchen, sweetheart," Devon replied. She stood as her daughter entered the big, warm room carrying a stack of books and papers that she deposited on the table before embracing her mother.

"How pretty you look today, Mama." Lindsay smiled.

Devon glanced down at her own beautifully fitted gown of jonquil silk. Emeralds sparkled on the choker about her neck, and her curls were caught up in a flattering silk bandeau. Lindsay, on the other hand, wore

a dark blue spencer over a simple gown of white muslin.
The girl's natural beauty outshone her mother's, even
without embellishments, but Devon couldn't help dreaming about the picture Lindsay would make in the new
clothing, jewels, bonnets, and slippers they would buy
in London.

"It's sweet of you to say so," Devon replied, casting
a meaningful glance toward Cassie.

"If you two ladies will keep an eye on the stew, I
think I'll pick some daffodils for the supper table," the
housekeeper said promptly.

Lindsay poured a cup of tea for herself and took a
chair opposite her mother's. "Oh, this day seemed end-
less! Jonathan Payton had the devil in him all morning
long. I could have thrashed him! Fortunately, I think he
exhausted himself, because by the time we did sums, he
stopped pinching Sally Arnold and quieted down." She
paused, her gray eyes alert. "Mama, is something both-
ering you?"

"Lindsay, I have something to tell you, something I
consider wonderful news. I only hope you'll agree."

"Well, good news would certainly be welcome in view
of last week's tribulations!"

"I can see that wary look in your eyes, child, so I
suppose it wouldn't do me any good to work up to this
gradually. The fact is that while we were in Philadelphia,
Senator Hampshire asked your father to go to England
on a diplomatic mission."

"What?"

"Now, let me explain, briefly at least. You see, because of the war, there has not been an American ambassador in residence in London. The president desires
that someone known to the British go there now . . . for
various reasons. There is concern that someone may be
selling American secrets, or influencing the powers that be
in a negative way, but it's only speculation. Our only
purpose in going may be simply to spread American
goodwill. All the other prominent Americans who also

are known and trusted in London are currently in Ghent, with the Peace Commission, so your father was a logical choice. At first, as you might imagine, he balked because of his business here, but in view of recent events, there is nothing to keep him in Connecticut.''

Lindsay was aghast. "Mama, how can you call this 'wonderful news' and expect me to echo your sentiments? I think it's dreadful! Why, Papa might be away for a year or more!''

"You didn't let me finish, sweetheart," Devon said gently, gazing into her daughter's eyes. "President Madison desires that *all* of us travel to Britain. He feels that your father's role will be most effective if he can seem to be a fairly neutral, family-oriented man. If he were to appear alone in London, while the war is going on, suspicions might be aroused.''

Stunned, Lindsay could only whisper, *"All of us?"*

"Don't you see, it's a wonderful opportunity for you! You need to get away from Pettipauge and see the world, Lindsay. London is like a fairyland for a girl your age. Handsome men, beautiful clothes, balls and assemblies—''

"You know that I consider none of those important for happiness. I'm accomplishing something here, Mama. I'm helping children to learn, to grow intellectually—''

"Wouldn't you hope that one day your students might be moved by what they've learned to venture out into the world and see its wonders firsthand? Don't you want them to be well rounded, to seek knowledge from experience as well as from books?''

"Of course, but—" Lindsay broke off as her mother's words sank in. Turning her head, she stared at the fire for a long minute, then whispered, "I have responsibilities . . .''

"Your first responsibility is to yourself, my dear, and in this case you also have a responsibility to your country. There is more to this journey than pleasure, as your father will explain. President Madison wants each of us to play a role in London." Reaching out, Devon touched her hand. "Besides, it's only for a few months—a year, at most. I'd hoped that you might be able to awaken a secret reserve of courage at the prospect of such an adventure."

"Courage?" Lindsay straightened her slim back. She was about to say "You might be surprised!" when a commotion in the front entry hall caused both of them to turn their heads.

"Devon? Are you here, *chérie*?" It was the deep, lightly accented voice of André Raveneau.

"We're in the kitchen, Papa," Lindsay replied, glad for the diversion. She met her father in the doorway and was wrapped in his strong embrace when she saw the other man approaching down the hall. Suddenly, her heart began to hammer madly.

"Loose me, *ma fleur*." André chuckled, turning to wave his guest into the kitchen. "I don't believe that you were present the last time I brought Captain Coleraine home. Ryan, allow me to present my daughter, Lindsay."

Though his smile was as devastating as ever, Lindsay recognized the dangerous glint in Coleraine's midnight-blue eyes. He held out a hand to her but spoke to André. "Miss Raveneau and I have already met. We introduced ourselves last week in front of the Griswold Inn."

Lindsay prayed that her cheeks didn't look as hot as they felt. "It's a pleasure to see you again, Captain." Then, to prevent him from gloating over the thought that he was keeping a secret for her sake, she added, "Papa, you must thank Captain Coleraine. In spite of his own trials on the day the British attacked, he still found time to see to my safety."

Ryan's black brows flicked upward almost imperceptibly. "Your daughter obviously inherited her parents' legendary bravery. It will come as no surprise to you to learn that a Raveneau attempted to repel the British singlehandedly, thereby ensuring the safety of your ships. Needless to say, my own efforts to inject a note of caution into Miss Raveneau's defense of Pettipauge were less than welcome. At the risk of sounding boastful, I would venture to say that I may have saved your daughter's life when I removed her from the fray." Ryan delivered this speech in a light, jaunty tone that suggested exaggeration for the amusement of his audience.

André glanced at Lindsay, who managed to smile and shrug innocently, thereby banishing his faint hope that Coleraine might be telling the truth. Obviously the man didn't know that Lindsay was actually nothing like the feisty rebel he had just described or that her parents would have been proud if she had behaved with such valor, however misguided. "That's quite a tale!" André heard himself chuckle. "How did you manage to convince Lindsay to abandon her crusade?"

Seething inside over Ryan Coleraine's smug little game, she spoke up first, laughing. "Oh, he tossed me over his shoulder and carried me off. Isn't that what heroes always do?"

Devon had risen from her chair beside the hearth and was watching the trio in the doorway with sharp blue eyes. Her interest had been piqued by the scene that she had just witnessed between Captain Coleraine and her daughter. Even Devon didn't really consider the notion that Ryan's story might be factual, but she did think that there was more to his past encounter with Lindsay than either of them was letting on. Unless Devon's intuition was faulty, it seemed clear that her daughter actually *disliked* this rakish Irishman. The prospect of Lindsay harboring a strong emotion, even if it was ill will, was encouraging.

"I should warn you, Captain Coleraine," Devon said as she walked over to join them, "my daughter does not enjoy being manhandled."

Ryan laughed and bent to kiss the hand she proffered. "I promise never to do it again." Lifting his eyes, he murmured, "It's a pleasure to see you again, madame. Your beauty increases."

"Not so rapidly as your charm, sir!"

André spoke up then. "You're aware, Devon, that I

have been meaning to have a talk with Ryan. When we met by chance at my warehouse, I remembered the mutton stew Cassie promised to make and invited the captain to join us for supper.''

She mustered a smile. "That's just fine, but Captain Coleraine may not consider hotchpotch of mutton to be the sublime delicacy that you do, my darling.''

"Impossible!'' her husband scoffed. "*Eh bien,* give me half an hour alone with Ryan in the study, then why don't you ladies join us for a glass of wine before supper?''

With that, the two men disappeared down the hall and Devon was conscious of a rising panic. Lindsay was not yet reconciled to the idea of going to London *herself*! How could Devon tell her that Ryan Coleraine would be joining their family, masquerading as her brother? All of her maternal instincts warned that such a disclosure at that moment would cause Lindsay to refuse to travel to Britain—or ever to leave Pettipauge at all!

"I don't like that man,'' Lindsay whispered distractedly.

"I noticed,'' Devon replied with a rather sickly smile. "I must say, though, I can't see what there is *not* to like. Ryan Coleraine seems to be the embodiment of a woman's dreams. He's— ''

"Oh, Mama!'' Lindsay hissed. "Spare me your fairy tales! I'm going up to my room. Not only must I prepare tomorrow's lessons, but there is this situation about London to consider.''

"Yes, of course.'' Devon's heart sank. Watching her daughter gather the stack of books on the table, she realized that the unfamiliar emotion that swept over her was helplessness. Of course, she ought to do something, but Lindsay's demeanor left Devon at a loss. "I know you'll see how important this journey to London is, sweetheart—for all of us.''

Lindsay passed by with her chin elevated. "Possibly.''

CHAPTER
4

April 15, 1814

"**D**ID SENATOR HAMPSHIRE MENTION WHETHER OR NOT I have a choice in this matter?" Ryan asked dazedly.

Watching the younger man swallow the rest of his brandy, Raveneau was reminded of his own reaction when this incredible plan had been presented to him. "I'm afraid you have me to thank for your involvement in this. There's no one else I would trust to impersonate my son and, of course, your appearance and age are also perfect. As for the matter of choice, I'd say that it wouldn't be advisable to decline." He ran a hand through his silvery hair and smiled sympathetically. "I felt backed into a wall myself the first few days after Hampshire talked to me, and I certainly considered refusing outright. This is not the sort of adventure men like you and me feel comfortable with, but we would be helping America, and considering the situation here in Pettipauge, it does seem preferable to waiting for the privateers to be rebuilt."

"I'm wondering if someone's tampered with your

brandy, sir. I could swear I'm having a truly bizarre dream!"

"Under the circumstances, perhaps you ought to call me André." Raveneau paused, then dryly added, "Or Father."

Ryan rubbed tanned fingers over his eyes and tried to laugh. "You know, I grew up in Britain. When I left nine years ago, at the age of twenty-two, I intended never to return. Certainly not under these circumstances!"

"You're from Ireland, though—"

"I lived in England those last few years," Ryan said enigmatically.

André thought back to the angry young man with an Irish accent and flashing dark blue eyes who'd come to him nine years ago to ask for work. Coleraine had explained that he had been first mate on a merchant ship out of Boston since arriving in America. He'd heard tales of Raveneau—the man, sea captain, and shipbuilder—and had saved for the journey to Pettipauge, determined to sign on. Ryan had brashly informed him that he intended one day to captain his own ship and eventually to own her, but in the meantime he'd swab decks to prove himself. During the intervening years, Ryan's keen intelligence, discipline, and talent had made his ambitions come true. Raveneau had come to trust and respect him more than any other man in his service, but now he realized how little he really knew of Ryan Coleraine.

"Are you concerned that people in London will remember you and expose our masquerade?" André asked.

"No . . . not particularly, though it's possible. I was a different person then, and so much time has passed that I doubt anyone there thinks of me anymore. Besides, I spent little time in London." He paused, considering. "It wouldn't be particularly difficult to alter my looks and personality just enough so that there would be little or no danger of recognition."

Raveneau laughed dryly. "Devon will be happy to

help in that area! She's an expert at these creative deceptions. . . ."

From the hallway, Devon called, "Did I hear someone mention my name?"

"Join us, *chérie*," her husband replied, rising to embrace her as she entered. It seemed to André that his wife had changed not at all during the thirty-two years of their marriage. She remained a bright, lovely, adventurous, curious, headstrong minx, and he loved her more than ever. Kissing her upswept curls, he remarked, "The hardest deception of all will be convincing people that you are old enough to be Ryan's mother."

"Don't be silly, André. Nathan may be only twenty-eight, but Mouette is at least Captain Coleraine's age." She took a chair and waited for the two men to sit down. "Now, first of all, we'll have to dispense with formality. I will call you Ryan and you must call me Devon."

"Or Mother," André put in with a straight face.

"You'll have to excuse me . . . Devon," Ryan said with a rather pained smile, "but I think I'm in shock. I'm still digesting this entire plan, and the fact is, I haven't yet agreed to participate in it."

She waved this off with a tiny hand. "You men! You're all so hardheaded. André was terribly difficult for days after Senator Hampshire discussed this matter with him, and he's only just begun to realize how entertaining this adventure could be!"

As he lit a cheroot, Raveneau slanted a wry smile at the younger man. "If you're wise, you'll take a piece of advice from a man who has lived with this woman for over thirty years. Once she packs a bit of snow together and starts it rolling down the mountain, there's nothing to be done. You might as well surrender, Coleraine."

"Do you always follow your own advice, sir?"

André and Devon exchanged a meaningful, laughing look before he replied, "I didn't say that *I* was wise!"

"André," his wife chided, "give the poor man an opportunity to make up his own mind! Come along with me into the kitchen. Cassie wants you to approve the hotchpotch of mutton.'' Firmly, she took him by the hand and drew him into the hallway. When they neared the kitchen, Devon paused to whisper urgently, "Oh, darling, I don't know what we'll do if Captain Coleraine doesn't come around almost immediately. Lindsay has made up her mind not to like him, and she herself hasn't agreed to come with us to London. Once she finds out that *he'll* be going, masquerading as Nathan, I shudder to imagine the ensuing scene!''

Raveneau rolled his eyes. "Why can't anything ever be simple?''

In the study, Ryan Coleraine was wondering the same thing. He was glad to have a bit of time alone to think, but he soon realized that his reactions to Raveneau's proposition were definitely mixed. He had no desire to return to England, especially in the guise of the Raveneaus' rich, fashionable son. The thought of playing that part, coupled with the prospect of sharing a family home, went strongly against his grain. A yearning for independence and a self-governed destiny had been his motivation for leaving Britain in the first place. These days, Ryan treasured nothing so much as his total freedom.

On the other hand, he felt that he owed America a great debt. Could he live with himself if he turned his back on a request from President Madison? And *could* one refuse such a request? Even Raveneau, who was twice as old and twice as powerful as Ryan, had come around.

Sighing, he sank back in the rose-upholstered wing chair and rubbed his bearded jaw. Since the *Chimera* had been destroyed the week before, Ryan had worked to suppress emotions he viewed as useless, chiefly, rage and restlessness. He'd been anxious for Captain Raveneau to return from Philadelphia, certain that the older man would be filled with plans to rebuild instantly—and perhaps even to seek revenge against the British. These new developments were totally unexpected, yet Ryan told himself that Raveneau would achieve the same ends though by different means. The ships would be rebuilt while he was in England, and in the meantime a subtler, more civilized form of revenge could be pursued. Sipping his brandy, Coleraine thought, Perhaps he's right. This assignment may prove more satisfying and challenging than staying around here to wait. At least we'd be busy . . .

"I'd hoped that you would have the good sense to politely refuse my father's dinner invitation and leave our home," a cool voice said from the doorway.

Ryan blinked and almost smiled as he stood to acknowledge her presence. "Ah, Miss Raveneau! I see that skirts have not improved your manners."

"All that my manners require is your absence, sir!" She stared at him defiantly, blushing under the apparent amusement in his dark blue eyes, then took a chair across the study. "Was my father called away by an emergency? I hardly think he would have left you alone with our valuables otherwise!"

Ryan feigned shock. "Miss Raveneau, have I been insulted?" He'd forgotten how stimulating Lindsay's company was. She might be infuriating and rude, but now that she couldn't cause trouble with the British troops, he was able to appreciate the fact that, unlike most women, Lindsay Raveneau never bored him. And she was physically stunning. Ryan's appreciative gaze swept over her simple white muslin gown, noting the graceful lines of the form it concealed, then lingered on her face. It featured pale, creamy skin accented by dawn-flushed cheeks; exquisite bone structure; a lush mouth, narrow nose; and, finally, those beautiful, intelligent smoke-colored eyes with their thick lashes and delicately arched brows. The crowning touch was Lindsay's mass of strawberry-blond hair, caught up in the simplest of loose Grecian knots that released soft, wispy curls to frame her face. She wore no jewelry, no powder, paint, lace, or satin, and Ryan thought that her beauty was only heightened by their absence.

"I am baffled by your question, sir," Lindsay replied frostily. "Did you expect flattery?"

The devil himself seemed to prompt Ryan's answer. "I had hoped you might find it in your heart to treat me with the same kindness you might show your brother. After all, soon we'll be living under the same roof—"

"*What?*" she cried. "I knew it! You're a madman!" Looking over her shoulder, Lindsay saw her parents appear in the entryway in response to the sound of raised voices. "Papa, you must ask Captain Coleraine to leave! He's ranting like a lunatic about how I should treat him like a brother as he will be living under the same roof as me and—"

Ryan's brows flew up as he cast a beseeching look at his hosts in the hope that they would perceive the truth of the situation. He and Lindsay were both on their feet, tense with antagonism, and he saw familiar sparks of fire in her smoky eyes.

"Sit down, both of you," said André Raveneau in a tone that Lindsay remembered from her childhood. "My patience and diplomacy are at an end. The fact is that none of us have any choice about this matter. We *must* go to England, like it or not, so both of you may as well dispose of your arguments." He turned to his daughter. "*Ma fille*, President Madison feels that it is very important that a young man be part of our family in London. As you know, Nathan is unavailable and, for many reasons, I have asked Captain Coleraine to go in his place. No!" He held up his hand to silence her. "I cannot begin to imagine why you have taken such a violent dislike to a man I hold in such high esteem, but unless you will tell me that he has done you an injury, it is of no consequence in view of present circumstances. You have treated a guest in my home with uncharacteristic rudeness and I would have you beg his pardon."

Lindsay widened her eyes in shock. "But, Papa, you don't understand! He—he—"

"You offer me evidence that he is dishonorable?"

"N-no, but—"

Raveneau cut her off with a steely glare. The air in the study was thick with resentment and confusion as Lindsay clenched her fists and forced herself to look at Ryan Coleraine.

"I apologize if I have been uncivil, sir."

He saw how her pride was suffering and experienced a pang of conscience. "Could we make this apology mutual? If you have been uncivil, Miss Raveneau, I have encouraged it. Neither of us could be held up as models of mature adult decorum based on this afternoon's encounter. However, I am willing to call a truce if you are."

Lindsay nodded stiffly, impatient to put an end to the scene. Every moment spent in Ryan Coleraine's company was sheer torture as far as she was concerned.

Looking over to find the Raveneaus watching them in consternation, Ryan offered a bemused smile and a shrug. "I'm afraid that what we have here is a simple case of two people who've gotten off to a bad beginning. Your daughter and I seem to have been at odds from the moment we met."

"I'm sorry to hear that, but you'll have to make the best of the situation. I realize that both of you resent being coerced into this—" André broke off suddenly and narrowed his eyes at Ryan. "*Mon Dieu!* Didn't Lindsay say that you told her you were going to be her brother? Does that mean that you've decided to agree to President Madison's plan? I can dispense with the threats I've been rehearsing?"

The younger man smiled dryly. "I thought it over and realized I would save myself a great deal of frustration by surrendering to the inevitable with as much good grace as I can muster."

"That doesn't mean *I* will," Lindsay announced defiantly.

"Oh, you'll surrender, *ma fille*," her father said in a dangerous voice, "gracefully or not."

"It would be humanly impossible for me to treat this—this *person* as I would Nathan! I cannot begin to imagine playing the role of loving sister to this—"

"Odious, high-handed, arrogant, vain, uncivilized *man*?" Ryan supplied helpfully.

"Oh!" she cried. "I see that you also listen at keyholes! Not that I'm surprised. Nothing could be too low for you!"

"Miss Raveneau, might I be so bold to suggest that if you do not want your private opinions to be overheard you ought to refrain from talking to yourself? When you unleashed that string of insults, I had just left the cabin and was still in the gangway!"

Devon decided it was time for her to step in. "Now, children, I haven't the slightest notion what this is about, but I must ask that you behave yourselves in this house!" she chided lightly. "I'm sure you'll learn to get along. Lindsay, you have always possessed great reserves of control and patience, and this is the time to call on them. In any event, it's a well-known fact of life that siblings frequently quarrel. I'm sure no one in London will be suspicious if the two of you appear to dislike each other. In fact, it may make our little charade all the more believable." She put an arm around her daughter and urged, "For now, though, let's all cry peace and seal it with a toast over supper."

As they started toward the dining room, Devon observed a silent exchange between Lindsay and Ryan. She cast a sulky look at him and he responded with a sardonically amused smile. Devon recognized the appealing gleam of deviltry mixed with anger in the Irishman's blue eyes but could not fix its meaning. The entire situation foiled her usually unerring female instincts. For the first time in years, Devon was at a loss to explain human behavior, and her frustration was all the worse because the person whose conduct baffled her the most was her own daughter. She and André had just gotten used to the idea that Lindsay would always be different, always poised rather than impulsive, thoughtful rather than emotional—and now, out of the blue, here she was, acting like a true member of the Raveneau family!

Devon had a disquieting feeling that, before their planned sojourn in London ended, she would discover whole new meanings for the word *adventure*. . . .

CHAPTER
5

May 2, 1814

"**I** FEEL AS IF I AM IN THE MIDDLE OF A BAD DREAM,"
Lindsay told her mother as she gazed around at the
trunks and bags that cluttered their small house in
Stonington.

"Nonsense," Devon replied briskly. "The only dream-
like aspect of this day is the beautiful sunrise over the
water. You should be excited, Lindsay! We're embarking
on a wonderful adventure that should only improve as it
progresses. Aren't you anxious to see your sister and
your nephews in London? There is much to look forward to."

"The prospect of spending the next few months with
Ryan Coleraine casts a dark cloud over the rest," Lindsay said stubbornly.

Devon was spared a reply by a knock at the front
door. "That must be Able with the carriage." However,
instead of Able Barker she discovered an earnest young
man with blond hair standing on the brick walkway in
front of the house. "Why, it's James Post, isn't it? What

are you doing in Stonington, James, especially at this hour?''

Smoothing his green waistcoat, James peeked hopefully at Lindsay. ''I would have come to say good-bye in Pettipauge, but I only heard last night that all of you were leaving for England, Mrs. Raveneau.''

James Post, a kind, industrious young man who had helped to build all of the Raveneau ships, believed himself to be in love with Lindsay. For nearly a year, he had pursued her with dogged devotion, and she had exhibited equal persistence in treating his attentions with friendly discouragement. Now, however, the sight of him made her heart swell with regret. If only she weren't being forced to go to England! How much more pleasurable it would be to spend her free hours with dear, sweet James Post.

''James!'' she exclaimed. ''How good it is to see you! Don't say that you have come all this way to see us off.''

He crossed the threshold to meet her. ''My only worry was that I would be too late,'' he told Lindsay, then turned to her mother. ''Mrs. Raveneau, may I walk Lindsay to the ship? I would be most grateful if you would grant me these few moments of her time.''

''You're far too polite!'' Devon laughed lightly. ''My daughter will do as she pleases, with or without my permission.''

''I'll see you at the ship, then, Mother.''

James held the door for her and Lindsay stepped through it onto Ash Street. Instinctively, she glanced back at the house where her parents had first lived after their marriage and continued to inhabit during visits to Stonington. It was simple and sweet, she thought, a typical one-and-a-half-story dwelling, long and low with a gambrel roof. Lindsay hadn't been away from Connecticut for nearly ten years. As soon as she had been old enough to protest, she had insisted on remaining behind with Cassie and Able whenever the rest of the family embarked on the sea voyages they loved so much. Now, gazing back at the little house, she was swept by a current of melancholy. When would she return?

"You certainly look pretty today, Lindsay," James was saying as he cocked an elbow for her to take.

"It's kind of you to say so." For reasons she couldn't fully explain, Lindsay had taken special pains with her appearance. She'd risen in the dark to bathe and to wash her hair before donning a fashionable new gown of peach muslin, its high waist and short, puffed sleeves edged with Belgian lace. Simple pearls accentuated the creamy softness of her throat, and Lindsay's beautiful gray eyes were complemented by a high-crowned bonnet of peach silk. To protect against the dawn chill, she had borrowed an ecru cashmere shawl from her mother.

"Pettipauge will be a dull place without you," James murmured, placing his hand over her slim fingers.

Lindsay turned to look at him. Why did he sound so ardent? They had known each other since birth, and though James's shyness and her own serious, solitary nature had kept them from being close, she had always thought of him as a friend. It was true that he had turned up to walk her home from school quite frequently of late and seemed to make a point of reading every book she mentioned, but it had never occurred to her . . .

"I wish you weren't going away!" he exclaimed suddenly. "I had just begun working up the courage to let you know how I feel. It's not fair!"

"Why, James! You surprise me." Lindsay spoke honestly, for she had never learned or cared to be coy.

"Sometimes I think you must be blind!" he cried, the floodgates opening at last. "How can you be unaware that every male you encounter is rendered speechless by your beauty? You're the most exquisite woman I've ever *seen*, Lindsay, in addition to being the most intelligent! If you'd ever given the slightest encouragement to any of the unmarried men in Pettipauge, you would have been besieged by suitors."

"Now you're being ridiculous. To suggest that dozens of men have been languishing in a sea of unrequited love, waiting for me to bestow a smile on them, is utterly silly!"

"Not a bit." James shook his head doggedly. "Though you might consider the notion that someone like me might have been afraid to approach you out of fear that you'd say that very thing. I can assure you, however, that my feelings for you are not 'silly'!"

Lindsay's head was spinning. "I beg your pardon, James. I certainly didn't mean to offend you! It's just that . . . I suppose I feel unworthy. It has never occurred to me that I might be the object of someone's admiration—or even affections."

"You've been too lost in your books. You're at an age now where you ought to give some thought to *real* people!"

Emerging from Ash Street, they turned north onto the main thoroughfare of Water Street, which was lined with wharves and tall-masted ships. The borough of Stonington was located on a tapering tongue of land that jutted out into Fisher's Island Sound and marked the separation of Stonington Harbor, on the west, from Little Narragansett Bay, to the east. This narrow village of barely two hundred fifty acres was one of the most picturesque on the eastern seaboard. Much of it was barely three blocks wide, affording spellbinding water views from nearly every dwelling on the tightly built lanes. Since the end of the Revolutionary War, Stonington had truly begun to thrive as a seaport. It acquired not only fishing but whaling and sealing vessels, too. Soon they were joined by packets engaged in coastal trade and trade with the West Indies. André Raveneau had moved his own shipbuilding enterprise to Pettipauge before Lindsay's birth, but he kept his two older, sentimentally favored ships anchored at Stonington. One was the privateer the *Black Eagle*, which he had commanded with such success during the Revolution, and the other was a larger brig named for his first daughter, *La Mouette*, which meant the Seagull in French.

Lindsay was happy to enter the bustle of activity on Water Street. She'd been surprised and flattered by James Post's revelations, but since she could not offer him any encouragement, distraction was welcome. Ahead of them, she could see the stately masts of *La Mouette* rising against the tangerine-and-lavender-layered sky. In spite of herself, Lindsay experienced a sudden thrill at the sight of seamen climbing the ratlines, bounding over the decks, and loading supplies up the gangplank. Drawing nearer, she spied her father standing on the quarterdeck. His silvery hair and loose white shirt were ruffled in the dawn breeze as he oversaw his crew, and though he didn't smile, Lindsay could sense his pleasure even from a distance.

"You've never been like the rest of your family," James said softly. "You have told me countless times that you care nothing for the sea. Why are you going?"

"I didn't really have a choice." Lindsay's tone was absent; her eyes were on her father.

"What if I were to offer you one?"

At that moment, a carriage drew up beside them. Driven by Able, it also contained Cassie, Devon, and all of their belongings.

"Good morning, Miss Lindsay!" Able cried exultantly. "It's an exciting day, isn't it?"

Shielding her eyes against the eastern sun, she smiled up at him, waving back at Cassie and nodding to her mother. "Good morning! I'll see you all on board."

As the carriage clattered off, Lindsay murmured, "It's getting late. Papa will be looking for me."

James was looking upset. He stopped to buy a basket of strawberries, which he presented to Lindsay, and they walked on in silence while he tried to decide what to say next. Lindsay, meanwhile, nibbled at a juicy berry and unconsciously scanned the crowd gathering around *La Mouette*. Suddenly, she spotted Ryan Coleraine striding forward to offer his hand to Devon. He was looking almost indecently handsome, his black curls tousled, his bearded face rakish and tanned. Clad in boots, biscuit-colored breeches, and an open-necked white shirt, Ryan moved with the grace of a panther. Lindsay was astonished to feel her heart skip.

Then, after escorting the captain's wife up the gangplank, Ryan returned to the dock. A woman stepped from the crowd to meet him, and the ease with which he slipped an arm about her waist told Lindsay that they had been together before the carriage drew up. Now, staring helplessly, she watched as they kissed. A tear sparkled on the woman's cheek, and Ryan smiled and erased it with a fingertip.

"Lindsay, I have to talk to you."

James! She'd forgotten all about him, which was no wonder since they stood just a few feet away from Coleraine and his paramour. Now, pointedly ignoring the Irishman, she gave all her attention to James.

"It's time for me to board, you know, but I want to thank you for coming all this way to see me off. That gesture, and the lovely things you said to me, mean more than I can tell you."

"Lindsay, you don't have to go!" he burst out. "Please, stay here. Come home to Pettipauge where you belong and marry me. I'll give you a good life, I vow it!"

She was surprised to realize that she wasn't even considering this offer, which ostensibly answered all of her prayers of the past fortnight. It seemed that a new part of Lindsay was emerging that actually welcomed the challenge of the adventure she was beginning, despite its uncertainties.

"James," she whispered, "I shall treasure your proposal. It's my first! But I cannot accept. I'm not in love with you."

"But you never cared for such things! You've told me that you think love is a myth."

"It may be that I have been too opinionated for my

own good," Lindsay replied gently. "In any event, you deserve a wife who will love you. Someone with a better temperament than I have. I don't know that I'm suited for marriage—at least not now. And as for this voyage—for better or worse, I am committed to go."

After kissing his cheek, she turned away and started up the gangplank. At the top, Lindsay reached out to the rail for balance before stepping down, but a strong, dark hand appeared to grasp her arm.

"Allow me, Miss Raveneau."

She turned her face just enough to glimpse his chiseled profile and the ironic arch of his left brow. "Why, Captain Coleraine, what a surprise." Lindsay's tone was dry.

With a swift, graceful movement, he preceded her onto the deck and lifted her down. "Didn't you notice? I was there all the time. But, of course, you were far too busy declining marriage proposals to greet your brother."

"Eavesdropping again, I see!" she retorted lightly, walking past him toward the quarter deck. "And I would have certainly greeted my brother if he had appeared on the dock! After all, Nathan's early return from the West Indies would mean that I wouldn't have to spend the next few months in *your* company!"

Ryan smiled grudgingly as he watched her stroll away. The chit had a sharp tongue, but she used it with style and the sight of her long, slim back and appealingly curved hips begged him to forgive and forget her less admirable traits. Thoughtfully, Ryan rubbed his jaw and decided that it was probably fortunate that they didn't like each other or this brother-sister charade would already be doomed.

As *La Mouette* sailed from Stonington Harbor toward Long Island Sound, Lindsay was unpacking a trunkful of books in her cramped cabin. After only a few minutes of bending and straightening in her muslin gown, she stripped it off and donned one of the sets of shirts and breeches belonging to Nathan that her mother had insisted she pack. "On a voyage of this length, you'd be foolish to wear dresses all the time," Devon had said. "On board ship, we all become family; it's not necessary to try to impress anyone or even to follow the usual rules of etiquette."

Lindsay smoldered with outrage when she thought of Ryan Coleraine appraising her backside that morning. Of course, the beast had no inkling that she'd realized what he was doing, and the circumstances made it impossible for her to confront him. Now she was determined to turn up in shapeless, unflattering boys' garb at every available opportunity. Let him leer at this! she thought angrily, pulling books from the trunk.

"Miss Lindsay, what are you doing down here?" Cassie cried, poking her head in from the gangway. "It's such a beautiful morning! The water's so blue and it looks like it's strewn with diamonds!"

Relenting to an unfamiliar urge to socialize and partake of this new experience, Lindsay smiled and let Cassie pull her toward the hatch. Up on deck, the sight was spectacular. *La Mouette* sliced through the sapphire-hued water, throwing up mists of fresh, salty water. Fisher's Island lay off the starboard bow, humped, enormous, and spring green against the blue sky and water. In the other direction, Lindsay could see the vague outline of Stonington and the Connecticut coast. She knew that before the sun set, they would be out of the sound and into the Atlantic Ocean.

"Lindsay!" her mother called from the quarterdeck, the captain's honored elevation at the stern of the ship. "Come and join us!"

Shielding her eyes, she saw only her parents and one or two ship's officers. Since there was no sign of her nemesis, Lindsay accepted the invitation.

"Give your poor papa a hug," Raveneau greeted her,

turning over the wheel to his first lieutenant. "I've been ignored of late!"

Lindsay laughed and returned his embrace. "Papa, I've been packing! Besides, you have spent most of these past few days on board *La Mouette*."

"Only to ensure that this voyage would be a happy one for you, *ma fille*. I even ordered this weather personally, trusting no one else to get it right. Do you approve?"

It was an old joke, dating back to a time when she had believed her father actually could perform such miracles. "Of course I approve! It's a perfect day!" Dropping her head back, Lindsay pulled the pins from her hair and freed a strawberry-blond waterfall of curls. The sky was astonishingly blue above her, and Lindsay suddenly felt utterly joyous . . . until she caught sight of a familiar figure high in the mainmast's rigging. Even from this distance, she imagined that she could see the laughter in Ryan Coleraine's eyes before he sketched a salute at her and returned his attention to reefing the topgallant sail.

"You're being too sensitive, you know," Raveneau murmured. "He may very well have meant that salute as a friendly gesture—and even if it was in jest, he doubtless does it to tease you. Why do you let the man chafe at you so?"

"I can't help it, Papa. I despise him!"

"Strong words, *chérie*," he cautioned. "And even if you do feel so strongly, you ought to endeavor to hide it from Coleraine. It seems to me that he's already treating you in a brotherly fashion. Knowing that he has the power to annoy you, he delights in using it."

Something about this speech of her father's irked Lindsay. His choice of words seemed ill-advised. Shading her eyes, she wrinkled her nose with distaste and looked back up the mainmast. Ryan was descending the ratlines now, and Lindsay found herself staring at the play of long muscles in his thighs, the hard curves of his buttocks, the narrow lines of his hips, the breadth of his shoulders, and even the play of sunlight on his crisp black hair. When she realized her own thoughts, she looked quickly away, her cheeks aflame, until Ryan dropped lightly to the deck before her and dusted off his breeches. To Lindsay's further consternation, she discovered that her father had gone to join her mother at the rail.

Eyeing her shirt and breeches, Ryan remarked lightly, "I hope you didn't dress up on my account."

She tried to arch an eyebrow. "Actually, sir, I dressed *down* on your account!"

"I'm sorry to hear it!" He laughed absently, then looked for Raveneau. "I know you'll think me cruel to deny you my company, but I must speak to your father. Excuse me."

Lindsay fumed as she realized that she was standing alone and that if she went to join her parents it would appear she was following him. Still, she had little choice and approached the trio at the rail just as a man who looked vaguely familiar to her mounted the steps to the quarterdeck. He was stout, with thinning dark hair, rosy cheeks, and a dignified manner accentuated by the large pewter tray of rolls he carried.

"Harvey!" Coleraine greeted the man with a grin. "Is it possible that those are—"

"Hot cross buns, sir" came the response in stentorian British tones. "I baked them myself this morning before coming on board."

"Captain Raveneau, have you met my steward, Harvey Jenkins? Harvey, you are in the presence of Captain Raveneau, his wife, and his daughter."

"A rare privilege, I assure you," Harvey intoned, nodding all around. "I regret that I cannot salute, Captain, but my hands are otherwise engaged."

The aroma of the hot cross buns nearly dispelled Lindsay's embarrassing memory of her last encounter with Harvey on board the *Chimera*. At least, thankfully, his face gave nothing away as he extended the tray and waited for each of them to partake. When Harvey had gone and the men had begun talking again, Lindsay leaned toward her mother and whispered, "I can't believe that he had the gall to bring his steward with him! Does he pretend to command this ship?"

Devon gave her a quelling look. In the ensuing silence, Lindsay heard her father say quietly, "It looks clear ahead?"

"No sign of another mast all the way to the ocean, sir," Ryan assured him, "but that's not surprising considering the fact that we set sail east of the British fleet that's anchored south of New London."

Raveneau nodded and gazed pensively out over the water. "It would seem that we're safe for the moment, but God knows what challenges wait for us in the Atlantic."

CHAPTER
6

May 4, 1814

"I DIDN'T EXPECT YOU TO BE AWAKE, SIR." HARVEY Jenkins stood in the doorway to Ryan's cabin, holding out an orange. "Considering the fact that you took watch most of the night, when you weren't even scheduled, and that Captain Raveneau sent you below to sleep, I thought that you would be in arms of Morpheus until early afternoon."

Propped against pillows at the end of his bunk, Ryan looked up from a slender, well-leafed book. "Why are you here, then?"

"I was going to leave this orange to provide sustenance upon your awakening."

He tried not to smile at the steward's curious turn of phrase. "My own mother never looked after me with half your devotion, Harvey." Accepting the perfect fruit, he wondered, "Where do you find these things?"

"I think of it as an occupational duty, sir, preparing properly for voyages like this. I dare to hope that I may be the finest steward on any ship."

"I'm sure you are, Harvey," Ryan concurred with a mixture of fondness and amusement. "It's just a shame that your talents are wasted on me."

The steward smiled at that. "Would you like breakfast now, sir?"

"Thank you, no. I think I may go up on deck for a bit."

When Harvey had gone, Ryan lay back against the pillows and tossed the orange into the air a few times, wondering at the restlessness that had kept him awake and driven him aloft last night and now prevented him from sleeping for more than an hour this morning. He told himself that the constant threat of British attack had him on edge, and that was true. Used to stalking other ships, Ryan was unnerved by this dangerous situation that demanded they escape detection by the British fleet.

He was further unnerved by the proximity of Lindsay Raveneau, but that was something he didn't want to think about. She had attempted either to avoid or to ignore him during these first days at sea, and while he certainly wasn't pining for *her* company, he found her behavior annoying in the extreme. Even during meals in the captain's cabin, which he had been invited to share as "one of the family," Lindsay tried to pretend he didn't exist. Last night, he'd pleaded fatigue and eaten alone.

Sighing, Ryan sat up and pulled on his boots. He then tucked his shirt into dove-gray breeches, raked a hand through his hair, and picked up the book and orange. Instinctively adjusting to the sway of the ship, he went out into the gangway.

"Silly thing!" scolded a feminine voice.

Against his better judgment, Ryan glanced into Lindsay's open cabin. Sunlight poured through the transom, striking sparks over the bright banner of her hair. Clad in what he thought of as one of her "schoolteacher dresses," a modest, unrevealing frock of pale yellow muslin, Lindsay stood on a chair in her stockinged feet.

Teetering precariously, she was trying to free a book from the highest-braced shelf.

"Come here!" she warned it.

"And I'd begun to think you didn't like me," Ryan remarked lightly, reaching up at the same time to pry loose the offending book.

Lindsay was so startled that she cried out, then lost her balance as the ship rolled to starboard. The chair tipped and she found herself in Ryan's arms.

"Must you always sneak up on me?" she demanded angrily.

"I thought I was coming to the aid of a damsel in distress! Your lack of gratitude could discourage my chivalrous inclinations," he chuckled.

"And your brand of chivalry could kill me! Now put me down, you beast!"

"I find it highly mysterious that two people as nice and intelligent as your parents could have raised such a termagant."

Thrashing ineffectually in his strong embrace, Lindsay threatened, "Loose me, or I'll scream!"

"How terrifying." He lowered his face to hers, one brow flicking upward as he felt her heart begin to pound against his chest. "Ask me nicely."

She glared at him, clenching her teeth against the string of epithets she longed to unleash. Her father would not appreciate it if she made a scene for all the ship to hear, so Lindsay tried to ignore the traitorous response of her body to Ryan's nearness and said coolly, "I would appreciate it if you would release me, sir."

"Not exactly heartwarming, but I suppose that will have to do," he decided. Walking over to the bunk, he dropped her lightly.

"I *detest* you!" Lindsay spat, struggling to sit up.

He nodded and reached over to pull her tangled skirts down over enticingly shaped legs. "So you've mentioned—with tedious frequency, I might add. I've been thinking, Miss Raveneau, that it might be advisable for you to consider polishing your conversational skills during this voyage if you hope to be a success in the drawing rooms of London. Somehow, I doubt that the British aristocracy would appreciate your incessant declarations of loathing."

Her only response was a low growling sound.

Ryan, meanwhile, turned his attention to the book he had pried from its shelf. "What are we reading? Byron? Oh, my, *this* is interesting!" Casually, he sat down at the other end of her bunk, leaned against the bulkhead, and opened the slim volume.

She was about to upbraid him for soiling her bunk when a better approach occurred to her. Laughing as if he had just told a highly amusing joke, Lindsay exclaimed, "Come now, Captain Coleraine, certainly you don't expect me to believe that *you* can *read*!"

His eyes were on the pages as he thumbed through them, but the corners of his mouth twitched slightly. "Shocking but true. And, at the risk of sounding immodest, I might add that reading is the least of my numerous talents."

"That boast strikes me as more ridiculous than immodest," Lindsay muttered, surreptitiously studying his rakish profile.

It seemed he hadn't heard her. "So, it was a craving for the pale, romantic Lord Byron that caused you to risk life and limb atop that chair! And for *Childe Harold's Pilgrimage* of all things. Tsk, tsk, Miss Raveneau. You give yourself away."

"I don't know what you mean," she replied primly.

"Don't you? You would have people believe that you're as dry as dust, without warmth or tears or dreams or passions, and yet you were about to immerse yourself in poetry that celebrates a debauched nobleman whose chief pastimes are riotous living and flagrant *love affairs*." Ryan reached for his orange and began to peel it while reading aloud. " 'Childe Harold through Sin's long labyrinth had run.' Boggles the imagination, hmm? 'With pleasure drugged, he almost longed for woe.' Now, Miss Raveneau, is it possible that you are able to find anything to identify with in such sentiments?''

Lindsay had been staring at his long, golden-brown fingers as they deftly made a spiral of orange peel. Now feeling Ryan's eyes on her, full of mischief, she retorted, "It is not necessary to identify with fine literature to appreciate its worth, sir."

He laughed aloud at that. "Ah, I see. You approach Byron from a loftier, more cerebral view than all those other females who swoon and spin fantasies of dark rapture over his poetry!" All too aware of the way she watched him peel and now eat the succulent orange, Ryan offered her a piece. "Hungry?"

When Lindsay took the segment, their fingers brushed. "It's too rare and delicious-looking to waste on the likes of you."

"You're welcome." He smiled.

At that moment, there was a commotion on the gangway and the young face of Drew, erstwhile first mate on the *Chimera*, appeared in the doorway. "Captain Coleraine? You're needed on deck, sir."

Rising lithely, Ryan looked back at Lindsay and sighed in mock dismay. "And we were having such a good time! Ah, well, duty calls. I realize that you must be desolate to see me go, but take heart! Now you have the orange all to yourself."

Lindsay caught the half-eaten fruit, still warm from his hands, and watched Ryan exit. Curious, unsettled emotions churned inside of her. The realization that she was beginning to *like* him rankled, and as for the other feelings he stirred up . . .

Straightening, Lindsay shook her head and sought distraction. An unfamiliar book lay at the far end of the bunk; on its spine, embossed in gold, was the name Wordsworth. Had her mother left it there? Puzzled, Lindsay reached for the beautifully bound volume and opened it. Inscribed on the flyleaf, in a strong, male hand, were the words: "Property of Ryan Burke Coleraine." The pages showed definite signs of use; this was a book that had been read and enjoyed many times. The first half of the book consisted of Wordsworth's long, autobiographical poem, *The Prelude*. Lindsay found herself looking at it with new eyes now as she realized how close Wordsworth's Lake District home was to Ireland. One particularly worn page contained the verse:

> Wisdom and Spirit of the Universe!
> Thou Soul that art the eternity of thought,
> That givest to forms and images a breath
> And everlasting motion, not in vain
> By day or star-light thus from my first dawn
> Of childhood didst thou intertwine for me
> The passions that build up our human soul . . .

Lying back, Lindsay cradled the book against her breast, broke off another segment of orange, and wondered just what sort of man Ryan Coleraine really was.

Ominous charcoal-gray clouds were scudding across the afternoon sky as Ryan ascended to the quarterdeck. He discovered Captain Raveneau leaning against the larboard rail, his expression grim.

"Take a look," the older man said, proffering a polished brass telescope.

In the distance, Ryan could barely make out the billowing sails and three tall masts of a massive frigate which flew an American pennant.

"Probably British, hmm?" he murmured.

"Since *we* are flying the Union Jack, I'd say that's a safe assumption!" Raveneau agreed with a grim smile. "This penchant for false colors begins to border on the ridiculous. One begins to feel *sure* that every ship's true nationality is diametrically opposed to the flag it flies."

"That frigate is enormous," Ryan assessed quietly,

still looking through the telescope, "and it's giving chase. What do you intend to do?"

"*Alors!* You know full well what I'd *like* to do! Nothing would please me more than to play with that overgrown monster for a few hours, then launch a creative attack and rid the ocean of one more British vessel. However," he sighed, "circumstances deny us such sport, which is precisely the reason I have prayed ever since we set sail that we might escape detection. We go to England as ostensibly peaceful, neutral visitors. There will be difficulties enough earning the trust of the powers that be in London without destroying one of their ships before we even arrive!"

Ryan winced, fearing what was coming. "Must we strike our colors and surrender?"

"Well . . . there's no point in making it *too* easy. Let them chase us for a while." Raveneau gazed off into the distance. "My only worry, if they overtake us, is the charts."

"Ah, that's right. Those charts could prove quite valuable to the British, couldn't they?"

André nodded grimly. "They're filled with information about strategic means of entry into harbors all along the eastern seaboard. I should have removed them before we set sail, I suppose, but they might prove the difference for our own survival someday. Well, no point in worrying now. The charts are hidden, and with luck no one will ever have cause to search for them."

"If anyone can outrun that frigate, it's you, sir," Ryan said reassuringly.

"We, you mean!" Raveneau smiled, then turned to his businesslike first lieutenant, Mason, and gave the "all hands" order.

Within moments, the decks and ratlines bristled with seamen clad in loose, knee-length trousers, striped jerseys and tarpaulin hats that had been waterproofed with tar or paint.

Coleraine knew that he was probably the most compe-

tent privateer captain in active service at that time, but
he felt no overpowering urge to offer advice to André
Raveneau. Although the older man may not have been
faced with this sort of challenge in recent years, he had
practiced for more than thirty years, and Ryan never
doubted that the outcome of this encounter would be
governed by Raveneau's sure hand. The marks of a
competent privateer captain were smart sail-handling and
clever maneuvering abilities, a sure judgment of wind
power and direction, and an intimate knowledge of the
capabilities of his vessel. Captain Raveneau was expert
in all three areas.

Freed of responsibility, Ryan climbed the ratlines to
join the topmen on the mast high above the slanting
decks to supervise the energetic pulling and hauling of
sails that accompanied Raveneau's orders to tack lee-
ward. The wind was with them, fueled by the burgeoning storm clouds. Ryan prayed that the rain would wait.

Belowdecks, Lindsay listened to the thundering of the
slatting canvas and the stamping of what sounded like
hundreds of feet as the sheets and braces were let go
and hauled. In no time, she had shed her gown, replacing it with Nathan's shirt and breeches. She then dashed
out into the gangway and collided with her mother, who
was similarly garbed.

"What's happening?" cried Lindsay.

"From the sound of it, I'd say that we've been spotted by the British!"

"Papa won't mind if we go above?"

Devon, already on her way, tossed a smile over one
shoulder. "Oh, certainly he'll mind, but if we stand our
ground, he'll doubtless be too busy to press the issue.
Better yet, he may not notice us for a while if we stay
out of the way!"

They clambered up the ladder and out through the
hatch. Lindsay's first impression on the gun deck was
that pandemonium reigned, but she soon realized that

each seaman was engaged in a specific activity. Spotting Drew, she demanded,

"Is there going to be a battle?"

Devon overheard and blinked in surprise at her daughter's excited tone.

"The captain says we should try to outrun them," Drew shouted above the din before he disappeared.

La Mouette heeled over as the shifted sails caught a fresh blast of wind and altered the ship's course. Lindsay had adjusted to the pitching decks her first day on board, and now she balanced neatly, standing with arms akimbo.

"Outrun them?!" she yelled at her mother. "Is this possible? My own father is turning tail? What has happened to simple bravery?!"

Hanging above, a yardarm braced between his chest and arms, Ryan looked down and watched Lindsay enacting an all-too-familiar drama on the gun deck. Hard droplets of rain began to pelt his face as he sighed and reached for the ratlines. He didn't need to hear what she was saying; the sight of her shouting and pointing in outrage was enough.

"Lindsay!" Devon was exclaiming. "What's come over you?"

"I want to see justice done! I'm tired of watching Americans roll over like befuddled dogs and simply *give up* without a fight!" Spinning around, she started toward the quarterdeck. "I'm going to talk to Papa!"

A hand caught Lindsay's shirt from behind, halting her progress. "I'd advise against that," Ryan said firmly.

The sound of that voice only increased her fury. Whirling, she challenged, "You have never had any right to dictate to me, Captain Coleraine, especially not *here*, on my family's ship in the presence of my parents! I am an adult, and demand that you treat me as such!" She tried to wrest her shirttail from his grasp. "Let *go!*"

"Not if you're going to storm the quarterdeck and deliver an ill-timed harangue to the captain!"

Lindsay looked imploringly to her mother. "Will you please tell this—this *person* to leave me alone? He has persisted in giving me orders and manhandling me since the day we met. Is it not plain to you why I detest him?"

The sight of her offspring, wet and wild-eyed amidst the melee on deck, inspired a strong mixture of emotions in Devon. It was as if she were looking at a stranger, for Lindsay had never behaved thus in the past, and yet, at the same time, it seemed that she was seeing herself thirty years earlier. The breeches, the ship, the tangled mass of golden-rose curls, and most especially, the unchecked temper . . . all of these recalled Devon's own early days with André. Unfortunately, she could not encourage Lindsay's intention to confront her father, at least not *now*. Marriage to André also meant that she had learned from him, as he had from her, and she had considerably more understanding of his judgment and wisdom than she'd possessed at eighteen. Also, Devon was his mate, his partner, and no matter how devoted she might be to her children, her husband had always come first, just as she was the most important person in *his* life.

"Lindsay, darling, you'll hate me for saying this, but I don't want you to bother your father right now. I understand your feelings, and I doubtless would have shared them at your age, but after thirty years, I've learned to trust the judgment of my husband. He knows what he's doing."

"Judgment?!" she cried, all the while trying to twist loose from Coleraine's grip. "Don't you mean *cowardice*? Have you forgotten that the British burned every ship anchored at Pettipauge? That they humiliated the town? I tried to console myself by thinking that if Papa had been there, *he* at least would have fought back, but now I'm not so certain!"

Ryan spoke up, hoping to end the conversation. "The issue is not cowardice, Miss Raveneau, but common sense. The entire village of Pettipauge might have been burned to the ground if we had resisted. I can assure you that if I'd thought there was a chance for victory, I would have risked my own life, but that chance was not there. As for our present circumstances, it would be folly to fight a British ship when we hope to be welcomed in London."

"If America had been governed by common sense, we would never have fought and won the Revolutionary War!" Lindsay shouted.

Slanting a bemused look at Devon, Coleraine murmured, "Perhaps you weren't aware of your daughter's bloodthirsty tendencies. . . ."

"I hadn't a clue!" she replied dazedly.

"How dare you join forces with this beast?" Lindsay accused her mother. A sudden blast of rain stung her face, bringing her near tears. Ryan was sufficiently distracted by the conversation so that when she jerked her shirttail free, his fingers tightened a second too late. Lindsay ran into the rain toward the quarterdeck, her dawn-colored hair streaming out behind her. Ryan was only a step short of catching her when Lindsay's foot struck a coil of rope and she pitched sideways, striking her head against the carved rail.

CHAPTER
7

May 5–10, 1814

FOR MORE THAN A DOZEN HOURS, *LA MOUETTE* AND HER two able captains led the pursing British frigate on a wild and exhilarating chase over the Atlantic Ocean. The storm joined in the game, moving behind *La Mouette* shortly after sunset so that the frigate was forced to fight twice as hard to keep up. The rain continued, but the wind was more manageable. Under the guidance of Raveneau and Coleraine, and with the skill of their crew, *La Mouette* gradually lengthened the distance between the two ships until the frigate had been left behind the western horizon.

It was past midnight, however, before Raveneau let his wife coax him below for some sleep. Approaching his daughter's cabin, he murmured, "I still find it hard to believe this wild tale about Lindsay's antics up on deck."

"I found it hard to believe when it was happening!" Devon exclaimed, her voice rising slightly. Whispering, she continued, "Your daughter behaved like an absolute hellion!"

" 'Twould seem that she takes after her mother after all. I seem to remember an incident long ago when you defied my order to remain below during a storm—and ended up falling and hitting *your* head against the deck. . . ."

"I fell because I was struggling to throw a line to you after you had dived overboard to save Noah Jackson! If I hadn't been there, you might have died!"

"I'm aware of that, *petite chatte*. I realized that day that a hellion might have redeeming qualities." Smiling, he wrapped an arm around her diminutive form. "I must say that I find this uproar about Lindsay's behavior rather disconcerting. Have you not always bemoaned the fact that she was so unwaveringly self-contained?"

Devon shook her head, gazing across the cabin to the polished mahogany bunk where her daughter lay, pale against the white sheets, apricot-hued tresses spread out in contrast. Cassie sat in a chair inches away, mending an apron. "It's just that this new aspect of her personality has displayed itself suddenly. Each time she rails at Ryan Coleraine, I am *stunned*! Today, I could hardly believe that I was in the presence of my own daughter."

"Well, the crisis has passed. Lindsay did open her eyes and smile momentarily, so we know she'll be all right. Somehow, *La Mouette* performed a miracle and escaped that British frigate—"

"The miracle was performed by you, my love," Devon put in.

"Don't forget that I had assistance from Ryan and the crew! In any event, we're all safe, and I am exhausted and know you must be, too, after sitting with Lindsay for a dozen hours. Are you aware that it's past midnight, *chérie*? Let's go to bed."

"Thank goodness for Cassie." She sighed.

The Raveneaus stepped into the gangway just as Ryan Coleraine came down through the hatch. Though the rain had nearly stopped, his black hair and beard were still wet and his white linen shirt clung to his hard-muscled chest. Quickly, he approached them.

"How is she?"

"Still sleeping, but the surgeon assures us that's normal after a head injury," André replied. "Did you receive the message that she regained consciousness momentarily a few hours ago?"

"Yes. If not for that encouraging news, I couldn't have remained on deck." A muscle tightened in his jaw. "If I had not relaxed my guard and let her get away from me, this would not have happened."

"Don't be silly!" Devon admonished in a heated whisper. "Lindsay is a grown woman, and you must not hold yourself accountable in any way for her actions! You were never assigned to guard her safety, and thus were not responsible for it."

Ryan sighed harshly. He wanted to say that, after his experience with Lindsay during the British attack on Pettipauge, he thought that he knew better than anyone what she was capable of in a temper, and he couldn't help feeling that with the knowledge came an implied responsibility. There was no point in verbalizing those thoughts to her parents, though. It was plain that they had not been acquainted with Lindsay the spitfire—until now.

"Would you mind if I look in on her?" he asked quietly.

"Go right ahead," Raveneau said. "Cassie, our housekeeper, is with her, and we were just about to retire for a few hours." Almost as an afterthought, he asked, "Is the situation still stable above?"

"Fine, sir." Ryan gave him a tired smile. "The men are still marveling over the fact that we eluded confrontation with that frigate."

"Why? Are not the two finest sea captains in America on board? Failure would have been a bigger surprise!"

After bidding the Raveneaus good night, Coleraine

cautiously entered Lindsay's cabin. He half expected
her to sit up and order him out, but she lay still and
silent in the flickering lantern light.

Cassie rose to meet Ryan halfway. "It's good to see
you, Captain Coleraine," she whispered. "Would you
mind staying with Miss Lindsay for a few minutes? I
should go and tell my husband that I'll be spending the
night here."

He nodded and then, alone with Lindsay, approached
the bunk. Clad in a fresh, snowy-white bed gown, she
was the picture of innocent, serene beauty. Ryan reached
over and ran a fingertip along one long, shining curl, and
his mind spun back to the moments just after Lindsay
had fallen. The instant that he had realized she was
unconscious, Ryan had quickly checked her pulse, then
lifted her limp form gently in his arms to carry her below
to her cabin. Devon, with a mother's reserve of alert
composure, had not panicked but sent a boatswain's
mate to fetch the surgeon before following Ryan through
the hatch.

The wind had whipped Lindsay's wet hair into his
face as he crossed the deck. He remembered that now,
along with the unfamiliar feeling of desperation that had
gripped him. It still surprised Ryan when he realized
how troubled he was by Lindsay's plight. She looked
angelic, with her lips parted and long lashes brushing
delicately sculptured cheeks, but he knew that she would
be incensed that Ryan was staring at her in her helpless
state.

Lindsay's right hand was turned palm-up on the bedclothes. Ryan felt a pang at the sight of it, so pale and
soft. On an impulse, he laid his own brown forefinger
over her cool palm and was surprised to see Lindsay's
fingers curl around it.

"Ryan?" she whispered, her lashes fluttering open.

"Yes, Lindsay, I'm here." He reached out with his
free hand to brush stray tendrils of strawberry-blond
hair from her brow. Lindsay turned her face against his

hand. "I'm sorry . . . I've been so bad . . . I shouldn't be so bad to you."

"Nonsense," he replied warmly, smiling. When she tried to turn toward him, Ryan gently gathered her in his arms. "You're going to be just fine and then you can be as bad to me as you like. I won't mind a bit."

She smiled dreamily, nestling against his chest. "You're so strong. . . ."

Ryan blinked. "You had better go back to sleep, little one, before you say something you'll regret later on."

After nearly managing a smile in return, she closed her eyes. For a long moment, Coleraine studied her sleeping face, then bent to kiss her brow gently. If Lindsay comprehended the touch of Ryan's lips, she gave no sign.

Peeking into her daughter's cabin, Devon discovered Cassie putting fresh linen on the bunk.

"Where is Lindsay? Ought she to be up?"

"She claims her headache has disappeared, ma'am," Cassie replied with a sigh and a shrug. "Insisted on dressing and going on deck, but I believe that Captain Coleraine intercepted her in the gangway."

"Well, four days have passed, so I suppose we couldn't expect to keep her down any longer."

"The reasonable girl I used to know would have been content to stay abed with a stack of books!"

Devon laughed. "What do you suppose has caused this transformation?"

"If I didn't know better, I'd say Miss Lindsay was in love, but of course *that's* impossible! The only eligible candidate is Ryan Coleraine, and we all know well enough how she feels about *him*." Cassie sighed again and shook out a fresh sheet. "The man has only to open his mouth and she takes offense. Of course, Miss Lindsay has led a rather sheltered life, and she's never had to associate with anyone she didn't like, so perhaps it's just these enforced new circumstances that've exposed this new side of her character."

"Perhaps . . ." It did seem to be the only logical explanation. "Do you know what, Cassie? As incorrigible as Lindsay can be these days, I like seeing her show spirit."

"I suppose you're right. There's no real cause for alarm as long as Captain Coleraine doesn't lose his temper and strangle the girl!"

"I'd better see to it that he isn't doing that very thing as we speak. She never appeared on deck, and Ryan isn't there, either. Where could they be?"

The sound of Lindsay's voice, raised in tones of outrage, answered Devon's question. Following it to the Irishman's cabin, she discovered the two of them seated at a small table, apparently engaged in a card game.

"You must be cheating!" Lindsay accused, her eyes flashing.

Coleraine lounged back in his chair and stretched his legs. A thin cheroot was lightly clenched between his white teeth as he reached out to discard a red king. One card remained in his hand, while she held two.

"It's typical of you, little sister, to assail my honor in an effort to distract attention from the real reason you're losing," he taunted sardonically.

"Don't say it, you rude beast!"

Ryan continued imperturbably, "It would be a sign of maturity for you simply to admit that your intelligence is no match for mine."

"What a *horrendous* thing to say!" Lindsay cried, coming halfway out of her chair. "Just because you have had more practice gambling, that does not mean that you are more intelligent than I. No doubt you have mastered *all* the vices!"

He feigned modesty. "You flatter me, Miss Raveneau, but I fear it takes a lifetime of practice to achieve that level of expertise."

"Wishful thinking!" she shot back, drawing an appreciative grin from her opponent.

"Gracious!" Devon exclaimed from the doorway. "It appears that you are recovered, my dear!"

"You have a way with an understatement, Mrs. Raveneau," Coleraine said dryly as he stood to welcome her. "Won't you join us?"

"Mama," Lindsay demanded, "have you ever encountered a more arrogant jackanapes in your life?"

"I don't mean to interrupt or disparage your intelligence, Miss Raveneau, but doesn't the word *jackanapes* usually refer to a male?" Ryan wondered, straight-faced.

"I'm talking about you!" She made a sound of extreme exasperation as the color heightened in her cheeks.

Devon looked on with a mixture of amazement and consternation. It was encouraging to see Lindsay so animated and rosy again, but she wondered if her behavior wasn't a bit extreme. Accepting the chair that Ryan held for her, she observed, "The pair of you are the outside of enough! Can you not exchange two consecutive civil remarks?"

"I hope you don't think I'm to blame," Lindsay protested, studying her cards. "You have heard for yourself how he goads me."

Ryan laughed outright at that, devils in his eyes.

"Perhaps he's just teasing you, darling. Try to rise above it." Devon's own mouth turned up under the spell of the man's charm. How could her daughter be immune? His looks alone were devastating: ruffled black curls, clear blue eyes under arched brows, aquiline nose, sculpted cheekbones, bearded jaw, white teeth, and finally those shoulders, trim waist, lean thighs, and strong, handsomely made hands. Devon suppressed a maidenly sigh and looked over to discover Lindsay scowling at her cards. Trying a different tack, she inquired, "Are you two playing piquet?"

Ryan nodded, trying to look serious as he waited for his opponent to make her final, fatal discard.

"I didn't know that you were familiar with the game, Lindsay," she pursued.

The girl looked up, smoldering. "Well, I wasn't until an hour ago!" At her wit's end, Lindsay discarded a diamond only to have Ryan show her the club he'd been guarding. The game was his.

"That's three out of three," he murmured. "Will you yield?"

"But there's been no wager involved, has there?" Devon interjected.

"Your daughter insisted, Mrs. Raveneau."

"But what could she have offered?"

"My gold-embossed volume of William Blake against his first edition of Shelley," Lindsay mourned, inclining her head toward the two books reposing on the edge of the table.

"I think that, in view of your unfamiliarity with the game, we should postpone the wager until a later date," Ryan decided.

She narrowed her gray eyes suspiciously. "My word is good, sir."

"Captain Coleraine is right, Lindsay. With practice, you'll doubtless win easily! Save the books you both love for a more balanced confrontation."

"No!" she cried. "I won't be treated like a child! I made a wager and I mean to honor it." Lifting her chin, Lindsay held out the book. "Perhaps a dose of Blake will be good for your soul."

"Well, anything's possible." Ryan smiled. He accepted the volume he knew she treasured only out of deference to her pride. "Please feel free to borrow this whenever you wish. In fact"—he gestured casually toward the bookshelves that were as filled as her own—"I hope that you will avail yourself of any of these books—on the off chance that there might be something interesting that you do not already own."

Lindsay found it far easier to deal with his insolence than his kindness. "You needn't patronize me. I intend to win my book back and gain possession of many of yours before this voyage ends.''

''I don't doubt that you'll try.'' He nodded, a spark of admiration in his eyes.

At that moment, when Devon was casting about wildly for a way to lighten the mood, André Raveneau appeared. ''Well, isn't this a cozy scene!'' he observed, bending to kiss first his wife and then his daughter. ''How are you feeling, *ma fille*?''

''Much better, Papa.'' She smiled, thawing visibly. ''When I awoke today, my headache had vanished!''

''Well, that's good news! It's wonderful to see you up and dressed. What's going on here?''

''Captain Coleraine has been teaching me to play piquet,'' she answered as lightly as she was able.

''Ah, *formidable*! I'm pleased that you two have declared a truce.'' He cocked an approving eyebrow at Ryan. ''I knew that with a little time and effort you could become friends.''

As if on cue, Cassie appeared with a tray of neatly sliced bread, meat, cheese, and apples surrounded by pewter mugs of red wine. ''I thought you all might enjoy something to eat,'' she explained, placing the offering on the table.

Ryan gathered up the cards as André took the remaining chair and lifted his mug to the other three. ''Here's to this newly formed family—and a successful adventure in London.''

Dutifully, they joined in the toast. Lindsay looked at Ryan under her eyelashes as she took a sip of wine and flushed when he dared to wink at her. Devon, meanwhile, was gazing thoughtfully at her new Irish ''son.''

''You know, we're nearly halfway to England,'' she said, ''and I think it's time to begin formulating a plan.''

''Really! A *plan*?'' André echoed, feigning surprise. ''Is it possible that you have one in mind already?''

''Be serious! I've listened to enough nonsense this past hour!'' Confronted with three startled, contrite faces,

Devon continued, "We can't just stumble into London, acting as we please, and expect to melt successfully into society. Lindsay, for example, must discipline herself to behave as a proper lady, which—until lately—has not been a problem for her. Far more important is Ryan's role. I've given quite a bit of thought to this. . . ." She turned her attention to him and was pleased to see that, aside from raised brows, he appeared serious and receptive. "Pretending to be Nathan should not be difficult since our son hasn't been to London for over ten years. When last seen there, he was a rather gangly youth of eighteen and could have undergone all manner of changes during the intervening decade. What concerns me more is finding a way to ensure your entrée into the best, and most influential, social circles—and, at the same time, seeing to it that the men you fraternize with are not on their guard when you're near."

Fascinated, Ryan leaned back in his chair and stroked his bearded jaw. "Please, don't keep me in suspense!"

"Well," Devon said with a smile, looking around the table, "I think that the perfect solution would be to make Ryan a fop!"

"I beg your pardon?" her subject murmured, hoping that he had heard amiss.

"You know, a fop! A witless dandy who cares only about the cut of his clothes, the style of his cravat, the shine on his boots, and the bloodline of his horses!"

This outburst elicited stunned silence from the two men and a slow, evil smile from Lindsay. André was the first to speak. "*Chérie,* has the wine gone to your head?"

"Certainly not! I've been mulling this over for days. Don't you see, if Ryan appears on the scene in London looking and behaving as he always does, he'd be the last person to overhear secrets. He seems far too sharp-witted and confident—aside from the fact that women would be entranced by him at first sight and the men would be fearfully resentful. The whole purpose of Ryan coming along was to mix with the younger set, where you,

André, would be out of place. A preoccupation with fashion would ensure him a position in society, while the rather superficial, slow-witted attitude of a fop would further his opportunities to eavesdrop on critical conversations!''

Raveneau considered this for a long moment before turning to the younger man. ''I hate to say this, but my wife does have a point.''

Ryan mustered a rather pained smile as he tried to picture himself mincing through the drawing rooms of London. ''I know, but that doesn't mean I like it!''

CHAPTER
8

May 26, 1814

T HE WIND AND WEATHER COOPERATED TO SPEED *LA*
Mouette's crossing to Britain so that on the morning of
May twenty-sixth, Captain Raveneau was able to announce that they would dock at Falmouth the following
day.

"Isn't it exciting? Before we know it, we'll be in
London!" Devon exclaimed to her daughter as they
shared a spartan breakfast of tea, biscuits, and jam in
Lindsay's snug cabin. Supplies were low, the fresh food
had been consumed weeks before, and everyone talked
of feasting once they reached England.

"I must confess that I'm a bit nervous," Lindsay said
in a small voice. "London will be so huge, so different
from what I'm used to. Furthermore, it's filled with
strangers—snobbish ones at that!—who likely won't welcome an American girl with open arms!" She paused,
then raised great gray eyes that shone with trepidation.
"What if they don't like me, Mama?"

"Half your problem, darling, is that you have never

been a social creature. From the time you could read, not so long after you began walking, as I recall, you would steal away from parties and we'd find you lying on your bed or under the big oak, reading." Devon reached over to clasp her daughter's hand. "You know that I have a deep love for books myself and that nothing could have pleased me more than your intellectual curiosity. However, it's important that you strive for balance in your life, never more than now. You're at an age when you should be exploring new places and people, Lindsay, and thinking about what you want from the future." She paused, smiling. "It's time, I'd say, for you to *live* life rather than read about the lives of others. I realize that the first steps of such an adventure can be precarious, but you'll soon be enjoying yourself and the new experiences that wait for you in England."

"And what about Ryan Coleraine?"

Devon, in the midst of spreading jam on a biscuit, glanced up in surprise. "Pardon?"

"Your new son!" Lindsay elaborated in acid tones. "The person I am supposed to shower with sisterly love!"

"What about him?"

"You know very well that there's a problem, and you and Papa have stubbornly refused to face it. I detest that man and I don't see how I can be expected to hide that fact from the world!"

"Darling, aren't you being rather dramatic? You only need to pretend to be Ryan's sister, not his lover!" Devon saw all too clearly the sudden smudges of color in the girl's cheeks. "Besides, I thought you two had grown quite friendly. The daily games of piquet, the sharing of books . . ."

"Mother, I've only tolerated him because I'm bored to tears on this ship! You know I hate the sea, I've told you often enough, just as I've told you that I loathe your precious Ryan, but you refuse to take me at my word!"

"You needn't shout, Lindsay. What purpose is served by this petulant outburst? If it is for my benefit, what response do you expect? I cannot send you home, can I? Nor can I undo Ryan's new role in our lives." Her blue eyes flashed. "You seem to suggest that our current and future circumstances are the result of some sort of elaborate plot to frustrate you! It would be wise, Lindsay, for you to remember that none of us asked to be here today—including Ryan Coleraine! I cannot tell you how disappointing it is for me to think that you appear to see life only in terms of the effect it has on you. Certainly this is not a trait that you learned from your parents! When I was your age, I had already learned that fortune would not always smile on me, but even unhappy turns of fate can be improved with the proper attitude. Self-pity is most unbecoming, my dear—learn to make the best of this opportunity!"

Lindsay paled. Her mother had always been careful not to criticize her for being different from the rest of the Raveneaus; on the contrary, she had quietly supported Lindsay's individuality. This unexpected dressing-down had a profound effect. "Oh, Mama," she whispered, "I can't bear for you to think that I am a selfish termagant!" Unbidden, memories of Ryan Coleraine calling her similar names returned to haunt her. "I think I am just frightened, and nervous, and those are feelings I'm not used to dealing with."

"Don't you see, though, sweetheart, it's time you learned!" Devon insisted in a gentler tone. "You can't live through books and hide from the real world. And I am convinced that once you begin to share life with real people, you'll be fascinated! Every new emotion will teach you something. You've always been nearly too poised and adult for your age—I suspect that you believed that you simply bypassed the turmoil one feels while growing up. You're a strong, intelligent girl, though, and I know you'll emerge a strong, wise woman if you muster your courage and plunge ahead."

"If you say this, then it must be true. Can I tell you a secret, Mama?"

"Silly girl, of course you can!" Devon impulsively leaned forward to kiss her daughter's creamy cheek.

"I've always thought that you were the most perfect woman God ever created. I used to dream about growing up to be just like you, but then it seemed impossible, so I think I decided that it would be safer to be *unlike* you."

"I'll accept the compliment, Lindsay, but I won't hear you disparage yourself! While you were growing up, so self-possessed and beautiful, I would think how you were the child *my* mother always wished for. I was always so undisciplined and emotional that when I looked at you I began to believe that you were probably God's quiet and sensible blessing on this adventure-craving family." Devon smiled rather wistfully. "So it seems that we all have foibles and worries that we manage to conceal from the rest of the world, hmm?"

Lindsay nodded, sipped her tea, and then stared pensively at the cup. "I suppose you're right."

Having become accustomed only lately to this particular distracted look, Devon said, "In any event, I think that we are more alike than either one of us knew before. Ryan seems to have brought out the 'me' in you."

"He drives me to madness!" Lindsay burst out.

"He appeals to you not in the very least?"

"I don't think so, Mama. He makes me feel . . . unsettled! There have been moments when he's been nice or has made me laugh with honest pleasure, but invariably he follows them with some horrid word or deed that makes me want to attack him and throw him overboard!" Lindsay paused, breathing deeply in an effort to calm herself. "I think he enjoys goading me until I lose control. . . ."

"And you are unused to that."

"Yes! Is that wrong? And am I wrong for disliking someone who torments me for his own amusement?"

"But, darling, do you not respond in kind?" Devon asked softly. "I have witnessed your verbal duels—you are an equal participant, not a victim. In fact, at the risk

of incurring your wrath, your father and I have both
remarked that you appear to enjoy sparring with Ryan.''

"*What?* That's ridiculous! How could I possibly de-
rive even a tiny bit of pleasure from the company of
such a taunting brute? Mama, he laughs at me! Half the
time he treats me as if I'm twelve years old!''

"Well, sometimes one enjoys exercising one's wits . . .''
Seeing that her daughter was about to interrupt with
another storm of protest, Devon held up her hand. "No,
no, that's enough. Obviously, I'm wrong and that isn't
the case here. I truly am sorry that Ryan's company is
such a trial for you, but, my dear, there's nothing to be
done. You'll have to make the best of it. No one expects
you to behave as if you adore the man, and I'm sure no
one will think it odd if two supposed siblings cannot get
along.'' Her cornflower-blue eyes twinkled as she added,
"In fact, you may be more believable as a sister if you
are ever looking daggers at Ryan. I'll be very surprised
if London's female population doesn't swoon when he's
introduced into the elite social circles. No doubt the
consensus will be that only a sister could remain immune to the man's looks and charm.''

Lindsay sniffed. "I suppose if one's taste runs to
savages . . .''

"Oh, he'll look anything but savage by the time he
appears in public in London. Which reminds me, I must
see that Ryan's beard is shaved today, just in case we
encounter anyone we know before we reach our house.''

Brightening, Lindsay inquired, "Can I watch?''

Devon stood and brushed stray crumbs from her simple pale blue frock. "I suppose so, if Ryan doesn't mind
an audience—and you promise to behave yourself.''

Following her mother toward the gangway, Lindsay
murmured, "I wish that I might wield the razor . . .''

Before Devon could scold her, Ryan Coleraine leaned
around the doorway. "Did I hear someone mention my
name?''

"Eavesdropping again?'' Lindsay asked.

"Children!" warned her mother, narrowing her eyes at both of them for good measure. "Now, then, Ryan dear, your appearance is very fortuitous. We were just about to go in search of you!"

"Why do I have the feeling that I should have hidden myself in an empty barrel? Does this have something to do with your plan to make me a fop?" Coleraine took a step backward into the gangway. "Madame, say that you won't squeeze me into a long-tailed coat and make me take snuff from an enameled box while I'm still on board ship! It would cause me no end of humiliation."

His display of mock terror amused Devon, but even as she laughed lightly, she caught his sleeve and held him fast. "Don't be silly, darling son . . . I only mean to shave your beard!"

"What?" Horrified, Ryan protected the lower half of his face with both hands. "It's apparent that you have been too long at sea, madame! You've been overtaken by strange fantasies!"

Off to one side, Lindsay mused, "How interesting. Don't you see, Mama, it's just like the story of Samson. Captain Coleraine is afraid that his manly powers will disappear if you rob him of this hirsute proof of his sex."

Noting the menacing glare Ryan slanted at her daughter, Devon laughed brightly. "Now, Lindsay, don't be foolish. Ryan was only teasing me, weren't you? And Lindsay is teasing you, Ryan!"

"Why, I wonder, do none of us look amused?" He arched a sharp black brow down at Devon.

"Well, it's just as you said. We've been too long at sea. But take heart! It's almost over, and soon you two will be enjoying yourselves in London." She attempted to pat Ryan's arm reassuringly, but it was hard and unyielding through the fabric of his shirt. "As for the shaving of your beard, I'm sure you realize that it is just a necessary precaution, in case we encounter anyone we know before reaching our house in London. Once we're there, we'll plead fatigue and begin preparing your masquerade in earnest, but for now we simply must take off that beard. It makes you look far too menacing and masculine.''

"Leave it to me, then."

"Nonsense!" Devon gave him her prettiest smile. "André has had several beards since we met and married, and I became expert at shaving them. No valet could be more skilled. Now, come along to your cabin, then relax and put yourself in my hands.''

"Such a request is a strong test of the affection I feel for you, madame,'' he murmured, ''but lead on.''

Devon passed him into the gangway, and Lindsay was following when he caught her arm and drew her back into the cabin with him. "So, I am afraid that my 'manly powers' will disappear along with this 'hirsute proof of my sex'?" Ryan hissed sarcastically, his grip tightening as he watched excitement and alarm mingle in her gray eyes. "Just to set the record straight, Miss Raveneau, this beard is *not* the only proof of my sex. Far from it! Do you wish further clarification? I wouldn't mind showing you—''

Her heart was thundering against her breastbone. "N-no! Of course not!" She tried to look defiant, praying that her cheeks were not afire. "Never have I encountered a baser man, sir. You are disgusting!''

"My apologies." Ryan tried not to betray his amusement. "I didn't realize that the prospect of seeing the hair on my chest would offend your maidenly sensibilities.''

Lindsay couldn't meet his eyes. She pushed past, raging at herself for falling into his trap, while Ryan followed in her wake, chuckling softly.

Lindsay had been looking forward to gloating while her mother bared Ryan Coleraine's face. She'd wanted to toss him glances both mischievous and innocent as he submitted, helplessly vulnerable, to the razor. However, he effectively took the wind from her sails with his well-timed confrontation in her cabin. After that, she didn't want to look at him and that was just fine with Ryan.

He managed to cajole Devon into allowing him to help with his own shearing. She let him look into a mirror as she first used scissors to trim the neat black beard back to stubble, then applied shaving soap with his fine boar-bristle brush, and finally took out the sharpened razor. Ryan was thankful that he shaved his neck each morning, so there seemed little risk that Devon could inflict a mortal wound. In fact, she had told the truth: She shaved him beautifully, and Ryan only took over in areas he felt were especially tricky.

When they finished, he rubbed off the stray bits of soap with a towel and gave Devon a dubious look. "Well? Will you still claim me as a son?"

She was staring in delight, one hand pressed to her mouth as she thought, My God, how handsome he is! Ryan's beard had always been neatly trimmed, conforming to the shape of his jaw, but still she had been unprepared for the rakish, masculine beauty of his face.

"Why did you ever cover this up?" She reached out to trace the line of his cheekbone and chin.

"Just modest, I suppose," Ryan replied flippantly. Glancing in the mirror, he winced. "God, I feel so exposed!"

"I was wrong about one thing. Removing that beard hasn't lessened the manliness of your face one iota . . . but, of course, it had to be done. London dandies do not wear beards." Devon gazed at him thoughtfully. "We'll just have to devise other means of making you look foppish. . . ."

"No patches, please," he begged with a smile. "I draw the line at beauty marks."

CHAPTER
9

May 25–27, 1814

Evening PROVED TO BE SO FILLED WITH ACTIVITY THAT there was no opportunity for the newly formed family to sit down together for supper. Lindsay spent hours in her cabin packing books and clothing, and she knew that across the gangway Harvey was performing the same services for his employer. Meanwhile, the two captains were on deck, charting a safe, sure course to Falmouth and discussing the morning's schedule with the boatswain and first mate.

It was nearly midnight when Raveneau appeared in the doorway to Lindsay's cabin.

"I'm to bed, *ma fille.*"

She smiled fondly at the sight of his handsome face. "Mama said good night barely a quarter hour ago, so you'll doubtless find her awake."

"Good. I've missed her this long evening." Wordlessly, he opened his arms and folded Lindsay against his broad chest. "I've missed you as well. Truth to tell, I look forward to our interlude in London. Certainly there is serious work to be done there, but we should also be able to enjoy ourselves as a family, and there is a great deal in England to enjoy!"

"I can't wait to see Mouette!" Lindsay admitted, filled with a new excitement.

"She may not recognize you, *chérie*. You couldn't have been more than fourteen the last time she came to America!"

"I know. Perhaps we can be friends now." It was sometimes hard for Lindsay to realize that her sister was thirty-two years old and the mother of two sons. Lindsay had only been seven when Mouette fell in love with Sir Harry Brandreth, a young baronet, during a family visit to London. She'd married him that same summer and lived in England ever since. The war had made visits impossible during the past two years, and now Lindsay wondered often if she and Mouette might become close since she had bridged the gap to adulthood. Oddly enough, she felt shy about meeting her sister again, for she barely knew her.

"That's the spirit," André said approvingly. "Concentrate on the happy prospects for our sojourn in London while you wait for sleep tonight." Hugging her close, he kissed Lindsay's rosy-gold curls.

She wrapped her arms around him and held fast, inhaling her father's familiar scent and enjoying the feeling that he would take care of everything.

"Sleep well, *ma fille*," André murmured gently, his steel-gray eyes soft as he met those of his daughter. "Pleasant dreams."

"You too, Papa. Give Mama a kiss for me."

"Now there's a favor I'll gladly grant!" Smiling, he kissed her brow once more, then took his leave.

Alone again, Lindsay paced across the slightly swaying deck of her cabin, wide awake. Finally, she decided to go above, pushing aside the realization that she would find Ryan Coleraine there.

Emerging through the hatch, Lindsay looked up to see a magnificent display of stars scattered over the night sky. The air was fresh, with only a trace of chill, and she let her shawl drop backward to reveal her half-bare upper arms and shoulders.

The gun and forecastle decks were quiet; in the starlight, she could see a few sailors propped against masts and rigging, half dozing. The wind was with them, filling the sails. Glancing upward to the quarterdeck, Lindsay recognized the tall, hard-muscled silhouette of Ryan Coleraine. He was leaning against the rail, forearms braced, gazing out over the shimmering blue-black ocean. She told herself that there was no other place to go and went to join him.

Unmoving as Lindsay approached, Ryan continued to look ahead even after she had reached his side. Then the corners of his mouth turned upward slightly as he murmured, "To what do I owe this honor?"

"My restlessness," she replied, copying his pose at the rail. "What a dazzling night!"

"Next you'll say that the stars look like diamonds."

"They do!" Lindsay felt no desire to take offense at his sardonic tone. On the brink of arriving in England, she was strangely giddy. "I should apologize for suggesting that the loss of your beard would unman you," she said magnanimously. "If anything, you are handsomer—in a most masculine way—without it."

Surprised, Ryan turned his head and stared at her, his brows raised. "How reassuring! Now I'll be able to sleep. I've been fretting all day . . ."

"No doubt." Lindsay gave him a happy smile, her teeth pretty and white in the starlight. "I seem to be in high spirits tonight. I don't think that you can annoy me."

"Perhaps I'd better not try, then."

"That would be pleasant."

Still leaning on the rail, they both looked back out at the sea and stars. Ryan indulged in a sidelong glance at

Lindsay and saw that she was still smiling. He was struck by the delicate beauty of her profile, from the cloud of strawberry-blond curls to the sweep of her lashes to the curve of her nose to the fine line of her chin, neck and throat. She truly was exquisite.

"Do you know the names of the stars?" Lindsay asked.

"Yes, of course." His tone was offhand. "Didn't you learn them from your father?"

"As a child, I think, but I haven't been to sea for a very long time. I didn't want any part of that family identity."

"Ah, yes, I remember. The black sheep. Or were you the white lamb and the rest of the Raveneaus black sheep?"

"A good question!" Lindsay laughed lightly. "But let's not rehash that tiresome subject. Won't you show me the stars? I can only identify the Big Dipper."

"Ursa Major, the Great Bear," he elaborated. "It's always there, you know, in this hemisphere. When I was a little boy in Ireland and my father showed me the stars, we called it the Plough." Ryan lifted a bronzed hand and outlined a different pattern through the dipper so that the handle slanted down to form a blade. "You see?"

Lindsay nodded, her gray eyes shifting from the stars, which were like diamonds scattered over midnight-blue velvet, to his deft, strong fingers.

"You know, the stars that one sees depend on the season, and even the month," he explained. "Cassiopeia is another constellation that never sets. It makes an *M* there to the north." He showed her how to draw a line from Mizar, the second star in the tail of the Great Bear, to find Cassiopeia. "Do you see the Little Dipper? That's the North Star at the end of its handle."

To Lindsay's surprise, she found that she was fascinated as Ryan went on to point out the constellation of

Cygnus, which made a cross, explaining that Deneb, one
of its major stars, was the Arabic word for *tail*. Then he
helped her find Boötes, which was nearly overhead. Its
brightest star, Arcturus, was a marvelous light orange,
and Ryan confirmed that this was the best time of year
to view it.

Several constellations later, Lindsay murmured, "You
love nature, don't you?"

He breathed deeply of the salty sea air and smiled.
"Don't we all? Why would you make such an observation?"

"I looked at the volume of Wordsworth you left in my
cabin. It was a celebration of nature."

After a moment, Ryan looked at her and smiled. "The
outdoors is the touchstone for my life. The sky, the sea,
the change of seasons, animals, flowers, trees . . . these
and all the rest are more wondrous to me than anything
money could ever buy, and they are constant. Wordsworth articulated it much better than I ever could, but
my feeling is that I can turn to nature when troubles
accumulate, and I'm reminded of the greater scheme of
things. When I can put aside petty everyday concerns,
the simple act of breathing gives me peace. Monetary
worries, politics, fashion, and the rest recede to their
proper place."

"I suppose that your philosophy must make it easier
for you to adapt with good grace to this charade we are
forced to perform."

He gazed down into her intent gray eyes and drew in
his breath. "Perhaps, but don't misunderstand me, Lindsay. I'm still very much a man and, being human, am
tied to the cares of our world."

"Yet you seem to be amused by the same things that
vex me intolerably!"

"My threshold for anger is doubtless higher than yours,
perhaps because I've lived longer. I have a temper,
though, as you well know."

Looking up at his chiseled face, Lindsay was all too

aware that her heart had begun to drum faster, her
cheeks were hot, and a strange tingling sensation seemed
to course through her veins. "Does it make you angry to
have to pretend to be my brother?"

"It may . . . but I'm not pretending yet. Until we
reach English soil tomorrow I am still Ryan Coleraine."
His right hand touched the soft curve of her cheek, then
traced Lindsay's bare neck. "I don't feel a bit like your
brother, and though I'll act the part once we reach
London, you'd be wise to remember that it's only a
masquerade."

Lindsay felt intoxicated by the stars, Ryan's voice,
and the warm proximity of his body. She yearned to
touch him, and she did so, reaching out to brush her
fingertips over the tiny black hairs on the back of his
hand. The thought of London was both exhilarating and
frightening, but for this instant Lindsay could escape.
There was no future, just these moments out of time on
a ship that bore no resemblance to her usual world.

When Ryan's arms encircled her waist, Lindsay melted
against him, craving the sensations his kiss had evoked
that wild morning in Pettipauge. How differently he is
made! she thought as he drew her against the length of
his body.

Just before she closed her eyes to await Ryan's kiss, a
sudden blaze of silvery light arced across the night sky.
Lindsay gasped in surprise and appreciation.

"Ryan! A shooting star!"

"Mmhmm." He was far more intent on the respon-
sive female body in his arms. "Comets are never more
beautiful than over the ocean, I think. A few hundred
years ago, an astronomer named Kepler wrote that they
dart through the night 'as the fishes in the sea.' I like
that imagery, since the sky and the water seem to merge
in the darkness."

He spoke softly and his breath was warm and intimate
on Lindsay's brow, setting off a chain of feelings, not
the least of which was an unsettling twinge that radiated

downward from the pit of her stomach. Somehow, though, she summoned the power to speak. "When I was little, I was staying one night with my grandmother in New London. I saw a shooting star and thought it was the most glorious sight—like a miracle! And then Gramma told me that comets were formed by the smoke of sin, set afire by God's anger."

"What a charming tale to feed to a child, especially one with an imagination like yours," Coleraine remarked dryly, meanwhile running one hand lightly over her back.

The delicious sensation made her shiver with pleasure, but her voice was still troubled when she said, "I was fascinated and horrified all at once. For years after that, I would sit in my window at night and stare at the sky, waiting and wondering what sort of sin would make God angry enough to send down a comet. Once, when I was eight, I told my father a lie and then fell asleep in my window seat that night while keeping vigil to see if a shooting star would appear." Lindsay laughed shakily at the memory and rested her face against Ryan's fresh-smelling white shirt. Through the fine fabric, she could feel the texture of crisp chest hair and hear the slow beat of his heart.

"So you've waited a long time to earn that comet, hmm?" he teased Lindsay gently, tipping up her chin to look into her luminous eyes. "What's your sin? Touching *me*?"

"Oh, no, no! I didn't mean to suggest that I believe in that story anymore!" Flustered, she blushed even more furiously when Ryan touched her hot cheek with his fingertip and silently lifted an eyebrow. "I mean, it's silly, isn't it! Intelligent adults could never subscribe to such a theory!"

"Still, in a corner of your mind, you're worrying that that shooting star was some sort of a sign, aren't you. A warning to deny yourself the pleasure of my arms." He pressed her closer, one hand sliding down over the curve of Lindsay's bottom. "Don't you think," Ryan murmured, his mouth grazing her temple, "that if comets were the smoke of sin that the night would be continually ablaze?"

Lindsay swallowed hard and managed to nod, nearly trembling with arousal.

"I prefer to believe," he went on quietly, barely an inch above her parted lips, "that if God chooses the moments when stars fall, He does so in a spirit of celebration. Perhaps He knows that you and I are enjoying a last night of freedom and wished to add a festive miracle for good measure."

"Yes," Lindsay breathed, yearning for his kiss. "I'm sure you're right. . . ."

"Are you?"

Coleraine's soft, enigmatic tone gave her pause, but his sculpted face and midnight-blue eyes were unreadable in the shadows. Slowly, their lips touched, and as reason fled, Lindsay closed her eyes and yielded to her unschooled feelings.

Sweet, he thought, luxuriating in the taste and texture of her sensual mouth. How many nights had he dreamed, unwillingly, of kissing Lindsay and feeling her melt against him? Now, as her arms found their way around his shoulders, he thought dimly that this would satisfy his cravings, enabling him to keep a proper distance in London.

The tantalizing play of his mouth only heightened Lindsay's desire. Now his lips were brushing fire over her eyelids, jawline, and throat, before returning to cling, gently, to her eager mouth. She was swallowing a moan when she felt his tongue touch her lower lip, then her teeth, until it grazed the tip of her own tongue. Unable to bear another moment of such torture, Lindsay pressed upward against Ryan's hard body and his mouth slanted over hers in response. Hot waves of sensation swirled down to her loins as they kissed and kissed, tasting and ravening, for long minutes.

Lindsay felt mad with passion. Her breasts tingled,

swelling as she pressed against the warm, strong expanse of his chest. Meanwhile, her hips sought Ryan's, driven by an instinct she hadn't known she possessed. The place between her legs was moist and yearning. She wanted to lie down with him right there on the quarterdeck.

Ryan's deft fingers explored Lindsay's back, fit themselves around the curves of her waist, hips, and derrière; then, as his mouth abandoned hers to explore the slim column of her neck, one hand slid upward over Lindsay's ribs until it touched a breast.

"Oh, Jesus," he whispered, feeling the puckered nipple through the thin muslin of her bodice. "I have lost my senses!"

She nearly panicked as she felt his body tense. "Ryan—"

"Lindsay, this is madness! We're on a ship with your parents—not to mention the men on the other decks!" Gripping her forearms, he held her away from him. "I never meant . . ." Ryan paused, looking from her stricken, beautiful face to the dark water. "It should have been just a kiss. A taste. Anything more would be not only wrong but insane!"

Suddenly Lindsay felt chilled; her shawl had fallen away to the deck behind her. Reason and pride returned in a sickening rush. "Of course. You're right!" She tried to disengage herself from the hands that still seemed to burn her flesh all too pleasurably. "You said it yourself this morning. We've been at sea too long and are both a bit mad. Why don't we just pretend that this . . . interlude never happened?"

Ryan stared down at her intently, wondering what she really felt. "Our dealings have ever been stormy in one way or another, have they not? Whether we can forget about tonight remains to be seen, but I do think that we can agree to keep it our secret."

"You have my word." Lindsay felt her composure return when he released her arms. Straightening her back, she put out her hand and saw Ryan's mouth curve ironically as he took it and they sealed their agreement.

Although she longed to look upward at the night sky, Lindsay realized that the last visible traces of the shooting star had disappeared long before, taking its secrets with it.

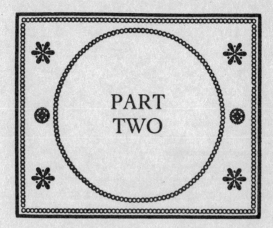

PART
TWO

This royal throne of kings, this scepter'd
    isle,
This earth of majesty, this seat of Mars,
This other Eden, demi-paradise,
This fortress built by Nature for her-
    self . . .
This precious stone set in the silver
    sea . . .
This blessed plot, this earth, this realm,
    this England. . . .

—WILLIAM SHAKESPEARE (1564–1616)

CHAPTER
10

Falmouth to London, England
May 27–June 1, 1814

At dawn, Lindsay climbed the ladder through the main hatch and discovered that *La Mouette* was safely anchored in the misty harbor of Falmouth. Her parents chatted with Ryan Coleraine, Harvey Jenkins, and Cassie and Able Barker on the quarterdeck, but she made her way to the bow of the ship, longing to survey her new surroundings undistracted.

In truth, Lindsay was embarrassed to face Ryan, especially in the company of her parents. It seemed that she hadn't slept all night, for now, on top of her worries about the unknown fate that awaited her in London, there were these horrid new snarls in her relationship with Ryan to ponder. In the cool light of morning, Lindsay felt like slapping herself for her behavior under the midnight stars. How could she have been so . . . *wanton*? Especially with Ryan Coleraine? He was the one man she wished to remain ignorant of her feminine desires, and yet she had clung to him, pressed herself against him, trembled at his kiss. . . . Almost as galling was the memory of all the other women who had succumbed to his charm. She had lowered herself into their company, reinforcing his already insufferable conceit.

That was probably the only reason he had kissed her at all. Ryan was accustomed to having a willing female in his arms, and after these weeks at sea his appetite must have been quite strong. She had been the only suitable woman available. . . .

Flushing anew with humiliation, Lindsay gripped the bow rail and looked out at the English shore. The small basin of the harbor was filled with at least two dozen ships, mostly packets, and was surrounded by softly undulating green hills dotted with grazing cattle. The first thing that struck her was the virtual absence of trees, for she was used to Connecticut's pervasive woods.

"That's Falmouth," an all-too-familiar voice said behind her shoulder, as an equally familiar tanned forefinger pointed toward an ugly cluster of little houses on their left.

Lindsay couldn't breathe for a moment, then pride reared up and came to her rescue. "So I assumed." She turned to face Ryan directly, trying not to notice how handsome he looked in snug buckskins, polished boots, and a tailored dark blue jacket. His cravat, tied simply yet expertly, was snowy-white in contrast to the bronzed line of his jaw, and Lindsay was keenly aware of the intensity of his crisp blue gaze. "Good morning. Should I call you Nathan now?"

He winced slightly. "Is that any way to treat a friend? The only peace I'll have these next few months will be when I'm alone with you and your parents. You must allow me to be Ryan Coleraine when no one's watching."

His tone was light, and she was relieved that he wasn't taunting her with veiled references to their midnight interlude. Still, it seemed to Lindsay that his turns of phrase were laced with double entendres. Or was she imagining things? Confused and upset, she turned back to the rail. "You can be whomever you please in private, sir. It matters to me not at all. Remember, though, that I shall have a new life of my own to deal with in London, and I only hope that I don't forget and call you by the wrong name."

His brows raised slightly at Lindsay's convincing air of detachment. "Perhaps we can say that Ryan is your pet name for me," he suggested, teasing gently.

Lindsay blushed involuntarily and cursed herself as she sensed his amusement. "I beg your pardon!"

"It's a common practice, isn't it? Little children garbling relatives' names and then continuing to use them out of habit . . . or affection?"

She was saved from replying by the approach of her parents. "Good morning, sweetheart!" Devon greeted her, adding a hug and a kiss. "Your father and I were just saying how relieved we are that you two are getting along."

André nodded. "Just don't take advantage of the situation, Coleraine! Lindsay is to be your *sister*."

Laughing ruefully, Ryan murmured, "If I should have a lapse of memory, I'm certain Lindsay will hasten to remind me."

Father, mother, and daughter stood together at the rail chatting about Falmouth and Pendennis Castle, which was situated behind them on a mound near the entrance to the harbor. Ryan drifted off to one side where he could look at Lindsay unobserved. In spite of her obvious uneasiness, she was more beautiful than ever, and he wondered what part her newly discovered passions played in her glow. She wore a short, fitted blue spencer over a dove-gray traveling gown that was highlighted by a pretty white ruffle encircling her neck. How soft and sweet-smelling her neck was, Ryan remembered with a pang. Lindsay's strawberry-blond curls were swept up and covered by a charming scoop-brimmed straw bonnet that tied under her chin, but a cloud of tendrils framed her delicate face and set off her long-lashed gray eyes.

Suddenly, she turned and met his eyes, and the rosy

color in her cheeks deepened. Ryan stared back unapologetically.

"Is everyone ready?" Raveneau asked. "It's time to go ashore."

"And thence . . . to London!" exclaimed Devon. "Of course we're ready! Who *knows* what adventures await us!"

The seven travelers followed a northeasterly route to London, the women traveling in a fine carriage that Raveneau hired in Falmouth, while Able and Harvey shared the box with the driver and André and Ryan rode on horseback. In spite of Cornwall's narrow, crooked roads that zigzagged up and down the treeless moors and softly rolling hills, their progress was rapid. Everywhere they saw evidence of Cornwall's abundance of mines but could not afford the time to inspect them. In Falmouth, André and Ryan had learned that the war with Napoleon was over, and rumors flew that the czar would soon visit London in the company of other members of European royalty. Devon was anxious that they reach the city as soon as possible. The social events surrounding the royal visit would provide perfect opportunities for the Raveneau family to take their place quietly among society, but first there were innumerable purchases to be made, tailors and dressmakers to be called in, and, most important, Ryan's role as a fop to be perfected.

And so they bowled through Exeter, then Bristol, admiring the countryside with its estates spreading wide and low over fine lawns contrasting with neat thatched farmhouses smothered in flowers. By the time they reached Bath, a beautiful town built of cream-colored freestone, even Devon was ready to relax and rest at the elegant White Hart Inn, where the food was delectable and servants anticipated their every need.

Out of Bath, the roads widened, and from time to time the River Avon could be seen below, curling amidst swaying willows and crossed here and there with moss-covered bridges of gray stone. Lindsay stared as they passed villas and mansions with classical façades and cool, creeper-framed windows, set among emerald lawns and trees. Everything seemed so tidy and well tended, even the most modest farms and the wildflower-drenched meadows. It appeared to her that the neat hedgerows, the fields of mustard turning from white to gold, the immense flocks of snow-white sheep, and the groves of chestnut merging into blue horizons had all been planned down to the last detail.

On the first day of June, Lindsay awoke from a midafternoon nap to discover that the view out her carriage window was vastly altered.

"We've arrived in London, sweetheart," Devon told her with a smile. "This is Oxford Street."

Too excited even to reproach her mother for not rousing her sooner, Lindsay stared in fascination as they rolled through the wide thoroughfare crowded with vehicles of every description. Her father and Ryan rode just ahead on horseback, chatting amiably as they took in their surroundings. Soon they led the way south on Park Lane, which skirted the eastern boundary of lush, enormous Hyde Park.

Park Lane was lined with magnificent homes and uniform town houses of brown and gray brick before which ran elevated flagstone pavements for the use of pedestrians, who were protected from the traffic by posts. The Raveneau carriage turned east on Upper Brook Street and soon drew up before a house in Grosvenor Square. Lindsay dimly recognized it from her childhood. Like most of the others she had seen, it was a sober yet elegant four-story structure with a freestone-bordered sash and white pillars on either side of the pedimented doorway. She smiled at the sight of the polished lion-mask knocker on the beautifully molded door, remembering the trepidation it had caused her as a child.

"We're home," André announced, opening the carriage door and holding out a hand to assist the ladies.

"I must be dreaming!" Cassie breathed. "Able, have you ever seen a grander place?"

While André and Devon assured the two servants that their town house was quite modest in comparison to most in this fashionable section of London, Lindsay stole a glance at Ryan Coleraine. He stood off to one side, lightly holding his horse's reins as he surveyed his new home with deceptive casualness. His top boots and buckskins were dusty, his face tanned, his black hair wind-blown. Feeling Lindsay's gaze, he turned and met it squarely, then strolled to her side.

"So, this is where we'll begin our new life together," Ryan murmured, a hint of suggestive mischief in his voice. "Who would have ever predicted this a few short weeks ago when I was carrying you over my shoulder down Main Street in far-off Connecticut?"

"Certainly not I," Lindsay replied lightly. "I find it astonishing—the sacrifices one can make to help one's country."

He grinned as the driver took his reins, and he and Lindsay started toward the house with her parents. Harvey and the Barkers brought up the rear. Realizing that this brief exchange had been the first opportunity he and Lindsay had had to speak alone since leaving Falmouth, it dawned on Ryan that he had missed her tart wit. In fact, though he hated to admit it even to himself, he liked Lindsay. She might be an infuriating brat far too often, but it was impossible to dislike or ignore her. It seemed to Ryan that even his moments of annoyance or anger with Lindsay were tinged with an affection that he hadn't experienced in the past.

As they reached the door, Lindsay touched her father's shoulder and asked, "May I knock?"

"Ah, of course—I remember!" André said with a chuckle. "You used to be afraid to touch the lion's mask, weren't you? And now you're all grown up and filled with courage, hmm?''

"I'd forgotten all about it," she replied, eyes atwinkle. "But now, remembering, I feel that using the knocker myself before entering this house as an adult would be rather symbolic . . ."

Her parents stood aside to give Lindsay room, and she stepped forward, pausing for a moment as the child that lived on in her rose to the surface. Then she smiled and lifted the lion's mouth, letting it fall with an echoing thud. A few moments passed and then the door opened slowly to reveal a bent, wizened old man clad in funereal black. Wisps of white hair were combed over the pale crown of his head, while his long face, covered with a network of tiny wrinkles, was dominated by tiny, keen blue eyes and an incongruously pink nose.

The little man stared for barely a moment, then opened the door completely and rasped, "Welcome home, Captain Raveneau, Mrs. Raveneau," as if their sudden appearance on the doorstep were nothing out of the ordinary.

"Hello, Roderick! It's so good to see you!" Devon went forward to kiss the butler's cheek.

"I realize that this must be a surprise," Raveneau said, shaking Roderick's hand with a familiarity that made the man highly uneasy, "but we weren't able to send word that would have reached you before our arrival." He followed his wife into the entry hall, then gestured to the others. "Roderick, you remember our daughter, Lindsay, and our son, Nathan, don't you? Doubtless they've changed considerably over the years."

Caught momentarily off guard, Ryan recovered without missing a beat. Although he realized that his appearance belied the persona he was to adopt, he managed all the same to raise an eyebrow lazily and relax his body into what he hoped was a fair imitation of bonelessness.

"How do you do?" he drawled.

The butler glanced from Lindsay to Ryan, then back again. "I wouldn't have known either of you." He paused to clear his throat. "But I'm glad you're both grown up. Far too headstrong in the past."

At that moment, two women approached from the back of the house. One was quite old, stern, and sour-faced. The other was younger, in her thirties, Ryan judged, and excessively plain though intelligent and kind-looking. Amidst the round of introductions that followed, he learned that the older woman was Mrs. Butter, Roderick's wife, and the younger woman was their daughter, Arabella. It appeared that the mother was now in charge of the kitchen, while Arabella had taken over the duties of housekeeper. These London servants seemed relatively unruffled by the sudden arrival of the Raveneaus, but it was apparent to Ryan that Mrs. Butter resented Cassie and Able's appearance in a house that she considered her own. When Cassie cheerfully announced that she had brought with her all of Captain Raveneau's favorite recipes, Mrs. Butter's mouth puckered into a tight knot.

"Indeed?" she replied frostily. "I have overseen meals for this family for thirty years without one complaint."

Devon intervened. "Cassie only wants to help, Mrs. Butter, and she and her husband were longing to return to England, where they were born. I'm sure you'll be happy to have some assistance with meals, since Arabella will be occupied with other household duties. No doubt Roderick will be glad of Able's help as well. We mean to bring this house alive! The Season has begun and our children are eager to partake of society. It will be a busy summer for all of us!" She turned to Arabella only to discover the young woman staring at Ryan as if she were having a vision. "Arabella, would you show Nathan and Lindsay their rooms? They may have forgotten the way after so long. Mrs. Butter, please assemble the rest of the staff, from parlormaids to potboy. I'll meet with them directly. Doubtless they've forgotten they have employers! And Roderick, please send a stableboy to fetch my daughter, Mouette. We're all very anxious to see her!''

Ryan rubbed a towel over the crisp black hair that covered his tapering chest, then tossed the damp linen next to the bathtub. It felt good to be shaved and scrubbed after the long days of dusty roads and quick, tepid baths in inns. Refreshed, Ryan was able to survey his surroundings without feeling as if he were in a dream.

It had been years since he had inhabited rooms so fine. Shrugging into a white muslin shirt, his gaze wandered over pale green walls and thick Chinese carpets with designs in cream and wine against a green background. The furnishings were in the style of Adam and Sheraton: a mahogany chest of drawers with a serpentine front, two painted and parcel-gilt chairs in front of the tall windows, a bachelor folding dressing table complete with mirror, a half-filled bookcase, and a handsome mahogany bed with cream and green draperies and Grecian keys carved into the tester-frame. It was an elegant, masculine room, probably owing more to Devon's taste than to Nathan's, since the man he was impersonating had been in his teens the last time he stayed here. The clothes hanging in the dressing room were out-of-date, and the few books on the shelves revealed only one aspect of Nathan's progressing character. They were all about ships, navigation, and astronomy, and Ryan looked forward to filling in the spaces with his own favorite volumes ranging from Shakespeare to Boswell to Sheridan to Pepys to Wordsworth.

"Ryan? May I come in?" It was Devon, knocking quietly at his door.

He fastened the last button on smooth biscuit-colored pantaloons and went to greet her. "Ah, Mother!" Ryan's voice was full of laughter as he opened the door. "How kind of you to call!"

"It's encouraging to see that you haven't lost your sense of humor," she told him, smiling as she followed

Ryan inside and took one of the chairs near the tall windows. The right casement was pushed open to admit a warm and fragrant June breeze. "Hold on to it. The ability to laugh at life will save you needless frustration in the weeks to come."

"Surely you don't mean to suggest that our sojourn in London might be less than constantly entertaining . . . ?" Ryan peered into the dressing-table mirror as he spoke, deftly tying his cravat in a simple yet elegant style, while his twinkling eyes belied his words.

"May I be frank with you?" Devon asked suddenly.

He straightened, his black brows raised, then took the chair opposite hers. "Of course."

"André and I are both very honest people; almost to a fault, I suppose. This entire charade goes against the grain for both of us since it is not being carried out for fun but in all seriousness. None of our family is good at lying, and I sense that you are not that sort, either." Devon paused and stared out the window for a moment, her apricot-hued curls glowing in the sunlight. "The fact is, though, that this must be done, for the good of our country. If there is a traitor in London's glittering nest, then he must be rooted out."

"I agree," Ryan replied simply.

"I know you do, or you wouldn't be here now. I just wanted to say these things to you so that you would understand that this is much more than a game as far as we are concerned. I *had* to call you Nathan in front of the servants because we must keep the circle of those who know the truth limited to our immediate family. I certainly trust the Butters, but I also am well aware that mistakes can be made, especially verbally."

"I understand." Ryan nodded.

"Good. And I suppose that you also understand that my plan to turn you into a full-fledged London dandy is more serious than fanciful. If we seem to be having fun with it, it's only because we're a family that loves to laugh, not because we are using you to provide amusement."

Ryan's blue eyes sparkled. "Are you anticipating another unbecoming scene between your daughter and me?"

"Well, partly, perhaps," Devon allowed. "Lindsay is young, younger than I was at her age. She has knowledge gleaned from books but little awareness of people and the world. I think that underneath the shield of antagonism she holds out in front of herself, she likes you."

He grinned. "I think you're right, Devon. And, if you'll promise to keep this a secret, I will tell you that I like Lindsay, too. We may not always get along, but we are already friends. To my mind, that's an unbreakable bond."

"I'm glad to hear you say so." She stared hard at Ryan, but his expression remained relaxed and half amused. "It's good to know that you are feeling a family bond. It may save Lindsay's life if you should be tempted to wring her neck in the future. However, at the moment, another trial awaits you. Our elder daughter, Mouette, is here, full of advice regarding your transformation into a fop. Can you endure it?"

Ryan laughed. "Madame, you are speaking to a man who has done battle at sea! How trying can conversation with another of your daughters be?"

CHAPTER
11

June 1, 1814

"**N**ATHAN!" A BEAUTIFUL, BLACK-HAIRED WOMAN RAN to Ryan the instant he appeared in the doorway to André and Devon's private sitting room. Throwing her arms around him, she hugged him hard, then drew back to grin mischievously at his startled expression. "How you've changed! I wouldn't have recognized you."

He took his cue from her playful demeanor. "I, on the other hand, could never forget my gloriously lovely older sister. How are you, Mouette?" Out of the corner of an eye, Ryan noticed Lindsay sitting near the window, watching intently. For her benefit, he returned Mouette's hug with decidedly unbrotherly enthusiasm. She began to giggle in his arms, finally pushing free and cuffing his chest. "I like you!"

"Remember, you're a married woman, *chérie*," André said wryly as he entered from the bedroom.

"Married but not dead, Papa!" Mouette's expression was merry as she stood back and looked Ryan over. "Mmm. My, my. Very nice! By the time we finish with you, you may lend a whole new meaning to the word *dandy*! I don't think I've ever seen a finer pair of legs on a man!''

Raveneau cleared his throat. "I beg your pardon?"

"Except of course, for you, Papa!" she amended. "That goes without saying."

Across the room, Lindsay shifted uneasily on the settee as she watched her sister and Ryan. Even though she was now grown herself, she still regarded Mouette as the perfect female; prettier, more self-assured, and more charming than she could ever hope to be. She was tall, but not too tall, and her body was slim and curvacious all at once. Her gown of pink-and-white-striped muslin was doubtless the very latest fashion, cut low in front to show the high curves of her breasts and ruffled at the hemline to display Mouette's well-turned ankles. No freckles dusted her rose-and-cream complexion. Her blue eyes sparkled with wit while the sun gleamed off her artfully arranged ebony curls. Even her laughter was beguiling. At least *Ryan* found it so. Lindsay could hardly believe that he would flirt so openly with Mouette in full view of her parents.

Of course, it wouldn't do him any good. Mouette might tease, but it was all in fun. She was happily married to Harry Brandreth, a mother of two boys, and, most important, a person of character. Even if it were fashionable for married people to engage in clandestine love affairs, Mouette would never do such a thing. Lindsay smiled a little to herself as she imagined Ryan attempting to seduce her sister and receiving a firm set-down. It would do him good!

Still, Mouette should not have encouraged him even this tiny bit. Lindsay wished she would stop touching his sleeve and laughing so gaily at each of Ryan's utterances.

Fortunately, distraction intervened in the form of afternoon tea. Arabella Butter wheeled in the cart herself, blushing deeply when Ryan nodded and smiled at her.

The family chose places in the grouping of gilt chairs and two settees upholstered in peach and ivory while Devon poured tea, adding milk or lemon according to each person's taste.

Ryan had seated himself next to Lindsay on one of the settees, amused by her show of indifference. He let his arm brush hers repeatedly, but her only reaction was the involuntary flush that spread over her cheekbones. Tiring of Lindsay's refusal even to acknowledge his presence, Ryan nonchalantly set down his cup and saucer and pretended to search for something in his left outside coat pocket. Since their bodies were nearly touching, it was easy enough to pinch Lindsay's backside lightly without being seen.

Her face turned instantly and stormy gray eyes blazed into his as she hissed, "Captain Coleraine!"

Ryan smiled politely. "It's kind of you to notice me, sister."

Across from them, Mouette was helping herself to a generous slice of gooseberry tart. "I shouldn't, I know, but this is an occasion!" she declared happily. "I've a weakness for tarts, just like Lord Alvaney. He is so fond of cold apricot tart that he has ordered his chef to keep one on the sideboard every day of the year! Do you remember Alvaney, Papa? He's quite wonderful, I think. Great fun, a consummate dandy, and he gives the most marvelous dinner parties. Alvaney's a great favorite at the clubs, especially White's. You remember their betting book, don't you, Papa? Some of the bets have become utterly ridiculous. Harry told me that last week, during a rain shower, two of the members bet on which of their chosen raindrops would first reach the bottom of the windowpane!" Mouette paused to giggle and taste her tart, then continued, "Silly, isn't it? I prefer Alvaney's style. A year or two ago, he wagered Sir Joseph Copley twenty guineas 'that a certain person outlives another certain person.' That's the way it's written in the betting book! Isn't that delicious? Of course, I haven't seen it myself; I have to rely on Harry for such gossip. Fortunately, unlike most men, he's quite obliging."

Mouette chattered on in an apparent effort to bring everyone up-to-date on all 'he current London news. Seeing that all eyes were focused on her sister, Lindsay shifted her cup and saucer to her left hand, then carefully slipped her right hand inside Ryan's slate-colored frock coat. His side was lean and hard, but she did her best, digging thumb and forefinger into the flesh under his waistcoat and shirt in an effort to return his pinch.

Ryan's reaction was less than she had hoped for. He found Lindsay's hand and brought it out; then, still holding her fingers, he inquired, "Have you lost something?"

Their eyes locked, his dancing with devils, hers smoldering like those of a sulky child. "Let *go* of me!" Lindsay yanked her hand away forcefully, only to find that he had released her so that she lost her balance for a moment, causing tea to splash into her saucer.

The others looked over at them curiously and Mouette laughed with delight. "Look, Mama! Isn't it cute? Already they behave like true siblings!"

Willing herself not to blush again, Lindsay reached for a seedcake and ate it rapidly. Her mother, meanwhile, appeared glad to hear the introduction of a more pertinent topic of conversation.

"Do you think, then, that we shall be successful in our plan to pass Ryan off as Nathan?"

"Nathan the dandy?" Mouette's eyes twinkled as she regarded Ryan Coleraine. "I don't mean to be outrageous, but since we are all family now, it seems best to speak frankly. Captain Coleraine is the *last* person I would think of as a fop. I mean, just look at the man. He is masculinity personified! However, if he means to cooperate, it may be possible. I happen to know an exemplary French valet whose employer was recently killed in the war. If we can borrow his services, I might be so bold to suggest that between the two of us, a physical transformation could be accomplished within the week. As for the rest . . ." Mouette shrugged impishly, her black curls glowing in the amber sunlight. "The rest depends on Ryan's dramatic abilities. We haven't much time, but if he will truly make an effort, success is possible."

"I think I am up to the challenge," Ryan assured her, trying not to betray his amusement. "At least, I will try my best."

"When does the czar arrive?" Devon asked her daughter.

"Well, you know Czar Alexander's sister, the Grand Duchess Catherine of Oldenburg, made an advance appearance—in March. She wanted to have a look-see at this foreign territory, we think. Harry says that she came early because of the Regent's desire to arrange a marriage between his daughter, Charlotte, and the Prince of Orange. They wouldn't look kindly on *that* marriage in St. Petersburg!" Mouette focused on Ryan. "Had you heard that my husband, Sir Harry Brandreth, was recently elected to the House of Commons? Papa is quite pleased, aside from political considerations."

André touched Mouette's arm. "*Ma fille,* all of this is highly entertaining, and no doubt useful, but first it might be better to deal with the more timely issues. *When* does the czar arrive?"

She lifted her eyebrows at her father, then softened. "Can I help it if I like to talk? I would have thought that my family at least could accept me without criticism!" Then Mouette laughed, diffusing tension. "All right, I'll be good. Harry says that Czar Alexander and King Frederick William of Prussia are due to land in Dover on June the sixth. I gather that they'll be accompanied by the ruling princes, statesmen, and generals of the greater part of Europe. You know, it's only been five weeks now since the last shot was fired, so the mood of celebration is still very intense. This royal visit should ensure the most festive summer that England has ever seen. I can hardly wait!''

"It will certainly provide the perfect opportunity for all of us to find a comfortable niche in society.'' Devon nodded thoughtfully. "In other circumstances, we, especially Ryan, might be scrutinized to the point of suspicion, but who will have time—or the inclination—to look at us with these glamorous foreign visitors in London's midst?''

"And we'll all have such fun in the bargain!'' exclaimed Mouette. "I don't even want to understand exactly what it is Papa and Ryan are *really* up to. I'd much rather concentrate on teaching my new brother to use a quizzing glass and a snuffbox and on introducing my long-lost, grown-up sister to the world of English men!'' She winked across the tea table. "What do you say, Lindsay? We'll be friends! I'll take you shopping in Bond Street and teach you to drive my curricle. I have the sweetest pair of grays all to myself! As for the men, well, I'll wager that you'll have them on their knees, queued up around Grosvenor Square just as soon as you make your first appearance in society. And it won't be at a dull evening at Almack's, either! Doubtless Prinny will give a sumptuous ball for the czar, and then there you'll be—''

A voice broke in from the doorway. "Mouette, my love, I've come to rescue your family from your unceasing chatter.''

Lindsay recognized her brother-in-law immediately, for he had changed not at all. Harry Brandreth had been classically handsome in his youth, and remained so, from his cropped golden curls to his long, perfect legs, currently encased in snug pale yellow pantaloons. Now, though, Lindsay wondered if the broad white smile he bestowed on them was a trifle insincere.

Mouette was at Harry's side in an instant, kissing him and linking her arm through his as they walked toward her parents. Devon embraced her son-in-law warmly, while André shook his hand.

"Good to see you again, Harry," he said. "And congratulations on your seat in the House. That's quite an accomplishment at your age."

"Thank you, sir. I can't tell you what a pleasure it is to see all of you here in London! Quite a surprise, coming home to hear that Mouette had gone over to greet her family! Not that I expected to find her at *home*—"

"Harry," Mouette broke in quickly, "say hello to Lindsay! Look, she's all grown up! And here's Nathan! Would you have known him?"

"Can't say as I would have!" Harry remarked, giving each of them a brief hug. "Makes me feel quite ancient, seeing the two of you. Last time I saw you, Lindsay, you couldn't have been more than fourteen! Seems to me that your legs were too long for the rest of you. You were forever bumping into the door frames because your nose was buried in some romantic novel. And Nathan . . ." Harry shook his head bemusedly. "Good God, you look as old as Mouette!"

"I beg your pardon?" challenged his wife in mock outrage. "Nathan looks much *older* than I do! So does Lindsay, for that matter!"

Harry smiled with indulgence and said to the others, "I've noticed that women begin spouting such nonsense past the age of thirty. Can't bear to face facts."

"I don't suppose you brought my grandchildren?" Devon asked eagerly.

"Arabella took them to the kitchen for gooseberry tart. Mrs. Butter said she didn't want them smearing it all over your good silk chairs."

"But we haven't seen them for years!" she protested. "Not since they visited Connecticut. Little Anthony was only a baby, and even Charles was just three. They've probably forgotten all about their grandparents—"

At that moment, two sturdy little boys came barreling

into the sitting room. "Where's Grandmother and Grandfather?" demanded the smaller child, a handsome blond of five.

"Can't you *see*, corkbrain?" his brother replied. "They're the old people!"

André arched an eyebrow at Devon, who blinked in surprise before kneeling to gather her grandsons into her arms. "Oh, children! How you've grown!" She stroked Charles's black curls and kissed Anthony's cheek.

"I'm eight years old, nearly nine," Charles announced. "I have my own horse!"

"Mama, how come you say Charlie looks like Grandfather?" wondered Anthony. "His hair is white!"

André chuckled. "I think that all of you ought to join us for dinner and we'll see if we can't sort all of this out then!"

"I suppose I ought to simply resign myself to the idea of living in a madhouse for the next few months." Raveneau sighed as he got into bed and lay back against starlit pillows.

"I suppose so," Devon echoed, her own sigh infected with laughter.

"A daughter whose personality changes with the wind, a son who isn't *really* my son, another daughter who cannot stop chattering long enough to breathe, two outrageous little grandsons—"

"Don't forget 'a charming, beautiful wife who provides an island of serenity amidst a sea of chaos,' " she teased.

"Are we speaking about the same wife? The one for whom life isn't worth living unless it is tangled with schemes?"

"They aren't schemes. They're *plans*!"

"Oh. *Pardonez-moi!*" He turned on his side and gathered her petite body close against his. "Devon, my love, tell me that you'll keep an eye on things and make certain the affairs of these children don't become impossibly snarled."

"Of course I will. Haven't I always?" Pressing light kisses along André's collarbone, she refrained from telling him that her instincts were on alert about Mouette and her marriage. As a mother, it hadn't been difficult for Devon to realize that her daughter's antic behavior had not been rooted in happiness. This was not the time to delve into this new problem, however, so instead she said, "Besides, they aren't children any longer! And though our daughters might allow some subtle attempts at guidance from me, I am quite sure that Ryan Coleraine will have none of it."

"Ryan!" André scoffed while his fingertips traced the line of Devon's back. "He is the least of my worries! Ryan's a grown man with a good head on his shoulders."

"Just so long as he doesn't get into trouble with women here. He has a reputation, you know, and if he becomes embroiled in an affair with someone else's wife it could prove the undoing of all our plans."

"Hmm. As a father, I'm more concerned about Ryan's relationship with Lindsay. He reminds me too much of myself."

"But Lindsay's nothing like me . . . is she?" Devon sighed in the darkness, remembering her daughter's recent flashes of fire. "Besides, she assures me that she cannot stand him. Wouldn't she confide in her own mother? And Ryan treats her with affectionate tolerance, as if she really were his sister. I don't think we have anything to worry about on that score." She snuggled closer to her husband and brushed her lips over the line of his jaw. "In any event, not at this particular moment."

"That's right." Raveneau's voice was barely audible. "The house is asleep and the night is ours."

Devon responded by twining her arms about his neck and drawing him down to her parted lips. "At this moment, I wouldn't care if they all *were* awake! Ryan and

Lindsay could be planning to elope to Gretna Green and I wouldn't lift a finger to interfere.''

"Don't place such a choice before me, sweetheart," André murmured, tasting the sweetness of her mouth and then the line of her throat. "It's frightening to think that I could so easily be distracted from my parental duties."

"It's only a matter of priorities," she teased softly as his hand found the curve of her breast. "I was here first."

CHAPTER
12

June 1–2, 1814

"I THOUGHT YOU WERE ASLEEP!" LINDSAY PEEKED INTO Ryan's partially open door, surprised at her own daring. "I went to the library for a book and glimpsed you sitting in front of the fire. . . ."

He looked up, smiling at the sight of Lindsay in a white silk and Alençon lace dressing gown that emphasized the lithe curves of her body. "Come and join me, dear sister."

Observing Ryan's bare calves, tanned and covered with crisp black hair, stretched out casually from the simple gray robe that hid the rest of his body, Lindsay hesitated. "I have a feeling that it wouldn't be proper."

"Oh, of course, and you and I have ever been sticklers for propriety!" he rejoined, laughing softly. "Don't say that you're going to turn spinsterish on me, brat! I've been counting on you to pinch me and make faces at me behind the backs of London society."

Lindsay melted under his potent, offhand charm. Besides, Ryan was treating her as he would a sister. His behavior was perfectly casual, without a trace of the passion that had marked their last night on board *La Mouette*. This was exactly what she wanted, wasn't it? Crossing the room, Lindsay curled demurely in the wing chair next to his and met his even gaze.

"Brandy?" Ryan offered, indicating his own glass and the decanter on the tripod table at his elbow.

"Please," she answered boldly.

He arched one black brow just a trifle, then poured a small amount of the liquor into a cut-glass tumbler and handed it to her. "You're fond of brandy?"

"Very." Lindsay nodded.

"That's reassuring. I'd rather not watch you cough it up all over these Chinese rugs."

"I suppose you're referring to my reaction to your Irish whiskey. Well, I can assure you that unless this is Irish brandy, I'll be perfectly fine." Defiantly, she swallowed her first taste of the stuff and clenched her teeth in an effort to conceal her horror. Did all strong spirits taste so foul?

"You approve?" Ryan tried not to betray his amusement.

"Of course. It's delicious." Somehow, she managed a smile.

"Have some more." Leaning over, he splashed more brandy into her glass and grinned. "It should thaw you out."

"For what purpose?"

Ryan gazed at her, enchanted by Lindsay's smooth fair skin with its new dusting of freckles across the bridge of her nose, the loose halo of her golden-rose curls, and her warm, challenging gray eyes. "Amicable conversation. What other purpose could I have?"

Color suffused her cheeks, but she gathered her wits in time to reply, "I thought perhaps you wished to quiz me about Mouette. I seem to recall you having a penchant for married ladies."

His blue eyes cooled. "I've never had a *penchant* for

anyone, Miss Raveneau—at least not since I achieved an age to know better.''

"Well, you and Mouette certainly seemed full of fast affection!" Lindsay took two hot sips of brandy in a row.

"Your sister is a charming, beautiful woman. Unfortunately, her husband doesn't appreciate her and thus she turns to other men for attention.''

"I beg your pardon!"

"I don't mean to sully Lady Brandreth's reputation, Lindsay, or to suggest that she's engaged in anything illicit. We all need reassurance from time to time, though, and Mouette is more needy than most." Ryan lit a cheroot and gave her a sidelong glance as he exhaled. "More deserving as well!"

"I'll thank you to change the subject before I lose my temper!"

"Certainly. What would you like to talk about?"

Caught off guard by his easy dismissal of what she perceived to be a burgeoning argument, Lindsay took a moment to slow her breathing and to think of a proper response. Finally, she said, "How do you like London?"

"My dear, I am British, in case you've forgotten. I lived here before coming to America and probably know the city better than your parents. As for liking it, it's a mixed blessing to be back. I left for a reason.''

"Is that what kept you from sleeping tonight?" she dared to inquire.

"I hate to dash your curiosity, but I won't tell you about my past here or anywhere else. It's none of your affair, but I can assure you that I don't lose sleep over it." Ryan sipped his own brandy, staring at the fire, then summoned a smile. "However, I will tell you what important problems kept me from sleeping tonight.''

"If they have anything to do with women, spare me!" Lindsay heard herself exclaim, then blushed in reaction.

"I can assure you that women were the farthest thing from my mind. I was pondering my new wardrobe.

Weston, the tailor, is coming here tomorrow, you know. Your mother has told him that I am ill and cannot come to Old Bond Street to be fitted. She and Mouette think, quite rightly, that I shouldn't be seen in public until my new persona is perfected.''

"I wasn't aware that you were a true fop at heart!" Lindsay taunted. "To think that you couldn't sleep because you were brooding about the cut of your new clothes. . . ."

He reached for her glass. "I think you've had enough of that. It's making you antagonistic."

"I'm an adult, Captain Coleraine! Leave me alone and I'll return the favor!"

He reared back, smiling. "My apologies, Miss Raveneau! Won't you call me Nathan?"

Lindsay was furious with herself for being so affected by his appealing smile and potent nearness. Each time his hand reached toward her, her heart constricted while her mind chastised her for her weakness. "I don't appreciate your humor, sir. Either cease teasing me or I shall leave."

His eyes were warm now as he gazed at her. "Don't do that. Believe it or not, I've missed your company during these past few days of travel. You've been far too well behaved."

When Ryan's fingers reached out to graze her wrist, Lindsay's heart skipped madly. "I'll stay," she managed to say, "if you'll be serious. What is it about your wardrobe that kept you awake?"

"It's not a topic that lends itself to serious conversation," he murmured lightly. "I was pondering the ways of the dandy and how best to carve out a place among them as quickly as possible."

"And?"

"And I decided that it would be best to break a rule or two without going too far out of bounds. Have you heard of Henry Cope, who must have everything green, from his cravat to his furniture?"

"No," Lindsay replied frankly, rather enjoying the brandy's effect.

"Well, Cope has his place in society, proving that there is still room for individuality in spite of Beau Brummell's code of dress and behavior. In fact, I think that a *bit* of individuality may work to my advantage. I don't propose to defame the name of Raveneau by being utterly outrageous, but I do think it would speed my access into society if there was something about me that was unique."

"I take it, then, that you don't propose to make your first appearance at White's in a blue frock coat with brass buttons, biscuit-colored pantaloons, top boots shined with champagne, and a deep white cravat tied in the Mathematical?"

Ryan grinned appreciatively. "You're quite perceptive, my dear! And you're right. Brummell's rules put me off. I'd rather be fashionable and different all at once." He paused to exhale a stream of smoke. "I could opt for a new mix of snuff or a different breed of horses, but clothing seems to offer the quickest route to being noticed. I don't mean to dress all in violet or wear feathers, but I like the notion of defying Brummell's gospel for color."

"Pink, perhaps?" Lindsay giggled, a dimple winking in her right cheek. "Chartreuse?"

"Now those are thoughts you might keep in mind for *yourself*! I, on the other hand, lean toward pastels. It's summer. Why shouldn't I wear light-colored coats? Dove gray, tan, sage green, or even pale yellow? I could contrast them with brocade waistcoats of a darker shade. What do you think?"

Lindsay's eyes ran involuntarily over his wide shoulders and tapering chest as she thought that he would look spectacular in anything he chose to wear. "It might work," she allowed.

"Thank God you approve!" Ryan sipped his brandy and gave her a sidelong smile. "Now I can sleep."

*   *   *

The next afternoon, Devon and Lindsay arrived back from a shopping expedition to Bond Street and handed their parcels to Roderick just in time to witness a scene in Ryan's rooms. Loud voices drew them to the doorway where they observed a group of people moving around agitatedly in front of the fireplace. One was Mouette, who stood slightly apart. Ryan leaned casually against the chimney piece while a tiny man with a red face and a French accent hopped on one foot, shouting at another man whose arms were filled with men's coats.

"I have told monsieur that it zimply will not do!" cried the Frenchman. "He will not listen! *Mère de Dieu,* zey beg me to help, zey ask my advice, and zen zis—zis *barbarian* brushes me azide as if I am *un insecte!*"

"No blue coats, he tells me," replied the clothing-laden man in a dazed tone. "I come all the way from Old Bond Street as a favor to old friends to fit a man I've never met, and what does he tell me? No blue coats! It's unheard of! Every man has blue coats!"

Overcome, Mouette put her hands over her ears and backed toward the windows. Ryan, meanwhile, smiled apologetically. "I assure you, I didn't say it to insult you, sir. If it means so much to you, I'll have a blue coat." Seeing the Raveneau women in the doorway, he lifted both brows just enough to indicate his bemusement. "Ah, here's Mother and my dear sister, Lindsay."

Mouette spun around. "Mother! Come in! Perhaps you can talk sense to—to Nathan! He's being horribly contrary."

"So I gathered," Devon murmured dryly. "It's so good to see you again, Mr. Weston!" Gracefully, she crossed the room and extended her gloved hand. "We can't thank you enough for coming over to fit Nathan. He hasn't been feeling very well, you know."

"My pleasure, Mrs. Raveneau," replied Weston, London's most fashionable tailor. "Has this illness affected his brain?"

She managed a rather sickly smile while darting a glance at Ryan. "I certainly hope not! Nathan, darling, I do hope you have listened to Mr. Weston's excellent advice."

"Absolutely, Mother. However, I was under the impression that these clothes were being made to be worn by me, not Mr. Weston."

The little Frenchman began to make choking noises, his bright blue eyes bugging out. Devon turned to look at him rather frostily. "I don't believe I've had the pleasure, sir."

Mouette rushed between them. "Mama, this is Monsieur Marcel Dindé, the wonderful valet I told you about. He's come especially to instruct Nathan, but I'm afraid that . . . they've gotten off to rather a bad start."

"Your son is an _idiot!_" Dindé screamed.

Devon arched an eyebrow. "I beg your pardon? I don't mean to make rash judgments, sir, but if you intend to instruct Nathan in the niceties of _your_ behavior, I cannot approve. Now, if you would be so kind as to take a chair, I will deal with Mr. Weston before continuing this discussion with you."

Clenching his fists and muttering in French, the little man obeyed. Devon then turned to her son and the tailor.

"Now, what's all this about blue coats?"

"Madame, as you must be aware, every well-dressed gentleman these days wears a blue coat with brass buttons and biscuit-colored pantaloons. It is almost a uniform! Your son, however, insists that he wants . . ." Weston paused to swallow audibly. "He wants . . . _pastel_ coats."

Devon looked at Ryan, who gave her a barely perceptible smile. "Am I not allowed to choose?"

Deciding that her intervention might be helpful, Lindsay came up behind her mother and whispered, "Trust him. We've discussed this and I think he's right."

"Kindly follow my son's instructions, Mr. Weston, and you will be paid accordingly."

The tailor heaved a sigh. "As you wish, madame." He turned back to Ryan, wincing. "Pale yellow, did you say? Sage green?"

"That's correct. Dove gray and tan, as well. And cream? What do you think, Lindsay?"

A bubble of happiness rose inside her. "Absolutely! And what about a very pale blue, perhaps with a hint of gray in it? That would go splendidly with your eyes, Nathan."

He gave her a dazzling grin. "You're showing signs of genius, my dear."

"It's a family trait, I believe." She beamed.

On the settee, Mouette and her mother exchanged surprised glances over the head of the sulking French valet.

"I'd better ring for tea," Devon remarked. "This promises to be a very *long* afternoon!"

CHAPTER
13

June 4–6, 1814

OVER THE NEXT THREE DAYS, THE RAVENEAU HOME IN Grosvenor Square was a hive of activity. Hoby, the bootmaker, who was also a Methodist preacher, came to fit Ryan for Hessians, top boots, and shoes for evening wear. That same afternoon, Rowland, the French coiffeur, came to cut his hair in the currently popular windswept style. Ryan rebeled against more than a trim, however, and when Rowland produced a bottle of Macassar Oil, a hair preparation of his own invention, he forbade him to remove the stopper. His crisp, slightly curly hair would have to do in its natural state, he said in a voice that brooked no argument.

The next day, Weston sent an assistant in his place to deal with the recalcitrant Nathan Raveneau. The young man brought a selection of the wardrobe Ryan had ordered, including four coats of superfine cloth, one of which was the dark blue he had finally agreed to. There were pantaloons for morning wear; buckskins, brocade, and plain buff waistcoats; embroidered cambric shirts; muslin neckcloths; and high stiff collars. Dindé nodded approvingly after helping Ryan into one of the coats, for it fit like a second skin. The young tailor's assistant assured them that the rest of the garments, including a selection of evening wear, would be delivered within three days.

Harry Brandreth accompanied his wife to Grosvenor Square the next afternoon. Bursting in on the family as they shared luncheon in the sunny morning room, he announced that he didn't have to be at the House and was prepared to take his brother-in-law round to the clubs to apply for membership. London was in a state of festive anticipation over the pending visit of Europe's royalty, and Harry suspected that even the bucks who ruled the world of fashion from the bow window in White's were likely to be expansive about admitting Ryan to their privileged circle.

Devon listened to these plans with a certain amount of trepidation. After sending Harry to the kitchen to sample Mrs. Butter's Bakewell pudding, she paced before André, Ryan, and her daughters. "I don't think Ryan is ready yet. Why, we haven't even taught him to use a snuffbox or quizzing glass! And then there's his accent and manner . . . !" She shook her golden-rose curls. "I'd counted on several more days to work with him. Ryan, we need to rid your voice of all traces of Ireland and teach you to behave like a fop. I'm afraid that there's a good deal more to this persona you mean to adopt than modish clothes!"

Reclining in his chair, Ryan regarded her languidly from under veiled lids and drawled, "You wound me, dear Mother. This will not answer!" His accent was upper-crust American, with a cultivated British undercurrent. All traces of his Irish heritage had vanished. "Let me assure you that your son is prime and bang-up-to-the-mark in every respect. How could it be otherwise?"

Four pairs of eyes stared at Ryan in stunned amazement. "How did you do that?" Mouette exclaimed between bites of turbot.

He looked at Lindsay, his blue eyes sparkling, and smiled. "I've told you all before that I lived in England for several years, long enough for the accent to rub off on me. The same is true of my time in America. I can combine the two speech patterns easily enough, and I've certainly observed enough fops in my day to imitate their behavior."

Lindsay smiled back at him, unaccountably pleased and proud, while her mother scolded, "You should have told me, Ryan, instead of letting me prattle on all this time about the lessons I meant to give you! Sometimes I think that you're having a joke at our expense."

"On the contrary, Devon, I'm sure there's a great deal you can teach me. The finer points of a snuffbox, for example. I've never used one, and I will need to practice. For today I shall simply have to do without."

Devon eyed him suspiciously. "Are you teasing me? *I* don't know how to take snuff! I'm not an eccentric old dowager, after all!"

André drew her down onto his lap and chuckled. "Not yet, at any rate. We'll solve the snuff problem tomorrow, Ryan. For now you probably ought to get rigged out for our foray into St. James's."

This first outing was viewed, especially by the dubious Dindé, as a test of the infamous pastel coats. Ryan invited Lindsay to make the choice, and she daringly picked one of pale yellow, which they paired with a new, snowy-white cambric shirt and a starched white high cravat. To placate Dindé, Ryan let him tie it in the Waterfall style but was alert to the movements of his fingers. A slate-gray brocade waistcoat, complete with fob and gold seal, snug white pantaloons, and gleaming Hessians rounded out the ensemble. When Ryan reappeared in the morning room for inspection, Lindsay thought that he had never looked more handsome. His black hair shone in the sunlight and his eyes were as blue and bright as the ocean on a cloudless day. Weston's superlative skill as a tailor was evident in the smooth, snug fit of the coat and trousers that showed Ryan's wide shoulders, narrow hips, and long, lean-muscled thighs to advantage. When he turned a white smile on the three ladies, Mouette pretended to swoon.

"I don't know if it's safe to turn you loose on the streets of London," she teased. "Respectable matrons will be throwing themselves from speeding carriages without a second thought, driven simply *mad* by the vision of such hitherto unimagined male beauty! Perhaps you ought to conceal a weapon to protect yourself."

"Only from you, Lady Brandreth," he shot back with cool amusement. "I'll take my chances with the rest of London's women."

"You look splendid, Ryan," Devon said, looking him over carefully. "The cravat is impressive, but are your collar points high enough for a true dandy?"

"Probably not, but I've heard tales of young swells cutting their ears on their collars, and I like my ears too much to risk doing them injury." His tone was light but distracted, and as he spoke his gaze sought Lindsay and lingered. She was curled in a tub-shaped lemon brocade chair next to the window overlooking the sun-drenched square. An open book lay in the lap of her simple, high-waisted gown of peach muslin, and burnished tendrils fell from a loosely wound Grecian knot atop her head. *"Childe Harold?"* he inquired softly.

Lindsay blushed. *"Sense and Sensibility."* She strove for a casual tone. "Are you waiting for me to join in this chorus of compliments? It's very bad for you, of course, but I suppose that this once it wouldn't do any harm to puff up your consequence since you're off to White's to face the mighty Mr. Brummell."

"Please don't compromise your principles on my account," Ryan said dryly.

"I don't mind. It's for a good cause." A dimple winked

beside her mouth. "You look very handsome. The bucks
of St. James's will pale in comparison."

"You'll never know what that means to me, coming
from *you*, dear sister!" Good-natured sarcasm infected
his tone, but he softened it with a smile and then bade
them all farewell.

Ryan went downstairs and found Raveneau in his
study, sifting through papers on his desk.

"Are we still off to White's, or has Harry changed his
mind?" Ryan asked, wryly hopeful.

André glanced up distractedly and murmured, "No,
he's around somewhere. In the kitchen, I think. I was
just wishing I had those maps with me here. They would
help me to better visualize the current naval battles. . . ."

"It's just as well, sir. The possibility that those maps
could fall into the wrong hands here in London is terrifying. Can you imagine what the British would do with
your maps of America's eastern seaboard?"

Raveneau nodded. "Doubtless the city of Washington
would be raided immediately—" He broke off at the sight
of Harry crossing the hall and entering the study.

"Secret charts?" Harry inquired, approaching the desk.
"May I have a peek?"

Looking irritated, André slipped the papers on his
desk into the top drawer and turned the key. "There's
nothing to see, Harry. Shall we go?"

Ryan lounged against a bookcase and proclaimed,
"Gad, sir, let's be away. I've been waiting my whole life
to go to White's! I'll be in my element at last, what?"

Once the front door had closed behind the three men,
Lindsay felt anxious. What if Ryan's first foray into
fashionable London went badly? Chances were that Beau
Brummell, society's arbiter of style who had popular-
ized the same blue coat with gold buttons that Ryan had
rejected, would be presiding over the bow window at
White's. If he greeted Ryan's pale yellow coat with

disdain, he certainly had the power to bar him from the club.

At teatime, distraction appeared in the form of Devon's, and now Lindsay's, couturiere. Dolly Jones was a stately, white-haired woman who had been making gowns for Devon for thirty years. An American, she had married a British soldier during the Revolutionary War and returned home to England with him. Today she came to Grosvenor Square to fit the evening dresses Lindsay and her mother had ordered, but first Devon insisted that she join them for tea and gossip.

Eventually, Mistress Jones joined Lindsay in her spacious bedchamber, which was charmingly decorated in shades of rose, cream, and china blue. Standing near the Sheraton field bed with its curved canopy, Lindsay held her book out in front of her and tried to read while Dolly tucked and pinned the bodice of her gown. Though some details remained unfinished, it was already exquisite. The white lace dress over a satin slip was trimmed at the bottom with a drapery of white lace entwined with pearls and roses and edged with a rondeau of satin. The bodice, cut low over Lindsay's bosom, was fashioned of rose-colored satin with a row of blond lace falling over the top, and the gown's short puffed sleeves were also of rose satin, slashed with white lace and finished with a fall of blond lace.

Glancing at her reflection in the pier glass, Lindsay murmured, "I must tell you, Mistress Jones, that this is the most beautiful dress I've ever owned. It makes me feel like a woman!"

"I would have been glad to reassure you on that point," a dry voice said from the doorway.

"You're back!" Lindsay exclaimed in surprise, barely catching herself before calling him Ryan.

Dolly Jones, her mouth full of pins, made a muffled sound of exasperation at Lindsay's sudden movement. "You musht hode shtill!" she commanded unintelligibly.

"I'm sorry, truly! Mistress Jones, have you met my

brother Nathan? He's just made his first visit to White's and some of the other clubs and I'm most anxious to hear how it went. Nathan, dear, do sit down and tell me everything!''

Tossing his hat and gloves onto a chair, Ryan crossed the room and kissed Lindsay on the cheek. Then, when Dolly's head was turned, he stole a glance down the rose satin bodice and grinned. "I agree with my sister, Mistress Jones. This evening dress is a fine piece of work.''

"Shank you,'' she muttered, managing a pin-filled smile.

To Lindsay's further dismay, Ryan then threw himself down on her bed and folded his hands behind his head. The pale yellow coat fell open to reveal a hard, tapering chest that was impressive to behold and accentuated by the white shirt, starched cravat, and snug gray waistcoat that covered it. Lindsay stared for a moment, thinking how appealingly clean and strong he looked.

"White's went well,'' Ryan was saying, smiling with his eyes closed. "I met Beau Brummell, as well as Lord Alvaney, Byron, Colonel Dan McKinnon, Sir Lumley Skeffington, and Lord Wellesley Poole, just to name a few. The bow window was a positive gallery of dandies.''

"You met Lord Byron?'' Lindsay gasped in disbelief.

"He was eating cheese.'' Ryan opened one eye, watched her, and raised the brow above it. "Hard to believe that he eats and drinks like other mortals, hmm? One can only wonder what other bodily functions he performs. The possibilities are utterly fascinating.''

Dolly made a choking noise while Lindsay's face turned pink. Ryan closed his eye again and tried not to smile. "Careful, Mistress Jones,'' he cautioned. "Don't swallow the pins.''

"Fortunately, Mr. Raveneau, I believe I'm finished. If you'll just remove the gown, Lindsay, I'll take it with me and finish it tomorrow. No doubt you'll be needing it for the round of parties that'll be given for the visiting royalty." As Lindsay disappeared behind a painted Chinese screen, Dolly looked at Ryan. "Are you looking forward to the celebrations, Mr. Raveneau? Perhaps you'll get to see Lord Byron drinking champagne!"

He grinned appreciatively. "Or burping."

"Nathan, stop being vulgar!" Lindsay cried as she reemerged in her simple peach-colored gown. "You'll give our family a bad name!"

He rose up on an elbow and pretended to ponder her words. "It's probably too late."

Laughing, Mistress Jones bade them farewell and left the room with Lindsay's evening dresses. Ryan resumed his prone position and had just closed his eyes again when he felt a poke in his ribs. "What now?"

"Tell me the truth. What was he like?"

Through his black lashes, he saw Lindsay perched beside him on the rose counterpane. "Brummell?"

She poked him again, frowning. "Lord Byron!"

"You're dangerously close to becoming a bore, my dear." He sighed. "Oh, all right. He's handsome enough, I suppose. Thin and very pale, with soulful eyes and hair that I'd wager he curls at night. We didn't form an intimate acquaintance, and if I have anything to do with it we never will, but he seemed agreeable enough. Clever but conceited. Just as Byron is unable to write a poem or a drama without making himself the hero, he makes himself the subject of his own conversations."

Lindsay made a moue. "I think you're just jealous."

His eyes opened. "Of *what*?"

"Well, of Lord Byron's celebrity. And his title, his aristocratic background, his education—"

"Let me bring this list of my shortcomings to a close. If I harbor any jealousy toward Byron it's because of the place he holds in your heart."

Startled, she stared at his face. Ryan could have been asleep for all the expression he betrayed. "Don't tease me."

The corners of his mouth turned up slightly, but he said nothing.

Casting about for another topic of conversation, Lindsay discovered one instantly. "Tell me about Beau Brummell, then. He approved of you?"

"I'd say so. There's a certain air of humor, of mock solemnity attached to his preoccupation with clothes. I think he sensed that I had purposely broken one of his fashion rules with this coat and rather liked me for it. He said to André, 'My dear Raveneau, have you not instructed your son that the severest mortification a gentleman can incur is to attract observation in the street by his outward appearance?' " Ryan paused to chuckle at the memory. "Then, feigning distaste, Brummell felt the cloth of my coat and looked me up and down through his quizzing glass. Finally, he said, 'I see you've been to Weston. That's a start, and I'll have to admit that the thing don't look bad on you. Do you truly like it, young Raveneau?' I assured him that I did, and he very nearly smiled before replying, 'Well, I do believe that what pleases is allowed.' Later, when we were leaving for Brooks's, the Beau approached me and suggested that I come to his house tomorrow at ten o'clock to watch him dress, thereby learning the proper way to tie a cravat. I accepted with pleasure but not too much pleasure. He's used to being fawned over, certainly by newcomers like myself, and my attitude of mingled respect and amusement must have piqued his interest. He said, 'You're like your father, I see! That's good. I'll take you round to Watier's and introduce you to Mildmay and Pierrepont.' "

"What does that mean?" Lindsay wondered.

"Watier's is the club formed by Brummell, Lord Alvaney, Henry Pierrepont, and Sir Henry Mildmay—the four most prominent dandies. It's become even more exclusive than White's, and Byron calls it 'The Dandy Club,' claiming that they persecute literary types." He paused, shutting his eyes again for a moment. "You know, all of this business goes against the grain for me. It's mildly diverting, as long as I tell myself that it won't last and that it's necessary for the success of the project your father and I are involved in. The sad fact is, though, that the cornerstones of London society are selfishness and snobbery. It's best to remember that this is not our real life, nor should it be."

Lindsay pondered this for a few moments, leaning back beside him and staring at the high, arched canopy. She wondered how Ryan had gained such insight into these people after only a few hours and if he might be right. What did that say for her own sister? Mouette did seem alarmingly frivolous these days, not at all the wise older sister she had expected to look up to.

Suddenly it dawned on Lindsay that she and Ryan were lying together on her bed, alone in the room. When his fingertips brushed her bare wrist, a shiver ran through her body followed by a wave of warmth. What if he rolled over right now, pinning her down and kissing her until she couldn't breathe or think? The possibility made Lindsay's heart pound with excitement. It seemed so long since they'd touched, since that night aboard *La Mouette* when they'd seen the shooting star and she'd been locked in his strong embrace . . .

"Mmm-unh."

It was a sleep sound, bordering on a snore! Lindsay stiffened and sat up, raging silently as she stared down at Ryan's slumbering form. The fact that he looked boyish and vulnerable only increased her fury. How dare he? She very nearly shook him and shouted the question aloud but realized that she would end up looking like a lovesick fool. And that she most surely was not!

Rising, she threw him one last contemptuous backward glance, then strode into the corridor. Her parents were emerging from their suite of rooms at that moment and smiled at her in greeting.

"Have you seen Ryan?" André asked. "Things couldn't

have gone better at White's. Harry says that his membership is certain since Brummell made his approval clear. Your friend handled himself magnificently; it was quite a performance!''

"He's not *my* friend!" Lindsay shot back, her gray eyes smoldering. "I detest the man!"

Devon and André glanced at each other, blinking in surprise. "Darling, what's brought this on?" her mother asked gently. "Did Ryan do something to insult you?"

"He fell asleep on my bed!" The hot words poured out even though she knew how silly they must sound.

"What's wrong with that?" inquired a baffled Raveneau.

"He's acting just like a *brother*!" Lindsay cried. Turning on her heel, she started down the hallway toward the stairs, adding over her shoulder, "I can't explain; you wouldn't understand."

When their daughter was out of sight, André looked down at his wife. "Do *you* understand?"

"I'm afraid I may." Devon sighed. "I'm going to give this situation the benefit of the doubt, however, and keep my own counsel for the moment."

"Thank you." He bent to kiss her lightly. "I was hoping you wouldn't tell me!"

CHAPTER
14

June 7, 1814

"WELL, WELL, THE *TIMES* ALREADY SHOWS AN ACcount of the king of Prussia's arrival in Dover," Raveneau remarked over his morning coffee as he shook out the newspaper. "It says that he docked yesterday afternoon and is expected in London today. Here's a sentence worth sharing: 'The public anxiety to behold these great sovereigns to whom so much of the present tranquillity of Europe is owing will no doubt receive full gratification.'"

"That must mean that they'll drive through town." Devon smiled.

"*That's* full gratification?" Ryan laughed. "I would have thought it implied something much more personal!"

"Isn't it time for your cravat lesson?" Lindsay inquired pointedly between sips of chocolate. "Your conversation makes me consider the notion of taking my breakfast in bed like most gentle ladies."

Ryan's brows flew up as he applied his napkin to his

mouth. "She's angry with me," he confided to André and Devon. "Trouble is, I don't know what I've done!"

"You've come face-to-face with one of life's great lessons and mysteries, son," Raveneau intoned, his eyes gleaming with silvery amusement. "Women don't *need* a reason to be angry with men."

"I'll have to start writing these things down." Ryan laughed. "I'll make a page for Beau Brummell's aphorisms and start another for yours, sir." Standing, he tossed down his napkin, then bent to kiss first Devon's cheek, then Lindsay's. "Try to forgive me, brat," he whispered. "Whatever it was, I promise never to do it again!" Then, picking up his hat, gloves, and new white-thorn cane, he disappeared out the front door.

Devon turned to her daughter, who was staring pensively at her buttered scone. "Are you still out of temper with Ryan because he fell asleep on your bed? Or is it because he treats you like a sister?"

"I don't want to talk about it." Lindsay stood up. "I'm not hungry. I'm going to my room to read."

"The town's in a state of chaos," Ryan announced upon his return. "Do you really think that we should venture forth to watch the entry of the royals?"

Devon looked up from her pretty satinwood writing table and smiled. "How handsome you look! My, my, did you tie that cravat yourself or is the Beau responsible?" Spontaneously, she opened her arms to him. How much he reminded her of André in his youth! Ryan, however, was less angry, at least under these circumstances. Devon delighted in his twinkling blue eyes and the humor that seemed to infect his every utterance. "Do you know," she said, holding his chiseled face in her hands, "I'm beginning to think of you as a son!"

"That's nice. Thank you." His smile was warm. "As for my cravat . . ." Ryan glanced in the mirror, touching it. "I tied it myself. Brummell swears that I'm doing as well as he, that I learned faster than any pupil he's had.

I'll wager that I could teach that little weasel Dindé a thing or two!"

"Speaking of Dindé, I wonder if we shouldn't persuade Mouette to find another place for him. There are Harvey's feelings to consider, and I also get the impression that you are not overfond of the man."

"Ah, Mother dear, how perceptive you are!" Ryan pulled up a shield-backed chair and sat down next to her desk. "Let us say that I have nothing against Monsieur Dindé, but his assistance is no longer needed."

Devon arched a delicate brow. "Or ever, methinks. Sometimes I am convinced that you must have been a dandy once, so at home are you in the role! It's hard to believe, considering the dashing, bearded Ryan Coleraine I knew in Connecticut . . ."

"Believe me, madame, I was never a dandy, at least not in this life! Put it down to my powers of observation, and possibly my talent for mimicry, and then put it away. The reasons are not important."

"You're right, of course. What matters is the undeniable success of your masquerade. All the rest is simple human curiosity."

"It's best to take me at face value. My past is just that. I often think of my first voyage to America as a rebirth. That's the wonder of the place: its innocent welcome to people who wish for a new beginning. I'm only here now because I feel I have a debt to pay to the country that took me in without questions or judgment."

Devon longed to meet his eyes, but Ryan was involved in lighting a slim, dark cheroot. "Well, it doesn't matter, does it?" she proclaimed brightly. "We all love you just as you are and whatever your past holds is your own affair, not ours."

His brows flicked upward. "Don't misunderstand me, Devon. I wasn't involved in anything criminal. I didn't come straight to Pettipauge from Newgate prison, if that's what you're thinking!"

"Not at all! And even if you had, it wouldn't matter.

Your life to us began the day you signed on with André, and you have proved yourself to be a man of strength and impeccable character. Why, even Lindsay likes you, and she doesn't like many people!"

"*Does* she, indeed," he said with a hint of irony. "I wonder."

"Well, that's between you two. Between *us*, I have a present for you. Mother to son, as it were." Devon pulled open the writing table's middle drawer and produced a tiny wrapped box. "Open it!"

He stared at her in amazement. "I'm touched. Do you know, I haven't had an honest present for years."

"All the more reason you should have one now, from someone who loves you." Devon was surprised to feel tears in her own throat as she watched Ryan carefully undo the wrapping and cast it aside.

"Good God." Ryan opened a velvet box to behold an exquisite Sevres snuffbox. "It's almost as beautiful as Brummell's!"

"No, it's *more* beautiful!" Devon laughed. "He'll be green with envy. Next thing you know, he'll be wearing yellow and dove gray"—she nodded at today's coat—"and asking *you* for advice!"

"Somehow I doubt that." Smiling, Ryan came halfway out of his chair to kiss her cheek. "This is a very thoughtful gift, and I'm sure it will bring me good fortune in whatever I undertake here in London."

"There's one more thing." Devon disappeared into her dressing room and returned with a glazed jar filled with a flaky brown substance. "Here is your snuff. This is Spanish Bran, a most popular variety and the one André thought you might prefer as long as you're forced to indulge. There are others, though: Masulipatam, Old Paris, Scholten, Bureau Demi-gros, Curaçao, King's Martinique, and Bolangaro, to name just a few. And there are stronger snuffs, such as Brazil, that are generally used to flavor other mixtures. Beau Brummell's quite an expert, I perceive. You may want to consult with him about developing your own mixture."

"I've been observing the Beau's method for taking snuff," Ryan remarked, taking a pinch of the Spanish Bran and sniffing it.

"One-handed?"

He nodded. "The left. But, as with my coats, I would like to absorb his style without imitating him. I'll have to work out a technique of my own."

Devon smiled her approval. "You're a very astute man, Captain Coleraine."

"It's a pleasure to hear my own name spoken. It's good to be reminded that I'm not really a Raveneau." Her slightly injured expression made him laugh. "I phrased that badly! What I meant was that it would be easy for me to slip into Nathan's place here and pretend that I actually am one of the family. You all have certainly made me feel at home, but I mustn't fool myself. I'm Ryan Coleraine, not Nathan Raveneau." His eyes twinkled suddenly. "Of course, your charming younger daughter would doubtless remind me of my true station if she suspected that I was becoming carried away with this charade!"

Privately, Devon wondered if that might be because Lindsay had feelings for Ryan that were not sisterly, but aloud she inquired, "Do you have a family here in Britain, Ryan? Parents in Ireland?"

"My parents died several years ago—and I buried the past with them." He stood up, abruptly distant. "If there's nothing else, I have a few matters to attend to before we venture forth to greet the czar of Russia, the king of Prussia, and their entourage."

"There is one more thing." Devon reached under the papers on her writing table and produced a long-stemmed quizzing glass attached to a black silk ribbon. "I thought you might be needing one of these. André received it as a gift some years back but never used it."

"Madame, you'll never know how much I appreciate

your thoughtfulness and kindness." Accepting the quizzing glass, Ryan held Devon's hand for a long moment,
his gaze rich with emotion.

Impulsively, Devon leaned forward on tiptoe and kissed
his cheek. "Some charades are more real than others,"
she whispered.

"Well," Ryan remarked to Harvey Jenkins before
exiting his rooms, "we're off to greet Czar Alexander
and his entourage."

"Mmm." Harvey peered at his master's cravat and
smoothed one edge. This entire expedition to London
had become a test of his patience. Harvey had been
steward and factotum to Coleraine ever since he had
taken command of the *Chimera,* and he had grown used
to a very different Ryan Coleraine in a very different
setting. Harvey had always been the expert on rules of
fashion and decorum, and his employer had either waved
him off or indulged him. Now, Jenkins found himself in
the company of an impeccably clad buck who insisted
on tying his own cravat and was suddenly wearing a
quizzing glass around his neck and carrying a Sevres
snuffbox! Add to that the indignity of sharing duties with
the rude little Dindé, and Harvey found himself in a
perpetual state of exasperated confusion.

"Why don't you come out, too, Harvey?" Ryan asked,
watching the manservant with gentle eyes.

"Oh, no, sir. I don't think so," he replied stiffly.

"You mustn't sulk, old man. I realize that this life
isn't what you're used to, but it's only temporary. Before you know it, we'll be back on the decks of a new
Chimera, bound for the West Indies! In the meantime,
why not make the best of this? Forget about me and
amuse yourself." Ryan paused, fingering the stem of his
quizzing glass. "You might start by inviting Arabella
Butter to accompany you out this afternoon to view the
arrival of the royals!"

Jenkins put his head to one side and considered. "Well, I *might* do, sir."

"That's better." With a grin, Ryan put an arm around the shorter, stouter man and they walked toward the doorway. "The girl likes you, you know. I've seen how she looks at you."

Harvey attempted to raise his brows in the manner of his master. "Gammon, sir! It's *you* Miss Butter gazes at, and well you know it!"

"I won't argue with you, Harvey, since you're always infuriatingly positive that you're correct. However, you might consider this in a different light. I'm giving you permission to steal the girl away from me!"

A grin spread over the manservant's face. "I see, sir!"

"There's one last thing I should tell you, in the cheering-up line, and then I must go. Mistress Raveneau has decided that there is no place for Dindé in her household. He's being dismissed."

"I can't say I'm sorry, sir." Harvey's grin widened.

"Neither am I!" Coleraine winked almost imperceptibly as he picked up his gloves and disappeared into the hallway. "Don't forget about Arabella!" he called in a stage whisper, then lightly took the stairs to the entry hall where his new family awaited him. "Sorry I'm late." Ryan drew on his dove-gray gloves. "Jenkins needed a bit of reassurance. I'm afraid this isn't what he's been used to during his years of service with me."

Lindsay stood off to one side, waiting for him to notice her extremely flattering new walking dress. Made of jaconet muslin, it was high-waisted, its fullness drawn in by welts. There was a pretty collar, welted to correspond with the trimming, and over the gown Lindsay wore a pale canary–colored spencer slightly ornamented with primrose satin. Atop her burnished curls was perched a French bonnet finished at the brim with more primrose satin and accented with a cluster of ostrich feathers off to one side. The final touches to her ensemble were gloves and shoes of the same soft canary hue. Lindsay liked them immensely and couldn't resist first pointing a toe and then pretending to readjust the fingers of her left glove.

"My, my, aren't we fetching today," Ryan whispered, his breath warm against her cheek.

Lindsay strove to appear aloof. "I don't know about *you,* but *I* certainly am."

"Now, children, you mustn't quarrel if you want to be allowed out in public!" Devon cautioned, laughing.

"That's right." Raveneau was opening the door and guiding his wife through it as he spoke. "Behave yourselves, or we'll lock you in the nursery for the afternoon."

Coleraine bit back an indelicate retort but indulged himself by eyeing Lindsay through his quizzing glass behind her parents' backs. The sight of her sudden, involuntary blush nearly made him laugh aloud.

"What a ridiculous piece of affectation *that* is!" she hissed.

"What?" Ryan feigned ignorance. "Oh, do you mean this?" He flourished the quizzing glass. "Guard your tongue, dear sister; it was a gift from your mother. *I* rather like it. It helps to make me feel like a different person."

"Let me assure you that you were *different* long before acquiring the toys of a dandy!"

Before Ryan could reply, Devon turned to speak to them. "I think we may as well walk. The fresh air will do us all good, and I have it on good authority from Harry that the best place to watch for the czar will be in Piccadilly, just a short stroll from here."

"But isn't the czar going to St. James's Palace?" Lindsay wondered.

"Certainly the Regent expects him to stay there, but Harry thinks that he will go first to the Pulteney Hotel where his sister, the Grand Duchess of Oldenburg, has taken rooms. In any event, I do not think we want to brave the crowds that are pouring out from the south-east of London. Ryan remarked on them to me when he came back from Beau Brummell's, and Harry says that the Prince Regent's gold and scarlet postilions, sent to meet the sovereigns, were submerged in the tumult. He was there himself and saw the mob set upon two separate vehicles approaching from Kent.''

"It's a scene of chaos, no doubt about it," Ryan confirmed. "The route to St. James's Palace is lined with coaches and carts, and wooden stands are filled on every street corner. The windows along the way are a sea of faces.''

"I find it rather mystifying that all of London would want to turn out to greet European royalty!" Lindsay said. "It's not as if the English have much in common with the Russians, and Prussians, and God knows who else. What's the attraction?''

Raveneau smiled back at his daughter. "You're sounding more and more like your mother in her youth!" He chuckled as they turned south on Park Lane. Across from them, lush green branches curved above the walls enclosing Hyde Park. "I think that the English are caught up in this precisely *because* they feel that these visitors are foreign and exotic. They don't know what to expect, but they want them to feel welcome. Plus, there's the desire for celebration now that the war is over. What better excuse than a visit from some of Britain's allies in the struggle against Napoleon?''

They continued in silence for a few minutes, enjoying the sunny June afternoon. Lindsay walked with her gloved hand snug in the crook of Ryan's arm, their paces matched. She liked the sensation of his tall, hard body against her slim arm and glanced over occasionally to watch the play of muscles in his white-clad thighs as he walked.

Soon, the quartet turned left onto Piccadilly, following the flagstone footpath that was crowded with pedestrians. It wasn't far to the Pulteney Hotel. Across the way was Green Park with its docile deer and cattle, the white-stuccoed Ranger's Lodge among the trees, and, in the distance, Buckingham House's redbrick façade framed by abbey towers and Surrey hills.

Joining the row of curious Londoners, who were obviously in a holiday mood, Devon said, "Did I tell you? Harry says that the banquet at Carlton House for the royals will take place tomorrow night, and he has acquired invitations for all of us. It's just what we hoped for! The perfect way to introduce Lindsay and Ry—that is, Nathan—into London society!"

"How could you forget to mention something so important?" Lindsay exclaimed. "What will I wear?"

"You'll have to pardon your mother," André murmured ironically. "Obviously 'Harry says' so much that her mind is overcrowded with his utterances."

Ryan leaned around Lindsay's back and whispered to Raveneau, "Since Harry seems to have knowledge about *everything*, we must be thankful that he is part of the family!"

"Mmm." André nodded absently, then straightened and stared into the distance.

"My forgetfulness has less to do with Harry than with the fact that I am unused to Lindsay caring about banquets, balls, or the proper attire for same!" Devon amended.

A slim, blond young man was wending his way through the line of people in front of them when he stopped suddenly and stared at Devon and André. "Why, it's Captain and Mrs. Raveneau, isn't it?"

Surprised, Devon smiled, nodded, and asked, "Have we met, sir?"

"Not since I was a child, I'm afraid, but I'd never forget you, madame!" He held out a pale hand. "I'm Lord Fanshawe. My parents are the Earl and Countess of Grimley."

"But of course!" Devon clapped her hands in delight. "We spent a week at your family estate in Oxfordshire the last time we visited England. You couldn't have been more than fourteen at the time. How lovely to see you! Lord Fanshawe, do you remember my daughter, Lindsay, and son, Nathan?''

"How could I forget? Miss Raveneau tried to compel me to read the complete works of Shakespeare in five days and continually threatened me with a comprehensive examination!" He swept off his beaver hat and kissed Lindsay's hand. "You've grown into a beautiful woman, Miss Raveneau," he murmured, staring at her with liquid brown eyes.

"Did you finally read Shakespeare, Lord Fanshawe?" she inquired, her cheeks warming under his appreciative gaze.

"Please, call me Dudley. And yes, I was forced to, at Oxford, and I must confess that I liked it no better. But at least there the course was being taught by a master who looked like a toad, so there was less to distract me.''

Ryan, who had been twirling his quizzing glass between his thumb and forefinger, lifted it to his eye and stared. "I beg your pardon, my good fellow."

Dudley Fanshawe looked over and blinked as he focused on a handsome, languid dandy in a pale yellow coat. "My last memory of you, sir, is the day that you challenged me to a race on my father's two best hunters. You sailed over an impossibly high hedge that I was too cowardly to attempt, ending the contest." He put out his hand, which Ryan accepted lightly. "So, we meet again. I don't think I would have recognized you."

"Nor I you, sir." Ryan glanced at Fanshawe's cravat with a nearly imperceptible air of disdain.

Discomfited, the young man turned to Raveneau and paid his respects, then nodded at the others and moved farther down the line of people. Lindsay instantly rounded on Ryan.

"Why on *earth* did you have to behave like such an idiot?"

"Part of the role, m'dear. Besides, I don't recall doing

anything out of line." Extracting his snuffbox, Ryan flicked it open, took a tiny pinch, set it below the base of his left thumb, and sniffed. "Did I?"

"Put that silly thing away!" Lindsay's voice rose to a pitch that caused bystanders to turn and stare. "And you can dispense with that foolish act with me!" she continued in a heated whisper. "I know the real you, and though I don't like him any better, at least he said what he meant!"

"Did I *say* something amiss to Lord Fanshawe? I don't recall speaking more than a half-dozen words to the man."

"Dudley Fanshawe is obviously a warm, sincere gentleman, and I won't allow you to make sport of him under the guise of this masquerade!"

Devon looked over, a finger to her lips. "Hush! Both of you!" she commanded. "There's a carriage turning at Hyde Park corner, and I'll wager it's the czar."

True to her prediction, a plain carriage drew up swiftly and unannounced in front of the hotel with its stone pillars and bow windows. A file of waiters dashed down the steps to form a line across the pavement before a tall, smiling man emerged from the vehicle. He paused to kiss his hand to a lady at a first-floor window, then disappeared into the hotel.

"I don't understand," Lindsay complained, still out of sorts with Ryan. "He came from the opposite direction of Kent!"

"The czar must have heard about the mobs waiting for him," her father replied, "and decided to skirt the city and enter by the western highway."

"Well, that was interesting, I suppose," Devon remarked. "At least we've had some fresh air—and some food for conversation tomorrow night at Carlton House."

"And we met Dudley Fanshawe!" Lindsay exclaimed, ignoring Ryan. "What a charming young man!"

As if on cue, Lord Fanshawe reappeared, pausing across from them on the pavement. His eyes were riveted on Lindsay as he tipped his hat, smiled, and said, "I hope to see you all at Carlton House tomorrow evening."

"We'll be there," Lindsay murmured shyly.

"I can't wait," Ryan put in in a bored voice.

Dudley looked perplexed but managed another smile before setting off in the direction of Green Park.

"Ouch!" Ryan gasped in surprise as an elbow poked his ribs.

"You are the only brat in this family!" Lindsay accused. "Thank God I don't have to put up with you for a lifetime!"

He looked around at André and Devon, the picture of innocence except for the devils dancing in his dark blue Irish eyes. "Was it something I said?"

CHAPTER
15

June 8, 1814

"T HEY SAY THAT THE GRAND DUCHESS OF OLDEN-burg can't abide Prinny," Sir Harry Brandreth murmured confidentially between long sips of champagne in the Crimson Drawing Room of Carlton House, the Prince Regent's own palace overlooking St. James's Park.

"Do they?" Devon responded politely. She and Lindsay had come over to join Mouette and her husband while André and Ryan chatted with a group of powerful Tories. Everyone looked dazzling and she had never seen Carlton House more lavishly decorated. Outside, its pillars were hung with thousands of lanterns and its screen was silhouetted by topaz and scarlet flares set between palm trees. Here in the Crimson Drawing Room, a spectacular chandelier glittered above them and they stood on a carpet of blue velvet adorned with the insignia of the Garter. Yet Devon felt that something was wrong. The heat was oppressive and Mouette wore an uncustomary expression of distracted melancholy. Meanwhile, Harry droned on.

"She feels that the Regent is used up by dissipation and that his much-boasted affability is licentious. And she has said that he and his brothers have a brazen way of looking at her. Of course, it's well known that the czar and his sister are very close, so his opinion of the Regent will doubtless be colored by the ideas she has formed during her two months in London. The czar has already snubbed Prinny by deciding to remain at the Pulteney Hotel with the grand duchess!" Sensing that his audience was less than rapt, Harry followed Devon's and Lindsay's gaze to Ryan's handsome figure. "I'm glad to see that Nathan had the good sense to dress properly for this occasion." Harry lifted his quizzing glass and scanned Ryan's spotless black frock coat, breeches, and impeccable white cravat, which were set off to advantage by his hard physique and gleaming back hair. "I was afraid he might turn up in a lavender coat or something equally outrageous."

Lindsay was surprised to feel a surge of indignation. "My brother is not a fool, Harry!"

Accepting another glass of champagne from a passing tray, he lifted a blond brow above flushed cheeks. "Of course he's not, dear child. He's a Raveneau, ain't he? No one has more respect for the attributes of your family than I! If Nathan has erred since arriving in London, it is only because he's misguided and head-strong, not stupid. I can see that I should have spent more time with him and offered a bit more advice. Coming from America, Nathan may not understand that there are certain rules here that it don't do to break."

"Apparently Beau Brummell doesn't share your view-point," Lindsay murmured. "He approves of Nathan. What more could he aspire to?"

"Oh, Lindsay, don't be so tiresome!" Mouette exclaimed petulantly. "You're sounding more like Nathan's wife than his sister!"

Sipping her champagne as a hot blush spread madden-

ingly over her cheeks, Lindsay managed to retort, "What
an *odd* thing to say, Mouette!"

At that moment, Ryan came up behind her and slipped
an arm around her waist. "The Regent has requested
that you be presented to him," he whispered, his voice
full of mischief. "Guard your virtue, sister dear."

Before she could answer, Lindsay found herself being
guided across the immense drawing room, which was
one of several in the palace. Ryan's manner was casual,
but his voice held a sensual undercurrent as he murmured, "I haven't had a chance to tell you how beautiful you look tonight. I'm hard-pressed to act fraternal in
your presence."

His eyes swept over her bare shoulders, the lace and
rose satin gown Dolly Jones had pinned in his presence,
then brushed the exposed curves of her breasts and
lingered on Lindsay's fine-boned, glowing face. The am-
ethysts in her upswept strawberry-blond curls paled in
comparison.

Blushing, Lindsay focused on the rotund figure of the
Prince Regent, who watched her approach from across
the drawing room. Her first impression was that of an
overgrown, self-indulgent baby, but she was soon distracted by his charm. Bright blue eyes beamed at her in
approval, nearly allowing Lindsay to overlook the florid
face of their owner.

"Your Royal Highness," Ryan said soberly, "I would
like to present my sister, Lindsay Raveneau."

"I am honored, Your Majesty," Lindsay said, bowing
her head as she sank into a curtsy.

He took her hand with plump fingers. "The honor is
all mine, Miss Raveneau. I wouldn't have thought it
possible, but I believe that you may be even more beautiful than your mother." He chuckled conspiratorially.
"Don't tell her I said so, of course! What you *may*
repeat is my sentiment that we are honored to have you
in London."

"Your Majesty is very kind," she answered demurely.

The Regent then presented Lindsay to his royal guests and it seemed that he was happy to have the distraction. Czar Alexander was blond and elegant in a bottle-green velvet uniform decorated with gold braid and diamond stars. Rumor had it that he was interesting and complicated, a mixture of progressive ideas and angelic mysticism. King Frederick William of Prussia was a bluff, gaunt man who had also snubbed the Regent in his own fashion. Although he had agreed to stay at Carlton House, he had spurned the magnificent suite of satinwood furniture, insisting on a simple camp bed.

Lindsay knew enough Russian to make conversation with the foreign guests, thereby impressing them favorably. She particularly won the favor of Field Marshal von Blücher, the snowy-haired chancellor of Prussia. The old hero, who had never wavered in his opposition to Napoleon and had been chiefly responsible for the drive toward Paris, fixed Lindsay with a twinkling eye.

"Are you enjoying London?" she asked him.

The field marshal cocked a bushy white brow at her décolletage. "Ah!" he exclaimed lustily. "What a city to sack!"

Instead of shrinking in embarrassment, Lindsay met his gaze and joined in his laughter. "If you mean to make me blush, sir, I should tell you that I am the daughter of a sea captain. I outgrew timidity long ago—in self-defense!"

Catherine, Grand Duchess of Oldenburg, was chatting with Countess Lieven, the alluring wife of the Russian ambassador and a leader of London society, but both looked up to acknowledge the Raveneau offspring.

"My dears, what a pleasure to meet you at last," murmured Countess Lieven, her eyes on Ryan. "Lady Jersey and I were just saying this afternoon that we must send you both vouchers for Almack's. We'll expect you at next week's assembly."

"Wednesdays, aren't they?" Ryan said. "We'd be happy to attend. But, Countess, how are they managing without you tonight? This *is* Wednesday, and Brummell whispers that you have allowed the waltz to be danced within Almack's hallowed walls."

"I'm certain that the assembly is very dull without me." Her smile was both arch and seductive. "Have you not heard, Mr. Raveneau? It is not fashionable where I am not."

"In that case, we are honored." Ryan's fingers pressed the small of Lindsay's back. "Are we not, dear sister?"

Before Lindsay could chime in with a comment that she was certain would sound clearly artificial and too sweet, the grand duchess linked arms with her brother and inquired of the Regent, "Your Highness, will we have the pleasure of meeting your wife, Princess Caroline, tonight?"

An awkward silence reigned. The Regent emptied his crystal glass of cherry brandy, then cleared his throat. "Uh, no, no, I'm afraid that's not possible." Desperate for a distraction, he brought out his snuffbox and took a pinch for effect, letting it escape before it reached his nose.

"I don't understand," the grand duchess pressed on. "I thought that tonight of all nights the princess would be present to greet the royal visitors who have traveled so very far."

Prinny's face grew even redder. The relationship between him and his unattractive, resentful wife had deteriorated to the point where he could no longer bear her company at all and she amused herself by attempting to embarrass the Regent in public. His position was made even more unnerving and humiliating by the fact that the people of London seemed to have taken Princess Caroline's side in the ongoing drama. And now, here were these European royals who would not allow the Regent to ignore his wife's existence. After all, she was the niece of George III and daughter of the Duke of Brunswick.

"I don't know if an introduction can be effected," he muttered. "My wife has been indisposed of late."

"Has she, indeed?" The grand duchess exchanged glances with the czar.

Lindsay's heart nearly went out to the squirming Regent, until she remembered his years of adultery with Mrs. Fitzherbert and Lady Jersey. Now it was said that there was a new woman in his life, a haughty Tory grandmother called Lady Hertford. Mouette whispered that he visited her every afternoon and that the Marquess of Hertford tactfully left them alone together. Furthermore, Lady Hertford was known to have a powerful degree of influence with the Regent.

Now, as if she sensed that she was the unspoken subject of conversation among the group of royals, the impeccably groomed but aging Marchioness of Hertford appeared at Prinny's side.

"Good evening, Your Highness," she murmured in cultivated tones.

"Ah, Lady Hertford!" With the irrational reaction of one in love, he happily faced his guests. "Czar Alexander, I would like to present my Lady Hertford."

"It is a great honor to meet the savior of Europe!" she declared.

The Russian ruler stared into space. The Regent, knowing him to be a little deaf and supposing he had not heard, repeated loudly, "This is my Lady Hertford!"

The czar continued to ignore them both, whereupon the lady made a deep curtsy, gave him the haughtiest of glances, and withdrew.

Lindsay took Ryan's arm, anxious to absent herself from the increasingly uncomfortable situation. He tensed his bicep in reply, then smiled at Countess Lieven. "Countess, would you care to speak to our parents? They have both been longing to see you since our arrival in London."

"No more than I have longed to see them!"

Curtsies and bows were made to the Regent and his

guests, then the trio started across the drawing room.
Beau Brummell accosted them midway.

"My dear countess," he murmured with an ironic
smile, "what was *that* all about?"

Countess Lieven lifted winged brows. "Czar Alexander refused to acknowledge Lady Hertford. 'Twas not
so significant, however, as the damning look she sent his
way before quitting his company. You know, George,
how much influence she has with our dear Regent. It's
my opinion that the fate of this visit was written in that
single glance."

Soon the guests adjourned with short-lived relief to
the Throne Room with its canopy of helmets and ostrich
plumes and its fender supporting the eagle of Jupiter
subduing prostrate dragons. Here Queen Charlotte, the
stiff and unpleasant wife of mad George III, took her
place under the canopy and received hundreds of satin-
clad ladies attended by men in court dress or uniform.
The old queen had borne fifteen children, nine of them
sons, but she had never relaxed the rigid etiquette learned
at the German court of her youth and thus these functions were invariably boring for the participants.

This particular evening was made more excruciating
by the stifling heat. Czar Alexander, left with nothing to
do but stand and watch, amused himself by quizzing
young beauties.

Finally, the Regent led his guests down the circular
double staircase, past the giant bronzes of Chronos with
his clock and Atlas bearing the map of Europe, to a still
more wonderful set of apartments below. They swept
left to the Library, the Golden Drawing Room and Gothic
Dining-Room, and right to the Anteroom, Dining Room,
and Gothic Conservatory. The open double doors between them made a continuous chamber three hundred
and fifty feet long. Its ceilings were spandreled in the
Gothic taste, its walls paneled with golden moldings and
shields, its fairylike chandeliers suspended from carved

monastic heads. Most magnificent of all was the conservatory, with a nave and aisles formed by clusters of carved pillars, stained-glass windows, and a ceiling with glazed traceries that flooded the marble pavement with moonlight.

"Well," Ryan murmured to Lindsay, "I believe I saw the king of Prussia gasp in amazement. Perhaps the Regent will feel better."

"I don't think so," she replied. "He looks awfully unhappy and strained to me."

"Doubtless all this food will cheer him up." His dark blue eyes swept the tables filled with dishes of gold plate that were laden with hot soups, roasts, all manner of cold food, and a fabulous assortment of fresh fruits including peaches, pineapples, and grapes. There appeared to be enough iced champagne for every citizen of London.

Lindsay accepted a glass from a servant's tray and drank it down. "I have a prodigious thirst!" she exclaimed, then hiccuped.

Ryan chuckled fondly. "I've missed you lately."

She lifted her chin. "We've been very busy—and you've been very bad."

"Bad?" He watched as she traded her empty glass for a full one and took a long sip. "I?"

"Yes. Thou." Lindsay giggled softly at her own wit. "Of course, it's no surprise. Your behavior has been objectionable since the day I met you."

"And you have liked me for it."

"What conceit!" Bravely, she gazed at his tanned, chiseled face and felt a strange weakness steal over her body. "I have told you that I despise you, and I never lie. I will admit that lately I have come to feel a certain contrary fondness for you, but that is in line with our new roles in life. It reminds me strongly of my feelings for Nathan."

"Ah, I see. Sisterly antipathy, hmm?"

"Exactly." Lindsay flushed and dropped her gray eyes under the heat of his gaze.

"Well, well!" A hearty voice spoke from behind them. "The Raveneau siblings! What a happy coincidence."

Ryan glanced over his shoulder to discover Lord Fanshawe staring at Lindsay.

"Hello, Fanshawe," he said shortly. "What can we do for you?"

"I wondered if your sister might consent to share a plate of fruit outside with me. The gardens are quite beautiful, filled with weeping willows, and although the peacocks may have retired for the evening, I do believe there may be nightingales in their place." He smiled warmly at Lindsay. "Do you have nightingales in Connecticut?"

"I—I don't think so!" Dudley Fanshawe epitomized the man she had dreamed about since childhood. He was elegantly slim and handsome, blond, cultured, and kind. Lindsay already felt completely at ease in his company. "I would love to eat pineapple in the gardens with you, Lord Fanshawe."

"Please!" He laughed as they walked away from Ryan. "You must call me Dudley or risk injuring my feelings. We're old friends after all, aren't we?"

"Christ," Ryan muttered under his breath. Lindsay had left him without even a parting glance and now she was halfway across the conservatory, beaming at that simpering Fanshawe. First she swooned at the mention of Lord Byron, and now she appeared to be captivated by a man who probably read the former's poems aloud and wept at appropriate intervals. What had happened to the sensible schoolmistress from Pettipauge?

Devon was chatting with Sir Lumley Skeffington, an old fop who wore false hair and painted his face, when she glimpsed her daughter walking toward the doors to the garden with Dudley Fanshawe, who was carrying a plate of pineapple. Looking around, she saw Ryan nearby.

The handsome Irishman was drinking champagne as if it were water. Excusing herself, Devon went to join him.

"Is anything the matter, Nathan dear? You are looking uncharacteristically out of sorts!"

He took her meaning but doubted that he could summon the patience to even play at his masquerade. "Am I? Well, it's damned hot in here, isn't it?"

"Are you well? It's not like you to snap at your own mother." Now Devon's sapphire eyes were penetrating.

"I apologize, dear Mother. Actually, there is something I should take care of and then I may feel more myself." To appease her, Ryan deftly flipped his quizzing glass upward and looked her over. "You're devilishly beautiful tonight. Did I forget to tell you?"

Momentarily thrown off guard by the spell of his smile, Devon caught his sleeve before he could escape. "Yes, you forgot, and yes, you are a brute," she whispered. "Have a care! Remember where you are and all who watch you!"

"Believe me, I shall," he said coolly. "My sister is in danger of making a fool of herself over that ridiculous Fanshawe. I only mean to offer her a bit of brotherly advice."

Watching him stride toward the doors to the garden, Devon felt an odd pang that mixed happiness with alarm. If André even suspected what she feared, he would be furious and the charade they had so carefully constructed would be over.

"There is a matter of family business that I would discuss with my sister," Ryan somehow managed to drawl lazily, taking snuff as he lounged against a willow tree.

"Can't this wait?" Lindsay asked in a tight voice.

"That's right," implored Dudley, "have some pity, old man! We haven't even gotten to the pineapple!"

"I'm afraid that this is more important than pineapple,'' he replied firmly, glancing skyward, ''or starlight. Come along, Lindsay.''

Fanshawe's face registered confusion as he watched the two of them leave in an obvious mood of mutual animosity. Lindsay had been so sweet, so soft as she'd swayed against him in the moonlight—and then the spell had been broken by Nathan Raveneau's abrupt appearance. Dudley had thought him too foolish to be overprotective, but perhaps he'd underestimated the man.

''I cannot believe that you are doing this!'' Lindsay hissed as they entered the conservatory. Ryan wore a congenial smile, but his fingers bit into the flesh of her upper arm.

''Don't make a scene,'' he counseled in a low voice.

Weaving through the warm, glittering crowd, Lindsay had little choice but to remain silent, but her temper rose apace. For his part, Ryan was beyond thought, beyond even noticing the pair of beautiful green eyes that marked his progress with fascination.

They passed the double staircase, then entered the library. Ryan led Lindsay to a doorway fitted obscurely into a wall of bookshelves, opened it, and thrust her into a tiny chamber decorated in crimson velvet, ivory, and gold gilt. Guttering candles and moonbeams afforded the only light.

''All right!'' she cried when he had shut the door behind them, ''explain yourself!''

He stared hard at her, but Lindsay did not quail. ''I am supposed to be your brother. I didn't want to witness the ruin of your reputation at the hands of Dudley Fanshawe.''

''That's nonsense and you know it! Lord Fanshawe is a perfect gentleman. But I suppose I couldn't expect you to understand that, since you don't know the meaning of the word *gentleman*!''

Ryan advanced. ''Don't be ugly, Lindsay.''

''Nothing else will do in your case, or so I begin to believe!'' Her thick-lashed eyes flashed silver.

"No doubt you'd prefer to be fawned over by your sweet Dudley."

His broad chest grazed the thin bodice of her gown, and Lindsay inhaled his faint male scent. "That's right. I would rather be treated as a human being, with the same intelligence and rights as a man. I prefer to spend my time with someone who is sensitive and caring. What is wrong with that?"

"Nothing." Ryan's voice was soft now as his brown hands closed over her forearms and moved lightly upward. "Nothing except that there *is* a difference between men and women, a point at which intelligence ceases to be a concern. A point where thought itself is obscured by a stronger force . . ."

"You haven't changed a bit. You're as insufferably arrogant as the day we met—" Jeweled clasps dropped from her hair to the carpet and Ryan's fingers sank into her burnished curls.

"The day you melted in my arms in your family's entry hall?" he mocked gently. "When you pressed against me and opened your mouth under my kiss?"

"Stop it!" She moaned.

"Lindsay, remember one thing." His large, dark hands framed her delicate face as he stared down at her. "I am *not* your brother. That is the one aspect of this charade that I will not tolerate."

Dimly, Lindsay realized that she should step back from him, but Ryan's touch was mesmerizing. Suddenly, his arms were about her and he was pressing her against the paneled wall. Their eyes met for a long moment before his hips and mouth joined with hers, demanding that she respond. It was a fierce kiss, and Lindsay felt powerless yet powerful all at once. His body was lean, hard, and muscular as she arched against it, greeting him involuntarily. Then Ryan drew back an inch or two, his breath warm across her cheek.

"Would Dudley Fanshawe kiss you like this?" he whispered harshly before his mouth slanted again across

Lindsay's. Ryan felt as if he could consume her, make her part of himself, as he kissed her with a fury that surprised even him. "Oh, Jesus," he groaned, drowning in the taste of Lindsay's mouth.

Lindsay felt as if her bones had melted away. She clung to Ryan's steely shoulders and shivered under the sweet torment of his lips as they burned a path down her throat and tasted each inch of her bare shoulders. Her nipples stood out in arousal against the thin satin of her bodice. Slowly, Ryan's hands slid from her tiny waist over the curve of her ribs until they cupped the fullness of Lindsay's eager breasts and she gasped aloud.

They kissed again, over and over. The sensation of his masculine body pressing her more delicate female form against the wall made Lindsay yearn to mate truly with Ryan. His hardness, fully roused against the fabric of his black breeches, tantalized her to the point of torment. When his fingers found the fastenings on the back of her gown and they opened, baring her breasts, tears came to her eyes.

"Oh, God, Lindsay," Ryan whispered, his voice now filled with emotion, "how I want you."

Her head, with its mane of golden-rose curls, fell backward as he lowered his mouth to one ripe breast. Lindsay sobbed when she felt warm, moist lips close over her nipple for the first time in her life. They were sinking in unison to the Persian carpet when a knock sounded at the door.

"Lindsay? Ryan? Are you two in there?"

Lindsay sat up, gasping. "My God, it's Mother!"

"I hear you, and I must insist that you come out," Devon declared in a low, firm voice. "André has gone in search of you both himself, and I can assure you that you do *not* want to be discovered by *him*!"

"We'll be right there, Mama!"

Ryan sighed as he quickly did up the back of her gown. "Wasn't meant to be, hmm?"

Common sense returned to her in crashing waves. "That, sir, is an understatement!"

Emerging into the library, Ryan and Lindsay saw Devon walking far ahead of them near the staircase. They followed her, each preoccupied with common thoughts and feelings, reaching her side at the entrance to the conservatory.

"I'll speak to both of you later," Devon whispered in deadly tones. "In the meantime—"

"Excuse me!"

The trio turned to find a woman of incredible beauty waiting nearby to be recognized. Tall and willowy, she possessed milky-white skin, glossy sable-hued tresses, emerald eyes fringed by black lashes, and a beautiful smile.

Lindsay glanced over at Ryan in the hope that he would speak some words of polite dismissal. Instead, she discovered him staring as if he beheld a ghost.

"Hester," he breathed.

Her smile brightened. Touching his arm with long, slim fingers, she teased, "How reassuring! I was convinced that you'd forgotten me, darling!"

CHAPTER
16

June 9, 1814

Lɪɴᴅsᴀʏ sᴛᴀʀᴇᴅ ᴀᴛ Rʏᴀɴ, ᴄᴏᴍᴘʟᴇᴛᴇʟʏ ɴᴏɴᴘʟᴜssᴇᴅ ʙʏ his disconcertion and confused by the situation at hand.

"It's good to see you, Hester," he said quietly, oblivious to the two ladies on either side of him. "Are you well?"

"As well as can be expected after more than six years, my dear. Have I changed?" Hester's sweet voice took on a rather brittle tone as she held a hand out on either side to display her charms. "You have. I confess I didn't believe my eyes at first, but then I heard your voice and . . . But that's enough for now about the two of us. Do, please, present me to your friends!"

"Ah, yes!" Ryan's dark blue eyes widened. "I would like you to meet my mother, Devon Raveneau, and my sister, Lindsay." Absently, he added in their direction, "This is Hester Moore, Countess of Chadwick."

"Your mother—and sister?" Hester's smile mixed amusement with disbelief. "It's a great pleasure to meet both of you!" She gave Ryan a knowing look. "Why am I not surprised by your sudden appearance in London—and the acquisition of a new family? No, no, don't panic, I won't breathe a word of it. But shouldn't you enlighten me further? Are you still Ryan Coleraine?"

"No—and yes. For the time being, I am Nathan Raveneau."

"Ah, of course. Well, you know that your secret is safe with me, darling. Waltz with me and we'll discuss this further."

"Hester, you know that we should not be seen together. Enough years have elapsed and I have changed enough so that I do not fear being recognized, but if people see me with you, they may remember. It's critical that that not happen."

"Well, then, come around the corner with me, darling, and we'll put our heads together and see if we can't arrange to meet later on. Francis has already left, pleading illness in that stifling throne room, so I ought to be able to slip away in an hour or less. It's past midnight now, isn't it?"

Lindsay was dumbstruck as she watched the two of them disappear around the corner of the deserted hall. Hester was gazing up at Ryan as if she owned him, one slim hand through his arm. He, meanwhile, seemed to have forgotten that Lindsay even existed, let alone what had just passed between them in the tiny crimson chamber off the Carlton House library.

"Hmm." Devon tapped a finger against her cheek. "I should have foreseen this, I suppose."

"I don't see why!" Lindsay cried. "Didn't he assure us that no one would know him in London? This is unforgivable! This is horrible! It's so very—awfully—"

"*Male,*" her mother supplied dryly. André came up behind them, then, and Devon turned to assure him that she had found Ryan and Lindsay safe and sound. "They had just retired to have one of their usual arguments," she said in an offhand voice. "However, we may have another matter to concern ourselves with of very real

importance. Ryan has just encountered someone from
his past, and from the looks of it, this lady does not wish
to remain there!"

Fuzzy from champagne and numb with emotion, Lindsay allowed Ryan to hand her into the elegant carriage
that would convey the family home to Grosvenor Square.
Her parents followed, the door was pulled shut, and
they rolled off down Pall Mall.

"Ryan," said André in an even tone, "I don't mean
to pry, but I think that the circumstances demand that
you explain exactly who the Countess of Chadwick is
and what she may mean to our situation here in London."

"You're right, of course." Ryan looked out the window, avoiding Lindsay's piercing stare, and cleared his
throat. "Well, there isn't much to say in that respect. I
knew Hester quite well when we were both considerably
younger. It's no secret that I have a past here in London, but you needn't worry that she will divulge the
truth of my identity." Slowly, he turned his head and
met Raveneau's eyes in the shadows. "This happens to
be a two-way street. You see, I am the conservator of a
few secrets of hers."

"I wish you had warned me that this might happen,"
André said sternly.

"As do I—now!" He pressed taut fingers to his brow.
"It was hard enough for me to come back here; I couldn't
bear to consider the possibility that I might encounter
Hester. Her husband's estates are on the northern border, very near Scotland, and I suppose that I expected
her to be spending most of her time there by now,
tending her children and doing needlework."

Lindsay made a rather rude noise that expressed dis-
gust and disbelief. Ryan ignored her.

"Sir, I did tell you, that first night we discussed all of
this in Pettipauge, that I had spent time here in London
and it was possible that I might be recognized."

"That's true. . . ." André's expression relaxed somewhat as he thought back. "However, you didn't mention knowing anyone in *this* particular circle of society!"

"That raises an interesting question!" Lindsay exclaimed. "How *did* you become embroiled in a torrid affair with a countess? Were you the cabin boy on her husband's yacht?"

Ryan looked at her for the first time, a glimmer of what might have been pain in his eyes. "How did you guess?" he replied in a tone that was both offhand and sarcastic.

"Well, certainly it's none of our affair," Devon put in firmly. "What matters is the present and the success of the task that President Madison has bade us to perform here in London."

"Of course, you're right," Ryan said, "which is why I must have some time alone with Hester to make it clear to her how crucial her silence is. She's a good person and will take me at my word without demanding a full explanation. Also, there is one other reason that has occurred to me for enlisting her friendship. Francis Moore, the Earl of Chadwick, is a long-standing Tory of enormous influence in the House of Lords. This was so before I left for America, in the days when the Whigs had all the power. Now that the political climate has shifted, God knows what office Lord Chadwick may hold and what he may know."

"And what Lady Chadwick may tell you?" André elaborated. "Hmm. Well, it's worth a try, but have a care! You don't want to arouse her suspicions. When will you see her?"

"Tonight, sir, if you'll allow me to use the carriage."

Lindsay barely heard her father's assent, nor did she remember anything else that transpired before she and her parents stepped from the carriage into a pool of yellow light made by one of the new gas lamps that bordered Grosvenor Square. She was only conscious of the hot flush that burned her cheeks, the pounding of her heart, and the thoughts and questions that clashed in her mind.

* * *

"Do you have any idea what would happen to my reputation if I were seen with you here?" Lady Chadwick whispered teasingly. "On Vauxhall Gardens' infamous Dark Walk, where young ladies venture in peril of being snatched up by amorous rakes?"

"No one will see you." Ryan paused under a willow tree and gave her an irresistible smile. "That's why they call it the Dark Walk. It's very . . . *dark*."

Hester tried not to laugh, then felt her eyes mist. "Nine years. It seems forever . . . and no time at all." She touched his sun-bronzed cheek. "After you left tonight, I nearly convinced myself I'd seen a ghost. I never expected you to come back, Ryan."

"Neither did I," he replied with heavy irony. "Tell me what has happened with you, Hester. Obviously, life has treated you well; you're even more beautiful than the day I sailed from London."

"I've been happy for the most part. It was easier to adjust once you left and I believed I'd never see you again. Francis has been a good husband; we've made a good home together, I think. After a time, I reached the conclusion that Father had been right in the decisions he made for me."

"Children?" Ryan asked softly.

"Three. Our daughter, Amanda, is eight. George is six and the baby, Maryann, is two. They're beautiful, Ryan, and they've changed my life. I'm wiser now, I think, and less selfish."

He gazed at her, indulging in a moment's reflection on what might have been, until a tear shone, diamond-bright, on Hester's cheek. Instinctively, he brushed it away with a fingertip and she caught his hand and pressed it to her face. "Tell me that you love Lord Chadwick," Ryan whispered. "Tell me that he deserves you."

"I love Francis." She nodded, inhaling the warm scent of his hand before she released it. "I do. And, of course, he deserves me! It was I who didn't deserve him in those first years, when he had to share our bed with your ghost! He's a good man. He was patient and gentle, waiting for me to let go of the past and give myself wholly to our marriage. Ryan, he must not know that you are back.'' She averted her eyes, murmuring, "He knows that my feelings for you were of a . . . different nature—more intense, if you will—than those I have for him. That doesn't make my love for Francis any less strong, but it's a quieter, more contented strength—''

"You needn't go on; I take your meaning," he said. "And you needn't worry that I'm feeling smug about this. What we shared was too rare for either of us to forget or repeat. I'm glad that you've found happiness in your marriage, Hester. In truth, it's a great relief to me, for now I no longer need agonize that I may have done the wrong thing.''

"*Have* you agonized? A small, spiteful part of me is glad to hear it. Without such penance, you would really have no right to inquire after my happiness or to look at me in that way that makes me want to cry! And I won't feel guilty that these children are Francis's and not yours. It could have all been different. You had the power to stop it and you would not!''

"Shh." Ryan touched a forefinger to her mouth. "We've been through all this, or have you forgotten? You said that you had let the past go, my sweet, and now that I know you are happy, I can do the same. It's too late now, and there's nothing to be gained from dredging up old arguments except fresh pain.''

Hester turned away and returned to the shadowy path. "Before we talk about the curious circumstances surrounding your visit to London, I would appreciate it if you could offer me some reassurance about Francis.''

"I am happy to oblige, my lady. I met Lord Chadwick yesterday at White's. Beau Brummell introduced me to him as Nathan Raveneau and he didn't flick an eyelash. He was most cordial, even slightly disdainful, though doubtless he didn't think I'd notice. That last I might ascribe to my new pose as a dandy.''

She gave Ryan a sidelong glance. "I'm relieved to hear it, and I'm sure you're right. One of us would have heard about it if Francis had recognized you."

"If you'll recall, my dear, he barely knew me to begin with."

"That's true . . . and you were ten years younger—and brash," she agreed.

"Exactly. Not some languid buck twirling a quizzing glass and offering him snuff." Ryan smiled and was gratified to see the corners of her mouth turn up in the moonlight. "Furthermore, I'm aware that I've changed in the nine years since I left London. Unlike you, dear Hester, I am not ageless."

"I shouldn't say it, but my innate honesty prevails. You may have changed, Ryan, but only for the better. That's the devil of the thing with men! They don't become truly attractive until their fourth decade. Unless, of course, they weren't attractive to begin with—and you certainly were."

He sketched a bow. "You are too kind, madame."

Hester sighed. "Tell me, then, what have you been doing in America and why are you here now?" Taking his arm, she added, "And if you are now a married man, wildly in love with your wife and the proud father of several babies, spare me the details. I am not so talented at offering magnanimous congratulations as you."

"Your generosity won't be tested this night because I have no wife—or babies, so far as I know. I've been living in Connecticut these last few years, when I haven't been at sea. I worked very hard, starting as a first mate on a merchant ship out of Boston, until I became captain of my own brigantine." He couldn't ignore the surprise in her emerald eyes. "Didn't think I had it in me?"

"No, of course, it's not that, but—"

"Never mind; I understand. At any rate, I led scores of privateering raids against my former countrymen, saved my earnings, and was about to buy the ship from my employer, André Raveneau, when the British attacked our port and burned every vessel in sight—mine included. It was then that Captain Raveneau asked me to pose as his son, Nathan, who is in the West Indies, and come with the family to London."

"But why?"

"I can't explain, Hester, except to say that I'm not involved in anything anti-British. I may have my faults, as you well know, but I like to think that I adhere to certain principles. I will always be a Briton. Let's just say that we need to discover someone who may be acting against America."

"Hence your role as a dandy," she mused. "To keep people off guard. Very shrewd!"

"Devon Raveneau deserves the credit. Would I *choose* to play the fool?"

Hester laughed fondly. "No, I suppose not. And what about the young lady I met tonight? What is her part in all of this?"

"She's the Raveneaus' daughter." His eyes flickered away.

Hester took a deep breath and lifted her chin. "I see."

"Look, I've been thinking about Lord Chadwick tonight. Is he still among the hierarchy of the House of Lords?"

"They say he may be the next prime minister."

"Indeed! I'm impressed. Hester, I hesitate to presume upon our, uh, friendship, but it would be invaluable if I could meet some of those powerful Tories."

"I don't believe I'm hearing this! Do you realize what you're saying?"

"Yes, but I had to ask." Ryan's smile flashed in the shadows. "Will you think about it?"

"You're an Irish devil."

"So you have always maintained." He grinned, lifting her hand to his mouth. "It's in the blood."

Hester prayed that he didn't feel her shiver at the touch of his lips. "Speaking of which, have you communicated with your family?"

"No."

"But your brother—"

"He is well? His family?" Ryan's tone was matter-of-fact.

"He has a son and a daughter, who spend most of the year in Europe with their mother."

"Well, at least there's an heir." Ryan gazed into the distance. "And now, leave it alone." Pausing on the pathway, he murmured, "It's late. I should see you home before Francis grows suspicious."

"Yes, of course." She caught the edges of his sleeves. "How handsome you look in your frock coat and white cravat."

"Thank you."

"Ryan, have you really changed so much? Aren't you even going to try to kiss me?"

"I had my turn, Hester," he said quietly, his dark blue eyes agleam in the moonlight. "I'm not a boy anymore, and I have no taste for cuckolding your husband." Ryan spared her a reply by taking her arm and starting back toward the carriage. In a lighter tone he added, "Make no mistake, my dear—I don't mean to suggest I'm not tempted!"

Hester's laughter mingled with the music in the night air and she leaned against him as they walked. "How lovely to realize that if we cannot be lovers any longer, we loved well enough to remain friends."

Ryan stopped for a moment, framing her face between his hands, then bent to graze her lips with his own. "Well said."

CHAPTER
17

June 9, 1814

SLEEP ELUDED LINDSAY FOR MOST OF THE NIGHT. OCCA-
sionally she dozed, but she was beset by dreams crowded
with vivid images and sensations. There were Ryan's
eyes, midnight blue, gazing at her in a way that made
her feel cherished, and then they were kissing, touching
intimately as their clothing dropped away. An instant
later, he would turn from her, embracing Lady Hester
Chadwick and forgetting Lindsay's existence.

Sunlight streamed into her bedchamber at six that
morning, just as it had each day since their arrival in
London, for Lindsay chose to sleep with her curtains
open so that she could doze and bask in the warmth.
Today, however, her dreams were too disturbing and
the rays of sun offered a brighter alternative. Unfortunately, when she opened her eyes, Lindsay remembered
that reality was not so different.

The day promised to be exceedingly warm, for already she felt damp in her muslin nightgown and the
tangle of bedclothes. Freeing herself of the sheet, Lind-

191

say then lifted her golden-rose curls so that they spilled
upward over the pillow, haloing her face. She closed her
eyes again, but the feeling of restlessness would not
pass. Her breasts felt confined within her nightgown and
she longed to bare her legs. Rebelliously, Lindsay removed the offending garment and stretched out across
the sunlit bed.

I must be mad, she thought. Still, it felt lovely, her
bare skin bathed in the pale gold light. Her eyes felt
heavy as she extended first one long leg and then the
other, viewing them through her lashes. Lindsay decided dreamily that they were quite pretty: slender and
shapely. She touched her hipbones, then the slightly
concave surface of her smooth belly, smiling. Gliding
splayed fingertips over her narrow waist, Lindsay slowly
moved them to brush the edges of her breasts. They
tingled instantly in response. She paused for a full minute, shocked, afraid, then tentatively touched first swollen
curves and then each taut nipple. Gasping, she drew her
hands away as sensations of forbidden pleasure intensified between her legs. The feeling of yearning was
almost unbearable and she blushed, ashamed and bewildered.

Quickly, Lindsay sat up, swung her legs over the side
of the bed, and drew her gown on again. She found
herself wishing that she could go back in time, back to
Connecticut when the household had risen early and she
had eaten breakfast in the keeping room while Cassie
bustled about. There had been a comforting discipline to
those days filled with books, students, and lesson plans.
If only the British—and Ryan Coleraine—had stayed
away!

Longing for Cassie, Lindsay put on a pale yellow muslin
dressing gown, ran both hands through her hair, and went
barefoot into the corridor. Everyone slept later in London, and surely no one but the servants would be awake
at this hour. It couldn't have been more than six o'clock.
She padded soundlessly down the hallway until, reach-

ing Ryan's door, she stopped in surprise upon finding it open.

He stood near the bed, its cream and green hangings soft and shadowy in the cool half-light that filtered through the curtained windows. Ryan had his back to the door, and Lindsay watched, frozen, as he removed and tossed his frock coat over a chair back. It was followed by a trim waistcoat of white brocade, a crumpled white cravat, and, finally, stockings and black breeches. She stared at his lean, brown, masculine legs, spellbound by their beauty. They were lightly covered with soft, curly black hair, and the slightest movement on Ryan's part caused muscles to flex in his calves and thighs. Lindsay thought that no painting or statue she had ever seen depicting the male form had looked quite so splendid.

Ryan raked tense fingers through his hair, then made a sound that was half sigh, half yawn. When he began to remove his shirt studs, she panicked, realizing that he'd be naked in a moment. Then what would she do? Lindsay took one sideways step and, instantly, Ryan's head turned.

"Good morning." His brows rose leisurely as he faced her wearing only his half-open shirt. "Up early, aren't you?"

Relieved that he hadn't asked if—or why—she had watched him undress, Lindsay struck a challenging note. "How would you know? Isn't the hour *late* in your case?" It dawned on her then how much time had elapsed since he had departed with the carriage. Silvery sparks kindled in her eyes. "You must be exhausted!"

Ryan inclined his head slightly, taking her measure and wishing he could read her mind. "There's no need for you to concern yourself," he said dryly. "I'll be all right."

"Oh, of course! You have the beauteous Lady Chadwick to coo and murmur over your infirmities!" She tossed back her dawn-colored curls and came toward him. "Furthermore, I find your conceit ludicrous! How dare you presume that I am concerned in the least whether you sleep or not? It matters to me not at all if you choose to spend your nights making love to married women! It wouldn't surprise me if you made a habit of such pastimes. Debauchery by night; sleep by day—the perfect life, I should think—"

Ryan reached behind her and closed the door firmly. "Kindly moderate your voice, Lindsay. You'll wake everyone in this house and all of Grosvenor Square in the bargain."

"Do you mean to instruct me on manners? What a joke! You could not presume to teach proper behavior to a tomcat! But, then, that's what you are, isn't it?"

He caught her wrists and stared down at her flushed, exquisite countenance, mere inches separating their bodies. "You betray yourself, my dear. You're awfully upset for someone who doesn't care what I do."

The nearness of Ryan's bare, tanned legs and half-exposed chest set her heart to pounding. "Let go of me! I hate you!"

"Lindsay," he said quietly, "I did not make love to Hester. We talked, I took her home, and then I went for a walk."

"Do you expect me to believe that? Not that it matters! Someone else might swallow your glib lies, but you underestimate my intelligence—"

"Not that it matters," Ryan echoed ironically, "but do you ever admit to *feelings* that overrule your much-vaunted intelligence?" Slowly he drew her against him and continued in a soft, sober voice, "I don't expect you to bare your soul to *me,* but do you ever search it privately? Honestly?"

Lindsay's gray eyes were huge in her now-pale face. She feared that he could feel her heart thudding against his chest through the thin stuff of her dressing gown. "Of course I do." Her voice was brave but barely audible. "I search my soul regularly and, though I hate to disappoint you, I've never discovered any emotions there that have any connection to you, sir."

The corners of his mouth turned up slightly. Their faces were so close that he could breathe in her soft, lavender scent. "I don't believe you."

"Are you calling me a liar?"

"I didn't call you anything. I would never disparage your character, my dear, only suggest that you may not be facing up to the truth."

"And what is *your* version of the truth?" Lindsay inquired haughtily.

"This." His lips were parted when they touched hers, tasting each soft, sensual curve until they opened to him, trembling. Ryan enfolded her body in his strong embrace as she melted against him, and dimly he registered an instant's surprise at Lindsay's sudden, eager response. Her hips arched upward; he could feel her breasts swelling against his chest through the muslin barrier separating their bodies. The sensation of her tongue exploring his mouth and Lindsay's urgent fingers on his shoulders, in his hair, drove Ryan mad. His own hands slid over her hips as their kisses deepened, and then he molded the curves of her buttocks with long, taut fingers. When the pulsing spot between Lindsay's legs was urged flush with Ryan's fully aroused manhood, she gasped in reaction.

"Good Lord!" Stepping backward, she was slightly surprised to feel him release her instantly. Eyes wide, cheeks pink, Lindsay involuntarily put her hands over her tender breasts. "Would you have taken me in my parents' house? What sort of animal *are* you?"

"Lindsay . . ." He took a breath, wondering if this were all a bizarre dream. "Christ! It's not as if I was forcing you! You were as tempted as I—so hot, I nearly forgot *where* I was! I—"

Her hand flew up to slap his lean right cheek. "You are a debased, conceited pig! Is it not enough for you to make love to a married woman in the middle of the night? Would you take my virginity for breakfast, right under the nose of my parents, who have taken you in and loved you as a son?"

"For God's sake!" Ryan ground out angrily, endeavoring not to shout. "Why do you insist on twisting things and blaming me rather than facing the truth?"

"What is *your* truth? That I seduced *you*?"

"Of course not." He put a hand out toward her, but Lindsay backed away. Sighing almost wearily, Ryan said, "The truth, if you would only confront it, is that I desire you—and you want me, too. It's nothing to be ashamed of, it's part of life! Haven't you realized that all the books in the would won't satisfy the craving you feel when we touch?"

Lindsay stared for a moment, speechless, then ran from the room.

"Well!" Devon put down her volume of William Blake when Ryan came into the sitting room. It was five o'clock, and it was his first public appearance of the day. "Up at last, I see!"

"Dear Mother, please don't rebuke me," Ryan said. He took the chair opposite the settee on which she reclined and lifted the lid on the teapot that remained with assorted soiled china on the low table between them. "Empty, I see." Boyish disappointment was written on his chiseled man's face.

Devon's heart softened. She couldn't help it; he was far too engaging and too like André. "I'll ring for more."

Ryan smiled his gratitude and picked up the *Times*. He could feel her questions thick in the air, and though aware that a few layers of paper would not stave them off, he did hope for a brief delay.

"You look very handsome in your riding smalls," Devon observed. Her blue eyes traveled over his immaculate fawn-colored coat and the doeskin breeches that were slightly wide at the hip but fit snugly down to the polished top boots that encased Ryan's calves. "Do you mean to ride in the park?"

He glanced up and smiled. "Hyde Park? I thought to, yes. Is it safe?"

"Now you *do* sound like Nathan! My intention was not to sound like a nosy, overprotective mother. I am merely curious."

"Curiosity noted." Ryan smiled again, politely, and pretended to be absorbed in the assortment of advertisements that covered the first page of the newspaper. Homes, cottages, rooms, and warehouses were for let or lease, but his attention was drawn to the various horses for sale. After a minute or two of silence, he remarked, "I think I'll go to Tattersall's tomorrow. I'd like to buy a horse of my own."

"What will you do with it when we leave England?"

"You're behaving more like a mother than my own ever did!" Ryan laughed. "I'll decide that when the time comes. Have you forgotten that I'm past thirty years of age, Devon? I've looked after myself for half my life, or so it seems. If it weren't for this rather ridiculous charade we find ourselves tangled in, I wouldn't be living here at all, you know. I'd have rooms of my own."

"You wouldn't be in London at all!" Her tone was light, but his little speech had made her uneasy for a reason she couldn't fully identify.

"Point taken," Ryan said, rather than go on with a conversation he was finding increasingly tiresome. With relief, he saw Cassie in the doorway with a fresh tray of tea and cake. She wore a familiar plain gown of figured ivory muslin and her ginger-colored hair was twisted up in a loose knot atop her head. The very sight of her was a poignant reminder of Connecticut.

"It's good to see you, Cassie. I've missed you!" He grinned and stood to take the tray from her. "Where have you been hiding?"

Her round face lit up in response to his kind words, then darkened. "It's that Mrs. Butter. She won't let me touch anything! If it weren't for my devotion to this family, I'd go to Kent with Able and stay there!''

Devon stared, aghast. "Cassie, why didn't you say something?''

"I shouldn't have needed to," she replied plainly.

"For heaven's sake, this isn't Pettipauge! It's a much bigger house and you know that I have had a great deal to do since we arrived in London!''

"That's why I haven't burdened you with our problems. We're only servants after all.''

Ryan cut a slice of the square cake and took a bite. "Mmm!" he exclaimed. "Now *this* tastes of America!''

A warm blush spread over Cassie's cheeks. "It's my own recipe for blueberry gingerbread. I had to bake it during Mrs. Butter's nap.''

"One hopes that she may nap more often," he murmured with a smile and a wink of encouragement.

"There, you see how much you're loved and appreciated?" Devon exclaimed. "Captain Coleraine is going riding momentarily and then you and I will sit down and talk this over. Agreed?''

Nodding, Cassie backed out the door. Devon watched as Ryan poured tea for them both, squeezed lemon into his own, and drank half the cup.

"You must have gotten home very late to have slept so long," she ventured.

His eyes met hers over the rim of his cup. "I didn't just awaken. I had to bathe, shave, and dress, you know. This damnable cravat requires a ridiculous amount of time to tie correctly.''

"I suppose so." She paused, then tried again. "Will you at least give me some clues as to the outcome of your interview with Lady Chadwick?''

"What aspect were you interested in? Social? Political? Sexual?''

"Ryan, you are being quite odious!" she cried, her cheeks pink.

He smiled wryly. "You look like your daughter when

you blush. No, don't scold me further; I'll yield. Lady Chadwick and I renewed our friendship quite successfully, and we may trust her to keep our secret. Politically, she has agreed to help in some rather roundabout ways by informing me of the receptions to attend where prominent Tories will be present. It was Hester who encouraged me to visit Hyde Park as often as possible. Seems that plenty of powerful men, as well as dandies, ride there at five o'clock." He took another bite of blueberry gingerbread and finished his tea, then gave her a sly look. "As to the last area of interest, there's nothing to tell."

"You wouldn't say so if there were!"

Ryan laughed. "Quite true." Picking up his hat and riding crop, he came around the table to kiss her cheek. "I'll see you later, Mother dear. Wish me luck."

The sound of his footsteps on the stairs had faded before Devon realized that she hadn't told Ryan that Lindsay had also gone out to the Hyde Park—in the company of Lord Fanshawe.

Lindsay was feeling reckless and gay seated beside Dudley in a beautiful *vis-à-vis* drawn by a pair of elegant grays, as they wound their way over the paths of Hyde Park. They passed, and greeted, the cream of London society, the men on the finest horses Lindsay had ever seen in one place, the women usually riding in neat, two-person equipages like her own.

When André had led her out to the stables before Dudley's arrival and explained that it was not considered proper for a female to be seen on a horse of her own, Lindsay had balked. But then the sight of the *vis-à-vis* he had just acquired for the use of his wife and daughter dissolved her anger. It was the most charming little carriage she had ever seen, with its hammer cloth, rich in heraldic designs, and its cozy interior. Best of all, a proper *vis-à-vis* only ventured forth with two liveried footmen and a coachman, all sumptuously garbed and sporting powdered wigs. Lindsay loved the fantasy, especially once they were in the park and it all became even more extravagant and whimsical.

"Good afternoon, Miss Raveneau, Lord Fanshawe!" It was the Duke of Dorset on his magnificent white horse. Affably, he doffed his beaver hat and smiled at Lindsay.

"It's a pleasure to see you, Your Grace!" she replied. "Isn't it a beautiful day?"

"It can't hold a candle to you, my dear." The duke's eyes swept from her beguiling bonnet of periwinkle satin, set off by a cluster of real pink roses, to the matching muslin day gown that showed Lindsay's lithe curves to advantage. "You're a fortunate man, Fanshawe."

"I'm aware of that, Your Grace."

The cherubic, white-wigged coachman snapped the reins then and they moved on. Paths curved past ponds, flowerbeds, and groves of trees under which grazed cows and deer. The *vis-à-vis* slowed so that they might nod to the Prince Regent, who, with his riding companion Sir Benjamin Bloomfield, had paused to converse with the Earl of Sefton and the ladies Molyneaux. Then, as they rounded the gentle crest of a hill, a stretch of empty pathway lay before them.

"Alone at last!" Dudley murmured with a pleased smile. He gazed at her with frank adoration.

Slightly disconcerted, Lindsay glanced around and pointed toward a stately elm with low-hanging branches. "Look over there, Lord Fanshawe!"

"Dudley," he corrected automatically, taking her hand in his. "Don't they have elm trees in America? They're a common sight here, I can assure you."

"No, no, look *under* the tree. There's a doe with the most adorable fawn!"

"Not half so adorable as you, my sweet. You're the loveliest woman in London, you know." He edged closer. "I'd begun to think I'd never have you to myself."

With immense relief, Lindsay heard a horse trot up

beside the little carriage. She was about to look up when a voice drawled, "Have her to your*self*? I'm afraid that's impossible, old man, at least as long as I'm around to uphold the proprieties!"

"Raveneau!" Dudley exclaimed, staring at the only man on Hyde Park's paths who was not clad in a blue coat with brass buttons. "What are you doing here?"

"Gad, sir!" Ryan raised his quizzing glass and struck an attitude. "I've come to chaperone my innocent sister!"

"Chaperone?" he spluttered. "Lindsay doesn't need to be chaperoned; she's with me!"

Languidly, Ryan lifted his right brow. "My point exactly, Fanshawe. That's why *I'm* here. One can never be too careful with the reputation of a beloved sibling." As the *vis-à-vis* began to roll onward, he trotted alongside on André's favorite black gelding. "In that line, I'd appreciate it if you would address Lindsay as Miss Raveneau. It don't do to relax the rules, you know."

Lindsay was torn between fury and mirth. Next to her, Dudley hissed, "Can't you do something? Tell him to go away, that you're perfectly safe with me!"

She looked up and had to smile at the sight of Ryan lazily examining his fawn-colored sleeve and flicking off an imaginary speck of dust. Then his eyes wandered over to meet hers, and for an instant, they betrayed a familiar glint of amusement. Sighing, Lindsay turned back to Dudley. "I don't want to hurt his feelings," she whispered. "After all, he's only trying to be a good brother and his concern is genuine."

He wanted to shout at her that her brother was a ridiculous *fool* who didn't deserve a place in her family, but bit his tongue.

"Lindsay," Ryan murmured with a yawn, "you're forgetting your manners. Have you no greeting for your brother? Aren't you glad to see me?"

She rolled her eyes at him. "Hello, Nathan. Of course I'm glad to see you, but you really didn't need to go to all this bother."

"Bother?" Ryan repeated as if he didn't quite understand. "Bother? Nonsense, m'dear! As long as there is breath in my body, I shall devote myself to your welfare. Quite frankly, I can't think of a better way of spending my time!"

Lindsay was barely able to stifle a giggle when, next to her, Dudley's shoulders sagged and she heard him moan in torment.

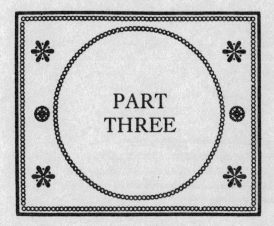

PART
THREE

The stars of midnight shall be dear
To her; and she shall lean her ear
In many a secret place
Where rivulets dance their wayward
    round,
And beauty born of murmuring sound
Shall pass into her face.

—WILLIAM WORDSWORTH (1770–1850)

CHAPTER
18

June 11, 1814

Devon Raveneau's lap was adrift with invitations. "I find it difficult to comprehend that there can be enough people in London society to give this many routs and assemblies," she remarked.

Across the morning room, Mouette sat in a ray of sunlight mending little Anthony's pants, recently split during a foray down the bannister. The blond little boy stood nearby, his head bent in concentration over a plate of cookies just procured from the kitchen by his Aunt Lindsay.

"Aren't you happy that the family has been welcomed so readily into society? You all were a tremendous success at Carlton House, and Harry overheard several eligible young men discussing Lindsay's charms at the clubs." Mouette snapped the thread and smiled mischievously at her sister. "Already she has Lord Fanshawe on the verge of a proposal! You have no idea how many fashionable young ladies have been angling to catch his eye!"

"A proposal?" Lindsay tried to laugh. "You exaggerate, Mouette."

"This is all well and good," Devon said absently, sipping her tea, "but I didn't realize that taking up residence in London would mean that we would have to attend all these tedious parties! Could President Madison have intended that we endure such unremitting torture?"

"Mama, what do you mean?" asked Lindsay.

"Oh, it's just unbearable. One receives an invitation like *these*"—she sifted through the pile for emphasis— "which state that the sender will be at home on a given night. You see, we have several for each evening. We would arrive in a home that has been virtually stripped of furniture to accommodate the crush and then try to squeeze ourselves into it. No one can sit, and there are no cards, music, and barely any conversation. It's much too crowded for such pleasures. This lasts a quarter hour, and then everyone goes to the hall door to wait for their carriages. Because there are so many, one spends more time with the footmen than abovestairs with the host and hostess. Finally, from this first rout, we would drive to the next, and the next, and so on. Sometimes, a half hour is passed waiting one's turn among the arriving carriages before one can even alight and enter!" She shook her head in remembered horror. "I swore that I would never attend another rout unless it was being given by a close friend or relative!"

Mouette laughed. "Well, *that's* reassuring since we are planning to give one on the twenty-fifth! Besides, Mother, I think you're being a trifle selfish. If you refuse to venture forth to mingle with society at these routs, how will Lindsay meet men?"

"I really wish you would stop that!" Lindsay cried. "I'm perfectly content."

"Are you in love with Dudley?" her sister pressed.

She was saved from answering by the appearance of Raveneau in the doorway. "Good afternoon, ladies," he greeted them, entering to kiss his wife's brow. "And Anthony, hello to you, too!"

The little boy was buttoning his pants but looked up to declare, "I'm not a lady!"

"You most certainly are not. What's been going on here?"

"Mama's been complaining that we may have to attend a lot of routs," Lindsay explained. "As you can see, the morning post brought scores of invitations!"

"That's a good sign." André nodded. When Devon looked up in alarmed surprise, his teacup in her hand, he took it from her and chuckled. "Don't panic, *ma chère*," he murmured, taking a place beside her on the mahogany settee. "You'll be spared the routs, for the moment at least. I just visited the House of Lords and received an invitation, ostensibly from the Regent, who seems to be afraid to venture outdoors in daylight much these days for fear of being jeered by the populace. At any rate, he's taking his visitors to Oxford on the fourteenth— this Tuesday—and asks that we join the party."

"Why would the Regent include us in such an illustrious group?" Devon wondered, putting out a hand to smooth back his silvery hair.

"The Whigs have stirred up so much public sentiment against him and for Princess Caroline that I think he is uncertain whom he can trust. Add to that the rather remarkable adulation the czar and his fellow visitors have been receiving here, and one may be assured that the Regent is currently feeling very insecure, indeed. No doubt we, as newcomers, appear to be relatively harmless to him."

"Hmm. And there's the fact that we're American," Devon mused. "Our presence would not only make Prinny appear magnanimous, but it would also add a certain spice to the group."

"I've always wanted to see Oxford," Lindsay said dreamily.

André smiled, then looked at his older daughter. "Did

I mention that Mouette and Harry are also invited? And where is my son, the newest buck of St. James's?''

"He went to Tattersall's at least two hours ago to claim his new horse," Mouette told him, careful not to say Ryan even in front of little Anthony. "He looked almost excited before his departure!"

"Better a horse than a woman," he replied dryly.

Lindsay pretended to rearrange the plate of cookies while inquiring, "Papa, what shall we do in Oxford? What's the reason for this journey?"

"I imagine that the Regent wishes to impress the czar and the various rulers. Who could fail to be impressed by Oxford? I believe that there are some formal plans, however. Degrees for the czar and the king of Prussia, a magnificent dinner at the Radcliffe Camera—"

"The circular, domed library?" Lindsay exclaimed. "I have seen drawings of it. It's the best thing at Oxford—at least I think it may be! Oh, I can hardly wait!"

"Neither can I!" cried a voice, infused with mock gaiety, from the corridor. An instant later, Ryan peeked around the door frame, one eyebrow arched above blue eyes that danced with devils. "I don't know what we're speaking of, but I did overhear those last words of Lindsay's, and, infected by the rare, unbridled excitement in her voice, I lost my head."

"I wish that you would," Lindsay muttered.

Devon pretended not to hear. "Come and join us. Have you brought your new horse safely home?"

"Indeed!" He came into the room, obviously full of high spirits, and sat down beside Mouette. "A finer piece of horseflesh I've never seen! His name is Brady, and he's a magnificent black stallion. We liked each other the moment we met yesterday. They told me at Tattersall's that Brady's never taken to anyone this way before."

"My goodness," Lindsay murmured, unable to stop herself, "it's a shame he's not female. This sounds like a match made in heaven!"

"Well, we'll all go down to the stables to meet this steed," André proclaimed, ignoring his daughter, "but first we should inform you of our plans for next week."

At the mention of the word *horse*, little Anthony had produced a wooden miniature from his pocket and was now showing it to Ryan, who inspected the toy with sober approval. After a moment, he looked up distractedly. "Plans?"

"We're going to join the Regent's entourage when he takes his European visitors to Oxford on Tuesday," Devon informed him brightly. "Isn't it exciting?"

Ryan's smile faded slightly, and then he blinked. "Did you say Oxford?"

"That's right!" Mouette chimed in. "We're all going! I for one cannot wait to escape from London for even two days. It will be a lovely diversion!"

"I've always wanted to see Oxford," Lindsay said again. "I've read so much about it, I half expect the town to be shrouded in a magical haze."

Ryan took a deep breath. "Well, I hope you all enjoy yourselves, but I'm afraid that I cannot join you. I have a previous engagement on Tuesday."

"How mysterious!" Devon lifted delicate brows. "Won't you elaborate?"

"I'd rather not." Determinedly, Ryan returned his attention to Anthony, bending his head to the boy's level and thereby avoiding the curious stares from the adults in the room. "It's a . . . private matter."

Lindsay's cheeks grew warm as she stared at his crisp ebony hair. A private matter? What else could that mean except an appointment—a rendezvous—with Lady Chadwick? The sight of her parents exchanging knowing looks only intensified Lindsay's mixed feelings of outrage and mortification. It galled her to realize that she cared what he did and to remember the scenes between them first at Carlton House and then in his bedchamber here. Worse, she had succumbed to Ryan's charm just hours later in Hyde Park when she should have ordered him to leave her alone with Dudley Fanshawe. It was horribly con-

fusing to think and decide things, then to forget all in
Ryan's presence. Now, Lindsay looked away from him
and gazed out the window at the garden court below,
wondering what was happening to her and why.

"You're being very difficult, Nathan," Mouette was
saying. "What shall we tell the Regent?"

Before he could answer, Roderick appeared in the
doorway, paler than usual and breathing hard from the
effort of climbing the long flight of stairs. "Lord Fanshawe
is here to see you, sir," he intoned with a bow to
Raveneau.

"Send him up, Roderick."

One or two minutes passed slowly before Dudley came
into the morning room. Clad in a dark blue coat of
superfine with brass buttons and snug biscuit-colored
pantaloons, his blond hair shone in the sunlight and his
light blue eyes gleamed with confidence. "Hello, all!"
he proclaimed, smiling at each family member in turn.
"Isn't it a fine day?"

"It certainly is, Lord Fanshawe," Devon replied politely. "Won't you sit down and tell us what brings you
to Grosvenor Square?"

"With pleasure, Mrs. Raveneau."

Lindsay felt a bit overcome as she watched him approach, then take a seat next to her on the settee.
Dutifully, she whispered, "Good afternoon, Dudley."

"It is now," he murmured, gazing first into her eyes
before letting his eyes drop to the low neckline of her
pale blue morning dress. "You're looking lovely as usual,
my dear Lindsay."

She tried not to blush when she glimpsed Ryan's
black brows arch upward. "It's kind of you to say so."

Arabella had arrived with a steaming pot of tea. Devon
poured and then, once their guests had taken a sip,
inquired, "Have you called for the sole purpose of gazing upon our daughter?"

Lord Fanshawe laughed as if she had made a great
joke. "Certainly that would be reason enough, my dear

Mrs. Raveneau, but, in truth, I had another errand. You see, I received a letter from my parents today. At their ages, they prefer life at Grimley Court, our family estate in Oxfordshire, to the social whirl of London. However, upon hearing that the Regent has planned a trip to Oxford, they have written requesting that I invite a select few from that group to visit Grimley Court on the fifteenth of June.''

"How kind of them," Devon said, wishing that her family were elsewhere.

"I inquired at the palace regarding the list of people traveling with the Regent and then decided that ten, with my parents, sounded like the proper number." Dudley squared his shoulders and grinned. "Straightaway it came to me that this family should be among those invited. That includes Sir Harry and Lady Brandreth, of course."

"Who will fill the last two places?" Mouette asked.

"I thought that the Earl and Countess of Chadwick might round the party out nicely. They are the right ages and jolly good company, don't you think? Have you all met them?"

Lindsay choked on her tea and Dudley looked on, unsure of what he should do. Finally Ryan stood and leaned over to strike her back lightly with his palm. "Steady on, brat!" he exclaimed, his words of encouragement underlined with an amusement that only she could discern.

When Lindsay had recovered her composure, she looked up to see Ryan taking snuff. Languidly, he commented, "I've just realized that I had my dates mixed. I'm free after all this next week and would be delighted to join my family for this outing to Oxford and Grimley Court.''

"I can't sleep."

"Mmm?" Drowsy and contented after lovemaking that had rivaled their early days together, Devon snuggled closer to André's chest. "Why not, sweetheart?"

"I'm wondering why Ryan suddenly changed his mind about Oxford. That empty-headed dandy pose might get him by Dudley Fanshawe, but he can't fool me. 'Dates mixed' indeed!" Raveneau reached for his glass of brandy on the bedside table and sipped thoughtfully. "It was quite obvious that he didn't want to accompany us, then thought better of it."

Wide awake now, Devon pushed back her hair and tried to read his face in the shadows. "I agree, but I thought that the reason for his turnabout was quite obvious, considering it came immediately after he learned that the Earl and Countess of Chadwick would be among those visiting Grimley Court."

"*Oui*, it would seem that he couldn't resist the opportunity to be near Lady Chadwick."

"Hester is very beautiful," Devon said tentatively, "and although Ryan has not been very forthcoming about their shared past, it does seem obvious that he still has feelings for her. You know that I have rather keen instincts about these things, and I am convinced that Lady Chadwick returns those feelings. I know that you don't want any scandal, and with Lord Chadwick along there is always that possibility, so I can understand your concern, and—"

"You're starting to babble, *chérie*," he interjected ironically. "And I fear you've underestimated me. Did you really think I would remain blind to the situation that's developing between Ryan and Lindsay?"

It seemed that her heart had stopped. Finally, Devon managed a weak "Pardon?"

"I have eyes. And I'm not so old that I've forgotten how people behave when they're falling in love."

"What are you saying?"

"Simply that I believe Ryan didn't want to go to Oxford for some personal reason. Perhaps people know him there. However, I don't think it was the prospect of being near Hester that overrode his misgivings; I think it was the idea that Dudley would have Lindsay all to himself."

Devon hardly knew what to do. It went totally against her temperament to play false with André, but if she agreed with him everything could be ruined. "Darling, I think your paternal imagination may be getting out of hand! When did you conceive this notion that Lindsay and Ryan are falling in love?"

"It's crept up on me, I suppose. I didn't *want* to think it, but the seeds were probably planted that first time I saw them together in our house in Pettipauge. There have been plenty of clues ever since, and I've reached a point where I can't ignore them."

"But they despised each other then! And they've argued most of the time ever since! It's only lately that they've struck a rather unsettled truce—"

Raveneau interrupted with a short, sarcastic laugh. "Do you take me for a fool, *chèrie*? I can assure you that I am not, nor have I forgotten our verbal battles during the months after we met. If memory serves me, we spent virtually all our time together either pretending we detested each other or else making love!"

She blushed in the darkness. "Lindsay has a completely different character from mine. You know perfectly well that she has always kept a tight rein on her emotions. She has told me that she does not even find Ryan physically attractive, that he isn't her type."

"He's too much like me! Sometimes I feel as if I'm watching myself thirty years ago and it scares me to death!"

"You're talking like a madman."

"If he lays a finger on my daughter—"

Devon's soft laughter was suffused with relief. "So *that's* what this is all about! You're worrying that Ryan's going to steal your daughter's virtue the way you stole mine! Darling André, you must remember that this is a completely different situation. I had no father to watch over me, but you are in the same house. Besides, I still think that you are wrong about the two of them. Didn't Lindsay tell us that he treats her like a sister?"

Raveneau gathered her near. "Yes, but—"

"Stop worrying. Dudley Fanshawe is exactly her type. He's well-bred, educated, gentlemanly, and fair-haired— the opposite of Ryan Coleraine. Her attention is on him, and Ryan's, for better or worse, is on Lady Chadwick."

"That comes with its own set of problems, but at least I think Fanshawe can be trusted not to ravish my daughter."

Devon realized that he was far from convinced but wanted to believe her for his own peace of mind. "Remember, too, that Lindsay is a good girl and far more level-headed than her mother. We raised her well and have to trust her." Even as she spoke, Devon remembered the interlude between her daughter and Ryan at Carlton House. Lindsay had assured her the next morning that they had only been arguing, just as Devon had told André, but her maternal instincts continued to sound a warning, which she tried to ignore.

"I suppose you're right." Raveneau closed his eyes, then muttered, "It's Coleraine I don't trust."

"Hush." She reached up to stroke his hair and felt him smile grudgingly against her brow. After a time, the cadence of his breathing told Devon that her husband was asleep, but she still lay, wide-eyed, turning people and events over and over in her mind. Finally, it came to her that she ought to follow her own advice. If Ryan and Lindsay *were* falling in love, there was nothing to be done about it except to trust to her daughter's judgment— and fate.

Besides, Devon thought with a small, sleepy smile, Ryan Coleraine was just the sort of man Lindsay needed. There'd be no escaping life and all its emotions with that dashing, irrepressible Irishman!

CHAPTER
19

Oxford, England
June 14, 1814

It was a day of rare glory. Under a cerulean sky, Oxford's spires were hazy and golden. High Street, the town's main thoroughfare, wound like a silvery stream past gabled houses and shops, Gothic college buildings and churches, and battlemented walls. This afternoon it was crowded with spectators. Members of the university were ranged on each side of the street in lines extending from St. Mary's church to Magdalen Bridge, all waiting, with other visitors, for the appearance of the Regent, the czar of Russia, the king of Prussia, Prince Metternich, and Field Marshal von Blücher.

"Oxford seems enchanted," Lindsay murmured to Ryan as they stood wedged between an undergraduate and a proctor. "It's exactly what I hoped for."

He smiled down at her lazily, tending to agree. The June sunlight was infused with a luminous glow that lent an aura to Oxford's pinnacles and spires as they crowded skyward. He'd come today against his better judgment, but now, standing next to Lindsay in this town he knew

215

so well, misgivings were pushed aside. Lightly, Ryan touched her cheek with one dark forefinger and murmured, "You look enchanted yourself today, my dear."

She beamed up at him. "Do I? That's the nicest thing you could have said."

It was true. Lindsay wore a charming new walking dress of thin muslin over a peach-colored sarcenet slip, accented by a triple fall of lace at her throat. The bottom of the gown was flounced with rich French work surmounted by a rouleau of muslin. With it, she wore a high-crowned peach and cream bonnet tied at the side with wide satin ribbons, straw-colored gloves, and cream kid shoes. The colors were a perfect foil for her bright strawberry-blond curls, which made a halo around her delicate face with its striking smoky eyes.

"I'm quite sincere, you know," Ryan whispered with a touch of mischief.

His words, and the warmth of his breath, made her blush. "I shall make a note of that, brother dear."

He chuckled and looked over her head in hopes of spying the Regent's party. Instead, his gaze lit on Lord Fanshawe peering hopefully in their direction. A dozen people, including the Brandreths and the elder Raveneaus, separated them, but Ryan had no wish to encourage the young nobleman's desire to make his way to Lindsay. He'd had quite enough of Dudley during their journey to Oxford.

"Do you see them yet?" Lindsay inquired. Several tall Oxonians, gowned and capped, blocked her view.

Without acknowledging Fanshawe, Ryan bent to reply. Pure chance, and a bit of subtle maneuvering on his part, had isolated him with Lindsay amidst this crush. They'd had so little time alone together lately, what with the hurried preparations for this excursion, that Ryan found himself even more intoxicated than usual in her company. Her soft, wildflower fragrance drifted up to him even as she tipped her head back and gave him a winsome smile.

A roar rose from the crowd. Lindsay stood on tiptoe to watch the Prince Regent and his illustrious European guests, all in full uniform, proceed on horseback around High Street's curves. Prinny bestowed regal smiles on the spectators, pretending that the cheers were for him rather than for the slimmer, more glamorous czar of Russia or King Frederick William of Prussia. As usual, Field Marshal von Blücher was a great favorite of the crowd, partly because of his colorful personality and partly because he had been a brave general during the war and the English longed to cheer a hero in the absence of their own Wellington, who remained in Paris.

"I wonder why the Regent does not realize how foolish he appears," Lindsay murmured to Ryan. "He behaves like an overgrown child, competing with these other sovereigns and trying to pretend that he cannot see that his own countrymen are more taken with these Europeans than with their own future king! It's almost pathetic."

Ryan's mouth quirked ironically. "As I understand it, Prinny's problem for much too long has been that he's attributed every wonderful event that has occurred in the world to his own great talent. No doubt, at this point, it is less painful for him to continue the charade, even with himself, than to face the truth."

Straining for a view as Blücher rode into sight, Lindsay made a small exclamation of surprise when she felt Ryan lift her off her feet from behind. He held her suspended six or seven inches off the cobblestones for a full minute. Rather than reprove him, as she knew she should have done, Lindsay chose to pretend it hadn't happened. Back on solid ground, she darted a smile at him that was almost shy.

"The field marshal looks tired," she observed.

Ryan longed to tease her or, better yet, to kiss her. The sensation of her slim form in his arms again had whetted a dangerous appetite. "So he does," he said instead. "And with good reason. As the popular hero of

the English, he's been beseiged since the first moment
they landed at Dover. And Blücher's a good-humored
sort. The courtyard at St. James's Palace has been constantly filled with crowds longing for a glimpse of him
and he's been obliging them every five minutes or so.
No wonder he looks fatigued!"

Ryan's arm had stolen around her shoulder in what
appeared to be a protective, brotherly gesture. Near the
Magdalen Bridge, the chancellor, vice-chancellor, noblemen, heads of houses, doctors, proctors, and delegated
masters moved forward. Lindsay's attention, however,
was not on the chancellor as he came forward to lay the
Bedel's staves at the feet of the Prince Regent. Her
senses were full of Ryan. Out of the corner of her eye,
she admired the shape of the tanned fingers that curved
around her shoulder and the cuff of his well-made fawn-
colored coat. Casually, she turned her head and indulged in a glimpse of the crisp black hair that curled
behind his ear. He was looking especially splendid today, from his high, snowy cravat to the fawn coat and a
snug waistcoat of cream brocade, and finally the champagne-hued pantaloons that hugged Ryan's lean-muscled
thighs and disappeared into gleaming Hessians. Lindsay expelled an involuntary sigh and instantly regretted it.

"Are you so moved by this ceremony?" he whispered
in amused tones.

"It's—it's just that the day is so lovely. Incompara-
ble, really."

"Mmm." The barest smile curved his mouth.

"At last!" cried an exasperated voice next to Lindsay. "I thought I'd never get through that crush!"

There was Dudley, looking warm in his usual dark
blue coat with brass buttons. Ryan knew an intense
longing to greet the man with sarcasm, but somehow
reason prevailed. Removing his arm from Lindsay, he
leisurely produced his snuffbox, flipped it open, and
held it out to the intruder. When Dudley declined, Ryan
took a fastidious pinch and observed, "No doubt my

sister appreciates the effort you've made to reach her side, Fanshawe." Glancing up, he added with a bland smile, "Unless, of course, it was I you wished to see . . . ?"

"Nathan is such a tease!" Lindsay put in hastily. Amenities were exchanged and then, casting about for an innocuous topic, she blurted out, "I wonder why they call High Street 'the High'?"

Proudly, Dudley straightened his shoulders. "Fortunately, my dear, you are in the presence of an Oxford graduate. Oriel College, 1812. You must feel free to bring *all* your questions about Oxford to me!" He paused for an instant, sensing danger from Ryan's direction, but when he looked over, he found that the man was merely gazing at him through his quizzing glass with his usual expression of blank stupidity. "Ahem! As I was saying, I cannot say for certain why the High is called the High, but I believe it is merely a custom here. Broad Street is 'the Broad,' Catte Street 'the Catte,' and so on. Even the River Cherwell is known as the 'Char.' You also should be aware that Magdalen is pronounced 'Maudlin' in Oxford, and the Thames, where it passes here, is called the Isis. Furthermore . . ."

Ryan dropped his quizzing glass, clenched his fists, and looked around for diversion, unable to bear another moment in the company of this insufferably pompous twit. The ceremony at Magdalen Bridge had ended and now, as if by fate's favor, he saw Lady Chadwick coming toward him, her hands outstretched.

"Mr. Raveneau!" she greeted him brightly. "How lovely to see you again! Might you spare me a moment's conversation?"

His irritation was such that he dispensed with manners and ignored both Lindsay and Dudley. "Nothing could give me greater pleasure, your ladyship."

She took his arm and they retreated under the arched entrance to Queen's College with its crowning cupola. Hester, garbed in an elaborate ensemble of pink and cream muslin and silk, gazed up at him with shining green eyes.

"I realize I'm being indiscreet, but I couldn't help myself. Francis has gone off to speak to the chancellor, and I acted on impulse. It has been simply unbearable, traveling in the same party with you and knowing that we will be staying together at Grimley Court and yet fearing that we might never have a moment alone!"

Ryan wasn't sure why he allowed her to talk this way or why it gratified him so. When she put her hand on his arm and he felt the sudden heat of Lindsay's stare from the High, an unfamiliar feeling of elation rushed over him. Still, reason's soft voice interfered.

"Hester, it's good to see you and to talk to you. I've told you before that I hope we'll always be friends, but you also know that we mustn't be seen together, nor can we afford the risk of conversing in private. Perhaps when all of this is over—"

"We can have tea together?" Tears sparkled in her eyes. "Don't worry, I shan't make a scene. I'm not the type to beg for favors, Ryan." She laughed shakily. "I did this to myself, didn't I? And what I told you at Vauxhall still holds true. I value my marriage and won't risk it. But seeing you with that Raveneau girl today . . . the way you look at her . . ."

"You're imagining things," he said harshly.

"Am I? I'd say rather that you are avoiding the truth! You'd do well to guard yourself when you and she are in society, Ryan, or you'll begin to hear the same rumors that have hounded Lord Byron and his sister."

"Lindsay is not my sister!"

Hester had taken a step away and now looked back over her shoulder. "No, that's true. But how many people know it? If you continue to woo her in public and she continues to respond, you'll both be the target of the most vicious sort of gossip!"

Ryan caught her arm. "Has it not occurred to you that you may have overreacted to the sight of us together? Brothers and sisters are frequently affectionate and cozy. Just as often, Lindsay and I quarrel before others in the manner of siblings. I think that you are making more of this because you know she is *not* my sister and because your residual feelings for me have kindled jealousy."

"Perhaps." Hester freed her arm and forced herself to meet his dark blue gaze. "People can sense things, however, and as an old friend, I am merely offering well-meant advice."

Ryan watched her walk away, then closed his eyes. He felt stifled by both the past and the present. The eeriness of returning to this place and of sharing Hester's company was difficult enough, but his present life was also fraught with complications. Where was the control and the freedom he had sought in America and enjoyed at sea? Oh, to be at sea again, on the decks of the *Chimera,* where the world extended only as far as the horizon! Instead, he found himself trapped between the past and the present, caught in a charade that was becoming increasingly difficult to carry off, surrounded by people who had power not only over his movements but his emotions as well. . . .

Slowly, Ryan summoned the strength to open his eyes. If he had the courage to confront death during ocean battles, certainly he could navigate the rough waters of his current existence. This was simply a different kind of challenge. After all, was Linday Raveneau, a mere female, more threatening than an attacking ship?

The comparison made Ryan smile. He felt confident as he turned back toward the High until he looked for Lindsay and saw that both she and Dudley Fanshawe had vanished.

"Oh, Dudley, this is heaven!" Lindsay exclaimed as she lay back in the punt. The wooden shell drifted lazily down the Cherwell River, propelled by the pole Dudley wielded as he stood at the far end.

"I'm delighted to hear you say so, Lindsay dear. Dare I hope that I am in heaven with you?"

She laughed rather uneasily, wishing somehow that he *weren't* part of this real-life fantasy. Looking away from him, she concentrated on the dainty willows that bent near the narrow river, whispering in the breeze, and on the lush sweep of meadows behind him. Never had she seen grass so vividly green, its beauty intensified by sprinklings of buttercups, bright red poppies, and lacy, pale golden meadowsweet. The river itself, a small tributary of the Isis, seemed to define the word *peace* as it murmured against the sides of the punt.

Dreamily, Lindsay turned her head and surveyed the ancient surviving walls of Oxford above which rose topaz-tinted spires and domes. "I love it here. If I lived in such a place, I don't think I could ever leave."

"Well, one has to get on with one's life," Dudley pronounced, guiding the punt toward a grassy bank. "Either that or become a don, I suppose, and I'm not that sort!"

Unsure of how to respond to that comment, Lindsay sat up slightly and inquired, "Why are we stopping?"

"That's Christ Church meadow," Dudley said, pointing absently to his right. "We've gone far enough—and I have a bottle of wine I thought we might open."

"Oh." She felt a certain trepidation but told herself that Dudley Fanshawe was a most reliable gentleman—unlike certain other men! Sitting up in the punt, Lindsay peeked over the meadow grass at the amber towers of Christ Church. "That looks like a magnificent place!"

"Christ Church?" Dudley shrugged as he drew the cork from the wine bottle and magically produced two glasses. "I suppose. Of course, it's an honor to attend any college at Oxford, but in terms of prestige, I suppose Christ Church ranks first. It's the grandest, at any rate."

"Is it very old?"

"Not as old as many of the colleges. Merton, you know, was founded in the thirteenth century. As I recall, it was 1264. Christ Church was begun by Cardinal Wolsey, though, during Henry VIII's reign when they had a tendency to overdo such things. Wolsey was building grander palaces than the king himself, but, of course, he fell from power and Henry ended up having them all, anyway. Christ Church, as well. It was the king, I believe, who united the college with the cathedral."

"How fascinating!" Lindsay accepted the glass of wine and took a sip. "It was very kind of you to take me punting, Dudley, and to suffer all my questions."

"At last you are calling me by my Christian name without being prompted!" He smiled. Carefully, Fanshawe slid down into the punt so that they sat close together. "It's been my pleasure to show you Oxford, dear Lindsay. I can't tell you how much it means to me to know that you are interested in becoming acquainted with the places that have shaped my life."

In the act of swallowing a bit of wine, she choked and took a huge gulp, then another before the spasm subsided.

"My dear, are you all right?" he inquired solicitously. Seeing his opportunity, Dudley put an arm about her and bent near, hoping that she might grant him a kiss in this moment of weakness and gratitude.

"All right?" drawled a familiar voice from the riverbank. "My sister will be perfectly well once she is restored to dry land."

Still coughing, Lindsay struggled out of Fanshawe's unwelcome embrace. "Nathan!"

He slowly lifted a dark brow. "None other. May I assist you?"

Dudley blinked in disbelief and muttered under his breath, "The man is like a curse, invariably turning up to plague me at the worst possible moment!"

CHAPTER
20

June 14, 1814

Ryan GAVE THE YOUNGER MAN A CHARMING SMILE. "I beg your pardon, Fanshawe? Did you say something?"

"No." He rolled his eyes.

Deftly, Ryan came down the steep bank and lifted Lindsay from the punt with ease. When she stood on the high ground of Christ Church meadow, he turned back to Dudley.

"I hope you don't think that I have been less than a gentleman, sir," the blond man intoned, balancing unsteadily in the slender punt.

Forcing himself, Ryan raised his quizzing glass. "Not at all! Why should I imagine such a thing? Fact is, my sister is notoriously prone to seasickness! She wouldn't tell you, of course, but as her brother, I felt it my duty to come to her rescue!" He gave him his best foolish smile. "I'd suggest that you return that punt, Fanshawe. Excuse us, won't you?"

Lindsay waved weakly from the bank, then Ryan took her arm in a hard grip and led her away.

"Surely you don't think that anything happened—" she began.

"Surely you don't take me for a fool!" he retorted angrily. "Your family didn't know where you were, your father is imagining all sorts of things, and you should thank God that I found you before he did!"

"If you're referring to the fact that I accepted a glass of wine and allowed Dudley to sit beside me—"

"Spare me!" Ryan shot back, his voice dripping with sarcasm. "I am well aware of your seductable nature."

Lindsay stopped and tried to slap him, but he easily caught her hand. "No more of that. I can't go round with a different bruise on my face every day!"

Suddenly the anger between them seemed to melt away and the humor seeped in. Lindsay pressed her lips together in an effort not to laugh at the thought of Ryan trying to explain his various slap marks, but a giggle slipped out. He caught both her wrists and tried to glare down at her, yet his own eyes were dancing. "Little witch!" They stood in the middle of Christ Church meadow surrounded by sun-dappled wildflowers and chestnut trees in full bloom. "Of course I know you weren't doing anything, but you were a fool to go!"

"You're jealous," she said impulsively.

"Of that ridiculous jackanapes?" He started off again with Lindsay in tow. "Don't insult me."

She decided to change the subject and pointed to the distant buildings. "That's Christ Church College, you know. I think it is magnificent! Dudley has been instructing me."

"No doubt," Ryan muttered dryly.

"Truly! I am utterly captivated by Oxford and eager to learn more about it." She lifted her chin. "I wish that Dudley were here now to tell me what I am seeing."

Before he could stop himself, Ryan said, "Believe it or not, brat, even an ill-bred boor like myself can manage to retain a few facts over the course of a lifetime." He lifted a dark hand and pointed, his finger moving from left to right. "That's Christ Church's hall, and the bell tower with the high, tapering curve is Tom Tower, named after Thomas à Becket. The tallest spire is that of Oxford Cathedral, which is also Christ Church's chapel. Satisfied?"

Lindsay held fast to his arm and nearly stumbled in the grass as she tried to match Ryan's stride. "How do you know all of this?"

"Never mind. I shouldn't have spoken at all." His profile was chiseled, remote. "I shouldn't have *come* at all."

"To Oxford or to find me?"

"Take your pick!"

"Well, then, why did you? I could be having a perfectly lovely time if you weren't so intent on spoiling it!"

"Drinking wine in a punt with that milksop Fanshawe?" he asked acidly. "Kissing him under the willows? How romantic!"

"You're impossible and unfair!" Lindsay cried. "Why do you hate him so? He's a perfect gentleman and has never said or done anything to offend you!"

"His mere existence offends me," he shot back unreasonably. "He's puffed up with his own consequence to the point of bursting, and it's all hot air. His title, his manners, his family estate, his Oxford degree—"

"I still say you're jealous!"

Ryan stopped suddenly and stared down at her with stormy midnight-blue eyes. "I'll say this only once, Lindsay, and then you'd be wise not to throw those words in my face again. I wouldn't accept Fanshawe's worthless, snobbish assets if they were presented to me on a silver platter. They don't count a damn toward character."

She couldn't help herself. "Well, of course *you'd* say that!"

He turned and walked away.

Furious herself, Lindsay lifted her skirts and ran after

him. As they emerged from the meadow onto the Broad Walk, which marked the southern boundary of Christ Church, they passed fellows in caps and gowns who turned to look curiously at Lindsay's lovely but unlady-like figure.

"Wait for me!" she cried at last. Ryan stopped but neither looked back nor spoke as she came up behind him. "You are the horridest man I know!" She gasped, trying to balance and remove a stone from her kid slipper at the same time. "Would you have me make a fool of myself before all of Oxford?"

"You're perfectly capable of accomplishing that without any assistance from me." When he saw that she was in danger of toppling over at the moment when her shoe was nearly back in place, Ryan put out a steadying hand. "You know," he remarked conversationally, "sometimes I could strangle you."

"And I, you!" Eyes flashing and cheeks pink, she gave him a murderous glance. "You are the rudest, crudest—"

Lightly, he waved a hand in front of her mouth. "Never mind the rest. It's all redundant. You've listed my short-comings so many times that even *I*, oaf that I am, have managed to commit them to memory."

As they resumed walking, Lindsay attacked from a different angle. "Furthermore, I am sick to death of your petty complaints about Dudley! What about your precious Heather? Don't you suppose that my sensibilities are offended by the sight of a married woman with children—and, I might add, with one of those silly, pompous titles you disdain—fawning over you like a schoolgirl? Even more unpleasant is the sight of you, fawning in return, for all the world to see! Is it any wonder that I accepted Dudley's invitation to go punting rather than subject myself to one more nauseating moment of such a spectacle?"

The corners of Ryan's mouth twitched. "Hmm."

He gave a mock sigh. "Sounds like jealousy to *me* . . . but then, what do I know about such things?"

She longed to scream and pummel him with her fists, but instead she cuffed his arm as forcefully as she dared. "This is simply— "

"Shh." Staring ahead, he caught her wrist in a grip that was firm yet gentle.

Something in his manner gave Lindsay pause. She swallowed her arguments and followed his eyes. They had turned north on St. Aldate's and were approaching Tom Tower, which loomed above the arched entrance to Christ Church's Tom Quad. The only person coming toward them at the moment was an elegant, tired-looking old man dressed in what Lindsay guessed were robes that bespoke a position of authority.

Almost inaudibly, Ryan muttered, "Jesus, I'm done for now. I was a fool to leave London."

While still some distance away, the old gentleman's head lifted a bit, his shoulders straightened, and a smile flickered in his eyes. Ryan returned Lindsay's hand to the crook of his arm and whispered. "Behave yourself." Then they walked forward. Before they reached the old man, a gowned student passed them from behind and removed his cap. "Good afternoon, Dean Jackson."

The dean nodded. "Mulcaster." Then, as the boy went on, he came to meet Ryan and Lindsay. "Hello, Coleraine." His smile was faint but suffused with affection. "You've changed, but, of course, I never forget a face. Yours in particular!"

They shook hands, and once again Ryan felt that strange rush of mixed emotions wherein the past tangled with the present. "Dean Jackson, it's good to see you. You're looking very fit."

"I have to be to maintain my legendary tact in managing that most unmanageable class of undergraduates: noblemen. Why do they all flock to Christ Church?" Ruefully, he shook his head. "I must say, though, I don't feel very fit at the moment. That ceremony in the

High was interminable! I confess that I slipped away before everyone adjourned to the Sheldonian to witness the czar and the king receiving their degrees." Now Cyril Jackson turned his keen gaze on Lindsay and waited.

"Allow me to present Miss Lindsay Raveneau." Ryan's tone barely betrayed his discomfort. "Miss Raveneau, you have the honor of meeting Dr. Cyril Jackson, dean of Christ Church."

"The honor is mine, I assure you," Jackson said gallantly. "How are you, Miss Raveneau?"

Totally confused, Lindsay extended her hand and told him of her enchantment with Oxford.

"Miss Raveneau is visiting from America," Ryan explained, hating the fact that he could not be honest with this man for whom he felt such deep affection and respect. "Her father owns the ships I have sailed these past few years, and, at his invitation, I accompanied the family to England for a few months."

"I appreciated your last letter, Coleraine, but you're a less than model correspondent. I believe it arrived more than three years ago! Fortunately, I have heard of your exploits at sea from other sources." His eyes twinkled. "Did I not tell you when you left Oxford that I would pursue you, as long as I live, with a jealous and watchful eye? I haven't forgotten you, you know, or your potential. I'm still waiting for you to live up to it. Woe be to you if you fail me!" Before Ryan, who felt as if he were choking, could reply, Jackson turned to Lindsay. "This young man could have been professor of astronomy by now if he'd remained at Oxford. He might have been a dean one day! But he chose to employ other talents, and who can blame a young man for seeking adventure and longing to conquer new worlds?"

Lindsay was speechless, but Ryan managed to reply, "I've had considerable success, Dean."

"Attacking English ships?" The old gentleman arched a white eyebrow. "Well, you doubtless feel a certain loyalty toward America after nine years, hmm? I don't suppose I dare to hope you've come back for good? You know how desperately we need men who are truly serious about the business of learning."

Ryan looked around, gazing through the arched entrance to Tom Quad as if it were the doorway back to his youth. "It's tempting, but I don't think so . . . at least, not at the moment."

Dean Jackson ran a critical eye over Ryan's garb. "You haven't turned into one of those dandies, have you? An out-and-outer? One of those self-indulgent, fancy fellows who insult their social equals and are offensively rude to their inferiors? I've seen too many of my students assume that role, getting it into their heads that they somehow have the right to criticize the entire universe, but I never would have thought it of you, Coleraine."

Dimly, Lindsay remembered the things Ryan had said to her about the social elite of London, disapproving of their selfishness and snobbery. "Ryan's not like that at all, Dean Jackson!" she said impulsively.

A smile warmed the old man's face. "I thought not, but a word of caution seemed in order."

"Sir," Ryan said, "I would be grateful if you could spare me the time for a private interview at your earliest convenience. There is a great deal that I would like to discuss with you."

"Certainly! I would be delighted. But the afternoon is nearly gone now, and there's that ponderous dinner tonight at the Radcliffe Camera for the Regent and his assorted guests. Can you come to my study at nine o'clock tomorrow morning? We'll have breakfast."

Ryan could hardly argue. Summoning a smile, he agreed, but as farewells were exchanged, he had to speak up. "Dean, I know that this will sound very odd to you, but I hope it will make more sense after we speak tomorrow. Until then, might I request that you say nothing of my presence in Oxford? And, if you should meet Miss Raveneau tonight, it would be a great favor to me if you would make no reference to your meeting here today."

"Deception?" The word dripped remonstrance.

"I give you my word that the situation is completely aboveboard and moral, sir."

"In that case, I'll agree, but you know how I feel about dishonesty. I expect you to explain yourself in the morning, Coleraine!"

"Yes, Dean." Ryan shook the old man's wrinkled hand. "And thank you."

After Dr. Jackson had disappeared into Tom Quad and Ryan and Lindsay had continued a little way up St. Aldate's in silence, Ryan suddenly stopped and pressed tense fingers to his eyes.

"Good God, I feel as if I'm eighteen again. My own father never had such power over me! Of all the people in Oxford, why did I have to encounter the single one who would recognize me anywhere, at any age, in any disguise?"

Lindsay's own thoughts were spinning. "Ryan," she whispered, stunned, "why didn't you tell us? Why didn't you tell *me*? You're a graduate of the finest college at Oxford and you've kept it a secret!"

He glanced down at her and sighed distractedly. "It was a different life. I've told you before that I began anew when I came to America. Oxford degrees don't win men places on ships, and aside from that, it's just not my way to go around boasting about such things. What's the point?"

She hardly knew what to say and, sensing his own preoccupation, remained silent as they made their way past Carfax and the medieval Church of St. Martin. Carfax was a corruption of the Anglo-Norman French for four ways, and it was the central point of the ancient town. Here, St. Aldate's met Queen Street on the west, The High on the east, and Cornmarket to the north, which was Oxford's shopping street. Ryan explained none of this to Lindsay; she had read it in her little guide book that morning when they came into town.

She walked beside him up Cornmarket and said nothing, trying, instead, to look around during this unplanned and silent tour. Finally, unable to bear it another moment, Lindsay caught his sleeve and beseeched, "Ryan, please, won't you talk to me? Can we not sit down somewhere and discuss this?"

A muscle moved in his jaw. "We're nearly to the Golden Cross. Your parents are waiting in their rooms for word from you."

"Then ask the innkeeper to take a message up to them. Please!"

The concern and bewilderment that were etched on her delicate countenance touched an unfamiliar place inside of him. "All right. There is somewhere I've been longing to go, and I'm so damned thirsty." His eyes gazed at the gabled rooftops. "Perhaps a bit of ale and civilized conversation might do me good."

Lindsay clasped his hands. "Wonderful! Thank you!"

"Remember," Ryan warned her with a quelling glance, "I said *civilized*. No more scenes!"

CHAPTER
21

June 14, 1814

Ryan and Lindsay went through the coaching entrance to the three-hundred-year-old Golden Cross. She waited in the cobbled yard while Ryan went inside and spoke to the innkeeper, then, minutes later, they were turning west on Cornmarket onto the Broad and she felt suffused with elation. Passing the golden-stoned, gable-roofed Balliol College and then the leafy gardens that guarded Trinity College, Lindsay was caught up once more in Oxford's spell. Ryan's company, the wonder of his marvelous secret, and the mystery of their destination only intensified the magical aura that enveloped her.

Students were everywhere, most of them costumed in flowing dark gowns worn over their suits and odd caps with flat square tops. They all seemed to be rushing about in the June sunlight, but perhaps it was due to the celebratory nature of the day. Ryan took Lindsay's arm, weaving deftly among the other passersby as he turned south on Catte Street.

"Everything here is so beautiful, so charming," she murmured. "It's like a town from a fairy tale—and yet it's the sense of history and the search for knowledge that make it a perfect place in *my* eyes."

"I hope you're not plotting to dress as a boy again to try to gain admission."

"Don't remind me of that silly rule. Why is it that men get to decide these things?"

Hoping to avert another tirade, he identified the massive Clarendon Building, which housed the Oxford University Press, then pointed to a fanciful building in the shape of a *D*, which was embellished with a great deal of carving and topped with a cupola. "That's the Sheldonian Theatre, which was designed by Christopher Wren. He took the shape from Roman theaters, and since they were roofless, the Sheldonian's ceiling is covered with a painting of the sky. You know, this is where degrees were conferred upon the visitors while you were out punting with Dudley. You could have seen it for yourself!"

Lindsay's sigh mixed wonder with regret. Before guiding her into a left turn down New College Lane, Ryan gestured farther down the Catte toward a circular building of amber stone crowned by a splendid dome. "Do you know what that is?"

"Radcliffe Camera?" she guessed happily. "Oh, it's just beautiful! Can't we go there?"

"You'll be there for dinner tonight, brat. I have a simpler destination in mind for now."

New College Lane curved this way and that, but Lindsay saw little of it because Ryan was soon leading her into a tiny alleyway barely wide enough to accommodate one person.

"What are we doing?" she exclaimed, looking about.

"Walking down St. Helen's Passage—also known as Hell's Passage,' he replied enigmatically. Beginning to enjoy her contagious high spirits, Ryan gave Lindsay a smile and reached back to take her gloved hand. It felt warm and tiny in his own. They followed the twisting alley through several turns, finally emerging into a tiny hidden world of cottages with steeply angled roofs that huddled around the imposing bell tower of New College. Otherwise, they seemed completely cut off from the rest of Oxford.

The largest cottage, built of stone, boasted a small swinging sign that announced: The Spotted Cow.

"God, how I used to love to come here," Ryan said with a sigh. "It's an inn by definition, but it's principally an alehouse."

Inside, he had to dip his head to avoid the low oak beams. The stone and timbered walls looked ancient, and even the tables were scarred and worn. Students were scattered throughout the Spotted Cow's two tiny public rooms, arguing or laughing over their mugs of dark ale. Moments later, Lindsay found herself seated at a corner table, her knees brushing Ryan's, and taking her first sip of English ale. The barmaid lingered over a nearby table, trying to catch Ryan's eye so that she might indicate her appreciation with a flirtatious smile.

"It's good!" Lindsay decided, laughing. "Strong . . . and rich."

"Be careful. It won't do if you're in your cups when I return you to your parents." His blue eyes were agleam with fond amusement as he watched her drink again, wrinkling her tiny nose.

After a third sip, Lindsay suddenly untied her bonnet and removed it, revealing the soft profusion of bright curls that escaped from the Grecian knot atop her head. "Oh, that feels heavenly! I'm going to take off my slippers, too. Is that all right?"

Her legs wiggled against his for a moment as she freed her feet, and Ryan chuckled. "As long as you draw the line there."

"I can't stop! The gloves must go as well!" She drew them off and tossed them into her bonnet with a flourish.

"The ale's going to your head."

"I like the Spotted Cow. It's very relaxing—and very old. Isn't it?"

His brows lifted slightly as he reached for her mug. "Yes, _very_ old. Five hundred years' worth."

"Oh, my. That's hard to imagine after America, where everything is so new. How could you leave a place like this?"

"The Spotted Cow?"

"Don't tease me, Ryan! Oxford! Dean Jackson said that you could have been a professor of astronomy! That means you must have been an excellent student. He obviously thinks a great deal of you, remembering you that way years after you graduated. I mean, it's a magnificent accomplishment just to earn a degree from Oxford—"

"Not necessarily." Ryan finished his ale and signaled for another.

"Let me say this! I'm about to humble myself, and since I may not do so again for years, you ought to at least listen!"

Ryan flashed a grin and cocked his head slightly in the way she found so appealing. "By all means, do go on."

"Well, I was going to say that you clearly made a mark for yourself here. You took your education seriously." Feeling her cheeks grow hot, Lindsay put her hands over her face and blurted out, "I'm so embarrassed! Every time I remember all the horrid, superior things I've said to you I could just die! I have put myself above you, insulting your intelligence when, in truth, _you_ should have been looking down at _me_! I wouldn't blame you if you beat me!" Lindsay took a breath that was half sob and waited for his response. When it didn't come, she peeked through her fingers to see the barmaid leaning over with his ale. The girl purposely brushed her breasts against Ryan's shoulder and smiled seductively. Lindsay's temper flared. "Do you _mind_? We would appreciate some privacy!"

Ryan was smiling at her with warm blue eyes. "You're

amazing, do you know that, Lindsay? I've never known a woman quite like you.''

"You must count your blessings," she whispered, her heart pounding with confusion, embarrassment, and the involuntary attraction she felt toward him.

"Don't talk nonsense. And, although I appreciate your apology, I'd prefer to forget it. I've said before that titles and degrees don't affect a man's true worth. I don't want you to change toward me because of what you've learned today; judge me as a person. As for the insults you've heaped on me in the past, I never took them to heart. They were just words, part of the game we play." His eyes held hers. "You've known all along that I am not stupid."

Lindsay's mind spun back to that first afternoon on the Point, when Ryan had casually mentioned the bit of Greek mythology that had inspired his choice of *Chimera* for the name of his ship. Over and over again, he had quietly proved his intelligence while she had stubbornly refused to acknowledge the evidence.

"I've been the stupid one."

"I don't want to hear any more of that nonsense. It's a waste of time, and we have very little of that right now. I do want to set you straight about Oxford, though, before we put the subject to rest." Ryan lit a cheroot and leaned back in his chair, stretching out his booted legs. "You're right about one thing—I did receive a wonderful education here, and I did take it seriously, but that's largely due to Dean Jackson's guidance. Fortunately, I had the sense to listen to him, but most students don't, and, for the most part, education at Oxford has been stagnating for a century. Spoiled young noblemen come here and spend their days in chapel, hall, the common room, and the pubs. Very little studying goes on. What makes it all worse is the way Oxford men hold themselves above all others. They're incapable of saying 'I don't know' and, in truth, they know damned little!" He paused for another drink of ale.

"Things are changing, though, I think. Dean Jackson has been predicting a period of reform for a long time, although I fear he won't live to see it."

"How sad." Lindsay was stunned by his words. "What a waste!"

"Well, I was loath to disillusion you, but at the same time, it was important for you to realize that Utopia doesn't exist—even at Oxford." He straightened. "And now, we should be getting back. You have a dinner to dress for."

"Ryan . . . you *are* planning to attend tonight . . . ?"

"You must see that I cannot. It was foolish for me to come to Oxford at all. I realized this afternoon that the risk of someone else recognizing me is too great to ignore. Radcliffe Camera will be jammed with hundreds of people who knew me during my years here."

"But that was a decade ago!" The prospect of going without him tonight made her heart sink.

"The danger still exists. I could be exposed in front of everyone." Then the corners of his mouth quirked as he picked up her bonnet and dropped it in her lap. "Get dressed now, brat."

She did as Ryan bade, trying not to pout. "But what shall we tell everyone?"

"I'll be ill. Something I ate." Standing, he took her hand and assisted her up. "You must promise me, Lindsay, not to tell anyone what you learned today. Not even your parents. My illustrious past at Oxford will be a secret between us."

The irony in his voice was lost on her as she sighed, caught up in the romance of sharing such a marvelous secret with Ryan. "I promise!" Lindsay vowed. They were halfway to the door before another thought struck her. "Ryan, Hester knows all of this, doesn't she?"

He put some coins on the bar as they passed, then allowed, "Yes, Lindsay, she knows."

"And she knows a lot of other things you won't tell me, doesn't she?" Her voice rose accusingly.

"Only because she was part of my past. I'd be happier if no one knew anything!" Ryan bent to pass under the low door, then guided her in silence back through the twists and turns of St. Helen's Passage. They were nearly out when he stopped abruptly and looked down into Lindsay's wounded gray eyes. "Let it go. Keep in mind that there is a great deal about my present life that Hester doesn't know. And, that's where I live—in this moment."

A smile rose from her heart as they continued on. Turning back onto New College Lane, Lindsay was so preoccupied that she didn't see Harry Brandreth and Lord Chadwick until her brother-in-law boomed, "Well met! Don't tell me that you two discovered the Spotted Cow?"

"A student directed us," Ryan drawled, lifting his quizzing glass. "Lindsay was feeling a trifle parched."

"I'm not certain it's the kind of place a well-bred young lady ought to frequent, Mr. Raveneau," Chadwick observed.

Lindsay intervened. "I only went once, so you mustn't scold, sir! Besides, I found it a delightful change from the formality of the day." Laughing, she took Ryan's arm. "Please don't think us rude, but we really must be on our way. Though he'd never admit it himself, my brother has suddenly become ill, and I must see that he returns to his rooms and goes to bed. You'll excuse us?"

Watching Lindsay and Ryan disappear around the corner of Catte Street, Harry shook his head and looked down at the shorter Earl of Chadwick. "I say, have you ever seen a cozier pair of siblings in your life?"

Francis Moore dabbed perspiration from his forehead with a snowy handkerchief and replied thoughtfully, "Can't say that I have, old man. Can't say that I have. . ."

"Admirable devotion, what?"

The earl slowly arched one eyebrow. "Quite."

* * *

"Lindsay, darling, could you spare me a moment?"

"Certainly, Mama. What is it?" Lindsay's voice was absent as she surveyed her reflection. Cassie had just fastened a choker of diamonds and pearls around her neck and inserted matching combs into her upswept strawberry-blond curls. She hadn't been certain what the effect would be, for her satin gown was all white and very simple. "What do you think, Mama? Should I wear sapphires instead?"

Cassie spoke up. "I told her, ma'am, that her hair and eyes are color enough. Not that she should wear just white *all* the time, but for a change—"

"You're right, Cassie, Lindsay looks stunning. Sophisticated and innocent all at once. All the other women will seem vulgar by comparison." Devon, garbed in a lovely evening dress of filmy white net over pale blue silk, sat down on the edge of the bed. "Would you mind leaving us alone, Cassie?"

"Of course not, ma'am!" Startled, she hurried from the room.

"What's this all about, Mama?"

"I was hoping you would tell me." Devon's tone was almost gentle. "What really happened today?"

"Ryan and I already explained. I was foolish enough to go punting with Dudley, and Ryan discovered us and brought me back. But then I begged him to sightsee with me and he grudgingly agreed. That's when we sent the note up to you and Papa so you wouldn't worry. We stopped for a bit of refreshment and Ryan felt ill suddenly, so we came back." Lindsay took a chair opposite her mother, thankful that there were no real lies involved. "I know I exercised bad judgment and I apologize, but certainly you don't believe I did anything seriously wrong?"

"My instincts tell me that there is a great deal more to this than either you or Ryan have said. Since he came into our lives, I have tried not to interfere in your relationship, even when you felt such unremitting antagonism toward him. You are twenty years old, after all. A woman. But, Lindsay, it is very hard for me to keep silent when I suspect that something is being hidden from me."

"Mama, I don't know what you mean!"

Devon shook her head. "Neither do I, exactly—and yet I think you know more than you will admit even to yourself. I suppose that my own worry is that a relationship is developing between you and Ryan that could complicate all our lives, especially given the mission the president has given us and the fact that we all live under the same roof. I am trusting you not to take advantage of the latter circumstance!"

Traitorous color warmed Lindsay's cheeks. "If you are suggesting that I am carrying on some sort of—of *love affair* with Ryan Coleraine—that we sneak into each other's beds after you and Papa are sleeping—"

"Don't overdramatize." Devon reached for her daughter's hand and found that it was ice-cold. "I simply want to remind you that *neither* of your parents is blind. I have tried to reassure your father and to forget certain incidents—like that night at Carlton House—for my own peace of mind, and because, as I said, you are a grown woman. I have longed for you to find love, darling, but as your mother I have a duty to beg you to use your head as well as your heart." She laughed shakily. "When the two of you disappear like that, I begin worrying. If your father were ever to discover you and Ryan in— a compromising situation, I shudder to imagine the consequences."

Lindsay rose to pace across her tiny room above the Golden Cross's courtyard. Horse hooves and carriage wheels clattered below. "I hope that Papa's imagination hasn't carried him off, too!"

"He has had his share of suspicions, Lindsay, which I have tried to allay."

"I think that you are both dreaming up these things

because Ryan and I have been thrown together in the same house. Why, you know that we have nothing in common—and I should think that you would be pleased that we've struck a truce of sorts until this charade is ended and we can all go home, back to our normal lives.'' Pleased with the sound of her arguments, Lindsay added, ''I must say, Mama, I find it a trifle odd that neither you nor Papa is worrying about Lord Fanshawe! He is the one who persuaded me to steal away with him in a punt on the River Cherwell! I can assure you, he is a very ardent and romantic man! Why is it that you are not concerned about *that* relationship?''

Devon stood up and smoothed her gown. ''Because,'' she said simply, ''there is no light in your eyes when you look at Lord Fanshawe.''

A moment later, standing alone, Lindsay realized that what her mother had left unsaid was far more meaningful than the words she had spoken aloud.

Propped against soft white pillows, Ryan slid his book under the covers when a knock sounded at the door. Harvey Jenkins, who had been brushing his master's coat, went to answer it.

''Good evening, Captain and Mrs. Raveneau. I trust you both are enjoying this exemplary June day?'' Harvey waved them in with a flourish.

''We'd be enjoying it more if your employer were well,'' André said as he and Devon entered, looking splendidly out of place in their formal attire. ''How are you feeling, Ryan?''

''Better, sir, I'm happy to report. Thinking back, I've decided it was the sausage cake I tried at luncheon in Henley. It had rather an odd taste.'' Valiantly, he struggled to sit up. ''You two are looking magnificent. I certainly wish I were going with you tonight!''

Devon crossed to the bed and felt his forehead. ''I don't remember any sausage cakes.''

"How fortunate. I doubtless got the only one. Probably left over from May."

"Ryan, dear, the sight of your chest is very . . . inspiring, but shouldn't you put something on if you're ill?"

"I don't have anything." He attempted a pale imitation of his usual rakish smile. "Clothing distracts me in bed."

Her delicate brows went up. "I don't doubt it." She lifted a nearly empty glass of brandy from the bedside table. "Brandy? On an upset stomach?"

"Harvey forced it on me, didn't you, Harvey? He swears it's a miracle cure." Harvey nodded agreeably from his place by the window.

Sighing, Devon narrowed her eyes at Ryan. "I suppose it's none of my affair, is it?"

"Never say so, Mother dear. However, I wouldn't have dreamed of disturbing your preparations for this momentous evening. So we mere men have just tried to muddle through in the sickroom. Haven't we, Harvey?"

"Unequivocally, sir." The manservant fussed with a spot of dust on the fawn coat sleeve.

"Is there anything you need?" Raveneau inquired, wondering why his wife was behaving so peculiarly.

"Nothing that Harvey can't see to," Ryan assured him bravely.

At that moment, first Mouette and then Lindsay appeared in the doorway. "Everyone's waiting downstairs," Mouette announced. "We should be going." Peeking into the room, she added, "Oh, my! Perhaps I ought to remain behind to nurse Ryan back to health! I don't suppose Harry would understand, though. Ryan, since you obviously won't be riding tomorrow, you must share our carriage and we'll regale you with stories about tonight!"

"A tantalizing prospect," Ryan replied with good-natured irony. "Think of me, languishing here in this spartan room, while you frolic at the Radcliffe Camera."

"We shall! Mama, Papa, come on!"

Devon turned in the doorway to look at Lindsay. "Are you coming?"

"I just brought Ryan a book I thought he might enjoy. I'll be down in an instant, I promise!"

"I feel too weak to read," the patient spoke up, "but, on the other hand, I could revive in an hour or two. . . ."

"Be quick, Lindsay," Devon warned as André gently pulled her into the hall.

Harvey Jenkins waited until he heard the family's footsteps on the stairs, then silently took his leave.

"Close the door," Ryan said, sitting up.

Lindsay blushed. "I can't stay—you heard them—"

"This will only take a moment. Come here."

The sight of his bare, hard-muscled chest with its light covering of black hair, his irresistible half smile, and his penetrating Irish blue eyes swept away her reason. "Ryan, I—"

He caught her hand and drew her down to sit beside him on the bed. "I just wanted to tell you that you look stunning. Ravishing. The sight of you is enough to make me wish I were going along, if only to keep that supercilious Fanshawe away from you."

"You smell of brandy." Lindsay smiled in spite of herself and reached out to touch his ruffled black hair.

"Do you think I'd be doing this if I were sober?" Leaning forward, he grazed her mouth with his. Strong, dark hands slowly encircled her satin-clad waist, then rounded Lindsay's back as he drew her against him and kissed her in earnest.

Warm arousal surged through her body, until she remembered all that her mother had said and realized that her family was waiting while she sat here in white satin, diamonds, and pearls kissing a naked man. Somehow, Lindsay managed to press her palms against Ryan's chest. When their lips parted, the sensation was almost painful.

"Ryan, I have to go!" Standing up, she felt dizzy. "I

brought you a book.'' She took a gulp of air. ''Boswell's *Life of Johnson*.''

An odd smile curved his handsome mouth as he accepted the volume from her hand and drew his own book out from under the bedclothes. ''Why am I not surprised?''

A chill ran down Lindsay's spine when she saw that they'd chosen the same title. ''Oh, Ryan—''

''You'd best be off, sister dear. Enjoy yourself.'' When she had reached the corridor, he called genially, ''Say something rude to Dudley for me!''

CHAPTER
22

Oxfordshire, England
June 15, 1814

"**D**ID WE TELL YOU THAT THE MILITARY HAD TO BE called to the Radcliffe Camera to quiet the students during the banquet?" Mouette asked Ryan.

"I think so, yes." He shifted uneasily, longing to stretch out his long legs or, better yet, to trade his place in this handsomely appointed carriage for one astride his new black stallion. Every time Ryan thought of Harvey riding Brady in his stead, he cringed.

Next to him, Devon wondered, "Are you feeling unwell again, my dear? It was very foolish for you to leave the inn this morning. I do hope that you didn't partake of any sausage cakes during your outing!"

He regarded her for a moment through narrowed eyes. Why had Devon been so suspicious of his "illness" from the first? These Raveneau women were altogether too sharp-witted. He never had a moment's peace in their presence, a fact that he was all the more aware of after two hours trapped in this carriage with Devon, Mouette, and Lindsay.

"I am not ill," Ryan said evenly, "merely . . . restless."

"Missing Brady, no doubt," Lindsay suggested, eyes atwinkle.

"Can you guess the reason for my sister's high spirits?" Mouette inquired. She was still determined to enliven their journey.

Stifling a yawn, Ryan answered, "Let's see. Is she overfond of carriage rides? Viewing a multitude of sleepy villages? Repeatedly rolling up and down hills?"

"My, aren't we testy!" Mouette scolded. "You really *must* be ill! Has it not occurred to you that Lindsay might be glowing because she was a great success at the Radcliffe Camera last night? I believe that all the men present, including the spectators in the gallery, were more dazzled by her beauty and wit than by the countless settings of gold plate. I confess that I was quite envious of my baby sister!"

Lindsay colored prettily and avoided Ryan's sardonic gaze. "Mouette, you exaggerate as usual."

"I don't know about that," their mother chimed in, watching Ryan from the corner of her eye. "Lord Fanshawe was more smitten than usual, the czar himself kissed her hand at length, and I was told that every man at Lindsay's table vied for the honor of conversing with her during dinner. I was glad that André and I were seated at a different table and that his back was to Lindsay so that he couldn't observe the stir she caused. Field Marshal Blücher attempted to propose to her! Of course, he'd had far too much cognac. . . ."

"How thrilling for you, dear sister." Ryan arched his black brows with the utmost nonchalance. "What did he propose?"

"Please," Lindsay begged, "can we not speak of something else?"

Ignoring her, Mouette went on, "Even the dean of Christ Church, an absolutely charming old gentleman, said that meeting my sister was the highlight of his evening!"

Lindsay's eyes met Ryan's in an instant of unspoken communication. "Dean Jackson could not have been kinder to me. He treated me as a daughter, and it is bad of you to imply otherwise, Mouette!"

"Is it?" Mouette tossed her glossy black curls. "I suppose that I grow wickeder with age."

Ryan looked out the carriage window at a poppy-drenched meadow and prayed that Grimley Court was at hand. It was reassuring to hear that Dean Jackson had not betrayed his earlier meeting with Lindsay but hardly surprising. Ryan's own breakfast conversation with the dean had gone well, yet he had left Christ Church feeling disquieted. Although the old man had professed approval of his former student's current life, there were undercurrents in his voice and eyes that Ryan recognized all too well. Dean Jackson had expected more. Oxford *needed* more.

Leaving Oxford had been a relief, but Ryan also felt a certain melancholy he could not afford to ponder. He told himself that Dean Jackson had a gift for subtly instilling guilt in his students, thereby helping them to reach higher, and that he himself was simply responding to old cues. Furthermore, Jackson was not God; his realm was Oxford, but did that mean that Oxford should take precedence in *everyone's* life? Ryan had carved out his own world. He was happy in it and with himself—or so he reasoned during the long carriage ride to Grimley Court.

Lindsay's increasing effect on his mind and feelings was also more than Ryan could bear to consider today. It was easier to shut her out, especially with Devon next to him watching for clues as to the state of his heart. In truth, at the moment, he wished he didn't have one.

"Have you heard," Mouette was exclaiming, "that the czar seems to be in love with Lady Jersey? Perhaps he is attracted to excitable, imperious women, but can you imagine a Russian with an Irishwoman?" She laughed, then quickly sobered, remembering Ryan's heritage. "No offense intended, of course."

"None taken, I assure you." His tone was absently polite. "Having met both Czar Alexander and Lady Jersey, I have trouble imagining that pairing myself."

Happily, Mouette continued, "Perhaps she has a taste for royals. You all have heard, I suppose, that she had an *affaire de coeur* with the Regent before his marriage—"

"Mouette!" her mother broke in. "You were only a child then, and Lindsay a baby. I cannot enjoy the sight of you appearing so worldly or instructing *me* as if I were a provincial old woman! Your father and I were in London and frequently in the company of the prince and Lady Jersey during their . . . romance."

"I'm sorry, Mama." Mouette leaned across to pat Devon's hand. "I confess, I do forget! At any rate, Harry says that rumor has it the Regent purposely lured the czar away to Oxford so that he wouldn't be present for Lady Jersey's midsummer ball tonight! The royal party is engaged to dine at Christ Church hall, so it seems that Prinny will succeed in his efforts to thwart the czar and his ladylove."

"Mouette"—Lindsay turned on her sister, exasperated—"how can you waste yourself, not to mention the time of this captive audience, on such utter nonsense? I cannot believe that you are a Raveneau! Have you been submerged in London society so long that your brain has begun to rot?"

Mouette gaped for a moment, speechless, then her beautiful blue eyes pooled with tears. "What—what a *hateful* thing to say!" Her voice broke. "Harry's right! You're a worse snob than anyone in England!"

As she stared in shock, it dawned on Devon that she had no point of reference for dealing with this sort of quarrel. Her daughters were both women now and this was not an argument over who had gotten more pie. Strangest of all was the realization that she identified more strongly with Lindsay, her baby, than with Mouette, who was a dozen years older than her sister. Of course, Lindsay had been wrong to speak out so harshly, but she had voiced Devon's own thoughts. . . .

The sky, gone slate, began to spit raindrops as the carriage turned up a curving drive lined with flowering chestnut trees. Not a moment too soon, Ryan thought as he gave Lindsay a quick sympathetic glance. He suspected what might be the matter with Mouette, but that didn't make it any easier to bear her nervous prattling.

Lindsay averted her eyes from his and looked out the window, watching for the first sight of Grimley Court. After all that she and Ryan had shared the day before, including the dizzying interlude on his bed, she was bewildered by his distant behavior this afternoon. Did he think that she was so besotted that she would simply fall into his arms when he willed it and that he might ignore her in the meantime?

"What a gorgeous house!" Devon cried spontaneously.

Lindsay focused her attention on an imposing Georgian mansion built of pale gray sandstone. Their carriage, along with the men on horseback and a covered landau containing the Earl and Countess of Chadwick, drew up before a grand portico that boasted colonnades, three Palladian windows, and a divided staircase whose two stone halves swept down to meet in the yard.

Privately, Lindsay felt that the house appeared quite cold and formal but decided it would do Ryan good to hear her join in her mother's and sister's chorus of ahs. "It's breathtaking," she pronounced.

Moments later, they were caught up in a whirlwind of stiff, liveried servants, followed by the equally stiff and proper welcome extended by the Earl and Countess of Grimley. Dudley attended Lindsay as she stepped from the carriage. Possessively, he tucked her hand through his arm and led her up the left staircase to the spot where his parents waited. They appeared very old and grand to Lindsay, and greeted her, and then her family, tonelessly. A suggestion of pleasure did seem to flicker over their faces when Lord and Lady Chadwick came up the steps.

As the butler led the Raveneaus into the cavernous hall, Lady Grimley drew Hester off to one side of the portico and whispered animatedly.

Lindsay tried to ignore the expressionless face of Ryder, the butler, as he led them through a succession of rooms, each more breathtaking than the last. Dudley did not relinquish his hold on her arm and he explained softly, "You see, Grimley Court was an early example of the scientific method applied to the English country house."

Having no knowledge of the English country house, Lindsay couldn't fathom what he was saying. She did like what she saw.

"The hall, that colossal room into which we entered, used to be the center of the house," Dudley went on, oblivious to Ryan's penetrating stare at his back. "Now we use it as a sort of vestibule and for banquets, which are rare occurrences these days. The salon, behind it, has become the great room where we tend to congregate."

Lindsay glanced back over her shoulder and saw Ryan flick his eyebrows upward in irritation. He'd been out of sorts all day and she could think of no other reason for it except that he was having second thoughts about everything that had transpired between them in Oxford.

The butler led them to three symmetrical apartments, each with an antechamber leading into a bedroom, two small rooms, and a back stairs behind the bedroom. Two front staircases, a chapel, and a library divided the apartments. The kitchens, cellars, and servants' hall were contained in the basement below.

Lindsay was too preoccupied to pay much attention, and soon she found herself alone in a glorious bedroom. Priceless paintings, including one of the Regent by Sir

Thomas Lawrence, were hung on pale green walls. The cream and gilt ceiling had been decorated by James Wyatt, and the bed, which dominated the room, was splendidly ornate, with a golden tester and green-and-pink-flowered draperies. She knew that she ought to find her parents and discover what the plans were for that evening, but she decided to lie down for just a moment. It was bliss to close her eyes, and instantly Lindsay sank into a deep, dreamless sleep.

After managing the clasp of Lindsay's diamond necklace, Cassie watched from the doorway as her young mistress dashed across the huge hall, lifting her pale blue silken skirts. She stopped quickly in the doorway to the salon, which also served as the dining room, and colored when she realized that she was the last to arrive.

"I apologize if I am late, Lord and Lady Grimley." Bravely, Lindsay went forward to greet them. "I confess that I fell sleep. Oxford must have been more exhausting than I realized."

"It's perfectly all right," Lady Grimley intoned in a voice that suggested just the opposite. "You'll find your place next to the viscount."

Lindsay paused for a moment, wondering who she meant, until Dudley rose to pull out her chair. Farther down the table, she glimpsed Ryan sitting between Hester and Mouette. Lady Chadwick was whispering something in his ear that caused his eyes to twinkle as he listened. He appeared oblivious to Lindsay's entrance. Sitting down, she felt her own mouth tighten in reaction. It took all her control to return the smiles of her parents and make polite conversation with Dudley, whose manner was decidedly proprietary. Tonight, he, like his father, wore a black frock coat with a snowy shirt and a cravat ruthlessly tied in the Mathematical.

Across from her, Lindsay saw that Ryan was the only

man who hadn't worn black. His coat was very pale
mauve, his waistcoat was ivory brocade, and his cravat
was elegant and immaculate. In contrast, his hair gleamed
like a raven's wing and his eyes seemed bluer than ever.
Each time he spoke to Lady Chadwick, she beamed
back as if to assure him that she found his unconven-
tional dress utterly enchanting. Watching from under her
lashes, Lindsay smoldered.

"That's turtle soup," Dudley informed her after a
servant placed a dish before her.

"Oh!" Lindsay looked down, uncomprehending for a
moment, then dutifully lifted her spoon and tasted. The
stuff was dreadful. "How very . . . delicious!"

The Countess of Grimley gave her a frigid smile from
down the table. "Do you have turtle soup in America?"
she inquired in superior tones.

Lindsay saw her mother's mouth whiten, so she replied grandly, "But of course, your ladyship! We have
everything in America except a king!"

Dudley and his father coughed in unison. Lindsay
reached for her wineglass, glimpsing Ryan's amused eyes
over the rim as she drank. Salmon appeared at one end
of the table and a platter of turbot surrounded by smelts
at the other. Serving himself, Lord Grimley muttered,
"Don't suppose that that young upstart Brummell showed
himself at Oxford!"

The Earl of Chadwick was glad for this conversational
opening. "Certainly not! As you've doubtless heard, he
and the Regent are on the outs these days. After all
those years, when Prinny doted on Brummell, I must
say I think it's high time matters were set right. The
man's only a clerk's son, but he began to act as if *he*
were ruling England. He would say the most outrageous
things to people of title and breeding, and if they took
offense, he contended that he could chase them from
society. It was inevitable, I suppose, that the Regent
would not only become jealous of Brummell's power but
irritated by it."

Harry, who had been looking preoccupied up to now,
spoke up. "I was there at Brummell's club, Watier's,
when he gave that ball a few months back. He and
Prinny were already feuding, so when the Regent arrived and cut Brummell dead, the Beau turned to Lord
Alvaney and said, 'Alvaney, who's your fat friend?' "

Lord and Lady Grimley gasped, while most of the
others who hadn't already heard the story wore, at the
least, expressions of shock and surprise. At this point,
André Raveneau attempted to inject a note of reason.
After chewing and swallowing a bite of salmon, he set
down his fork and remarked, "I think that George
Brummell may be his own worst enemy. It's true that
the Duke and Duchess of York have become his patrons
in the absence of the duke's brother, but I believe that it
is also true that Brummell has begun to gamble reck-
lessly. Doubtless many of you here tonight think that I
have no right to form an opinion, being newly arrived
and American, but I believe that Brummell's downfall
will come not as a consequence of the Regent's disfavor
but as a result of his gambling."

Saddle of mutton, fowls, ham, and tongue had arrived
at the table, accompanied by side dishes of potatoes and
vegetables. They all looked singularly unappetizing to
Lindsay. Next to her, Dudley spoke up. "Although the
man is no friend of mine, he is a countryman, and I
feel that you may be doing him a disservice, Captain
Raveneau. I know several members of White's and
Watier's and all have told me that Brummell has recently doubled his income by gambling."

Raveneau arched an eyebrow. "I know. And I'm also
old enough to be aware that he is already in dangerous
territory. Gambling is a treacherous business. Success
accelerates the pace, and then there is only one way to
go—down."

Harry blanched, stabbed a boiled potato, and stuffed
it into his mouth. Next to him, Devon surveyed the

company. Lady Chadwick had returned to flirting openly with Ryan, and he seemed more than glad for the distraction. Fortunately, Lord Chadwick appeared oblivious to his wife's behavior. Lindsay, on the other hand, watched them at intervals from under her long lashes while pretending to converse with Dudley. Sighing, Devon thought that she knew the signs all too well. She looked into her husband's warm gray eyes and thought back to all the times she had tried to pretend indifference to him. Mouette had begun to prattle again about the rumors concerning the czar and Lady Jersey; Harry was lost in thought as he pushed the tasteless vegetables around his plate. Finally, Devon's eyes moved to her hostess. Lady Grimley, pale, straight-backed, and thin-lipped, wore no expression at all until she sensed Devon's curious gaze. Then she looked at her guest and the corners of her mouth turned up in the coolest of smiles.

"Would you care for more mutton, Mrs. Raveneau?" she inquired through her teeth.

Sensing André's amused smile from across the table, Devon tried to keep a straight face as she replied, "It's delicious, but no, thank you."

Some distance away, Lindsay felt that she was in the middle of a bad dream. Perhaps she hadn't awakened from her nap after all? The sight of Ryan's blue eyes fixed on the countenance of Lady Chadwick made her feel both angry and ill. They seemed to be having a marvelous time, whispering and laughing together.

"I happen to think that Byron is at least as controversial a character as Beau Brummell," Dudley murmured close to her ear.

Lindsay roused herself. "I must inform you, sir, that I admire Lord Byron excessively." For an instant, her mind spun back to the day Ryan had teased her so mercilessly about Byron in her cabin aboard *La Mouette*. She saw herself toppling from the chair into his arms and then being tossed onto the bed. Had she really been angry when he dropped down beside her and read aloud, mockingly, from *Childe Harold*? Looking back, she felt an odd current of warmth and suspected that, even then, she'd been captivated by his brash charm.

"You should be warned, then, my dear Lindsay," Dudley was saying, "that Byron is quite disreputable in his dealings with women! I have heard rumors that would scorch your sweet ears. In their stead, you might take to heart the words of Lady Caroline Lamb who said that Lord Byron was 'mad, bad, and dangerous to know.' She, I can tell you, was an authority! I cannot fathom why you females are so taken with men of this type!"

Only half listening, Lindsay's heart jumped at his last words. Immediately, her eyes went to Ryan. He looked utterly splendid: tanned, chiseled, and elegant, his blue eyes dancing with devils as he listened to something Hester was saying. Silently, Lindsay repeated the phrase "mad, bad, and dangerous to know." She realized that it applied perfectly to Ryan—and also that, rather than heeding its implied warning, she was feeling more attracted to him than ever.

Hester looked over, her necklace of emeralds glittering in the candlelight. "Are you all right, Miss Raveneau? Yes? I do hope I'm not being rude monopolizing your brother this way, but I find him very diverting. I was just telling Nathan about my daughter, Amanda. She is eight now and very full of herself. Truly a charmer. Of course, the fact that she has ebony curls and sapphire eyes does nothing to curb her self-confidence. . . ."

Something in Lady Chadwick's tone and gaze sounded an alarm inside Lindsay's brain. An eight-year-old raven-haired, blue-eyed daughter? The night at Carlton House when Hester and Ryan met again, she'd said that it had been nine years since their parting. Lindsay's cheeks flamed as she reached a natural conclusion. Ryan Coleraine had fathered the Earl of Chadwick's first child!

"I say, sister dear," Ryan murmured lazily, lifting his

quizzing glass, "you don't look at all well. I do hope you haven't been so foolish as to nibble on a sausage cake today."

Lindsay lifted her chin and her gray eyes were wintry. "I assure you that I am perfectly fine. Never better, in fact!" Running a hand down Dudley's arm, she beamed at him a bit madly. "How could it be otherwise when I am seated next to the most charming, intelligent, *handsome* man in Britain?"

Watching Dudley succumb to her spell, Ryan's face darkened. "How, indeed?" he muttered coldly.

CHAPTER
23

June 16, 1814

RYAN STARED BROODINGLY INTO HIS NEARLY EMPTY SNIF-
ter of cognac and listened to the spatter of raindrops
against the windows of his bedroom and the wind howl-
ing through the chimneys of Grimley Court.

With tense fingers, he loosened his cravat and sent it
sailing across the bed to lie atop his discarded jacket.
The clock atop the mantelpiece struck midnight. On
either side, candle flames guttered, then leaped as a fresh
burst of wind found its way out through the fireplace.
Ryan's mouth hardened. What was Lindsay doing?

When the boring dinner, followed by the obligatory
ceremony of port and cigars for the men, had come to an
end, the Earl and Countess of Grimley had retired and
the rest of the sleepy guests gratefully followed suit.
Hester had looked more reluctant, but she had little
choice except to go with her husband. Lindsay and
Dudley openly declared that they were not tired, then
slipped away to the library, ostensibly to review the
Grimley collection of books.

Now it was midnight. The house was quiet except for the sounds of the storm, yet Ryan had not heard Lindsay and Dudley come upstairs. Bitterly, he imagined the two of them in the darkened library. Were they lying on one of the great Chippendale sofas, kissing passionately? Unwilling to rein in his imagination, Ryan's rage smoldered and flared brighter by the moment. If that smarmy coxcomb dared to lay a hand on Lindsay . . .

Soft, girlish laughter drifted in from the hallway. Every muscle tensed, Ryan drained his cognac and slowly got to his feet. His own door was ajar and through it he saw them in the doorway to Lindsay's suite of rooms. Her hair was loosened, making a golden-rose halo around her delicate face, and Dudley was bending over her. Ryan ignored the blush that suffused Lindsay's cheeks and the uneasy expression she wore as she endured the viscount's kiss. All he knew was that a white-hot rage possessed him at the sight of her being touched by another man. His emotions, fueled by the fine cognac, were too raw for Ryan to analyze—or subdue.

When Dudley wandered off dreamily in the direction of his own apartments on the other side of the staircase, library, and chapel, Ryan waited to hear the faint click of his door, then entered the corridor. Reason was lost to him as he tapped once on Lindsay's door.

She opened it slightly while shaking out her long, burnished curls. "Dudley, you must—" Her voice broke off at the unexpected sight of Ryan.

The danger of being overheard was all the reason he needed to enter uninvited and close the door. "I want to talk to you. Privately."

"Don't be ridiculous! You can't barge in here at this hour of the night!"

"Really?" One black brow flew up sardonically. "I was under the impression I just did exactly that."

Lindsay backed away, all too aware of her vulnerability and the potency of his attraction. Her heart had felt bruised and numb ever since dinner, but her body responded traitorously to the sight of Ryan. His ruffled hair gleamed in the faint candleglow, his eyes were as wild and dark as the Irish Sea, and dimly she noticed that his hard, male chest was half exposed and the muscles of his thighs were outlined against the snug fabric of his breeches.

"You must go," she announced. "Someone will hear us."

"I doubt that. The only other rooms on this side of the house are your parents', and mine are in between. In any event, everyone's been asleep for at least an hour—except for you and your lover."

Somehow, Lindsay resisted the bait. Although the rapid rise and fall of her breasts gave her away, she sounded credibly calm as she replied, "Obviously, I cannot force you to respect my wishes. I had considered the notion of revising my conviction that you were a coarse brute on the basis of the new information about your educational background. This is most instructive. I must not forget that even an Oxford degree is no guarantee of breeding or good manners."

"Oddly enough, I went to Oxford in search of knowledge rather than manners. Being polite is not in my nature—unless it is engendered honestly." Ryan took another step toward her, then laughed softly when Lindsay instinctively backed up again. "At any rate, I came here not to discuss my lack of breeding but *yours*."

"You must be drunk. What can you possibly mean?"

"I am referring, my *dear*, to the ruthless little game you are playing with that thick-skulled Fanshawe. What do you hope to gain by it? A title?"

Lindsay gasped. "How dare you!"

"Not a very original retort, darling, but then an evening with the viscount has doubtless dulled your wits. It must be something of a relief to be adored unconditionally. Needn't you give *anything* in return? Perhaps he settles for a chaste kiss at the moment, but I trust you realize that once you're his wife, you'll have to fulfill some carnal obligations.''

"You are odious and vile!" Lindsay whispered heatedly.

"Merely stating the truth, my dear."

"Overstepping the bounds, you mean! How *dare* you speak to me about carnal behavior when you yourself are carrying on with a married woman?" Silver sparks flashed from her eyes.

Ryan caught Lindsay's slim, pale wrists. "I can take care of myself, but I have serious doubts about you." He stared down at her, their faces so close that their breath mingled. "What kind of a game are you playing, Lindsay? I cannot believe that you are serious about Fanshawe. How can you even consider lying for the rest of your life with such a passionless twit? Flowery speeches and flattery may impress you now, but let me tell you that they're a poor substitute for the embrace of a real man."

She felt dizzy with rage and longing. "It's—it's none of your affair—"

His mouth hardened. "*Isn't* it?"

Lindsay opened her mouth, but no sound came out. Instead, she found herself being enfolded almost roughly into Ryan's steely embrace. And then she couldn't speak because he was kissing her.

Lindsay tried not to touch him, but the sensations his mouth evoked went far beyond any token resistance her mind could put up. Her hands fluttered only once before rounding his shoulders. Similarly, Ryan's anger was also quickly forgotten. All either of them knew was a consuming hunger for the other. After the first fiery moments of passion, Ryan's lips and arms grew gentler as he sensed there was no battle to fight. Lindsay was on his side.

Her mouth was incredibly sweet and soft. He kissed the full lower lip, tasting, while his hands shaped the supple curves of her waist and hips. "Oh, Lindsay . . ."

His voice was edged with a moan. "Do you have any idea what you do to me?"

She opened smoky, gold-flecked eyes and gazed up into his splendid face. "I know what you do to *me*," she whispered as they exchanged butterfly kisses. "I feel that I've gone mad, that you've put a spell on me, that I . . . can't get enough . . ."

Lindsay's low, sensual voice unleashed a fresh torrent of passion in him. Ryan's mouth covered hers and their tongues met, caressing, even as her fingers sank into his gleaming hair and his arms gathered her against the length of his body. The outside world didn't exist. They sank down onto the plush Aubusson rug before the dark fireplace, the room illuminated only by the wavering flame of one candle, while raindrops fitfully splashed against the windowpanes.

For long moments, they kissed wonderingly, pausing at times to gaze into each other's eyes before resuming. The sensation of touching Ryan was bliss for Lindsay. Her fingers gloried in the texture of his hair, the sculpted contours of his face, and the broad strength of his shoulders. Their bodies intertwined as if this mating had been preordained from the instant of their own conceptions. When Ryan's fingers flicked open the fastenings on the back of her filmy gown, Lindsay didn't panic. Her own hands fumbled joyously with his buttons.

Ryan paused to blink at her, surprise and love mingling in his expression. "Aren't you going to push me away?" he whispered gently, kissing her. "Tell me I'm a brute? A cad? And, worst of all, a *man*?"

Smiling dreamily, she ran the tip of her tongue over his lower lip. "Yes, I'll tell you you're a man . . . and I'm a woman . . . and it's time we were together."

"At last we agree." His dark hands lowered the bodice of her gown. In the flickering candlelight, her breasts were pale and ripe, the nipples puckered with longing. "Jesus, but you're beautiful."

Lindsay drew her arms from the puffed sleeves and

stretched like a sensual cat when his lips began a warm and leisurely exploration of her breasts. The feeling of his mouth, gently kissing and sucking, drove her mad. Tingling currents of arousal spread downward to her womanhood and instinctively she arched against him. He was now lying between her legs, hot and hard even through his breeches and the fabric of her gown, and Lindsay sensed dimly that both of them were spinning past the point of no return.

Her fingers sank into his hair and he came back to kiss her mouth again, so deeply and ardently that she was breathless. She pulled at his shirt and then it was gone. Ryan's lips seemed to scorch her delicate flesh. He kissed the bridge of her nose, the curve of her cheek, the length of her neck, and the hollow at the base of her throat. Lindsay, meanwhile, was experiencing sensations she'd never dreamed of. She was wet and aching between her legs, moving against Ryan's hardness with an involuntary rhythm. She touched him wonderingly: his arms and chest were golden brown, hard and warm all at once, and the mat of hair on his chest was soft.

"My darling," Ryan whispered hoarsely, "you must tell me now if you have second thoughts. I fear the moment of truth is at hand!"

An incandescent smile lit her face. "I want you, Ryan. I want *us*."

He gazed down at her with warm sapphire eyes and paused to smooth back Lindsay's tangled strawberry-blond mane. Then he knelt to slip off her gown, drinking in the sight of her curved hips, long, slim legs, and the auburn curls at their apex. "Dear God," he murmured, "you're exquisite."

She had been thinking much the same thing as she stared at his tapering chest. He was the very image of an Irish pirate. A thin line of black hair bisected the muscled ridges of his belly, and when Ryan removed the rest of his own clothing, Lindsay saw that it pointed to the very impressive proof of his manhood—and his desire

for her. She reached out to run her fingertips down the
hard edge of Ryan's hip, touching first the taut curve of
his buttocks and then the line of his thigh. No sculptor,
she thought, however brilliant, could capture such perfect male beauty in marble. For this was a warm-blooded,
living man; the man she loved.

Without thinking, Lindsay said it aloud. "I love you,
Ryan."

He covered her body with his own and that alone was
the stuff of rapture. His dark hands framed her face. He
kissed each smoky eye, lingered over her sensual mouth,
then whispered, "I love you, Lindsay."

Her thighs opened. She felt swollen yet fairly abuzz
with new sensations. Slowly, he touched her there, skillfully and gently, until she sobbed against his mouth.
Then Ryan came into her with the utmost care, biting
the inside of his mouth in an effort to contain his own
intense pleasure. She was so taut, so warm and wet . . .

"Am I hurting you?"

"It feels wonderful . . . better than wonderful. I never
dreamed . . ."

"Sweet Lindsay." His mouth closed over hers and
their tongues met at the same instant that he thrust
inside, joining their bodies completely. She moaned,
passion and pain mingling, then her hips found Ryan's
slow, building rhythm and her fingers clutched his muscled back. Together, they moved in a ritual of love as
old as time itself. Hot, pleasurable tension built between
their thrusting hips. Lindsay thought it might drive her
mad as she panted against his neck. Then, suddenly, the
spiral of passion exploded in what felt like a million
sparkling stars cascading out from the very core of her
being. She let out a moan of primitive surprise, her slim
form trembling against the strength of his body. Feeling
her reflexive contractions, Ryan smiled and kissed her
damp hair, then allowed himself a climax that left him
drained and breathless.

They gasped for air together, half laughing with joy.

Lindsay adored the feel of him still inside her, warm and pulsing. Ryan rolled onto his back, taking her with him, their bodies still joined, and reached up to caress her tumbled curls and glowing face.

"I had no idea . . ." she murmured, bending to kiss Ryan's mouth.

"To tell you the truth, neither did I." He chuckled.

"I was . . . all right, then? I mean, I know you're used to more experienced women—"

"It's never been like this, Lindsay, with anyone else." Wrapping his arms around her, he held her against him so that their heartbeats mingled. "Are you in any pain?"

"I never felt better in my life!" Her voice was muffled against his chest.

Gradually, reality seeped into Ryan's consciousness. Was it possible that this had actually happened in a house filled with other people—not the least of which were Lindsay's parents?

She felt him stiffen slightly and a shadow fell over her heart. Then Ryan gently turned them both sideways, just enough so that he could withdraw carefully.

"What's wrong?" Lindsay managed to whisper brokenly.

"It's just beginning to dawn on me how incredibly mad I've been to take you *here*—in the house of your suitor and under the noses of your parents!" Reaching for his breeches, he found a handkerchief and ministered to Lindsay as if they had always been intimate. "You know that I would love nothing more than to spend the rest of the night in bed with you, my darling brat, but the harsh truth is that I must get out of here as soon as possible. If anyone should knock on either of our doors, we'd never be able to explain!"

Goose bumps spread over Lindsay's naked form as she watched him pull his clothing back on, then hold out his hands to her. "Come on, angel, get up. God, but you're beautiful!" Briefly Ryan held her against him. "Don't look at me like that! Have you forgotten that nearly everyone in this considerably crowded household thinks we are brother and sister? I'd say that we've taken enough risks for one night. Where are your nightgowns?"

Wearing an expression of utter dejection, Lindsay pointed to the dressing room. Ryan went in, rummaged around, then returned to pull a shapeless white garment over her head with a sigh of relief.

"That's better. Now be a good girl and scrub your teeth, wash your face, and get into bed." For a moment, he cupped her delicate face and stared down into her great gray eyes. "Don't despair, Lindsay. We'll steal some time alone to talk when we get back to London, but for the moment, it's necessary that we put what happened between us away. You do understand, don't you?"

She couldn't stop shivering. If she'd felt she could wrap her arms around him and stay safe in his embrace, it would have been easier to bear. However, as things stood, Lindsay was embarrassed by her body's betrayal. She disengaged herself, backed away, and pasted on a tremulous smile.

"Of course I understand! We—we both lost our heads! I expect it was all that wine at dinner. And you're perfectly right; you must go back to your room immediately before we're found out!" Lindsay managed a hiccup of laughter. "It wouldn't do for you to be called out by both Dudley *and* my father, would it!"

He was unsettled by her manner. "Don't misunderstand me, Lindsay—"

"Misunderstand? You are not talking to a child. I am nearly twenty years old, and I do not lack for intelligence. I understand exactly what transpired here tonight, and you needn't be concerned that I shall swoon tomorrow morning at the sight of you. Even if there were not so many practical considerations, I would have no desire whatever to inform the world of tonight's . . . uhm . . . lapse."

Ryan knew her well enough to recognize what was happening now, but he couldn't afford to stay and sort it out. Instead, he stared at Lindsay long and hard and reached out to caress her cheek with the backs of his fingers. "It was not a lapse, and well you know it!" he scolded gently. "Try to get some sleep, and we'll—"

Weakening at his touch, Lindsay watched as Ryan suddenly inclined his head. "Shh!" he warned, raising a tapering, dark forefinger.

"*You* were talking, not I!" she whispered, bristling.

"I think I heard something. I'd better go." Then, unceremoniously, he gripped Lindsay's forearm and pulled her against him, kissing her already bruised lips. "We'll finish this in London. Sleep well, angel."

A moment later, Lindsay was alone in the huge sitting room and trembling again. Dazedly, she wandered into the bedroom where more candles had been lit by a maid.

Ryan had called her angel. Remembering, she felt a welcome rush of warmth but then found herself wondering if it was merely a standard endearment that he used whenever he had made love to a woman. . . .

White curtains billowed at the windows; the wind blew in and then retreated like a living thing. Lindsay found herself drawn to a window, its casements thrown open, wondering numbly if the stars were out tonight. Stray raindrops stung her face as she searched the sky and watched dark clouds obscure and then reveal a glimmering crescent moon. More clouds hid the stars. Fitting, Lindsay thought morosely.

She was about to turn away from the window when she noticed a shadow move on the lawn below. Staring, she recognized Harry's blond head and then saw another man come into view. It was the Earl of Chadwick. There was something furtive about their movements that put Lindsay on guard, and she grew more suspicious as minutes passed and they continued to converse with heated intensity. At times, she could hear one of their voices break above a whisper, and Lord Chadwick repeatedly poked Harry's handsome chest. Finally, Chadwick produced what appeared to be a letter and handed it to Lindsay's brother-in-law, then they turned in opposite directions and disappeared.

What could it mean? Lindsay's heart was beating in her throat as she considered the possibilities. Lord Chadwick was one of the most powerful Tories in the House of Lords, while Harry had a new seat in the House of Commons. Could politics be a factor in their meeting?

One thing was clear: She had to tell Ryan. Crazily, she searched for a pink silk dressing gown and went out into the corridor without a thought to her appearance. Lindsay found that, aside from the puzzle of Harry and Lord Chadwick, she could hardly wait to see Ryan again and be near him. Boldly, she knocked at his door.

There was a long pause and then from inside came the voice of Lady Chadwick. "Ryan darling, aren't you going to see who it is?"

CHAPTER
24

June 16, 1814

Before Lindsay could run, the door swung open and Ryan stood before her. Hester was a blur across the room.

"Lindsay!" he whispered with sharp surprise.

"I must speak to you. A . . . family matter. When you're free . . . ?"

Before he could respond, she turned and dashed away to her own rooms. Shaking his head, Ryan looked back to find Hester in the corner by his bed pouring herself a glass of cognac. Her green eyes tilted upward slightly as she regarded him from under long lashes.

"I hope you don't mind. It's very bad of me, I know, but I need the extra courage." She smiled. "Let me fix you a drink, too."

Ryan buttoned his shirt up to his collarbone as he watched Hester approach with the two crystal snifters. When she handed him his and clinked her own against it, he knew a strong sense of disorientation. How bizarre to have just made love to Lindsay for the first time in a strange house and now to be alone with Hester in the same unfamiliar surroundings. When her fingers brushed his own, he nearly flinched.

"Darling," Hester was murmuring, "do you remember the first night I drank brandy with you? It was in your rooms in St. James's. If my parents had known that I was there alone with you—"

"I remember." Ryan averted his eyes and took a deep swallow of the cognac. "Hester, is it wise for you to be here alone with me now? Your husband is in the same house and he could wake up and discover your absence at any moment."

Daringly, she leaned forward enough so that her brow grazed his chest. "Francis isn't asleep; he went downstairs a little while ago."

Ryan's blue eyes widened. "But that means that he could return at any time and search you out. I do *not* think that this is the proper place or time for that sort of confrontation! Hester, you must tell me what it is you want and then go back to your own rooms." Firmly, his fingers closed around her arm and he moved her away from him.

"I had to talk to you." Realizing that he was in no mood to while away the time nostalgically, Hester seized the moment. "I know that tomorrow we all return to London and I wasn't certain when I would see you again. Ryan, ever since the night we talked at Vauxhall Gardens, I've been unable to think of anything except you. When I told you that I was content in my marriage, I wasn't being entirely truthful . . . though I didn't realize that until later." She laid a slim hand on his sleeve. "Tonight, sitting with you at dinner, I felt as if the years had fallen away, and afterwards I couldn't sleep. Finally it dawned on me that I was feeling the same way I did when we first fell in love a decade ago."

"Hester, don't do this to yourself. We both agreed that we're better off as friends now." Ryan wished that he might sound more sympathetic and caring, but the fact was that this was the last thing he needed at the moment. He longed to be alone if he couldn't be with Lindsay, to lie in the darkness and relive every word, every moment of their time together. The situation was muddled enough without Hester injecting a whole new set of complications into his life! Still, he looked down at his old lover and tried to muster sympathetic concern. "You have a family to think of. We both have new lives . . ."

Her green eyes cooled. "I knew it."

Ryan winced slightly, sensing her meaning. "Pardon?"

"It's that girl. Lindsay. Well, I suppose it was inevitable since the two of you have been thrown together for weeks, but really, darling, I should have expected your standards to be higher!"

A muscle clenched in his jaw. "I can't imagine what you mean." Privately, he thought that she sounded like a bitter, frustrated, middle-aged woman—a role he would never have imagined her in. "Hester, I won't say that I wish we could continue this discussion. Frankly, I think it's a waste of time and energy, and, worse, it's dangerous. Your husband will be missing you. There was a time when I would have relished the thought of fighting a duel with him but no longer."

She felt as if Ryan were twisting a knife in her heart. The sight of him, grown even more appealing and handsome with age, made her ache with longing. Hester could feel the warmth of his body through the fabric of his shirt. She breathed in his masculine fragrance and longed for the sensation of his mouth covering her own, his beautiful hands touching her body. . . .

"Ryan," she whispered brokenly, "have you really forgotten what was once between us?"

"Of course I haven't forgotten." Softening, he brushed a fingertip over the side of her cheek. "It was marvelous then, but both our lives have changed. We can't go back."

Desperation overwhelmed her. Her hands crept up to his shoulders and her lips sought his. Ryan's mouth was unyielding, but he was kind enough not to draw back until a knock sounded at the door and it swung open.

"I refuse to wait at your convenience a moment longer!" Lindsay announced, bursting into the room. "I hope it isn't asking too much to insist that you cut short this tête-à-tête? Besides, I heard Lord Chadwick come upstairs a moment ago and I would think that the countess might be wise to return to her own rooms."

Ryan held Hester at arm's length. "Lindsay's right. You'd better go."

Cheeks flushed, the older woman glanced from one to the other. "Of course. I—well, good night." Tilting her chin, she managed to smile in both directions as she exited.

Ryan closed the door. "It's not what you think."

Too incensed to listen or think, Lindsay wanted to scream but instead whispered heatedly, "Please, spare me your weak explanations! I have eyes! You would do well to remember, Captain Coleraine, that I am not some insipid English twit during her first Season in London! I am a strong, intelligent *American* woman, so you would be wise to disabuse yourself of any notions of treating me otherwise!"

The corners of his mouth quirked. "My darling, I learned all that the day we met!"

Rounding on him, Lindsay poked his chest with her forefinger. "Don't you dare to call me darling! Perhaps I made a fool of myself tonight, but I won't apologize for that, either! I have the same needs as any healthy adult—"

Ryan was losing patience. "Stop this." He caught her wrists and held them even as she struggled. "Behave yourself. I appreciate all that you are saying, and the emotions that prompted this tirade, but I can't let you continue. Kindly give me the same credit for intelligence that you give yourself. Do you think that you can sweep in here, jealous, and tell me that you made love with me out of lust? Lindsay, you could rant and rave until dawn and never convince me of that. And if you'd use your head, you'd realize that nothing could have happened between Hester and me just now."

Gasping for breath, she let her head drop against his chest. "Oh, Ryan . . ."

He caressed Lindsay's silky, burnished hair, then tipped up her chin. "Look at me. Can you honestly say that you didn't *know* what my feelings were when we lay together? Even if I hadn't said it aloud, you should have sensed that I love you, angel."

Her eyes were smoky pools of emotion. "I—I don't have anything to compare it to. And you have such a reputation as a rogue . . ."

"I never knew any of those women the way I know you. You and I were enemies, and then friends, long before I dared to consider what I felt."

Unable to stop herself, Lindsay pressed, "What about Lady Chadwick? Was she not a great love?"

His eyebrows flicked upward as he glanced toward the ornamented ceiling. "I will tell you what I told Hester just before you came in. That was another lifetime, another world, and I have changed and grown a great deal since then. Because she and I were young, the passion seemed intense, but I can see now that it lacked depth. Do you want to know what makes the relationship I have with you so magical and new for me?"

Lindsay's anger melted with each word he spoke. Now her face glowed as she gazed up at him. "Yes."

"It's the sense of friendship between us; the camaraderie, the sparring, the laughter . . . the fact that we don't have to be loverlike to enjoy each other's company. And yet, isn't that the ideal situation for lovers? When you and I are engaged in a discussion about a book or playing cards or arguing furiously, I feel a wholly new sort of passion that has more depth than anything I've experienced before. I've been used to wooing women, but lately I've found myself far more aroused during the wildest arguments with you than ever before in my life. . . .''

"Yet you've rarely acted on that passion," she reminded him quietly.

"To be honest, it frightened the life out of me! I didn't know what would happen if I gave in to it. Perhaps I had to feel more certain that you felt the same."

Resisting the urge to melt into his arms, Lindsay instead spun away, her golden-rose hair frothing out to halo her face. "Old habits die hard, though, don't they? You just told me that you resisted your feelings for me. Aren't you used to doing just that with women and turning to someone else to keep your feelings at bay? What about Hester? How could you be alone with her—and *kiss* her—just minutes after—after—"

"She's confused," Ryan said quietly. "I felt that I had to hear her out. I owed her that much."

"Did you owe her a kiss as well?" Lindsay heard herself burst out. "Or was that in deference to your daughter?"

He stared, uncomprehending. "What?"

"Amanda! Frankly, I find it very strange that you could get Lady Chadwick with child and then desert her, but, of course, I don't know the circumstances. Perhaps she didn't tell you? Yet why else would you have begun a new life in America? I can only hope that you will see fit to enlighten me about that period of your life if you intend to continue *our* relationship!"

Ryan sank down into a chair by the fireplace and reached for his brandy. Sighing, he muttered, "I'm not Amanda's father."

"I didn't think you would admit it." She glanced away.

"Lindsay, I suddenly find that I am very tired. Unless you think that we can actually resolve this matter within the next few minutes, why not let it alone? I think you may see things differently in the morning."

Anger welled up inside her. "Fine. It's most instructive to learn that you are the type of man who simply turns away when a conversation becomes serious—"

"It's two o'clock in the morning, for God's sake!"

Lindsay ignored him. Perching on the edge of the bed, she declared, "In any event, I did not come here to discuss your love life. I came to tell you that I saw Lord Chadwick and Harry talking in the garden after you left my rooms."

"And?" Ryan was slightly irritated to realize how eagerly his eyes drank in the sight of her there in her modest nightdress and clinging silk dressing gown. How bizarre—yet how natural—that they should be talking thusly, at this hour of night. He could almost imagine it as a daily occurrence. . . .

"Must I spell it out for you? Why should Harry and Chadwick meet alone, secretly, on the grounds at such an hour? Plus, their demeanor gave every indication of subterfuge. They were obviously having an animated, though whispered, conversation, and when it ended, Lord Chadwick passed something to Harry."

"And I suppose that you know what this means?" Ryan asked ironically.

"Of course not!" Her voice rose. "I only thought that you should hear about this in case it might have some significance."

"I see. Well, I appreciate your concern, but it's probably misplaced. I find it difficult to envision Harry and Francis as spies."

"I didn't say they were! Ryan, if you think that I brought you this information merely as an excuse to intrude on your little . . . tryst with the countess, kindly disabuse yourself—"

"Why?" he broke in and, rising, came toward her. "Because you don't care what I do? I don't mean to overrule this pose of cool bravado, darling, but I know you too well—and you should realize that it's much too soon to expect me to forget, even momentarily, our own tryst tonight.''

Lindsay's heart began to pound in her ears as she realized that she couldn't back away from him, nor did she want to. "I lost my head," she murmured weakly.

One brow curved high above his dark blue eyes. "You lost more than that, angel."

The sensation of his warm breath on her averted face made her feel faint. Why, *why*, did he have this effect on her? As his hands, so strong and masculine, slid up her arms, Lindsay blinked back tears. Swallowing audibly, she twisted to meet his gaze. It was like jumping into the middle of the ocean. "Oh, Ryan . . ."

"Forget Lady Chadwick, Lindsay." His voice was rough yet gentle at the same time. "I have."

She moaned artlessly, lips parting, as he began to kiss her. Lindsay had never guessed that kissing could be so sublime an experience. Dudley's mouth had reminded her of wet marble. Now her hands crept helplessly up Ryan's chest to clutch at his shoulders while his palms framed her face. In a moment, he'd be beside her on the bed.

From the doorway, a soft, familiar voice murmured, "Mad, bad, and dangerous to know," followed by a deep sigh of resignation.

Lindsay literally jumped, panic-stricken, away from Ryan and off the bed, clutching her dressing gown together at the same time. "Mama!" she croaked.

Ryan said nothing, but his mouth hardened and his brows drew together as he straightened and looked at Devon Raveneau.

She wore only a billowing white nightgown with a lace collar around her neck and her hair was loose, making her look more like Lindsay's sister than her mother. There was nothing childish about her expression, however. It was deadly serious. "I realize that I've displayed very bad manners walking in on you two this way, but I had grown tired of playing the cat to your mice. Few things frustrate me more than *knowing* something in my heart but having the truth denied to me repeatedly. Worse, it's been painful and frankly worrying to me that the denials have come from my own daughter and a man I've come to care for as if he were really my son.''

Lindsay's eyes were huge and luminous in her pale face. She couldn't move or even relax her grip on the edges of her dressing gown, which she held tight across her bosom. Ryan, however, appeared self-assured as he walked over to stand beside Lindsay and rest a hand lightly on her shoulder.

''I don't think we've set out purposely to deceive you, Devon. The truth is that neither of us was certain what the situation was between us; we've been confused and frustrated ourselves much of the time. It's only tonight that we've begun to sort things out.''

''I *see*,'' Devon said in measured tones, then sighed. Her well-honed instincts told her that her daughter was no longer a virgin. She hardly knew how to proceed or even what to think and feel. She was terribly fond of Ryan Coleraine and yet, as a mother, she could not help but see warning flags when she considered his past, his reputation, and his way with women. Devon knew that he was a good person at heart and yet, as a man, might he not have been captivated by the challenge of winning a girl who had professed from the first to despise him? And what about the adventure of wooing her under the noses of her parents—and all the people who thought them to be brother and sister? Devon sighed again. ''I don't have to tell you that it has bothered me enormously not only to keep my suspicions about you two from my husband but also to allay his own as they crop up. And I wonder if you have any idea how he would have reacted if he had walked in here tonight instead of me!''

''Do you imagine that Lindsay and I hatched a plot to fall in love whilst keeping her parents in the dark?''

Ryan demanded in a low, intense voice. "Or perhaps it is I alone whom you suspect? If so, allow me to assure you that there has been no conscious subterfuge involved. Every encounter between Lindsay and myself that has taken a romantic turn happened spontaneously, and I know that we have both resisted the feelings that have grown between us for the very reasons you named. Personally, I am all too aware of the seriousness of my business here in England and of the trust you and André have placed in me. I would never set out to damage either of those aspects of my current situation, but at the same time, my heart has been increasingly occupied with Lindsay."

Lindsay herself felt as if there were a whirlpool of conflicting emotions inside her. When she opened her mouth, only one word would come out. "Mama . . ."

Devon's heart twisted. "Since André isn't here to speak as Lindsay's father, I feel a responsibility to ask you in his place exactly what your feelings are, Ryan. You both realize that you're playing a very dangerous game—you're risking the ruin of everything we set out to accomplish by traveling to England. But much more important than that is the safety of Lindsay's heart."

"Tonight we spoke of love for the first time. We've spent so much time fighting our feelings, taking two steps back for every one forward, that it's as if we're just beginning."

"Indeed?" Devon's eyes and tone sent hot blood to Lindsay's face. "Perhaps my daughter is too shy to discuss the state of her heart in front of you, Ryan. Lindsay, you and I will talk when we return to London. In the meantime, I can only warn both of you that you *must not* allow even a glimmer of romance to show through when you are in the presence of others. In fact, if you're wise, you'll postpone it completely until the family's business in England is finished."

Spoken like a true mother, Ryan thought wryly. Aloud, he said, nodding, "That's good advice. We'll certainly do our best to keep our heads until it's safe for me to court your daughter openly.''

''You realize that means you can't be stealing into each other's rooms? Especially in a house filled with guests who believe you to be brother and sister?''

Lindsay found her voice at last. ''I've certainly gone to Nathan's room to talk in my nightclothes before!''

Her mother fixed her with a penetrating stare. ''I think you *know* what I mean. And now it's time for us to return to our various beds before someone else hears us and comes to investigate. Lindsay?''

Ryan led her over to join her mother and then, at the door, kissed each of them on the cheek. ''Good night, ladies.''

He watched them separate and go into their rooms on either side of his own. Shaking his head, he doused his lights, pulled off his breeches and shirt for the second time that night, climbed into bed, and wondered if he'd have time to sleep at all after sorting through all the events of the evening.

Devon, meanwhile, was slipping under the sheets next to her slumbering husband. Bathed in a pool of moonlight, she stared out the window and swallowed another sigh. Telling the two of them that they must suppress their feelings and desires had been an exercise in futility. If Devon weren't so keenly aware of the spellbinding power of new love, she wouldn't be nearly so worried. . . .

André made a low sound in his sleep and reached for her. Snuggling against her husband's warm, hard body, Devon remembered their own stormy beginnings. If she could manage now to step back and consider Lindsay's situation as a woman rather than as a parent, she might be able to get to sleep after all.

Down the hall, Lindsay alone had not yet gotten into bed. She paced in the darkness, her eyes drawn against her will to the place on the rug where she and Ryan had made love. Blushing at each memory, Lindsay was torn between happiness and the shame she felt when she recalled the look on her mother's face. Mama *knows,* she thought over and over again. She knows what I've done! How can I ever face her again? And how can I look at Ryan in the morning?

As it turned out, the dawn brightened Lindsay's world. While bathing and dressing in a pretty heather-tinted round dress decorated at the neck and hemline with ribbons of ivory satin, she looked out over the park surrounding Grimley Court. A plummy-orange sun shone through misty clouds, spreading its glow over rich green hills that shimmered with dew. Birds sang in the hedgerows and from the shelter of weeping willow, oak, and sweet chestnut trees, while stags and rabbits appeared in search of a leafy breakfast. Beds of jewel-toned flowers decorated the lawn; there were pink hollyhocks, pansies, moss roses, scarlet pimpernels, delphinium, stock, lavender, and many more that Lindsay couldn't name, all basking in the peaceful beginnings of the new day.

Cassie had informed her that there would be a large breakfast served downstairs, and Lindsay was summoning up the courage to emerge and face the others when a knock sounded at her door.

"Who is it?" she asked, while her heart seemed to skip alternate beats.

"It's your papa, *chérie.* Do you remember me?"

Throwing open the door, she went straight into his comforting, familiar embrace, pressing her face against the broad expanse of his chest. "Oh, Papa, I've missed you. There are always so many other people about!"

Raveneau chuckled and held her away from him. "Hopefully all of this will be over before very long and then our lives can return to normal, hmm?" He flashed a white smile. Clad in a perfectly tailored blue frock coat, cream-colored pantaloons, and an impeccably tied cravat, André was handsomer in his sixties than most men decades younger.

Lindsay smiled with a touch of irony at his words. Normal, she thought, ¬uspecting that her own life would never be the same again. That was fine, though. At least she was experiencing it firsthand these days rather than vicariously through her books. "You're looking splendid today, Papa." She reached up to brush back a stray lock of his silvery hair. "Have you come to escort me down to breakfast?"

"Bien sûr," Raveneau replied with the warmest of smiles. Then he paused to gaze down at his younger daughter. She was acquiring a womanly glow that made her look more than ever like her mother. How quickly they grew. "England seems to agree with you, Lindsay. I believe you're becoming a woman at last."

"Had you given up hope, Papa?" Her great gray eyes met his eyes of slate.

"Don't be silly. A rose that opens slowly is the most exquisite." Raveneau pressed a long kiss to her brow, then gave her his arm and they walked toward the sweeping staircase.

Entering the salon with her father gave Lindsay courage. Everyone else, except for the Earl and Countess of Chadwick, was already present. Devon got up to kiss her daughter, and when Lindsay saw the love in her eyes, she felt like weeping. Dudley, behaving in the proprietary fashion of a man who has finally won a private kiss from the girl of his dreams, rose to pull out the chair next to his, sliding it forward when Lindsay was seated. She spoke to the Earl and Countess of Grimley, who looked pale and pinched in the early-morning sunshine. Mouette called to her and Lindsay leaned forward to send her sister a smile. Finally, unable to avoid it a moment longer, she glanced at Ryan.

The sight of his dark blue eyes staring at her over the rim of his teacup sent a flush spreading over her body and reminded her of the dull ache between her legs.

Suddenly, she felt hot there, too, stingingly so. For one involuntary instant, Lindsay remembered the two of them naked and straining together; remembered his damp, chiseled face above her; remembered the sensation of being filled, the rhythm of his thrusts and her answering hips, the abandon of their kisses. . . .

"Will you have tea, miss?" It was a footman at her elbow.

Somehow Lindsay managed to refrain from flinching in surprise. "Yes, thank you."

Next to her, Dudley solicitously added lemon, knowing by now exactly how much she liked it. She gave him a smile.

"Have I done something to offend you, dear sister?" Ryan asked quietly from across the table.

Feeling her mother's casually watchful gaze, Lindsay mustered a bright smile. "Certainly not, Nathan! What a question!"

He helped himself to a mutton chop and some herring as the platter was presented to him. "Well, I *am* your only brother and you *were* ignoring me . . . but perhaps that's to be expected now that you've ventured out into the world of other men." Ryan looked at Dudley with sleepy eyes. "Are you aware, Fanshawe, that my sister's only passion was books until she came to England?"

"Something of the sort," Dudley muttered.

"You'd better help yourself to breakfast," Ryan remarked, turning his attention back to Lindsay. He buttered a muffin and dipped it into his egg yolk. "Have a sheep's kidney; it'll do you good. You look as if you didn't sleep much last night! Fanshawe, I hope you were a gentleman and returned my sister to her rooms at a respectable hour. It would be such a bore if I had to call you out in defense of Lindsay's honor. . . ."

Dudley couldn't speak; his mouth was full of quail pie, but his eyes bugged out, betraying his reaction to this speech. Lindsay, on the other hand, wanted to laugh with joy. The sight of Ryan, so gloriously male and handsome, lifting his quizzing glass to survey her erstwhile suitor made her heart sing.

"Nathan, do stop." She tried to sound stern. "You are the outside of enough!"

The quizzing glass turned in her direction and his black brow arched above it. "Am I?"

Lindsay prayed that she wasn't blushing as she bit into a strawberry and returned Ryan's secret half smile.

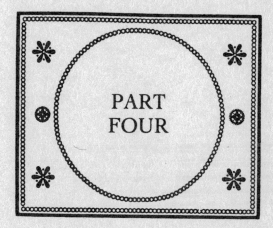

PART FOUR

True love's the gift which God has
    given
To man alone beneath the heaven:
It is not fantasy's hot fire,
    Whose wishes, soon as granted, fly;
It liveth not in fierce desire,
    With dead desire it doth not die;
It is the secret sympathy,
The silver link, the silken tie,
Which heart to heart and mind to
    mind
In body and in soul can bind.

—Sir Walter Scott (1771–1832)

CHAPTER
25

June 20, 1814

GLANCING AT THE NOTES OF HAND THAT WERE ACCUMU-
lating at Michael Angelo Taylor's pudgy elbow, Ryan
let out a sigh of consternation and put down the dice.
"You've won far too much of my father's money, Taylor. Why don't we end this now and you can buy me
dinner with your newfound wealth?"

The influential member of the House of Commons
smiled good-naturedly, which accentuated his perma-
nent port-induced flush. More fond of gossip than gambling, he took pity on André Raveneau's son. The boy
seemed a good sort, even if he wasn't very well en-
dowed in the top story. Taylor figured that Captain
Raveneau wouldn't give his son money and turn him
loose in White's if he didn't expect him to drop a few
quid, but it didn't seem altogether sporting to win every
last shilling. No need to draw blood, after all!

"Right-o, young Nathan! I hear there's a tolerable
dish of boiled fowl with oyster sauce being served to-

night. We'll share a bottle or two of claret to console you.''

When they were seated in the dining room and Michael Angelo Taylor had drained one glass of claret and poured another, he smiled at Ryan. "Who's your tailor, boy?''

"Weston.'' Ryan glanced down at his honey-colored jacket and cream and gold brocade waistcoat, biting back a smile. "He doesn't entirely approve of my orders. . . .''

"Dark blue's the style, you know,'' Taylor advised him confidentially. "Blue coat with brass buttons and buff-colored pantaloons. Coming from America, you may not be aware.''

"I appreciate your telling me, sir.'' To cover his amusement, Ryan ceremoniously took snuff, offering the Sevres snuffbox to Taylor.

"I hear you were in Oxford with the Regent and all the others. Tell me about it!'' Taking a pinch, he snuffled loudly.

Ryan was rather taken aback by the older man's unabashed curiosity, even though he had been forewarned. He gave him as colorful an account of the events in Oxford as he could muster, then Taylor leaned forward.

"Did you hear that Prinny tried to keep the czar from attending Lady Jersey's midsummer ball Wednesday last by seeing to it that he dined at Christ Church that same night?''

Studying his boiled fowl, Ryan allowed, "Yes, I believe I did.''

"Then perhaps you *haven't* heard that the czar took his leave in the middle of that dinner, drove through the night, and arrived at Lady Jersey's ball at three in the morning—''

At that moment, Lord Byron, who was being seated at a table next to them, leaned over and declared, "I saw him there myself, Taylor, in a starless blue coat and kerseymere breeches whisked round with the Jersey, who, lovely as ever, seem'd just delighted with majesty's presence as those she'd invited!" The poet chuckled and reached up to smooth his carefully waved hair. "Do you like it? I vow, these foreigners inspire me no end!"

Ryan tried to smile but was certain his expression betrayed his true opinion of Lord Byron. Meanwhile, Brummell had been standing in the shadows waiting for the poet to finish before joining him at the table. Now he sauntered forward, his brows elevated slightly.

"Old story, George," he murmured. "You're becoming quite tiresome. In fact, if you do not promise to cease reciting that boring verse, I shall have to see to it that you are expelled from the club." The Beau glanced over at Ryan and Taylor. "You shouldn't encourage him, you know. He's far too conceited as it is." He paused for one beat, then added, "Hello."

Ryan couldn't help smiling even though he knew that the gleam in his eye betrayed more of himself than he liked to show. "It's good to see you, Brummell. You're well?"

"Tolerably." Lifting his quizzing glass, he appraised Ryan's coat. "Hmm. It's nothing I would wear but not altogether offensive to the eye. At least you rebel in a tasteful manner, young Raveneau." One nostril flared as he surveyed their meal. "I must speak to Raggett about the menu. That looks *deplorable*." Bending at the knees, Brummell sat down gracefully and turned his attention to the wine.

Michael Angelo Taylor's white hair glittered in the candlelight in contrast to his rosy cheeks. Leaning forward, he whispered, "Did you attend the Guildhall banquet on Saturday?"

Barely suppressing a sigh, Ryan replied, "Yes, I did."

Taylor beamed. "I was ill. Do tell me about it! Is it true that the grand duchess insisted on accompanying the czar, thereby forcing Prinny to go alone rather than sharing a carriage? And that they were an hour late? And that there were crowds lined up along the route who shouted to the Regent, 'Where's your wife? Love your wife!'?"

Ryan longed to cut the conversation short, but he hoped to lead Taylor into other areas and didn't want to offend him. "So I heard."

"Well? Tell me about the rest of the evening."

Gritting his teeth, Ryan strove for brevity. "When Czar Alexander and the others arrived and the royal procession started into the banqueting hall, the czar stopped in the middle to speak to Lord Grey and Lord Holland."

"Two of the Regent's bitterest enemies!" Taylor laughed and rubbed his hands together.

"Indeed. The atmosphere was chilly thereafter, though the hall was unbearably hot. I would have given anything to be elsewhere. Toast after toast was made, followed by appropriate songs from the fiddlers and opera singers in the gallery. Finally, the grand duchess declared that if that caterwauling did not cease, she would be sick."

"Lovely!" Michael Angelo Taylor's face was redder than ever. "And then?"

"Well, notes were passed to and from the Russian ambassador, and the Regent had to appeal to the grand duchess to allow the national anthem to be sung. She balked but eventually gave in. I heard the prime minister mutter, 'When folks don't know how to behave they ought to stay at home!'"

There wasn't a scrap of meat left on the carcass on Taylor's plate. Licking his lips, he poured the last of the claret into his glass and leaned forward again. "I suppose you heard about the row at the opera, where the Regent and his wife were both present—in separate boxes?"

"Yes, I did."

Taylor continued as if he hadn't heard. "There was great applause when the Princess of Wales appeared in her box. The czar bowed to her, which forced her husband to follow suit and prompted an absolutely wild and enthusiastic reaction from the audience. Would you not think that England would give up hoping for a happy ending for those two? In any event, Prinny pretended to assume that the cheering was for him and bowed repeatedly until it ceased. One might assume that there was an end to it, but when Princess Caroline left, the mob surrounded her carriage, offering to burn down Carlton House if she wished!"

Ryan couldn't have cared less. Sipping brandy, he chose his words carefully. "That's quite a story, Mr. Taylor. You would seem to be privy to all sorts of information!"

The older man finished his brandy and signaled for another. "I might be."

Careful to keep in character, Ryan took a pinch of snuff and regarded him languidly. "Lord Chadwick was with us at Grimley Court this past week. I suppose you are well acquainted with the man?"

"Well enough to know that he thirsts for power. Francis intends to become the next prime minister, and he just might achieve it. The past year or two, he's given Prime Minister Liverpool and Foreign Secretary Castlereagh plenty of information that has proven quite valuable in carrying out our struggle with—" Taylor broke off, suddenly remembering, and mumbled, "America . . ."

"Don't worry, old man," Ryan exclaimed, chuckling in a way that suggested he was not very bright. "I don't bother with politics. Such a bore! Besides, I feel much more at home here than in America!"

"Who could blame you, dear boy?" Taylor took a huge bite of apple tart and chewed contentedly. "It's not terribly civilized there, is it? Of course, your family has turned out splendidly, but you've spent a great deal of time abroad, hmm?''

"That's true. We've had our house in Grosvenor Square as long as I can remember, and of course my sister has been married to Sir Harry Brandreth for some years. . . ." He took a sip of brandy and pretended to search for something else to say. "You must know Harry, being in the House together, what? How is his career coming along? I do hope that my sister Mouette can look forward to a secure life with him. God *knows* he hasn't much else to offer, unless one counts that golden sort of beauty as a positive attribute. . . ."

"Oh, well, I don't think you need to worry about Harry," Taylor replied rather distractedly. "He's coming along nicely. I'd say that he's quite ambitious, too, but because he's lazy he takes a different approach. Harry may not be in constant attendance in the House, but he's ingratiated himself with some of the powers that be. The Earl of Chadwick, for one!" Plate cleaned and brandy drained, he consulted his watch. "I don't mean to rush off, dear boy, but my wife's mother is visiting and I ought to put in an appearance this evening."

"I understand." Ryan rose with a lazy smile. "Thank you for dinner, Mr. Taylor."

"Not at all, Raveneau! I do hope your father won't be put out about your losses today." The older man got to his feet and patted his swollen belly. "Good night, then!"

Ryan watched Michael Angelo Taylor weave slightly as he left the room. His own thoughts were far away until he sensed that someone was watching him. Turning, he met Beau Brummell's perceptive gaze.

"I wonder, Raveneau, whether you are having us all on," the Beau drawled.

Relaxing his body, Ryan raised his quizzing glass. "My dear Brummell, what *can* you mean?"

Leaving White's, Ryan nearly collided with Sir Harry

Brandreth, who was looking slightly worse for wear. His curly blond locks were tousled, his blue eyes bloodshot, and his breath smelled of brandy.

"My brother!" Harry exclaimed, slapping him on the back. "Dear brother! Come and join me in a game of faro!"

"I'd like to, Harry, but I've already lost my limit for today." That in itself was a lie of sorts, for Ryan had allowed Michael Angelo Taylor to win. "I hope you won't think me impertinent, but are you certain that you're up to gambling? I wonder if you might not regret it in the morning?"

Chuckling, Harry leaned against his brother-in-law for support. "Can you keep a secret, Nathan, old boy?"

"Certainly." He was hard-pressed to remember the role he was supposed to play. Apart from his growing suspicions about Harry, he felt an obligation to Mouette and the Raveneau family. However, to be on the safe side, Ryan took out his snuffbox and delicately indulged. "Do you want to talk to me outside?"

"Why the bloody hell would I want to do that? I just came in!"

"The air might do you good."

"Nonsense. All I need is a brandy and a good game." The sentence was slightly slurred. "Don't worry about me, though. I can afford it. Look!" He pronounced the last word in a loud whisper and withdrew a thick packet of ten-pound notes from his coat. "You see? I can afford to lose a bit. Mouette'd only spend it in any case, so what's the difference? Don't tell her, though. I know she's your sister, but the truth is that she can be a terrible shrew when she puts her mind to it!" Harry laughed as an afterthought, slapped Ryan on the back again, then staggered away toward the tables.

Ryan raked a hand through his hair, wondering what to do. Out of the corner of one eye he glimpsed Raggett, the proprietor of White's, and motioned to him. Raggett was an honest sort who was known to sit up with club members during all-night games.

"My good man . . ." Ryan pretended to stifle a yawn. "I realize that this must be a terrible bore for you, but could you possibly look in on my brother-in-law from time to time? I'm not certain that he's responsible for himself, and I'd hate to hear that he's gambled away his home and family!"

"Certainly, sir." Raggett made a small bow, even though he considered himself superior to this ridiculous dandy. "In fact, I'll try to encourage Sir Harry to go home as soon as possible."

Ryan's dark blue eyes were distant. "Thanks, old man."

The windows of the town house on Grosvenor Square were ablaze with light as Ryan approached. He'd walked the mile or so home, lost in thought, oblivious even to the stars that gleamed above like diamonds against a dark velvet background.

Arabella Butter met him at the door. "Hello, sir! How are you tonight?"

"I'm fine, Arabella. And you?"

"Quite well, sir!" The sight of him still sent shivers of pure female lust down her spine, but even that sensation had lessened since Harvey Jenkins had begun to pay his attentions to her. "The rest of your family is upstairs in the ballroom."

"Pardon?"

"You've missed all the fun, sir. They're *waltzing!*" She pronounced the word as if it were some exotic, though enticing, tribal dance. "My mother's outraged, but personally I think it looks quite fun!"

A slow smile spread over Ryan's face. Trust the Raveneau family, he thought, to provide the perfect antidote to his overserious mood! "Arabella, is there any champagne in the house?"

"Why, yes, sir."

"Bring me a bottle, would you? And four glasses."

Moments later, after shedding his jacket and waist-coat, he took the stairs by twos and approached the third-floor ballroom. A lilting waltz drew him onward, and from the doorway he glimpsed Devon sitting at a beautiful piano. Stepping inside, Ryan saw Lindsay turning rather haltingly in the arms of her father. In spite, or because, of her unsure movements, she was giggling softly.

For a moment, Ryan leaned against the door frame, champagne in one hand, a cluster of glass stems in the other, and watched. Lindsay wore the simplest of white muslin gowns, cut rather low over her breasts and tied beneath them with a yellow ribbon. The short puffed sleeves showed off her graceful arms, and the loose Grecian knot of strawberry-blond hair atop her head displayed the beautiful line of her neck to perfection. Ryan's eyes warmed with love and longing. They had scarcely been alone since returning to London. He was determined to unravel the mystery they had come to solve so that he could speak openly to her father, and Lindsay had been busy with engagements of her own. Viscount Fanshawe continued to call, but Ryan wasn't worried. Even when hours passed without a word between them, he could gain instant reassurance by looking into Lindsay's expressive gray eyes.

"Ah, Ryan!" André Raveneau called, dancing in his direction and then coming to a halt. He gasped for breath, laughing. "Just the man I'd hoped to see! I've been dancing with this girl all evening, and I think it's your turn!"

Across the ballroom, the piano music had trailed off. Hoping to allay Devon's fears, Ryan held up the champagne and glasses. "I'll have my turn with Lindsay, if she'll let me, but first let's drink a toast. Come and join us, Devon!"

The ballroom was lovely and delicate without being too grand. The pale pink walls were decorated with raised swirls of white plaster, while the arched ceiling continued this fantasy. There were gilt chairs lining the walls, and all four of them sat down in them, feeling very small and somehow decadent as Ryan eased the cork from the bottle of champagne.

He poured frothing portions into each glass, then said, "I would like to propose a toast . . . to the people I love better than my own family."

Devon was shocked to feel tears sting her eyes. Seeing the emotion in her daughter's face, she murmured, "And to the successful completion of our task here in England."

"Hear, hear," said André, raising his glass. They all drank, and then Raveneau looked at Ryan. "Any news?"

"Yes, but it can wait until morning. Right now, I would love to relax and perhaps learn to waltz with my friend, Lindsay."

Raveneau put his head back against the wall and laughed softly. "More welcome words were never spoken! We've danced until my legs ache, but she cannot quite relax. Perhaps you'll have better luck."

Finally, Lindsay turned almost shy eyes to Ryan. "It seems that we're going to attend the assembly at Almack's this Wednesday. That means I only have two days to learn to waltz!"

"I'm sure that you wouldn't be the only person who couldn't waltz, brat," he replied gently. "If the czar weren't so fond of that dance, I suspect that most of those very proper people at Almack's would still be unsure whether it was at all seemly to waltz at all!"

André poured more champagne all around, draining the bottle, then stood up. "I suggest, my darling wife, that you and I take our glasses to bed and leave these two young people alone to debate the merits of the waltz." Gazing at Devon, he arched an eyebrow suggestively. "Shall we?"

There was little she could do beyond darting a brief warning look at Ryan. "Certainly, darling." She kissed Lindsay's cheek, then Ryan's. "Good night, you two. Behave yourselves." Then, in the doorway, she paused. "But wait! How will you dance without music?"

Ryan's laughter sounded dangerously warm and low to her. "Oh, don't worry," he replied. "We'll manage somehow."

When they were alone, he longed to take Lindsay in his arms, and kiss her endlessly, but he held himself back. "How've you been, angel?"

She gazed into his dazzling blue eyes, sipped her champagne, and swayed in his direction. "I'm wonderful . . . now. I've missed you."

"I've missed you, too. But at least we see each other every day. You realize that I'm concentrating on solving this thing so that we can come out in the open? Your mother was right, you know. We can't go on deceiving your father, and I cannot go on pretending to everyone else. I'm growing tired of this masquerade, especially where it extends to you."

"Ryan, have you learned anything? I wish that you would look into my suspicions about Harry and Lord Chadwick."

"I have been." He stared past her for a moment. "And I fear that you may be right. In fact, though I couldn't say so then, I've had my doubts about Harry for some time. That was part of the reason I came along to Oxford."

"I beg your pardon?"

Ryan laughed and kissed her hand. "And, of course, I wanted to be with you. But be serious for a moment, Lindsay. If it's true, how can I ever tell your parents? It would destroy them—and Mouette, of course. What would become of her?"

"You underestimate my sister—and my parents. Mama and Papa have never been overpartial to Harry; I've always sensed that. As for Mouette, she's a Raveneau. She's strong—and if this is true about Harry, she'll survive." Then, like a woman in love, Lindsay's thoughts returned to the matter at hand. "You don't talk as if you've missed me at all!"

He grinned. "Of course I have. How do you think I feel when I see you go off with that twit Fanshawe?"

She laid a slender forefinger over his mouth. "Shh. You know that I am not encouraging him, Ryan, and neither can I brush him off so quickly. You trust me, don't you?"

Her mouth, so ripe and sensual, drove him mad. "Yes, of course I trust you. That's not the point."

Lindsay smiled in a new way; it was the smile of a woman in love. "You needn't say it. I know what the point is."

"Let's toast to that, then." His eyes slanted up a bit at the corners in a slightly devilish manner that Lindsay had come to adore. "Here's to the day when we can tell your father and all the world how we feel." Leaning forward, he grazed her lips with his.

They toasted, sipped, and then he stood and held out his arms to her. "Shall we practice your waltz?"

Lindsay giggled softly, then put her hand over her mouth to conceal a tiny burp of champagne bubbles. "But, Ryan, there's no music! Besides, how do you know the waltz?"

"Trust me, angel. There's very little that I *don't* know!"

She thought that he looked beautiful in his champagne-hued breeches, snowy shirt, and artfully tied cravat. His ebony hair was wind-ruffled, setting off his keenly sculpted face and sapphire-blue eyes with their fringe of black lashes and winged brows above. When he held out his hand, tanned and rough from years spent aboard ship, Lindsay put her own slim fingers into it and allowed him to pull her to her feet.

Ryan grinned down at her. "Can you hear the music?"

She beamed back. "Yes—yes, I can!"

His arm rounded her back, sweeping her into his arms. "It's easy. Just count one-two-three and turn with the music. You see?"

Lindsay felt fluid and graceful. Her feet found the rhythm, one moving behind the other, then reaching out, and it seemed that she was dancing on a cloud. She dropped her head back, gazing at the ceiling. "This is fun!"

Ryan's head bent to press a scorching kiss on her arched neck. "Good. As long as you keep hearing the music, the fun will continue for the rest of our lives. . . ."

CHAPTER
26

June 21–22, 1814

AT BREAKFAST THE NEXT MORNING, RYAN STIRRED HIS tea, tasted it, and then remarked, "I thought I might visit the British Museum today. I've never seen the Rosetta stone!"

"Hmm!" André grinned around the London *Times*. "Sounds nearly as exciting as the visit Devon and I are paying to an old friend in Islington. I captured Captain Silas Longheart's ship back in 1782, and he was obliging enough to perform Devon's and my wedding. Silas is nearly eighty now. We've kept in touch and I gather that his health is failing. It seemed only right that we go up there to see him." He glanced at Lindsay, who was pouring a cup of chocolate. "I don't suppose you want to come along?"

She looked slightly pained. "Well, Papa, it's not that an afternoon in Islington doesn't sound vastly entertaining, but . . ."

"You're welcome to inspect the Rosetta stone with me," Ryan said casually. With the edge of his spoon, he

gently cracked a boiled egg, ignoring the stare Devon
suddenly turned in his direction. "That is, if you haven't
any other plans."

Lindsay pretended to consider his invitation. "Actually, I've been meaning to go to the museum. As a
teacher, I should find it particulary worthwhile."

"Well, good." Raveneau folded the newspaper and
drained his tea. "We all have constructive plans for the
day. Devon, we ought to leave soon, you know. I thought
we might bring a luncheon in to Silas; it would doubtless
be a great treat for him."

"I'll speak to Mrs. Butter, darling," she replied, "and
I'll be ready to go within the hour." Watching André
rise and go upstairs, Devon narrowed her eyes at Ryan,
then at Lindsay. "Very neatly done!"

Coleraine stared right back at her. "Are you worried
that I'll try to take advantage of your daughter at the
British Museum? Lift her skirts amidst the Egyptian
artifacts?"

She flushed, looked away, then sighed. "No. Of course
not. I apologize. I suppose I'm overreacting—and I
shouldn't begrudge you two an afternoon together, should
I?"

"No, Mama," Lindsay answered. "We'll be careful."

Shaking her head, she murmured, "It's just that so
much shows in your faces, in the way you look at each
other . . ."

"I doubt whether any of the smart set will be wandering around the museum today," Ryan said reassuringly,
then stood up. "And you needn't worry that I'll take
advantage of your absence to force my attentions on
Lindsay. Now, if you ladies will excuse me, I must go
upstairs and do battle with a cravat."

"How very disgusting!" Lindsay murmured to Ryan,
her eyes fixed on a stuffed yet seemingly half-decayed

badger. "Did we come to the British Museum to look at such things?"

"Shh." He had to bite the inside of his lower lip to keep from laughing aloud. Grasping Lindsay's elbow, he guided her, along with the rest of their group of fifteen, past rows of inexpertly stuffed birds.

"And why did we have to wait for a fifteenth person? Have you ever heard a sillier rule? Fourteen of us were forced to wait for more than half an hour, and then the rest of the fifteenth person's family had to be left behind because of this ridiculous group-of-fifteen rule!"

"Lindsay, do stop!" He pulled her aside, gripped her bare upper arms, and tried not to laugh down at her. "If we make a scene and are expelled from the tour, they may all have to go back and wait for an even fifteen before they can start again!"

For one brief, mad moment, she felt almost faint. Ryan's face was so devilishly handsome, his Irish blue eyes gleaming down at her with boyish mischief, that Lindsay longed only to lean upward and kiss him.

"Don't think it," he cautioned, arching a brow. "Come along, Miss Raveneau, and fix your mind on higher matters."

The German guide, or cicerone as he liked to call himself, set a brisk pace as he led the group through more rooms of stuffed birds and animals, then past weapons, dresses, and ornaments of savage tribes. Lindsay barely had time to widen her eyes at some particularly curious objects before they were swept onward to a display of antiquities from Herculaneum.

"Herculaneum?" Lindsay stage-whispered to Ryan. "Where's that? Greece?"

"You're incorrigible, brat," he replied, his breath warm against her ear.

"Am I? No one's ever said so before, but it's a quality I've always aspired to."

"For the record, Herculaneum's in Italy." Stifling his

laughter, Ryan shook his head and pointed toward the cicerone.

Her mouth made an *O*. "Of course! It's near Pompeii. How silly of me!"

The cicerone craned his neck and pursed his lips in Lindsay's direction. "I do not mean to interrupt, fraulein, but perhaps you might close your mouth so that others will be able to hear my descriptions of these artifacts from Pompeii that we are approaching!"

"Oh, yes!" Lindsay replied with enthusiasm. "That was very near Herculaneum, wasn't it? I find this *extremely* fascinating, Herr von Tiebolt, and I promise to be quiet as a mouse from this moment on!"

Ryan's senses reeled with astonishment and love. He wanted nothing more than to pull Lindsay into an alcove and kiss her senseless, but there didn't seem to be any alcoves handy at the moment.

They both turned serious during the exhibit from Pompeii and even more so when they were able to pause in front of the Rosetta stone. It featured a treble inscription on a large block of dark porphyry: one in hieroglyphics, one in the common language of Egypt, and one in Greek. All three said the same thing, therefore each served as a glossary to the others and proved the key to deciphering hieroglyphics. Herr von Tiebolt hurried them along, however, promising that there were great Roman and Greek marbles to follow. Lindsay caught only a glimpse of the Egyptian sarcophagi and statues before they were out of the room.

In America, Lindsay had read about and gazed at drawings of ancient statues, but this was the first time she had ever actually seen such works of art. There was a breathtaking statue of Diana, and then Lindsay was taken aback to see a bust of a woman looking at her with an expression that mingled indignation and terror.

"How unusual to see such a look on a statue from that period!" she whispered to Ryan. "They are usually so placid! I wonder what upset this poor woman so?"

"Perhaps she saw a chimera," he replied absently.

Lindsay stared up at his fine, angular profile, sensing his feelings. "You miss her, don't you?"

He glanced at her, then away, but gradually brought his eyes back to hers. "The ship, you mean? Yes, I suppose I do. There's been little time to brood over that loss, what with *all* that's been happening here in England." One side of Ryan's mouth quirked mischievously.

Lindsay would not be diverted. "By the time we get home, you'll have a new *Chimera,* you know, and she'll be even more wonderful because she'll be up-to-date! Everything will shine, the wood will be perfectly smoothed—"

"Don't go on if your intention is to cheer me up, angel. I enjoyed the feeling that the *Chimera* was worn and supple. It used to seem that she had acquired wisdom and experience with age, like a woman of the world." Without looking, Ryan's fingers entwined with Lindsay's. "It's like the difference between a new house that still smells of paint and seems untried and one that creaks in familiar places and has acquired a cozy, golden glow. Or the difference between a soft, worn, satiny blanket and one that still scratches!"

"Ryan, I *know* what you mean," she replied simply. "The *Chimera* was your friend and your partner, and she can't be replaced by an untested imitation."

"I *beg* your pardon," intoned the cicerone, pursing his lips in their direction. "Sir, if you and this young lady have something important that must be discussed during our tour, I will have to ask you to go."

"All right," Ryan replied pleasantly. Still holding Lindsay's hand, he turned to leave.

"Are you aware that you will miss seeing the museum's rare manuscripts, including forty-three volumes of Icelandic literature?"

Coleraine glanced back and said somberly, "Please. This is already hard enough." With that, he made good their escape, emerging with Lindsay into the sunlight.

"How ill bred they must think us," she remarked, opening her parasol as she looked down Great Russell Street. "You are very bad, you know."

"So you've told me, Miss Raveneau." Smiling up at the sky, Ryan sighed. "Glad that's over. I might have enjoyed it if we could have viewed the exhibits at our own pace, choosing what to skip and what to linger over, but I would *not* have chosen Herr von Tiebolt as a browsing companion."

"Yet we did have fun."

"Of course we did. And we may have enriched our minds a bit at the same time . . . though I'll probably suffer for the rest of my life as a result of being deprived of those Icelandic manuscripts."

Lindsay laughed softly and tucked her gloved hand through his arm as they strolled. "Our cicerone interrupted when I was about to ask you what effect your lack of enthusiasm about the new *Chimera* might have on your future. Are you thinking of not returning to Connecticut, Ryan?"

His blue eyes were far away. "I haven't given it a great deal of thought. As I've said, the goings-on *chez* Raveneau have kept me pretty well occupied. There's a lot to take into consideration; after all, it's only been this past week that I've dared to hope you might care to *share* my future. If we manage to make a success of this madness between us, you'll have an equal say in the circumstances of our life together."

Lindsay flushed slightly, torn between worry that he was unsure of their love and delight that he meant for his wife to be an equal partner. "Well, as you said, there's a great deal to sort out. I only asked because I like to know how you feel about things, what you're thinking. The sea has been your life for so many years—"

"And let me guess. You always swore that you would never marry a sea captain." Feeling safe in this neighborhood, which was a good distance from Mayfair, Ryan bent to kiss Lindsay's nose under the brim of her

Angoulême bonnet, a garland of moss roses encircling its high crown.

"I've shed some of my own prejudices," she replied meekly. "Before I met you, I thought I knew exactly what my future held. Now the one thing I'm sure of is that I *don't* know."

"That's why our plans are best deferred until we've untangled the other business here in London. Who knows what could happen by summer's end?"

He's *not* sure about us, Lindsay thought despairingly. A sigh was welling up in her when Ryan suddenly slipped an arm around her waist and said, "What shall we do now? It's a beautiful day. Why don't we walk home? We could buy some fruit and wine on the way and make a detour through Hyde Park."

Her heart lightened. "Might we walk along the Serpentine and have a small picnic?"

Lindsay leaned her head against his shoulder and Ryan inhaled her fresh scent. What he really longed to do was take her to bed for the rest of the afternoon. The memory of their coupling on the rug at Grimley Court was still sharp and arousing. That brief taste of Lindsay's abandon had only served to whet his appetite for more, but for the time being he had to be content with tantalizing crumbs . . . a stolen, hungry kiss; the sight of love and longing in her smoky eyes; a sudden touch of her hand on his arm or back; the pressure of her breasts against his chest when they danced. Had she any idea of her power over him? Never before had Ryan felt this way about any woman, for this was much more than lust. He wanted her so much because he *loved* her. True, the memory of her body haunted his dreams, but he also yearned to give Lindsay pleasure, to have her moan again against his mouth and wildly return his kiss, to smile suddenly in that way that lit the darkness, to return his caresses shyly until she felt at ease with his body, to tell him what she liked best. And he wanted to hold her in his arms in the afterglow, then sleep through the night, embracing . . .

"Ryan?"

"Hmm . . ."

"You didn't answer. Can we have a picnic along the Serpentine?"

"Of course we can. We'll do anything you want, angel." He was about to drop a kiss on Lindsay's sensual, upturned mouth when he glimpsed a familiar figure across Bedford Square. Instantly, Ryan straightened and moved away from Lindsay. "Shh. Look, it's Lord Chadwick with Lord Liverpool, the prime minister. We can only pray that he didn't see us before." Meanwhile, Ryan was also remembering everything Michael Angelo Taylor had said about Francis passing information to Liverpool and Castlereagh that had helped in the war with America.

They paused to chat with the two men, acting like a typical brother and sister. Lindsay related the tale of their expulsion from the British Museum, blaming "Nathan," and laughter ensued.

Ryan glanced casually at Lord Chadwick, wondering if the earl had observed him and Lindsay during those suspiciously intimate moments. And, again, he wondered *what* information Francis was privy to—and how he had obtained it.

"I think this is extremely barbaric—and farcical!" Lindsay announced as she stepped from the Raveneau carriage outside Almack's Assembly Rooms in King Street off St. James's Street. "How dare these women presume to pass judgment on anyone else? Who exactly do they think they are?"

Devon, looking like a girl herself in white silk trimmed with forest-green satin, recognized the signs. Unable to show her true feelings for Ryan Coleraine to the world, Lindsay vented her frustrations by criticizing whatever

else was at hand. This was not the time for a mother-
daughter chat, however. Instead, Devon came up beside
her and gave her a meaningful pinch at the swell of her
hip. "Shh! Behave yourself!" she whispered.

Indignation, now mixed with embarrassment,
only heightened Lindsay's considerable beauty. Her
strawberry-blond mane was wound into a loose Grecian
knot atop her head, freeing frothy curls to set off the
exquisite beauty of her fine-boned face and luminous
gray eyes. Her long neck curved downward into creamy
shoulders and the first curves of her breasts, a view that
was accentuated by a narrow necklace of sapphires.
More sapphires gleamed in her hair and ears and were
set in the ribbons that defined the bodice of her gown
and the tucks in her short sleeves. All else was of the
finest gossamer white muslin.

André and Ryan exited the carriage and joined the
ladies. With Raveneau present, not to mention countless
other spectators, Ryan was careful yet direct. Placing
his right fingertips firmly against the small of Lindsay's
back, he smiled and whispered, "Think, angel. I know
you're capable."

Though she had no qualms about standing up to Ryan,
even since their relationship had shifted toward romance,
Lindsay took note of the steely tone in his voice. Realizing he was right, her face softened and she glanced up at
him. "Point taken, sir."

Ryan, for once, wore conventional garb, since one of
the main rules of Almack's was that men must wear
knee breeches and a white cravat. He was clad in impeccably tailored black with white stockings, shirt, and
white satin waistcoat. Lindsay thought that the severity
of his clothing only served to set off his tanned, chiseled
features, ruffled ebony hair, and piercing blue eyes. As
they went into Almack's, her own gaze swept the room
and she instantly saw that there wasn't a man present
whose looks could match Ryan's. How she longed to let
all these people know that they were not brother and

sister but lovers. Instead, Lindsay was forced to endure
the stares of dozens of females, each pair of eyes fixed on
Ryan Coleraine.

"Good evening." It was Lady Cowper, the most popular of the seven *grande dames* who ruled Almack's.
"So happy to see you here at last. I'm certain that we
issued vouchers for the entire Raveneau family the moment you arrived in London!"

André gave her a smile that sent her pulses racing.
"Lady Cowper, you must forgive us, but we felt that we
couldn't make an appearance until we were able to waltz!"

"Oh, Captain Raveneau, you are much too charming!" she tittered, allowing him to kiss her hand. "And
your son has grown into such a handsome man!"

Devon slipped between the two men, took André's
arm, and smiled as the ladies Jersey and Castlereagh
joined Lady Cowper. "It's lovely to see you all again!
Have you met our children?" Greetings were exchanged,
then they drifted into the assembly rooms. One by one,
the other patronesses appeared to extend their rather
stiff greetings: the kind Lady Sefton, the haughty Countess Lieven, who was the wife of the Russian ambassador, Princess Esterhazy, and Mrs. Drummond-Burrell.

Like a dutiful son, Ryan brought cups of lemonade
back to his family, then stood with them and regarded
the company through his quizzing glass. Devon watched
as a Scotch reel was concluded, the dancers looking
rather bored. Even the orchestra from Edinburgh, con-
ducted by the celebrated Neil Gow, appeared on the
verge of a collective yawn. Then Viscount Fanshawe
appeared to alleviate the Raveneau family's boredom, at
least momentarily.

"Lindsay, my dear, how good it is to see you again!"
His blond head bowed before her. "I have stopped
several times in Grosvenor Square, but on each occasion you have been out. Mrs. Butter has always insisted
that you are riding in Hyde Park, but yesterday she
surprised me with the news that you had gone to visit

the British Museum. Why did you not send word to me? I would have been delighted to introduce you to its wonders!''

"Oh, well . . ." Blushing slightly, Lindsay avoided Ryan's eyes. "If I had known that you were so attached to the place, I certainly would have called upon you, Dudley, but as it was, this excursion was simply a whim of Nathan's. And, in the end, he behaved very badly and we were turned out before the end of the tour. . . ."

"I plead guilty," Ryan chimed in, his tone ironic. "Lindsay was deprived of viewing the forty-six Icelandic manuscripts."

"Forty-three," she put in, feigning annoyance.

"You see, Fanshawe? She probably would have forgiven you, but she'll never forgive me!"

Devon longed to slap Ryan. What sort of game was he playing? But she clenched her tiny hands as Lindsay accepted Dudley's invitation to dance. They moved onto the floor as the orchestra struck up an English country dance.

Watching Lindsay attempt to copy the other dancers, Ryan couldn't help smiling. " 'Twould seem that your daughter needed to learn more than the waltz," he murmured in Devon's ear as they saw Lindsay tread hard on Dudley's foot.

"You're sounding rather smug tonight, my dear," Devon replied. "What would you say if I told you your old lover was making her way toward us?"

He caught a glimpse of Hester in the crowd. A small diamond tiara gleamed against her upswept sable curls. "I would say, Mother," he replied quite grimly, "that I am about to waltz with my dear sister and haven't time to speak to Lady Chadwick."

As if Ryan had willed it, the orchestra struck up a waltz just as Dudley delivered Lindsay back to her family. Her eyes met Ryan's and they went off to dance without speaking a word.

"That's odd," Dudley murmured, watching them. "I could have sworn that Lindsay had no talent for dancing."

Remembering her inept performance two nights before, André replied, "So could I!"

For several long minutes, Ryan and Lindsay and Czar Alexander and Lady Jersey were the only people waltzing. The two couples swirled about joyously, years apart yet enjoying themselves equally. Lindsay's soft muslin skirts swirled out behind her as she laughed up at Ryan, her breasts caught up against his chest. Watching them, Devon knew a sense of dread.

"My mother insists that the waltz is a shocking excuse for hugging," Dudley muttered.

"Mama, I must speak to you." It was Mouette, whispering harshly in her ear.

"I didn't know that you and Harry were here!" Devon exclaimed in surprise.

"Shh!" Mouette, her eyes shadowed, looked left and right. "Please say nothing to Papa. Just come with me."

The two women slipped into an arched alcove and Mouette instantly began to speak in nervous tones. "Mama, Harry has heard some very alarming rumors about Ryan and Lindsay! Something must be done before everyone whispers that they are engaged in the same sort of relationship as Lord Byron and his sister!"

Devon's heart thudded in alarm. "What are you talking about?"

"You know perfectly well, Mama! People are saying that Ryan and Lindsay's love for each other may be something more than should exist between siblings. They are saying it's *unnatural*!" Her blue eyes strayed to the dancing couple, who seemed to be laughing over some secret joke even as they turned in perfect, graceful time with the waltz. "Just look at them!" Mouette's voice rose. "Everyone will be saying that—"

"Stop it!" Devon felt like shaking her daughter soundly. "You talk as if it's true, and yet you know full well that Ryan is *not* Nathan!"

"But no one else knows it! Mama, you must *do* something!"

"I am. I've tried. And they are trying. I cannot believe that they would have behaved in a manner that would arouse suspicion. Where did Harry hear this rumor?"

"From the Earl of Chadwick!" Mouette declared triumphantly. "He told Harry that he and Lord Liverpool—the prime minister!—saw them with their own eyes! Fortunately, Lord Liverpool surmised that what he witnessed was merely a display of familial affection, but Lord Chadwick knew better. Mama, what are we going to do?"

CHAPTER
27

June 23, 1814

"I HAVE A LUNCHEON ENGAGEMENT AT WATIER'S WITH Lord Liverpool," André told Ryan as the two men descended the stairway together. "I certainly hope that this conversation is more productive than the others I've had lately. I've begun to worry that one of our ambassadors at the peace negotiations may cross the channel to find out how we're progressing—and I don't know what I could say!"

Ryan's legs ached from waltzing and he felt only half awake even though it was noon. Coatless, he wore riding boots, fawn breeches, and a snow-white shirt without a cravat. "I—I may have something to tell you in this area, sir, but I would appreciate a few more days to confirm my suspicions. . . ."

Raveneau stopped on the stairs and looked over his shoulder with flinty eyes. "I thought we had agreed to share information all along, Coleraine. For all you know, I may be aware of something that would complete the puzzle for you!"

"It's a bit more complicated than that, sir. Please, trust me for the moment. I only mentioned this at all so that you wouldn't feel so discouraged about our lack of progress."

"Well . . ." André took his hat and gloves from the waiting Roderick and sighed. "There isn't time to go into it now, but we'll talk at the first available opportunity, *n'est-ce pas?*"

"Certainly." Coleraine smiled until the older man was out the door, then threw up his hands and went in search of Lindsay. Unfortunately, he encountered further complications in the form of Devon Raveneau, who was just emerging from the second-floor morning room.

"I wish to speak to you at once, Ryan. Lindsay is on her way. I was only waiting for André to leave." Her blue eyes narrowed slightly. "You realize, I hope, that I refuse to go on deceiving my husband much longer?"

Clenching his fists, Ryan took in her immaculate cream gown and rather severely coiffed hair. Obviously, Devon was in a serious mood. Lindsay appeared at that moment, clad in a soft morning dress of green sprigged muslin, her burnished curls tumbling over her shoulders.

"Good morning, Ryan." She widened her eyes at him for an instant, then crossed to kiss her mother's cheek. "Mama, you wished to see me?"

"It's nearly noon, my dear," Devon told her, indicating the place beside her on the sofa. "I take it you are fatigued after your exertions at Almack's . . . ?"

Accepting a cup of tea, Lindsay looked warily from her mother to Ryan. "I enjoyed myself, if that's what you mean. Aren't you pleased that I learned the waltz so well? The czar told me that I outshone Lady Jersey!"

"It is not your talent for waltzing that concerns me," Devon replied in sober tones. She paused, then her face crumpled slightly. "Oh, Lindsay, what has happened to you? There are moments when you seem a stranger! In the past you have often appeared to be the most sensible member of our family. What has become of that girl?"

Lindsay's gray eyes were unwavering. "I suppose that she came out from behind her shield of books and summoned the courage to become a woman."

Ryan's eyebrows rose above the rim of his teacup, but he said nothing.

"Don't misunderstand me," Devon went on in a strained voice, "I want you to be happy. Of course I do! And I hoped that you would blossom during our time in London. But this . . . relationship between the two of you is causing complications that become more tangled by the day."

"Mama, we promised you at Grimley Court that we would be circumspect, and we *have* been! Ryan has scarcely dared to kiss my cheek since the night you spoke to us—"

"What you two do in private is not relevant to this problem!" Devon burst out. "Can you not realize that each time your eyes meet, you kiss? Do you imagine that people are blind? Mouette told me last night that rumors of *incest* have begun to circulate!"

Lindsay gasped, spilling tea into her saucer, and looked at Ryan. His own expression was deadly serious. "Did Mouette say where she had heard this rumor?"

"Harry told her. Apparently, he spoke to the Earl of Chadwick who, along with the *prime minister,* must have witnessed a highly suspicious display of affection between the two of you recently."

Ryan and Lindsay locked eyes. In a small voice, Lindsay said, "It really wasn't much, Mama. We were on the street—"

"How circumspect of you!" Devon shot back.

"It was my fault," Ryan said. "We had just emerged from the British Museum. The sun was shining, I was elated to have Lindsay to myself, and I thought that no one would see us in that rather distant neighborhood—"

"Very foolish!" Devon cried, trying to refrain from raising her voice. "Moreover, your explanations are meaningless. They cannot erase the damage that has been done. There is only one solution and that is for both of you to *swear* to me that you will not display even an iota of affection for each other outside of this house! And even here you cannot so much as smile at each other unless you are alone in a room with the door closed—a circumstance that I would consider ill advised at best!''

Lindsay's heart was pounding. "Mama, I've never seen you so angry—''

"Then take note of it!" Her eyes blazed. "So much can be lost as a result of your headstrong passion. Every step that has been made toward discovering whether someone has betrayed America could be erased. Even more important to me, however, is André. I live in fear that he will hear these rumors and discover that all three of us have lied to him! I am his wife, and we have not built a marriage of more than thirty years on a foundation of deceit. Either the two of you put your passions on the shelf until our business in London is resolved or I shall go to André with the truth." Devon lifted her chin angrily. "I think that both of you know him well enough to realize that he would put a stop to this nonsense once and for all!''

Lindsay's mind reeled. Had her mother forgotten how it felt to be in love, really in love, for the first time? She expected Ryan to be furious about Devon's dictatorial attitude, but he leaned back quietly in his chair. Finally, he rubbed long fingers over his eyes and murmured, "Will you at least allow us to go on talking?''

Devon stood up. "I am going to Mouette's to help her prepare for the rout she and Harry are giving this Saturday night. You two may engage in conversation, but keep the door closed and your hands to yourselves!''

With that, she swept out of the morning room, firmly closing the door behind her. Lindsay gazed at Ryan, her mouth trembling a bit as tears gathered in her eyes. After a moment, he held open his arms and she rushed into them.

"It's impossible not to hold you," he whispered, caressing her silky titian curls. "We simply must be very certain that we are completely alone. . . ."

"Mama is acting like a stranger!" Lindsay exclaimed thickly. "One would think she had never experienced love herself, when just the opposite is true! She and Papa were not even married when Mouette was born! How dare she pass judgment on us—"

"Only because we are putting others in danger, angel. It's a tricky situation, and I am more determined than ever to resolve it as soon as possible."

"I wish that we could simply put that entire mess out of our lives for several days. I long to walk down Park Lane and Piccadilly with you, proudly showing my feelings. I want to ride with you in Hyde Park without thinking that I cannot smile at you with real affection or even put my hand out to touch yours. . . ."

"Is that all you want?" Ryan's voice was husky and appealing. He held her on his lap with both hands around her bottom.

She ran her fingers through his crisp hair, stared into his eyes, then brushed his lips with her own. "You know it's not. Oh, Ryan, will we ever be free of this coil?"

Shifting in his chair as arousal intruded, Ryan made a sound that mingled laughter with a moan. "Get up; I can't stand it!" He set her on her feet and held her away from him. "To answer your question: Yes, of course we'll free ourselves, but first there's work to be done. We have to discover—"

A knock sounded at the door. Ryan stepped behind the chair to make certain that the evidence of his longing for Lindsay was hidden, then called, "Come in!"

Arabella Butter appeared, wiping pale hands on her apron. "Mama isn't feeling well, and Harvey has offered to assist us in taking her to the physician's. It's very sudden, a terrible pain in her belly!" Her brow was knit with fear.

"Hurry, then, Arabella!" Lindsay exclaimed. "You should not have even bothered to tell us!"

"Well, I've already roasted the chestnuts for chestnut soup and have started them stewing in veal broth, ma'am. If I leave, there'll be no soup for dinner tonight!"

"Nonsense!" Lindsay assured her. "I'll finish it. Is there a recipe?"

"Yes, ma'am!" Arabella's plain face wore an expression of utter relief. "If you can read Mama's handwriting, it's on the worktable in the kitchen."

"Then, go!" She watched her spin away, then glanced at Ryan. "Well? What are you looking at? Come and help me make chestnut soup!"

He followed obediently, but when Arabella was safely down the stairs, he grabbed Lindsay around the waist just as they passed under the doorway. "I never realized that you could be so dictatorial." He chuckled.

Lindsay leaned back against his hard body for one indulgent moment. "I promise to consult you in the future . . . unless, as in this case, there is only one possible solution!" Turning her head, she gave him a brief kiss, then struggled free and started down the stairs.

"I see," Ryan responded ironically as he followed her, "and who decides what is or is not a situation with only one possible solution?"

"Don't be so silly." Barely sparing him a backward glance, Lindsay entered the kitchen and looked around for the recipe. Absently, she added, "Such things are obvious."

"To you, no doubt," he muttered dryly under his breath.

"I beg your pardon?" Lindsay slipped a starched white apron over her muslin round gown and turned so that Ryan might tie it for her. "Did you say something?"

The corners of his mouth twitched before he lifted her hair and kissed the nape of her neck. "I forget."

"We are not completely alone, you know. Cassie and Able are somewhere about—"

"They went to Covent Garden."

"Oh. Well, there are housemaids cleaning the bedrooms."

"Believe me, I'm aware of that. Do you imagine that we would be in the kitchen otherwise?"

Her cheeks flamed as she disengaged herself from his tantalizing embrace. "Ryan, I hope that you don't imagine, since our—our . . . interlude at Grimley Court, that I would continue to behave in that . . . manner."

Lazily, he lifted one black eyebrow and perched on the edge of the table. "Of course not. I thought that next time we might try a proper bed."

"Ryan Coleraine!" Lindsay gasped in outrage. "You talk as if you think I could be some sort of—"

"Wife?" He caught her wrists with long, tanned fingers and pulled her struggling body back against his own. "Does it shock you to contemplate the joys of our marriage bed?"

She grew still, but her face burned and her heart pounded so hard that she was certain Ryan must be able to hear it. Their eyes were inches apart as she whispered, "I—I didn't know you meant—"

"To marry you? Good God, did I forget to ask?" He put on an expression of boyish contrition. "I've assumed too much, hmm? Well, I can only hope it's not too late to make amends."

Lindsay stared as he gracefully dropped down onto one knee. "Miss Raveneau, would you do me the honor of consenting to become my wife?"

She pulled at his hands. "Ryan, do get up before someone sees you!"

"Not until you give me an answer. Should I elaborate? Very well, then. Miss Raveneau, I love you better than my life, and I want nothing more than to spend the rest of my days as your husband." His mouth scorched the tender insides of her wrists. "For better, for worse, to have and to hold . . . ." While murmuring this last phrase, Ryan looked up at her from under his thick black lashes and flicked one eyebrow up and down suggestively.

Lindsay felt faint with love and longing. Most of the men she had met were utter bores, and now she wondered dizzily if Ryan had somehow appropriated the appeal of at least ten of the other males in London. "You must get up," she murmured weakly. "This is very silly!"

"Silly?" he feigned devastation. "My dear Miss Raveneau, I am completely in earnest! You have dealt a crushing blow to my masculine ego, from which I may never recover. . . ."

Unable to help herself, Lindsay laughed softly and ran her hand over his gleaming, ruffled hair. "Of course I'll marry you, if you'll have a brat like me. *Now* will you get up?"

Ryan kissed his way up her slim arms, rising slowly from his half-kneeling position. He laid his cheek against the bodice of her gown and sighed softly. The sensation of his warm breath through the muslin fabric caused Lindsay's nipples to tauten. Ryan said nothing but smiled as he kissed each one in turn, then moved upward to her bare throat. Her back bent, her body supple and yielding under his hands, her arms wound about his neck and then Lindsay was lying back over the bleached worktable.

Sheer passion won out for a long minute as he kissed her, savoring each sweet inch of the inside of her mouth. Lindsay's breasts pressed upward against his chest and Ryan yearned to unfasten her gown. Her buttocks met the edge of the high worktable and he was standing between her legs, feeling her soft warmth against his aching hardness. If only he could undress her and . . .

"Ryan, we mustn't." She moaned against his open mouth.

He nearly laughed when he felt Lindsay's hips arch upward in contradiction to her words. "I know, angel." After one more sensual, lingering kiss, he drew back, smiling, and arched an eyebrow at her. "But soon, hmm?"

"On the kitchen table?"

"When we're married? Oh, absolutely. You won't be able to peel a potato in peace, my darling. Or answer a letter"—Ryan's lips gazing hers—"or bathe, or read a book, or ride in the park—"

She widened her eyes in mock horror. "You would come between me and my horse—in Hyde Park?"

"I would consider it!" Helping her up, Ryan pressed one last kiss to her throat, then watched, smiling, as she skittered away and began to read Mrs. Butter's recipe aloud.

"Let's see. Arabella said that the chestnuts are already stewing in veal broth. "Using a towel, she lifted the lid on a pot and sniffed. "Hmm! Well, now we need to take a piece of bacon, a pound of veal, a pigeon beaten to pieces—"

"Who's going to beat the poor bird?"

"We'll take turns." A dimple winked next to her mouth. "It says here that we also need an onion, a bundle of sweet herbs, a piece of carrot, and a little pepper and mace. We lay the bacon in the bottom of a stew pan, then put the meat and other ingredients over it and set it over a slow fire."

Ryan rolled up his sleeves, tied a towel around his lean hips, and they carried out the instructions together.

"I suppose that you are hoping that Harry will do something suspicious at the rout he and Mouette are giving tomorrow night," Lindsay remarked as she peeled the skin from an onion.

"Well, certainly. I abhor the idea of telling our suspicions to your father until I have some sort of proof to offer." Sighing harshly, he cut up the veal. "Of all the people in England to suspect, why did it have to be Harry? A member of your own family! It seems to me that I have to be damned certain before I point a finger at him! As it is, your father is pressing me for information. Perhaps he thinks I don't really know anything and am simply putting him off."

"With any luck, Harry will say something to Lord Chadwick at the rout. Perhaps they'll go off together and we can follow them."

"*We?*"

"Ryan, you're cutting that carrot into awfully big pieces!"

He narrowed his eyes at her. "Forget the carrot. And forget any notions you have of coming with me if I have to follow Harry. If you want to help, you can start by having a talk with Mouette." As he spoke, he sliced each chunk of carrot into thirds. "Why not visit her tomorrow to help with last-minute details before the rout? It seems to me that you two are long overdue for a sisterly conversation. See if you can't persuade her to confide in you about her marriage—and any unusual behavior she's noticed on Harry's part."

Lindsay nipped a piece of carrot and chewed thoughtfully. "That's a good idea. I'll send a note over as soon as one of the footmen turns up." She paused then, watching Ryan chop the onion into tiny bits. "Why do you suppose Harry is doing this? What has he to gain?"

"Money, for one thing."

"But wouldn't he have to pay for the information he gives Lord Chadwick?"

"I've been pondering that one and I half suspect that this may all be a sham on his part. He may be fabricating secrets, telling the Tories that he is privy to information via his father-in-law."

"But that's awful! Why would Harry do something so immoral and dangerous? What need does he have for that sort of money?"

Ryan shrugged and sprinkled a handful of herbs over the veal and vegetables. "I have an idea that Harry has taken to gambling. And I also suspect that he is unsure of himself underneath that façade of blustering good looks. Added wealth, plus the promise of power among the Tories, must bolster his confidence."

"I think you may have overdone the herbs," Lindsay murmured, staring into the pan.

"You told me to put in a handful!"

"I don't think the author of this recipe counted on a cook with such *large* hands. . . ."

"If I'd known you were going to be so critical, I'd have left it all to you! As I recall, you *begged* for my assistance and expertise." Ryan's fingers slid around her tiny waist, drawing her hip against his, while his mouth grazed her temple.

Lindsay was about to take issue with his memory but laughed instead. "You're—"

His lips interrupted her, slanting across hers as he gathered her body full-length against his own. Finally, when she was breathless and weak, Ryan raised his head and gave her a smile that was provocative and boyish all at once. "I'm what? Wonderful? Irresistible?" He kissed her again. "Wonderfully irresistible?"

"Mmmph!" was all Lindsay could say as both lowering retorts and giggles were smothered under Ryan's persuasive mouth.

Long, indulgent minutes passed before either of them heard the sound of shoes tapping across the kitchen. Finally, Lindsay opened one gray eye and saw Cassie and Able standing in the doorway to the stillroom, which opened onto the garden. Ryan seemed to sense their presence at the same moment. Gently, he set her away from him, then faced the Barkers with what he hoped was a repentant expression.

"What can I say? I lost my head." Ryan looked over at the blushing Lindsay. "Can you forgive me, Miss Raveneau? I give you my word that I will never force my attentions on you again."

"Of course." She appealed to Cassie and Able. "Please, don't tell Mama and Papa about this! It would only upset them, and it was probably as much my fault as Ryan's—"

Cassie sniffed shrewdly. "I'm not getting involved, so

you can save your stories for someone more gullible.
You're adults and ought to be able to work out this
muddle without any interference from the likes of us!"
Passing them, she added, "At least I *hope* you can!
Come along, Able."

When they had exited through the dining room, Lindsay pressed both hands to her mouth to stifle a sudden
fit of laughter. Swaying against Ryan's wide chest, she
felt his hand come up to cradle her face and smooth
back loose burnished curls.

"Cassie's right," she whispered at last. "This is a
muddle!"

"And we don't seem to be very adept at circumspec-
tion, do we," he replied ironically. "All the more reason
to clear up the confusion about Harry so that we can
turn to more *important* matters, hmm?"

Lindsay nodded weakly. "Let's finish this impossible
soup, then I'll write a note to Mouette."

Longing to kiss her again, Ryan stepped backwards
instead. "Right. Of course. Where were we?"

"You just added a bushel of herbs, darling."

"You mean a pinch."

"Look, there's no time for your mutinous arguments.
Just do as I tell you!" Lindsay's dimples teased him
again as she surveyed the recipe. "Oh, good. It's time to
beat the pigeon to pieces!"

Biting his lip to keep from laughing or kissing her
again, Ryan picked up the small, plucked bird and began
to joint it. "God, what have I gotten myself into?"

She rubbed her nose against the edge of his jaw.
"Into? That's easy. You've gotten yourself into love,
Captain Coleraine!"

Ryan's eyebrows went up. "Ah-ha. I suppose that's
why I'm suffering and having fun all at the same time?"

"Exactly!" Lindsay grinned, then widened her eyes
in alarm. "Ryan, what are you doing to that pigeon?"

He paused in the act of hitting one of the legs with a

wooden mallet. "I'm beating it to pieces, just as you ordered."

"They don't mean it literally!" Lindsay was about to launch into a tirade when she saw the laughter in his dark blue eyes. "You shouldn't tease me, you know. It's very bad of you."

Chuckling, Ryan enfolded her in his arms and kissed her brow. "Don't forget 'mad' and 'dangerous to know.' "

"And delicious!" Standing on tiptoe, she kissed him sensually. For one brief instant, Lindsay imagined what her mother would do and say if she could see them now, but the sensation of Ryan's tongue touching her own banished all thoughts.

Behind them, the meat, vegetables, and herbs had begun to bubble in the stew pan. Soon it would be time to add more broth, French bread, and then the chestnuts. "We forgot the pepper and mace, angel," Ryan muttered softly against her mouth.

Lindsay yearned only to make a meal of this man she so adored. "Are they important?" she wondered in dreamy tones.

"Probably not." He couldn't help chuckling at the sight of her languid expression. "But it might be advisable to add them all the same."

"Particularly since the Butters are coming in from the carriage!" Cassie announced from the doorway.

They broke apart again just as the stillroom door opened to admit Mrs. Butter, who was supported by the wizened Roderick and Harvey Jenkins. The old woman sniffed loudly, surveyed the kitchen scene, and demanded, "Who's been tampering with my recipe for chestnut soup?" She glared at Cassie. "It's you, I'll wager! Since the day you arrived from America, you've been lurking about, waiting to get into my kitchen! Well, it won't answer! If you think I'm a sick old woman, you have another think coming!"

"You mustn't blame Cassie!" Lindsay exclaimed, stepping forward. "If the soup doesn't smell right, it's my fault. Nathan and I were trying to help in your absence—and Cassie's only just returned from Covent Garden!"

"*Smell* right?" Mrs. Butter echoed sarcastically. "I can tell you one thing, Miss Proper American Lady! Things haven't smelled right around here for quite a while!"

With that, her family led her off to bed. Harvey remained stranded in the kitchen with the others, clasping and unclasping his hands. Finally, he glanced at his employer, pursed his lips, and raised heavy brows in an unspoken yet eloquent question. Ryan turned away.

"There's nothing wrong with this soup," he muttered stubbornly, lifting one lid and then the other. "All it needs is some pepper and mace—and besides, it smells fine to me. It just isn't finished yet!"

Looking from Cassie to Harvey and then at Ryan's back, Lindsay didn't know whether to laugh or to cry.

CHAPTER
28

June 25, 1814

"W ON'T YOU HAVE A SHREWSBURY CAKE?" MOUETTE invited, taking a large bite of her own. "They're still warm, and our cook has just made this fresh raspberry jam."

Deciding that it would be best to enter into her sister's mood, Lindsay smiled and accepted the plate Mouette proffered. "It looks delicious. Thank you."

"Thank *you* for coming over here to help me! There's so much work to be done today and one can only trust the servants so far." She stirred her tea and spread clotted cream over another cake. "You're growing into an exceptionally tasteful woman, my dear. If you're smart, you'll marry Lord Fanshawe and settle down right here in London. With his family's wealth, you could probably have an even grander house than this."

Lindsay's smile began to falter. They sat in an exquisite sitting room that adjoined her sister's boudoir. The twenty-foot-high gilded ceilings and walls painted the color of beeswax framed fashionable pieces of satin-

wood furniture by Sheraton. There were valuable paintings, Aubusson carpets, and cut-glass bowls of yellow
roses, and yet Lindsay sensed that something was missing. This was just one of dozens of fabulous rooms in
the Brandreth house, but no amount of money could
purchase the love and happiness that were necessary to
transform mere rooms into a home.

"Well, I'm afraid I'm not in love with Dudley," she
explained quietly.

Chewing the last of her second cake, Mouette fingered
her necklace of pearls and rubies. "You ought to be. He
has a great deal more to offer than that renegade sea
captain."

"Have you forgotten that our father was a renegade
sea captain and still is, to some extent?"

Mouette shrugged. "No, I haven't forgotten, but Papa's
different. Besides, even he could not provide the sort of
life I now have."

Choking back angry words, Lindsay took a deep breath.
"Where are Anthony and Charles?"

"Their nanny has taken them to St. James's Park to
see the cows." She spooned more sugar into her tea.
"At least I think that's where they went. Oh, well, it
doesn't really matter as long as they're not underfoot.
Children can be such a nuisance! I am so thankful that
we can afford to pay a nanny and a governess—"

"Mouette!" Lindsay had to bite her tongue to keep
from shouting exactly what was on her mind. Instead,
she thought madly, trying to make sense of her sister's
erratic behavior. Mouette was eyeing the last Shrewsbury cake, and for the first time Lindsay took note of
her more rounded face and the generous cut of her
morning gown. She was exhibiting so many signs of
strain that it seemed obvious that there were indeed
some serious problems within the Brandreth marriage.
Softening, Lindsay moved over to sit on the gold-and-
ivory-striped settee next to her sister. "I'm sorry, I

didn't mean to raise my voice. It's just that I love you and I'm worried about you, Mouette.''

"I'm sure I don't understand. You have scarcely been around me enough to feel such concern for my well-being. Besides, I have everything any woman could want!" There were tears in Mouette's huge blue eyes.

Lindsay put an arm around her shoulders. "You can talk to me, you know. I won't even tell Mama or Papa. Is it Harry, Mouette? Are you unhappy in your marriage?"

The older sister saw such love and sympathy in her sibling's eyes that her defenses crumbled. She rested her forehead against Lindsay's shoulder, then relaxed slowly as she felt the caring and warmth in her embrace.

"Yes, it's Harry. Has it shown?"

"Only to your family, darling. You needn't worry that all of London is talking about you. Won't you tell me what is wrong, though?"

"Promise you won't tell Mama? I've always felt so intimidated by the success of our parents' marriage!"

"I promise."

Mouette seemed to shed the sophistication acquired during her years in London as she spoke, and Lindsay felt that she was discovering her for the first time. "He's been away more and more the past two or three years, dining at his club almost nightly—and even leaving late at night! He insists that he is merely strengthening his connections with the powers that be in the House, that it's important for all of us that he build a firm foundation for his political career, but . . ."

Lindsay stroked her sister's glossy black curls. "Yes?"

"But Harry's been spending so much money! And yet there always seems to be more to replace it. I may seem a scatterbrain to you, but I have managed the family finances since the day we were married and I can tell you that it frightened the life out of me when he announced last year that he wanted to take them over. I wouldn't—I *couldn't*—allow it! He tells me that he wins

money at cards with Lord Liverpool and Lord Chadwick and the others, but I find that so hard to believe.
Harry has ever loved to gamble, but he's never had a
talent for it. I've seen him at the tables!''

"What is it that you suspect?"

Mouette shook her head miserably. "I don't really
know. For a time, I felt certain that he was having an
affair. He would come home at all hours from these
'political meetings' reeking of liquor, his cravat askew . . .''
Tears spilled onto her cheeks and she wiped them away.
"I was *ill* worrying about it! I tried everything. I bought
new furniture, new clothing, I tried a different coiffure,
I brought him breakfast in bed—but nothing worked.
Now I'm less certain that another woman is at the root
of this. Since the day we married, I have sensed that
Harry harbors a feeling of insecurity. He's done well in
life, and God knows that *I* love him just as he is, but he
is forever looking around at his peers and worrying that
he hasn't a weighty title, that he isn't wealthy enough,
that he isn't as dashing as Papa, that I care more for
material things than for him, and now he belongs to the
wrong party and can never advance very far in the
House."

Gently patting her back, Lindsay murmured, "What
do you think he's been doing, then?"

Mouette heaved a huge sigh. "I'm not sure. That's
what worries me so! He won't *talk* to me, Lindsay, and
I'm wise enough to know that that's the first big step
toward an empty marriage. What's worse is that I become so nervous I eat too much and spend too much
and complain or nag too much, and that makes everything worse. I don't know . . . my suspicions shift from
day to day, depending on Harry's behavior. Sometimes,
when he doesn't touch me for a week or more, I become
convinced again that he is in love with someone else.
Then I decide that gambling is to blame for all of this. I
don't know. I just don't know.''

"Does he ever ask you what Papa says about the war between America and England?"

Raising her eyes, Mouette stared at her sister, then blinked. "What a question! As a matter of fact, we *have* been known to discuss the war from America's viewpoint. Why?"

"Oh, nothing. I just—" Lindsay broke off thankfully when the Brandreths' housekeeper appeared in the doorway to inform her mistress that the man with the flowers had arrived.

Mouette also seemed happy for the distraction. "Wonderful! Let's go down and look, Lindsay. It's getting late, you know, and we mustn't linger here any longer. Why, the rout begins in just six hours!"

While dressing that evening, Lindsay racked her brain for a means of speaking to Ryan alone. Cassie was there every minute, helping her slide into an exquisite gown of white *gros de Naples* ornamented at the bottom of the skirt by a broad band of plaited white satin wreathed in pearls. The corsage was cut low to accentuate Lindsay's creamy breasts and made a deep V to bare half of her back. More plaited and pearled satin topped the gown's short puffed sleeves, and a wide satin sash was tied in a long bow at the back. Tonight, Lindsay wore a necklace of emeralds and topaz, as well as a slim band of emeralds that encircled her upper right arm. More emeralds shone in her ears, and Cassie was now carefully pinning pale yellow rosebuds into her mistress's luxuriant upswept curls.

"You smell quite wonderful, Miss Lindsay," Cassie observed. "Must be that scent we put in your bath."

Lindsay's gray eyes were distant. "I suppose so, Cassie."

"It'll all work out somehow, you know. I can feel it."

She was afraid to ask what the housekeeper meant.

Still, Cassie had seen her kissing Ryan. What else could she be referring to?

"How did you find your sister?" the older woman was asking now.

"I'm not quite certain. Rather troubled, I think." Lindsay looked straight at her now. "Don't you still have to help Mama dress? I would feel so much better if I could speak to Captain Coleraine before we leave for the rout."

Cassie sighed and pushed back her own damp curls. The night was warm. "Go ahead, then. I'll see that your parents are occupied." Watching Lindsay back away while smiling gratefully, she muttered, "I should have known that day he carried you off down Pettipauge's Main Street. If any other man had dared to do such a thing, you probably would have seen him dead."

"Ryan is a bit more difficult to get rid of," the girl said, laughing.

"Just the man for you, then, hmm?"

An incandescent smile lit Lindsay's countenance. "Yes, I think so!"

Alone, then, yet still basking in her young mistress's glow, Cassie considered the transformation Lindsay had undergone. Before Captain Coleraine burst into her life, she had been much too serious for a girl of her age, beauty, and promise. She had hidden from life then. How could Cassie disapprove of a man who had drawn Lindsay out into the sunlight and taught her to laugh and to enjoy being a woman?

Sitting near the cold fireplace in his room, Ryan smoked a thin cheroot and sipped a small portion of brandy. His feet, shod by Hoby, were propped on a footstool, and his dark blue frock coat was slung across the bottom of his bed.

"What would Beau Brummell say?" admonished a voice from the doorway.

Ryan paused in the act of rubbing his eyes and laughed

suddenly. "Ah, angel, you've appeared just in time. How lovely you look!" Standing up, he arched a brow at her. "Don't forget to close the door."

She did so, then crossed to pick up his coat and shake out imaginary wrinkles. "Tsk, tsk!"

"Thank God I'll soon be able to go back to my old ways." Ryan slipped his arms around her waist, and she touched her nose to his shirtfront and breathed in its fresh, masculine scent. His cravat was tied in an intricate, unique style, and snug pale yellow pantaloons skimmed his long, lean-muscled legs.

"Your old ways?" Lindsay whispered half playfully. "Never *quite*."

A slow smile spread over his face. "I imagine the new ways will be far more enjoyable."

They kissed lingeringly, then Lindsay pushed herself away with a small moan. "It's nearly time to leave for Mouette and Harry's. Cassie promised to keep Mama busy, but it's quite possible that Papa might appear. We should open the door and talk quietly—and sit in separate chairs!"

Ryan nodded and went over to reopen his bedroom door. "Sit down, then, and tell me about your afternoon."

She took a wing chair across from his and softly described all that had happened between herself and Mouette. Listening, Ryan sipped his brandy, then nodded grimly when she had finished. He handed the snifter to Lindsay and she took a swallow, made a face, then handed it back.

He smiled in spite of himself. "That reminds me of the morning you hoisted my bottle of Irish whiskey on board the *Chimera*. I thought you'd pass out right there."

"You underestimated me, sir!"

"Truer words were never spoken, brat." He chuckled softly. Reaching out, Ryan lifted her hand and kissed it with warm lips. "I never would have believed that morning what the future held for us. But that's another conversation, and for the moment we must concentrate on Harry Brandreth."

"Poor Mouette!" her sister whispered mournfully.

"Yes." He rubbed the edge of his jaw. "And I fear her lot will not improve anytime soon. Fortunately, she's a Raveneau and ought to land on her feet once she learns to navigate alone again."

"Does any of this surprise you?"

"No, but it's good to have our suspicions confirmed. I think that Mouette has her husband figured out pretty well, except for the source of his money. She suspects that he has a fatal weakness for gambling, and she understands about his basic insecurity and need for acceptance within the House. In spite of her own problems, she's gone to the heart of Harry's quite skillfully." His penetrating blue eyes held Lindsay's. "Angel, do you think that Mouette loves her husband?"

"I—I'm not certain. Why? Would that matter?"

"It could . . . but perhaps I'm better off not knowing. Will you help me tonight?"

"Have you a plan?" she asked excitedly.

"Something like that. I would like Harry to think that I am overimbibing. When you see me near him with a glass, make a point of scolding me so that he can hear you. All right?"

"Won't you tell me what you mean to do?"

"Shh." Hearing footsteps in the corridor, Ryan laid a dark golden forefinger over her mouth and she bit it lightly in rebellion. "Behave yourself. It's time for us to join our parents, dear sister. This promises to be a highly educational evening."

"I hope so!" she whispered, watching as Ryan paused to pick up quizzing glass and snuffbox from the table beside his bed. "I'm longing for a huge, exciting adventure that will unravel this mystery once and for all!"

After waiting in the crush of carriages outside the

Brandreth house in Belgrave Square, the Raveneaus alighted and stood in line once again to be received by their host and hostess.

Harry looked a trifle flushed, but Mouette, though pale, was beautifully garbed in champagne muslin and rubies. Her husband held up her hand to display a magnificent ruby and diamond ring.

"Aren't you going to show them my gift to you, darling?"

"Of course." Mouette glanced almost painfully at Lindsay, then smiled at her parents. "Isn't Harry generous?"

Raveneau looked dubious but managed a polite nod, while his wife murmured the appropriate compliments. They were starting toward the drawing room in order to allow others to enter the narrow entry hall when Mouette put her hand on Devon's arm.

"Mama, I remembered the disparaging things you said about routs earlier this month, so I decided to alter the usual formalities. I hired four musicians to play—violins, flute, and harpsichord. And the servants will be passing among the guests with trays of food, just little cakes and bits of fruit and cheese, but I thought it would help. There's champagne, too—more than enough!"

Devon gave her a warm smile and patted her cheek. "Very wise, sweetheart. I'm certain your party will be a great success—and will create a whole new fashion!" Lifting her nose, she added, "I can already smell the roses!"

"Champagne, you say?" Ryan repeated, peering through his quizzing glass. "Bravo, sister dear! I have a prodigious thirst tonight."

Watching Ryan strut after his family into the drawing room in search of refreshment, Harry smirked. "I hate to say it, Mouette, but your brother is a raving fool. Can't understand how your parents produced him!"

The next group was lingering in the doorway, turning over hats, canes, and reticules to the porter. Mouette's nerves were just frazzled enough for her to speak to

Harry without due consideration. "Nathan's not really such a fop. It's largely an act, you know."

"I don't take your meaning."

"Oh, never mind." She wanted to bite her tongue. "I can't really explain yet." Gratefully, Mouette stepped forward to greet the new surge of guests. "Good evening, Mrs. Drummond-Burrell, Lord Alvaney! How kind of you to come! And Lady Castlereagh, have you had news from your husband? How are the peace negotiations progressing in Ghent?"

Inside the spacious drawing room, Lindsay was looking around. With its soft gas lighting, mirrored pale lime walls, and ceiling decorated with a complex pattern of circles, the room looked elegant and inviting in spite of the fact that all of the furniture had been removed to accommodate the crush of guests. From an alcove, the lilting strains of a Bach concerto wafted through the air.

"Have a tart," Ryan offered, appropriating a pastry filled with strawberries from a passing tray. The sight of Lindsay eating it, and then licking berries and cream from her rosy lips, made him clench his teeth. "I wish you wouldn't *do* that." He groaned, reaching for two fluted glasses of champagne from another footman's tray. He handed one to Lindsay. "I may need this after all."

"Look, there's Lord Chadwick," she murmured near to Ryan's ear, admiring the black curls that brushed it. "Perhaps you ought to go and speak to him before more rumors begin to circulate about our unnatural relationship. . . ." Even as she spoke, Lindsay noticed Hester on the other side of the room watching them through narrowed emerald eyes.

"Hmm. I suppose you're right. No telling what he might say to me if I lead off with the proper inane remarks." Casually, his hand touched the inside of her upper arm in a caress that sent shivers of arousal down Lindsay's spine. "Don't forget to let Harry know that I'm drinking too much."

"I shan't." Watching Ryan cross the crowded room,

she could only hope that her expression didn't betray the decidedly unsisterly emotions she felt. With his crisp raven hair, broad shoulders, lean hips, rider's hard legs, and impeccably tailored clothes, Ryan Coleraine was easily the best-looking man among the several dozen present.

"I have a confession to make," a quiet voice announced from Lindsay's right side. "I think I'm falling in love with your brother."

"I beg your pardon?" Startled, she looked over to discover Lady Emma Thorneycroft, a sweet-faced girl of seventeen who was in the midst of her first Season. The two of them had chatted several times while riding in Hyde Park. Lindsay had always thought it rather odd that Lady Emma had singled her out to pursue as a friend, but now it was making more sense. "My brother?" she echoed in tones of surprise. "But isn't he rather old for you?"

"I think he is perfect." Lady Emma sighed, her doe eyes and toffee-hued curls shining softly in the gaslight.

Lindsay looked at Ryan, who was lounging against the chimneypiece while taking snuff with languid grace. "Well, I must agree that Nathan is very handsome, but—"

"I know what you are going to say. Mr. Raveneau seems a fop, but I truly believe that there is a great deal more to him than that. Sometimes I watch him when he isn't aware of my regard and I perceive that there is a very real man hiding under that façade." She sighed again.

"No doubt you imagine that you are just the woman to bring those qualities to the fore," Lindsay murmured.

"I think he only needs a woman whom he could trust." Lady Emma nodded. "Please, won't you present me to him?"

"Well, I—" At that moment, a hand touched her other elbow and she glanced over to find Lord Fanshawe smiling adoringly at her. Lindsay had never been so pleased to see him. "Dudley! How handsome you look tonight!'' She then looked back over at Emma, her eyes intensely apologetic. ''Would you be terribly offended if I excuse myself for just a few moments? There are pressing matters I had promised to discuss with Lord Fanshawe, but when we finish I shall certainly introduce you to my brother—if you still wish it.''

''Oh, of course!''

Lindsay reached for a glass of champagne and gave it to the girl, who politely wandered away, sipping the heady potion.

''My darling,'' Dudley whispered ardently in Lindsay's ear, ''how I've missed you!''

''Well, I've been rather preoccupied with some family matters.'' She inquired after his parents, then chatted on about this and that before glancing over at Lady Emma again. The girl's cheeks were pink from champagne now. ''Dudley, would you do me an enormous favor?''

''Name it, my goddess!''

Lindsay's eyes nearly crossed at that endearment. ''I have promised to help my sister with one or two things, but in the meantime I'm quite concerned about Lady Emma Thorneycroft. Do you know her?''

He shrugged. ''We've met. Quite a fetching girl.''

''The thing is, Lady Emma has told me that she has developed a *tendre* for Nathan. Surely you can realize that her hopes are—''

''*Doomed,*'' Dudley supplied sarcastically.

Forcing a smile, Lindsay managed to reply sweetly, ''That's a rather strong word, Dudley, but probably apt. In any case, I would be so grateful if you could distract her from Nathan for a while. I don't think they've even spoken before, so this is obviously a passing fancy on her part. She might forget all about it if—well, if another *man* paid her a bit of attention, however polite.''

Dudley straightened his shoulders and puffed out his chest, eyeing the lovely Lady Emma. ''Say no more, my dear. I take your meaning and I shall be pleased—and, indeed, proud!—to perform this favor for you!''

No sooner had he sauntered off than Lindsay saw Harry weaving his way through the crowd toward Ryan and Lord Chadwick. Looking in the other direction, she was relieved to discover that her own father had engaged Lady Chadwick in conversation. Lindsay started toward Ryan from another direction, and his eyes found hers over the heads of the other guests. He winked almost imperceptibly and took another glass of champagne from a passing servant.

Lindsay suppressed a smile that turned inward and spread a tingling warmth throughout her body. Their plan was already working! Together she and Ryan would succeed, and then they could come out in the open and announce their love to all of London!

CHAPTER
29

June 25–26, 1814

T HE REGENT'S ARRIVAL WAS ANNOUNCED IN STENTORIAN
tones by the majordomo, and the crowd parted to allow
him to enter. Accepting a glass of champagne, Prinny
feigned boredom as he looked around for someone to
talk to. The sight of lords Liverpool and Chadwick next
to the fireplace brought out his contrary streak. He'd
suffered enough humiliation at the hands of those damned
royal visitors. Tonight he would salve his ego by watching the cream of the Tory party bow to him.

"Ah, Sir Harry!" the Regent murmured, approaching
the cluster of men. "What's a Whig doing among this
stellar group of Tories?"

"How can our two parties hope to compromise if we
do not talk, Your Majesty?" Harry murmured, inclining
his head. "And I am the host, after all."

Beads of perspiration had already begun to form on
the Regent's brow, and his corseted stomach strained
the confines of his waistcoat. "True, true. I must say,
this is quite a rout! It's a great relief to see only English

faces and hear only English voices after being subjected to those foreigners, hmm?'' His eyes fell on Ryan then. "Gad, sir, my pardon! Of course I didn't mean you. I was referring to those barbarians from Europe who could scarcely make themselves understood! Thought they'd never go back to where they came from!''

"I must agree, Your Majesty, that it's a relief to have London quiet again,'' Lord Chadwick said.

Prinny glanced over, certain that a subtle insult was intended. Few things had galled him more about the presence of the czar and his entourage than the fact that everywhere they went, they had been cheered wildly by *his* countrymen! Pretending to take snuff, he returned his attention to Harry. "I must say, Brandreth, that I appreciate the fact you didn't ask Brummell tonight. Most respectful of you.''

Lindsay hovered outside the circle of men, wondering how she could interrupt about Ryan's drinking before Dudley appeared to reclaim her. How warm it was! She sipped her own champagne, uncertain whether she felt heady from its effects or the excitement of the evening.

Fortunately, at that moment, the Regent moved away to chat with a more adoring group of women. Lords Liverpool and Chadwick were greeting Colonel Dan McKinnon, a large, agile man with a genial personality and snapping black eyes. Seizing her chance, Lindsay slipped between Ryan and her brother-in-law.

"Wonderful rout, Harry!''

His sandy brows elevated slightly. "You know better than to heap compliments on me, Lindsay. I think you probably helped Mouette more than I did.''

"I'll wager you chose the champagne, though, hmm? It's really excellent.'' Her smile faded as she looked at Ryan. "Perhaps a bit *too* excellent. Nathan, I've seen you take at least six glasses. You mustn't have any more or you'll do something horrid that will embarrass our parents no end!''

Ryan eyed her through his quizzing glass, drawing in

his lower lip in a fair imitation of a fish. "Lud, sis, you're becoming a termagant!"

Hot blood rushed to Lindsay's cheeks as she remembered the times he had called her that much earlier in their relationship. It was just the response Ryan had hoped for and his eyes glinted for an instant. "If I am, my dear brother, it must be because your unsavory behavior demands it!" With that, Lindsay gave him a frosty look and swept away.

"Women can be such a bore," Ryan drawled to Harry, "especially when they're relations, what?"

"Indeed." Harry drained his own glass of champagne when he saw a footman approaching with another tray. "Will you join me?"

"Delighted, my dear fellow." He had surreptitiously poured the rest of his last glass into one of the tubs of roses and now placed the empty flute on the tray and took a full one. "I must say, this is such a pleasure—getting out and all that. My family's agreeable enough, as families go, but I do get bored listening to Lindsay rattle on about Lord Fanshawe while Father drones on about the war. Every time he receives a communication from America or Ghent, he takes it upon himself to explain every detail and possible ramification to me." Yawning, Ryan sipped more champagne, set his glass down, and took snuff with exquisite care. "Frightfully dull, don't you agree?"

Harry's sky-blue eyes sharpened. "Well, I would imagine so, but not having heard Raveneau's words myself, I can scarcely judge. I must confess that I have been known to find the politics of war rather intriguing. . . ."

"Egad! Let me relate Father's latest speech—for these scenes between us can hardly be called conversations—and you may judge for yourself!" Ryan looked for his glass again. "This very afternoon a letter arrived from the secretary of the navy—a lot of bosh about Commodore Barney and our flotilla of gunboats going to Chesapeake Bay to blast the British out of the water."

"Barney?" Harry repeated with studied unconcern. "Who is this chap?"

"Oh, some tremendous hero from the Revolutionary War. I gather he was captured several times by your side and eventually imprisoned here in London. He escaped and lived here for a time before finding his way back to Philadelphia. What followed is a very long story, but suffice it to say that Barney was able to rebound by capturing a British sloop-of-war called the *General Monk*."

"Ah, yes, I remember," Harry muttered as if to himself. "He sailed her to France and received a kiss from Marie Antoinette. And, later, didn't your Barney serve as a commodore for the Frenchies during their war with us?"

"I, er, believe so," Ryan replied with the dimmest expression he could muster. In truth, he was a friend and admirer of the feisty commodore. "I seem to remember my father saying something about Barney feeling that the American navy slighted him, and so when hostilities commenced between our two countries, he took command of a privateer. During one four-month voyage, however, he took no less than eighteen prizes and soon had the military powers that be begging him to return."

"Hmm!" Thoughtfully, Harry mused, "And now, puffed up with his own consequence in that way that is so uniquely American, the old hawk is circling over Chesapeake Bay? Well, it's a rather interesting story, but it's nothing to me. After all, our own Admiral Cockburn has been making a fine showing, what? Certainly it's frustrating for the House of Commons to languish across the ocean, but someone has to look after the day-to-day business of England. We can only trust our military to do their best." He glanced at Ryan, who had once again turned his champagne into the roses and now pretended to drain the glass. "Well, in any event, it's all neither here nor there, hmm? The peace commission in Ghent may have already solved the whole bloody mess!''

"Absolutely, Harry, old boy. Politics bore me to tears. Much rather get into a good game of faro! Why don't you and I slip away to White's after a bit?''

Brandreth ran a hand through his blond curls. "Nothing I'd like better, Nathan, but your elder sister would have my head if I were to desert our first party of the Season! Which reminds me, I've been neglecting my duties as host. Must circulate, you know!''

An expression of grim satisfaction crossed Ryan's face for the barest instant as he watched Harry go in search of the Earl of Chadwick. Then, feeling someone watching him, he let his eyelids drop lazily.

"Having fun, darling?" Hester whispered next to his shoulder.

"You know me. I thrive on gatherings like this," he replied sardonically. "How have you been?"

"As well as could be expected since we last met at Grimley Court. How are *you*—and your *sister*?"

"Never better." Distractedly, Ryan watched Harry's golden head above the crowd. He was moving in the direction of Lord Chadwick. Wondering how he himself could escape from Hester and eavesdrop on the two men's conversation, Ryan was suffused with relief when he glimpsed a cluster of upswept strawberry-blond curls studded with yellow rosebuds just a few paces behind Harry. Thank God for Lindsay! He saw then that she was gathering little cakes and whole strawberries from a tray, pretending to be interested only in the food as she continued to follow Harry. Soon both of them were out of sight behind a wall with shell carvings that led to the alcove where the musicians were now playing Vivaldi's Concerto in B Minor.

"I had a letter from your brother," Hester was saying.

"Indeed? I hope he's well" came Ryan's absent reply.

"Actually, he's not, I'm afraid. In fact, I'd like to see you alone to discuss this matter. Are you free tomorrow?"

"It's unlikely, Hester. Look, you know as well as I that, for all intents and purposes, I renounced my family ties when I left for America. Blake seemed perfectly happy to see me go then, and I can't imagine what we would have to say to each other now."

"Ryan," she murmured, surprised by his sharp response, "it *was* your idea. Blake would have worked something out with you—"

"It was too late then, and it's too late now. I have a new life—two, in fact!" His laughter was edged with cynicism. "Leave it alone. You ought to be concentrating on your own affairs. How is everything between you and Francis?"

"Beastly." Hester gazed into her champagne, her thick lashes lowered, then took a long sip. "He's rarely home— always off at the House or White's or Watier's . . . doing God knows what. His increasing neglect only makes me miss you more." Glancing up in the hope of eliciting a sympathetic, caring response from him, she saw that Ryan's eyes were fixed on Lindsay Raveneau. The girl was weaving her way through the crowd in their direction. "Well, at least one of us isn't lonely these days!"

He turned an intent blue gaze down on her face. "Have you no idea what Francis is doing or what he might be involved in?"

Part of her longed to confide in him, hoping that her secrets might draw Ryan closer, but she sensed that it was far too late for her, too. Why should she help him? Whatever he was seeking involved Lindsay, too, and Hester couldn't bear to aid their cause. "No." She dragged her eyes away from him. "No idea."

Lindsay squeezed her slender body between the backs of an earl and a marquess to stand before them. "Good evening, Lady Chadwick. I hope you're enjoying yourself."

"I can't recall a more wonderful experience," Hester retorted coolly. "And you, Miss Raveneau?"

"Actually, I don't feel quite the thing." She widened

her eyes slightly at Ryan. "Dearest brother, I believe you have my medicine? I ought to take a dose to combat this queasiness."

"Ah, yes, of course!" The picture of brotherly concern, he felt her brow and frowned. "Hmm. Come with me, Lindsay. I left your medicine in the library."

After bidding the sulky Hester a good evening, Ryan put an arm around Lindsay's slim shoulders and guided her through the crush. They escaped into the entry hall, then ducked into a narrow anteroom.

"I heard every word Harry and Lord Chadwick exchanged!" she declared excitedly. "Oh, Ryan, if we take care not to make a wrong step, we might be able to untangle the entire coil this very night!"

"All right." He strove to keep his voice low and to think calmly. "Just tell me what you heard, Lindsay."

"Harry told Chadwick that he has something of great import to tell him. The earl suggested they meet in the arbor at the Flora Tea Gardens at half past midnight! Oh, Ryan, we'll have proof at last and this charade can be ended once and for all!"

"Shh." His eyes gleamed in the shadows as he touched a finger to her mouth. Lindsay kissed it sensually. "One step at a time, angel. Where is this place?"

"Off Oxford Street above Hyde Park. Opposite Lancaster Gate, as I recall. Mama, Mouette, and I went to a lovely concert there one Tuesday night when you men were off at White's. Don't worry, I'll show you the way."

"You'll do nothing of the sort," Ryan whispered harshly. "You'll go home to bed like a good girl."

"I beg your pardon, sir! I am going with you."

"Absolutely not. I forbid it."

"This dictatorial behavior is so typical of your sex! You may *forbid* me until you're blue in the face, but the fact remains that I am a grown woman and you have no authority over my actions."

He narrowed eyes that were the color of a stormy

ocean at midnight. "Look here, Lindsay, this may very
well turn dangerous. What if we were caught? Those
two could be armed, and I suspect that they might be
quite ruthless in their efforts to ensure our silence. I
love you too much to subject you to such peril."

Realizing that Ryan would never agree, Lindsay pretended to see reason. "Well, perhaps I am behaving
rashly. I would rather go with you, but if I can't, I'll
settle for a kiss." She backed into a dark corner, pulling
him with her.

This is too easy, he thought. The deep shadows prevented him from seeing her eyes, which he had learned
to read quite well. "Why don't I trust you?"

"I'm sure I can't imagine." Lindsay slid her hands
inside his frock coat and caressed the hard contours of
his sides and chest. "I think perhaps you have a suspicious mind. That's a troublesome quality in a husband
. . . but you have other, more *positive* attributes that
should compensate."

"You're a minx," he muttered.

"Not a brat?"

"That as well . . ." His voice trailed off as she stood
on tiptoe and sighed against his cheek.

This woman had the most sensual, tantalizing, sumptuous mouth he had ever kissed, bar none. When she
nibbled gently at his lower lip, then touched the tip of
her tongue to his teeth, Ryan groaned and caught her up
in his arms. Kissing Lindsay was better than a banquet
in Paris and a case of champagne. He'd never tasted
anything more delicious.

Her hands were wandering over Ryan's wide, strong
back, fueling his passion. After long minutes of raven-
ous kissing, Lindsay dropped her head back and his
mouth blazed a path from her throat to her breasts. She
slid one slim hand downward to touch the hard ridge in
his snug trousers.

"What the hell are you doing?" He groaned.

"Touching you." Her smoky eyes held his in the shadows. "I was curious."

"*Curious?* Jesus, I must be as crazy as you are! What are we *doing*?"

"Don't you know?" A subtle purr underlied her whisper.

"Stop it! There are dozens, probably *hundreds* of people just across the hall—including your parents! God knows I really must be in love because I never mislaid my wits this way in the past. We've got to compose ourselves and return to that gathering before someone comes in search of us." Grasping her arm, Ryan drew Lindsay back into the half light and scrutinized her appearance. Tanned fingers readjusted a dangling rosebud and pulled up the bodice of her gown so that less décolletage was visible. "Try not to look so . . . aroused."

Lindsay nearly laughed aloud and stared pointedly at the hard proof of his own arousal. "Physician, heal thyself!" she teased.

"Why don't you take a vow of silence and go back to the drawing room?" he ground out in menacing tones. "I'll follow in a moment."

She gave him one last provocative smile from the doorway, then slipped out of the room. Sighing with relief, Lindsay said a tiny prayer that Ryan had been so successfully distracted that he'd forgotten all about her determination to accompany him to the Flora Tea Gardens.

It was a little past midnight when Ryan saddled his black stallion, Brady. Horse and master always looked splendid together, but tonight the effect was even more striking, for Ryan was clad all in black and his hair gleamed like a raven's wing in the moonlight.

Walking Brady out of the stables, Coleraine glanced up at Lindsay's window and sighed. There was still a candle lit, and he could see a shadow moving behind the curtains. Under his breath he muttered, "For God's sake, go to sleep, Lindsay."

Hiding in a clump of hawthorn bushes, Lindsay watched Brady and Ryan leave the stableyard, then craned her own neck up to look at the illuminated window. "Thank you, Cassie," she said, grinning. Standing up, Lindsay hitched up the roomy breeches she'd been forced to filch from Harvey Jenkins's chest, then started off at a run. Fortunately, since she was on foot, she could take a more direct route to the tea gardens. An alleyway behind the Raveneau house led directly to Providence Court, which opened onto North Audley Street. From there it took less than a minute to reach Oxford Street. Keeping to the shadows, Lindsay easily covered the distance to Hyde Park's Lancaster Gate, reveling in the night's excitement and the liberating sensation of running in breeches.

On the edge of the Flora Tea Gardens, she paused to catch her breath. Ryan would be along soon, so there wasn't a moment to spare. There were still a few people wandering over the lawns and through the sylvan glades surrounding the main buildings of the tea gardens, but for the most part the place was deserted.

It was easy enough to locate the huge arbor, its arching trellises covered with climbing roses, honeysuckle, and wisteria all in full bloom. Their scents filled the balmy June air. Lindsay chose a dense, high boxwood hedge next to the arbor and crouched behind it, waiting.

Meanwhile, Ryan was tethering Brady amidst a grove of trees behind the tavern. He then tucked a pistol into his breeches and set off, his fine leather boots nearly soundless as he crossed the green. Spying a young couple approaching from the trees ahead, he inquired where the arbor was and they pointed the way for him. It was still early when Ryan reached the leafy, fragrant bower and took up a position behind the vine-covered trellises that crisscrossed the back of the arbor.

All his instincts told him he was not alone, yet his

eyes and ears could not confirm his suspicions. It was time for Harry and Lord Chadwick to arrive, so Ryan couldn't afford even to move, let alone investigate.

Harry emerged from the shadows first, strolling leisurely toward the arbor. He looked around, then withdrew a flask from his breast pocket and drank deeply. A cloud passed over the moon just as the Earl of Chadwick came into view.

"Fancy meeting you here." Harry chuckled softly.

"Spare me your feeble attempts at wit and get on with it," Chadwick hissed. Drawing his cloak closer about his slight form, he looked left and right from under a beaver hat.

"I'll be happy to get on with it as soon as you tell me what you intend to pay me."

"That depends on the worth of your information, Brandreth."

"I've told you that I won't settle for a shilling less than two hundred pounds."

"I have it, but I'm not turning it over to you until I hear what you have to say. To be honest, I've been waiting for a communication from Admiral Cockburn regarding the information you've sold me so far. Because of the distance and time involved, I really have no idea whether the information you've imparted thus far has been of any value or not!" Chadwick agitatedly took snuff. "Now that I know your father-in-law, I find myself wondering more and more whether he would confide all of these so-called secrets to a bumbling imbecile like you!"

Harry went red in the moonlight. "Are you insulting me, Chadwick?"

"Don't be an ass, Brandreth. Next you'll be calling me out. What a joke! Just tell me what you feel is worth two hundred pounds and we'll go from there."

Drawing himself up, Harry intoned, "I have very fresh news regarding the American campaign in the Chesapeake Bay. They think they have a 'secret weapon' that could win the war for them! Have you heard of a Commodore Joshua Barney?''

Icy calm with rage, Coleraine stepped around the corner of the arbor, his pistol pointed at the two conspirators. "I think you've said *more* than enough, Harry. I hope you two won't mind cutting this little meeting short and coming back to Grosvenor Square with me for an interview with Captain Raveneau?"

Knowing the delayed firing time and inaccuracy of the pistol, Chadwick felt perfectly safe in drawing out the knife he held under his cloak. He lunged straight at Ryan, surprising the two other men with his agility and ruthless strength.

"Let it go," he snarled, pressing the blade to Ryan's corded neck. "I said, Drop the pistol! I can assure you, old man, that I have no qualms whatsoever about killing you outright."

"That's doubtless your intention, anyway," Ryan replied in deadly tones.

At that moment, a slim, masked figure emerged from the other side of the arbor. The young man's hair was concealed by a hat pulled low over his ears and he was clad, like Ryan, all in black. In his hands, he held a large pistol.

"Halt!" the figure commanded in rather unconvincing bass tones. "Release that man or I shall shoot!"

CHAPTER
30

June 26, 1814

Ryan, HIS HEAD FORCED BACK AT AN AWKWARD ANGLE while the sharp blade of a knife pressed against his throat, hardly knew whether to laugh or cry at the sight of Lindsay brandishing a pistol.

"And who might you be?" Lord Chadwick sneered. "Raveneau's bodyguard?"

"Never mind that," Lindsay retorted gruffly. "I may not be very strong physically, but I can assure you that I am highly skilled with a pistol. If you value your life, unhand Mr. Raveneau!"

Harry had been sidling toward her as she spoke and now Lindsay couldn't decide what to do. If she turned the pistol on him, or even went so far as to wound him, Chadwick might well go ahead and kill Ryan, then take his chances with her.

"Halt, sir!" she thundered at Harry.

He laughed softly. "I have an idea that this mysterious masked stranger just might be my adorable sister-in-law. You wouldn't shoot *me*, would you, Lindsay? Mouette would never forgive you!"

"I'm warning you . . ." Lindsay pulled the hammer back with her thumb. "And as for your wife, she would probably thank me!"

"Harsh words, my little hellion. I find such devotion to your brother quite touching. One might also suspect that your relationship ran deeper! I have heard *rumors* . . ."

Ryan, meanwhile, was burning with rage and frustration. He couldn't even speak without risking the blade, and it would certainly do Lindsay no good if he were dead. His entire body was tensed as he watched Harry taunt her, edging closer, and then he held his breath when Lindsay put a finger over the trigger.

"I'll shoot you, Harry," she warned with deadly calm. "I won't aim to kill, but one never can be quite sure with these pistols, can one?"

Brandreth cocked his handsome blond head at her, measuring her, then smiled as he made his decision. "You're feisty for a female, m'dear, but you don't have it in you." Jauntily, he strolled toward her, then froze as Lindsay pulled back on the trigger. The pistol clicked but didn't fire. Harry's eyes narrowed. "Little witch!" he hissed.

She stared at the pistol in horror and heard her heart pounding in her ears. Harry lunged at her, wrenched the weapon away, then angrily struck her over the head with it. Stars flashed before her eyes as she sank to the ground.

"Shall I kill her?" he asked Chadwick.

"Don't be a fool," the older man returned coldly. "All we need to do is to incapacitate the pair of them, then we'll be safely away before they awake."

Although he longed to take the risk and fight back, Ryan knew that the odds were stacked too heavily against him. When Harry approached, brandishing the pistol, he recognized the contempt in Ryan's midnight-blue eyes.

"You're a swine, Brandreth," he dared to whisper, his nostrils flaring.

"And you are a fool, Raveneau." With that, Harry brought the butt of the pistol down over his head and Ryan crumpled to the ground.

Although stunned, he was not unconscious. Lying limp, he prayed that they wouldn't decide to slit his throat after all. Instead, he heard Chadwick mutter, "Well, this has turned into a right mess, and we have troubles enough without risking being arrested for murder. Although, if I could be certain that no one else knew about us, I wouldn't hesitate to kill these two. . . ."

"What do you intend to do, then?"

"We'll go away—immediately. I had planned to rendezvous at sea with my intermediary, a courier who will be en route to America. As much as it pains me, I suppose I must allow you to accompany me, if only to keep you from telling what you know to all of London."

"My marriage is finished," Harry moaned. "The Raveneaus will see me dead if I stay here."

"Quite. For myself, this sort of thing could get very messy. It might spell the end of my career in the House if a controversy erupts now. After the war's been won and I have proved a credit to our cause because of my spying activities, it would be different. Once your meddling in-laws leave town, I could return and plead my case without their arguments. The solution seems to lie in dropping out of sight for a time. There's a large debt I've put off collecting. The debtor himself lives not far from our destination at sea. No doubt he'd hide us until the Raveneau family returns to America."

"There's nothing else to be done, then, is there?"

"Nothing except elude the Raveneaus. You realize that if they capture us, they could take us back to America to stand trial as spies?" Chadwick stared down at Ryan's prone body. "Or they might save themselves the trouble and simply do away with us. I can't imagine that your father-in-law will be pleased to learn of your treachery, Brandreth.''

"Well, then, let's be off before these two awaken. I only wish we had some rope with which to tie them up!''

"The less evidence they have against us, the better. Since Nathan Raveneau doesn't have any inkling of our plans, he'll never find us. Let's be away now.''

His voice fading into the distance, Harry replied, "Besides, Nathan's too stupid to outmaneuver us. I wouldn't be surprised if that blow to the head destroyed whatever intelligence he had to begin with.''

Listening to the sound of their footsteps die away, Ryan clenched his teeth as raw fury coursed through his body. Somehow he remained motionless on the ground, counting off the minutes, then slowly raised his head and looked around. In the distance there was only blackness; not even a shadow could be seen. Across the arbor, Lindsay had begun to moan softly. Lithely, Ryan got to his feet and crossed to her side.

"Angel, can you hear me? Lindsay?'' Cradling her head against his thigh, he looked for blood in her hair and was relieved to see that the blow Harry had dealt hadn't been as serious as he'd feared.

"Ryan?'' she murmured groggily.

"I'm right here, sweetheart, and you're safe. Can you open your eyes?''

Her sooty lashes fluttered once, then lifted to reveal focused gray eyes. Lindsay even managed a tremulous smile. "Are you terribly angry with me?''

"Are you joking? I'm far too relieved—and worried—to be angry. Thank God you're all right. When I saw Harry strike you with that pistol butt, I wanted to kill him— and I may yet," Ryan told her grimly. "How do you feel, angel?''

"My head hurts and I'm a bit dizzy, but otherwise I'm all right." She basked for a moment in his intensely concerned and loving gaze, then murmured impishly,

"I'll wager that you yell at me once you're certain I'm not injured."

"Nonsense," Ryan returned gently, kissing her brow. His blue eyes stared distractedly into the darkness. "My only concern is getting you home—and then figuring out how to track down those two scoundrels. If Brandreth and Chadwick imagine that they can escape so easily, they're in for a tremendous surprise."

"I cannot believe that you followed me after I specifically ordered you not to!" Ryan shouted at Lindsay from across her bedroom.

Propped against thick pillows, her burnished curls cascading over her shoulders, she smiled. "I knew that you would scold me." Pretending to examine a fingernail, she added, "Besides, I didn't follow you. I took an entirely different route and arrived before you did."

"That's not the issue!" he raged, approaching the bed.

"What is the issue?" Lindsay inquired sweetly.

"The issue is that I cannot go through the rest of our lives worrying that you will be forever disobeying me—"

"Disobeying?" she repeated in mocking tones. "Do you intend to be my master?"

"No, of course not, but—"

"If that is the arrangement you have in mind, Captain Coleraine, you may as well search out a different wife because I happen to believe that my intelligence and opinions are a match for any *man's*."

"I am well aware of that, Lindsay. It's just that—"

"I will not be bullied by you or anyone else!"

Exasperated, yet half amused and quite captivated, Ryan clamped a dark hand over her mouth. "My darling brat, will you do me the courtesy of allowing me to speak?"

"Mmph!" Her delicate brows flew upward.

"Thank you very much." Keeping the hand in place,

he narrowed his eyes at her, but they sparkled with humor. "I am simply concerned that you might get yourself killed by rushing off wildly into dangerous situations after I have warned you not to. I worry that I will spend the next, uh—"

"Sheventy yearsh," Lindsay supplied in muffled tones.

"Seventy years looking over my shoulder in fear that you are about to leap out of the shadows brandishing a pistol!" Removing his hand, Ryan bent to kiss her tenderly. "Angel, you could have been killed tonight."

"So could you," she whispered mutinously.

He arched a black brow, hoping to silence her. "It wasn't the place for a female, though, especially one masquerading as a boy! Those men were playing by a deadly set of rules."

"But, Ryan—" Although her head had begun to throb, she would never have admitted it to him. "If my pistol hadn't jammed, this would have all turned out very differently. I would have wounded Harry and Lord Chadwick would have been forced to release you. It wasn't my fault that the silly thing wouldn't fire! What if I'd saved the entire situation? I'll wager you would be showering me with kisses of gratitude right now rather than scolding me!"

"I have never doubted your intentions, Lindsay, but even if all had gone perfectly and we had captured those men due to your courage, I would still be upset with you for taking such a risk. You must promise me that you won't do anything so foolish again."

"No."

He reared back in surprise, staring, and raked a hand through his ebony hair. "Pardon me?" The words were barely audible.

"I will not promise any such thing. I couldn't! If, at some point in the future, I believed that you were in danger and I could help, I would have to break my word. I'm sorry, Ryan, but if you have your heart set on an obedient wife, you'll have to look elsewhere."

Shaking his head, he closed his eyes and made a sound that mingled laughter with a sigh. "I should have known, that night on the wharf in Pettipauge, when you appeared in the thick of battle to throw buckets of water on that fire . . ."

Lindsay's heart went out to him. She knew he didn't mean to be a dictatorial male, that he was only concerned for her safety, but there were simply certain matters about which she could not compromise. Still . . . "Ryan?"

Warily, he opened one blue eye. "Yes, dearest brat?"

"I will promise not to rush into anything without considering all sides of the situation—including your feelings and the possible danger."

"That sounds ominously conditional, but I suppose I should be happy for what I can get, hmm?"

She traced the line of his cheekbone and jaw with slim fingers. "You've known from the first day we met that I'm unmanageable. At least I haven't surprised you after it was too late."

"You surprise me constantly, but I know what you mean." Tenderly, he bent to kiss her, his hands framing her face. "And, in all honesty, I must admit that that's half your charm. Every day with you is a challenge; I never know what to expect!"

"I love you so very much, Ryan." Tears gleamed in her gray eyes.

"And I love you, angel." He kissed her again, tasting, then deepened the kiss as she began to respond. Ryan had shed his coat when they came home and now Lindsay's hands caressed his back and shoulders through the thin fabric of his shirt. Her tempting breasts pressed against him as he leaned nearer, but then suddenly he sat up. "How do you do it? You're the first woman I've ever known who could cause me to completely abandon reason!"

"I didn't do a thing!" she cried defensively. "*You* kissed *me*!"

"Well, I shouldn't have." Standing, he rubbed his eyes and tried not to smile. "Your parents will be home at any moment, and the last thing I need tonight is your father challenging me to a duel! In the meantime, we—I mean, I—have to figure out what to do about Brandreth and Chadwick."

"What can we do?"

Glancing over at her widened eyes, Ryan ignored Lindsay's reference. "Well, first of all, I shall have to talk to your father and fill him in on all of this now that I have confirmed my suspicions. Obviously, he can't go to Lord Liverpool since there is a possibility, however minute, that the prime minister was aware of this pay-off arrangement. And it will be hard to prove anything without confessions from the two perpetrators, but obviously someone must be alerted in case—"

A chill ran down Lindsay's spine. "In case what?"

"In case something happens to me after I go in search of Harry and Chadwick."

"Ryan, what do you intend to do?" she cried apprehensively. "We don't even know where they've gone!"

"I heard them say a few things after they thought I'd been knocked unconscious," he replied, pacing across the bedroom. "They're going to rendezvous with a courier at sea, near the home of someone who is indebted to Chadwick and will hide them if necessary. I simply have to find out who this person is and then give chase."

"Next you'll tell me that you're going to see Hester!"

Ryan stopped to look at Lindsay over one shoulder while the corners of his mouth quirked ironically. "Exactly."

"What do you want from me?" Hester asked agitatedly. She paused at the window of the library in the huge Chadwick mansion overlooking Green Park and sighed. "Really, Ryan, it is the outside of enough for you to burst in here at this hour of the night and tell me this wild tale—"

"It's quite true, I assure you. As for bursting in, I waited for *you*, Hester. Where've you been? With Byron? That's the current rumor, you know."

"My private life is none of your affair anymore, my—I mean, Ryan. You have made it quite clear that you want nothing to do with me. And, under the circumstances, I don't see why I should even consider helping you trap my own husband."

"Perhaps because, in spite of your transgressions, you are a person of character." Quietly, he crossed the rich Turkish carpet and put a hand on her shoulder. "I know you, inside and out, and I've loved you. Circumstances may have forced you to compromise your basic principles on occasion, but underneath you haven't changed. You couldn't live with yourself if you allowed Francis to get away with this, Hester."

"Francis is my husband!" she exclaimed, spinning around to face him. "I shall share, to some extent, whatever fate befalls him!"

"That fate is inevitable, though. Don't you see? He may run away and try to hide, but the eventual outcome will be the same. And Francis has ruined himself. It's neither your fault nor mine. The blame belongs to him."

Hester's senses swam under the compelling spell of Ryan's nearness. She wished that they could simply sweep away the last nine years and begin again . . . or even go back in time for one brief interlude. "Oh, Ryan," she breathed, afraid to look at him, "how could I have let you leave me? If only I had stood up to my father and Francis and—"

For a moment, he was reminded of Lindsay, who vowed never to be bullied by anyone, and a smile warmed his heart. Then Hester's unfinished sentence sank in. "And *who else*?"

Hester felt weak in the knees and leaned against him. Ryan held her for a moment, as if to bolster her courage, then guided her over to a silk-upholstered sofa. She accepted the glass of sherry he poured for her and drank it gratefully. "I really mustn't tell you. It's such a coil. . . ."

"That's why you *must* tell me. Hester, we can't undo the past, but we do have control over the present. You must trust me."

She turned wet emerald-green eyes up to him and nearly wept at the sight of his beloved face so near—yet so unattainable. "I've made such a lot of mistakes, Ryan."

"As have I, my lady," he said matter-of-factly. "And yet I've learned that it's never too late to begin anew. This is your chance."

When his firm, golden-brown hand covered hers, Hester felt a rush of strength. "Francis conspired with your brother to see to it that you left England," Hester whispered. "You see, Francis learned that Blake was illegitimate. He shouldn't have succeeded to the title at all. By rights, you are the Marquess of Clifden. Blake's been a pretender all these years."

Ryan's dark blue eyes widened, then narrowed, and he sank back against the sofa. "Hmm. Well, that's interesting, but what does it have to do with this current situation?"

"Don't you *care*? All these years, that stunning Irish castle and its lands could have been yours. Blake's known since your father's last illness that he was not the legitimate heir, yet he kept it from you!"

Thoughtfully, he rubbed one side of his mouth. "Well, Blake had counted on that all his life. He married and had children believing that the title would pass to him, and since I was merely the second son, I didn't bother with a family. Of course, I would have married *you*, Hester, particularly if I believed I had so much to offer, but I think now that our lives worked out for the best."

"How can you say that?" Her sable hair gleamed under the soft gas-lit chandelier as she reached out to touch his face. "And how can you be so nonchalant about Blake's deception? If not for him, you would never have left Britain! You would have assumed the title of Marquess of Clifden and moved into the castle! Think of what your brother has done to your life!"

"I am, and that's why I'm not angry. Of course, a part of me resents his deception, but I don't regret one minute of the last nine years, Hester. This may sound trite, but my new life in America made a man of me." Ryan gently pried her hand from his face and held it briefly before returning it to her lap. "Right now I'm more interested in Blake's connection to your husband and Harry."

Sighing, she looked away. "I'm sure, given the debt that Blake owes Francis for forcing our wedding and thereby disposing of you, that my husband was referring to Blake as the person who owed him a favor."

Ryan bit his lip, considering. "That sounds logical. Clifden Castle would be an ideal place to disappear to for a few months. But I have to be more certain before I sail to Ireland! Why would this fellow spy choose so remote a place to rendezvous?"

"Do you know, a great deal is beginning to make sense to me now," Hester mused. "Francis has been going off for a fortnight or more at a time during the last few years. He owns a handful of ships docked at Falmouth and, two summers ago, purchased one that sails out of Galway Bay. He's told me that his journeys have been to take care of business regarding that ship, but that explanation never sounded quite plausible. Letters arrived from time to time from Galway, and when I asked about them, he said that they were from the ship's captain—and yet I never saw them afterward in his desk. I didn't think much about it at the time, but now . . ."

Ryan stood up. "He's been cautious, selling secrets to a spy who sails from Ireland. Little chance of the man turning up here to expose him, hmm?"

She followed him to the door. "Ryan, there's something else I must tell you if you intend to go to Ireland. Blake has been very ill. He wrote me that he thinks he may be dying—and his wife has gone off to France with their children, both of whom grew up to be quite contemptible. He's all alone, and I would say that it's impossible to predict what Blake will do if Francis calls in his markers. . . ."

PART
FIVE

And Earth, Air and Light
And the Spirit of Might
Which drives round the stars in their
    fiery flight;
And Love, Thought, and Breath,
The powers that quell Death,
Wherever we soar shall assemble
    beneath!

—PERCY BYSSHE SHELLEY (1792–1822)

CHAPTER
31

June 26–28, 1814

"Hélas!" RAVENEAU EXCLAIMED, HIS GRAY EYES stormy, "why didn't you come to me with this from the first?"

Ryan glanced across the dining-room table at Lindsay who, like her parents, wore bedclothes and a dressing gown, then shrugged. "I suppose if I truly were Nathan Raveneau, I might've done. As it was, I didn't feel I had the right to accuse a member of your family without proof."

At that moment, Cassie appeared with a tray filled with steaming cups of tea, plus a decanter of brandy and four small snifters. Setting it down before Raveneau, she quickly made her exit. Although it was nearly three in the morning, all four opted for brandy and took a first sip in unison.

Devon spoke next. "Weren't you aware that our affection for Harry didn't run deep?" More than anything else, it hurt her to see her husband excluded from the intrigue surrounding this situation. It was just what André would have enjoyed at this point in his life.

"How could I know?" Ryan replied earnestly. "He is married to your daughter! There were her feelings to consider, too, and the effect all of this would have on her life and those of your grandsons. If I had accused Harry and then been wrong, imagine the consequences!"

Raveneau leaned back in his chair, brows knit, and sipped his brandy. A meaningful glance from Devon told him that he was merely resenting his exclusion from the adventure. "All right, then, *mon ami*," he murmured. "I understand. If it had been anyone else, you would have told me?"

"Absolutely!" Ryan declared with conviction.

"So you want to go after Harry and Lord Chadwick? Do you really believe they are bound for Ireland?"

"Lady Chadwick seems to think so, and I must believe that since we have no other clues. From what she's told me, it sounds as if they'll rendezvous with the courier in Galway Bay, then, if I haven't caught up with them by then, they'll go to a man living nearby who owes Chadwick a large favor. Chadwick hopes that this person will provide refuge until the scandal here subsides and we have returned to America." Ryan paused for a sip of brandy. "Of course, I hope to apprehend them before they leave Falmouth, but it may be necessary to sail to Ireland. Will you allow me to take *La Mouette*, sir?"

"Of course. Ideally, I'd like to accompany you, but I realize that one of us should stay here in case something else crops up that must be dealt with. It's plain that you're the person to go since you are familiar with Ireland."

"As a matter of fact, I grew up near Galway," Ryan remarked casually.

Devon was looking thoughtful. "Are you certain that Lady Chadwick can be trusted? It seems to me that she might wish to mislead you in order to protect her husband."

Feeling Lindsay's gaze on him, Ryan cleared his throat.

"I think not. Let us say that Lady Chadwick has kept certain secrets for too long and, like Mouette, has been dissatisfied with her marriage. I'm confident that she was honest with me."

"I take it that you are unwilling to share these secrets," Raveneau surmised.

"Not because I don't trust all of you but because this information is . . . confidential. Whatever honor I have left requires that I respect the privacy of the parties involved until this situation is resolved. You understand?"

"Of course we do," Devon said firmly. "And we also have a high opinion of your honor and your character, Ryan! You know that both André and I have come to care for you as a son."

A smile flickered at the corners of his handsome mouth. "That's good to know." Reaching out, he caught Lindsay's hand in his own. "You see, there is something I would like to ask the two of you before I leave for Ireland."

André's brows went up. "Yes?"

"I find that I am in love with your daughter. Would you do me the honor of granting me her hand in marriage?"

"Mon Dieu!" Raveneau shouted. "I knew it! I begin to think that you have a very devious character, monsieur! First you keep me in the dark about the nefarious conduct of my son-in-law, and then you court my other daughter while living in my own house! I sensed that you had designs on Lindsay, but my dear wife assured me that I was imagining things! Why is it that no one will tell me the truth?"

"There was no point, sir, until we could be sure that my masquerade as Nathan Raveneau might be coming to an end," Ryan replied frankly. "And you needn't worry that I have been compromising Lindsay's honor under your roof. Your highly suspicious wife has been keeping a close eye on us."

Raveneau glared at her accusingly. "You knew!"

"Not exactly, sweetheart," she said soothingly. "I knew that there was romance in the air, but not marriage. Isn't it exciting?" Devon was quick to divert him. "Surely you couldn't wish for a finer husband for your daughter! He's just like you, after all!" Her blue eyes sparkled teasingly.

"Hmm." André drained his glass of brandy and poured himself a bit more. "I suppose that's true. *Eh bien,* I will agree to this marriage on one condition."

A euphoric Lindsay cried, "Name it, Papa!"

"You all must promise never to keep anything from me again!"

Ryan reached over to shake the hand of his mentor and future father-in-law. "You have our word on it, sir."

Lindsay, clad in a muslin nightgown and matching peach-tinted robe, sprang out of her chair and rushed to hug each of her parents. Then she went over and sat right down on Ryan's lap. Her left hand ruffled his glossy hair, then curved around his broad shoulder, while her right caressed his cheek as she kissed him. "It will be a perfect marriage!" she told her parents. "We're both unmanageable, just like the two of you!"

Daybreak had not yet begun to lighten the eastern sky when Harvey Jenkins appeared in his master's rooms. Ryan was packing fresh shirts, breeches, and underclothes into supple saddlebags along with a flask of brandy, his shaving gear, and a pistol.

Hearing the familiar footsteps of his manservant, Coleraine turned and raised a finger to his mouth. Harvey closed the door.

"You aren't thinking of going without me, sir?" he accused in injured tones.

"I'm afraid so, Harvey. You need to look after Miss Butter, don't you?"

A blush warmed the plump man's cheeks. "Well, that's

true, sir. We are planning a wedding, but my first obligation is to you!"

"Nonsense! I'm just going off for a few days, Harvey. I need to look into a matter or two in Ireland, and you remember what happened the last time you went there. It was so damp and gloomy that you suffered from the ague for weeks!"

"Not really, sir. It only *seemed* like weeks."

"Whatever. The fact remains that you didn't like it there. What kind of employer would I be to force you to accompany me on a journey to a place that makes you sick?" His teeth flashed for an instant in the soft morning light before he leaned down to pull on an older pair of dark brown top boots. When Harvey made no response but continued to stand by the doorway looking bereft, Ryan crossed to pat his back. "This doesn't mean a thing, old man. I'll be back soon, and we'll go on as before. You should know enough to trust me by now."

"Indeed I do, sir."

"Good. Look after everyone here until I return, all right? You know where to find me if an emergency should arise."

"Yes, sir." His bearing was stolid. "I'll do as you bid . . . if you'll promise to take care of yourself."

"Of course I will." Ryan laughed softly, half hugging the rotund manservant and patting him on the back again. "And don't worry. I'm taking a groom with me, so I won't be alone."

He went into the hall, saddlebags slung over one shoulder, and paused outside Lindsay's door. Slowly, he eased it open. Lindsay was huddled under the covers in the great four-poster across the room. She would be furious if he left without saying good-bye, but at the same time he couldn't face another drawn-out scene with her. Better simply to leave quickly and return as soon as possible. Closing the door, Ryan turned to find Harvey watching him.

"She's sound asleep. I don't want to disturb her," he whispered to the manservant. "Will you tell her I said good-bye—and that I love her?"

"Certainly, sir."

"And tell her to start planning our wedding. I hope to be back within a fortnight and do not intend to wait a moment longer than necessary to make Lindsay my wife."

"I will convey those sentiments to Miss Raveneau, Captain. And"—Jenkins put out his hand—"congratulations."

"Thank you, Harvey." With a sigh, Ryan headed through the quiet house down to the kitchen, where he snatched a large walnut muffin. In spite of the long journey ahead and the potential of danger, he was filled with energy. Clad in worn, snug buckskin breeches, a comfortable linen shirt, and a blue coat from his days at sea, Ryan felt almost lighthearted as he breathed in the sweet, fresh dawn air and crossed the stableyard with long strides. By the time he reached Brady's stall, his thoughts were occupied with planning the journey ahead. To his surprise and pleasure, he discovered that the stallion was already fed and saddled. Glancing around, he saw a wiry young man in baggy breeches and a broad-brimmed hat that hid his face as he cinched the strap on a dappled mare's saddle.

"Good work, lad. What's your name?"

"Ian, sir," the boy replied in husky tones.

Deciding that Ian was shy, Ryan made one effort to put him at ease, then forgot for several hours that he wasn't alone. "You may as well call me Coleraine, Ian. That's my real name, as you'll learn soon enough." He swung gracefully onto Brady's back and patted the black stallion's sleek neck. "I hope you're a damned fine rider because we have great distances to cover over the next few days and I can't wait for you."

Mounting his own horse, the groom gazed at the Irishman with intent gray eyes. "Yes, sir," he replied, but Coleraine wasn't listening. He was already entering the stableyard, nudging Brady into a trot, his mind on more pressing matters.

André Raveneau opened his eyes to find the bedroom still shadowed. Devon was curled against his back, warm and purring like an exhausted kitten, but for some reason he was wide awake after less than two hours' sleep. For a moment, he lay motionless, listening, then eased out of bed to follow his instincts.

Had there been a noise outside? Raveneau dressed quietly and emerged into the hallway. Ryan's door was ajar, the room empty. Probably he had only heard the Irishman leaving for Falmouth, and yet it couldn't hurt to investigate. . . .

Silent as a cat, André descended the stairs and felt the hair stand up on the back of his neck. Someone was in the house; someone who didn't belong there. His pistol was in the study. Opening the door, he came face-to-face with Sir Harry Brandreth.

Clad in traveling clothes, Harry was standing next to the desk, his hand in the top drawer. At the first sight of his father-in-law, he smiled, thinking to bluff his way around the older man, but Raveneau's steely, piercing gaze told him that it was too late. He'd already heard the truth.

"I expected you to have run from London hours ago," André said coldly. "What are you doing in my house?"

Harry summoned every ounce of mad courage he possessed, knowing that if he faltered now the game would be over. Raveneau was a formidable adversary. Slowly, he walked over to face him, then slipped one hand inside his coat to draw out a pistol, which he pressed to his father-in-law's hard belly.

"You ought to be asleep, sir. I've waited all night for this house to go dark."

"May I ask why?" Raveneau inquired coolly.

"I'm afraid that Nathan and Lindsay's interference has forced me to leave London for an extended period of time." Harry's full upper lip curled contemptuously. "I will be needing something of value, something that I can sell so that I won't starve during my enforced exile. You wouldn't want me to starve, would you, Captain Raveneau?"

André's only response was an eloquently arched brow.

"Patriot that I am, I would like to help my country in the bargain, so I decided to take what I have longed to possess since your arrival in London. I understand that a certain Commodore Barney means to thwart the British fleet along America's eastern coastline. I knew about your mysterious maps, and my faithful wife has explained to me that they show little-known entries into all of the major American ports; ways to slip in without detection or to navigate harbors that aren't thought to be deep enough for larger vessels."

"Brandreth, I've always thought that you were an ass, but it's clear that I was far too generous in my estimation of your character."

"Now, now, let's be civil. I don't want to be forced to hurt my own father-in-law!" Smiling, Harry jabbed the pistol against him for emphasis. "As I was saying, I imagine that your charts would be of great value to the British military. If we do attempt a raid on Washington, your charts could make all the difference in the world, don't you think? So why don't you show me where they are?"

"Do you really believe I would be foolish enough to have those charts here in London?"

"What do you mean? Where are they?"

"I have them locked up on board my ship!"

Grimacing, Harry narrowed his eyes. "Fine. You'll show me where they are. I suppose I would have had to take you with me, anyway. If I left you here, the others would find you when they awaken and give chase. As it is, they won't be certain where you've gone. Get your coat, Captain Raveneau."

Ryan's day passed in a blur of winding roads, hilly countryside drenched in wildflowers, and hedgerows covered with songbirds. The travelers stopped only when necessary to rest and water the horses, stretch their own legs, and partake of food. Ian would stay outside to look after the horses while Coleraine went into the inns and brought bread, cheese, fruit, and ale back to him.

Throughout the day, Ryan was so preoccupied that he barely remembered that the groom was along. This wasn't terribly difficult since Ian was usually a quarter mile or more behind, praying each time he came to a crossroads that Coleraine hadn't turned. Coming into a village, the groom was forced to look hard at every inn in search of Brady's distinctive black form. Then, perhaps a quarter hour later, Ryan would emerge from the inn and find Ian with the two horses, head bent as he rubbed them down.

"I see you found us" was his usual distracted greeting, to which the groom would mutter a monosyllabic reply. Coleraine would then pass along some food, mount Brady, and be cantering back onto the road while Ian struggled to stuff bread and cheese into his pockets while jamming an ill-fitting boot into the mare's stirrup and hoisting himself up into the saddle.

By afternoon, they had passed Basingstoke and were deep into the verdant, peaceful county of Hampshire. The villages, with their thatched cottages and colorful gardens, were charming, but there was no time to pause and appreciate them. Ryan was intent on getting as near to Salisbury as possible. He had made up his mind to reach Falmouth in less than three days.

Night had fallen when Ryan reined in an exhausted yet valiant Brady in front of the White Star Inn in the tiny village of Lapcombe Corner. Salisbury was so near he could almost touch it through the darkness.

Dismounting, he ran a hand through his dusty hair and had started toward the stables before he remembered the groom. If the boy couldn't keep up, there hardly seemed any point in having him along! What use would he be fending off highwaymen or caring for Brady if he was never there? At that moment, Ryan glimpsed the silhouette of a gray horse and slight rider approaching the White Star.

"Ian!" he called, a note of irritation in his voice. "Is that you?"

Slowly, the mare turned toward him and finally stopped a few feet away. The young groom fairly toppled from the horse's back.

"Are you all right?" Ryan bent to see the boy's face, but the darkness and his broad-brimmed hat made a good look impossible. Tired, hungry, and impatient, he turned the reins over to Ian and said gruffly, "I'll go inside and bespeak rooms for us. You can wash up then, and we'll have a hot meal before bed."

"I'd rather sleep in the stable, sir," the groom replied in a husky monotone.

"Don't be an ass. You'll need a bath, a decent bed, and a good night's sleep, or you'll be even more worthless tomorrow than you've been today." With that, Coleraine turned and strode off toward the cheerily lit inn, unaware of the fact that his young groom was sticking a pink tongue out at him from the shadows.

Craving a drink, Ryan paced back and forth in the spartan room. Finally, he decided he couldn't wait any longer for Ian and opened the door to the hallway. The boy was standing there, fist raised as if he'd been about to knock.

"What're you doing, lad? Come on in! Jesus, but you are a sad sight! I've already put on other clothes so that I won't cover the taproom with dirt, and the innkeeper's wife has offered to wash them for me. Strip yours off and I'll pass them along as well."

Ian stared at the floor and mumbled, "I couldn't share a room with you, sir. I didn't know you meant—"

"I can assure you, I didn't! This was the last room. I for one will sleep far too soundly to notice you." His black brows arched in exasperation. "Give me your clothes, Ian! I haven't all night! I'm starving and Mrs. Craddock has promised us pork stew with boiled potatoes. I saw a joint of mutton and fresh-baked bread in the kitchen as well."

The groom continued to stare at the floor for another long minute, until Coleraine, out of patience, reached out to grasp the wide brim of his hat.

"No!" A slim, pale hand came up involuntarily to keep the hat in place, brushing the Irishman's strong fingers in the process.

Ryan stepped backward as if he'd been burned. A sick sensation washed over him as realization dawned. "No. Please, God, no. I'm imagining things . . ."

The groom sighed, then slowly straightened and lifted a delicate chin. Huge gray eyes met Ryan's disbelieving blue gaze.

Lindsay attempted what she hoped was an engaging smile. When she pulled off the hat, lustrous golden-rose curls spilled over her shoulders. "Hello, darling. It's me!"

CHAPTER
32

June 26–27, 1814

Ryan's face was a portrait of pale shock, incredulous disbelief, and impotent rage. He spoke not a word. Lindsay's smile faded as she studied her beloved's expression and saw the way his lean brown hands clenched and unclenched at his sides.

"Aren't you glad to see me?" she tried again in more cautious tones.

His eyes were nearly black and flashing menacingly. Lindsay imagined that she could see smoke escaping from his flared nostrils.

"Ryan?" She backed toward the door. "Won't you say something?"

He opened his mouth, breathing with an obvious effort at control, and the first sound that he uttered was a low growl. Finally, in cold, measured tones, he said, "I don't trust myself!"

"Darling, aren't you overreacting just a bit?"

"Overreacting?" Coleraine looked around as if searching for something to smash. "Miss Raveneau, if I were you, I'd count myself fortunate to be *alive* right now!"

The frigid anger in his voice sent a chill down her spine, and for the first time it occurred to Lindsay that she might have gone too far. Was it possible that her attempt to share this adventure with Ryan might have cost her his love? Her eyes swam with tears.

"For God's sake, don't cry!" he shouted, pacing across the room. "It will only make matters worse. I can't believe this is happening! After we just discussed this very subject less than twenty-four hours ago!"

"I haven't forgotten," she replied. "I promised you that I would consider carefully—"

"This is insane!" Ryan interrupted, his eyes blazing. "What good does such a promise do me if you turn around, dress as a boy, and follow me that very night? I might as well conduct these discussions with a chair for all the progress I make with you! I can only imagine the little scene that ensued after you went to bed last night, knowing that I planned to leave for Falmouth. Did you pause momentarily and have a dialogue with yourself?" He mimicked her: " 'Hmm. Ryan's off to Ireland! I can't bear to think of him having an adventure that I cannot share. But I did promise to consider every aspect of the situation. He probably wouldn't want me to come, but I can surely calm him down. I'll shed a few tears, then kiss him, and before we know it, he'll be thanking me for practicing yet another deception!' "

Lindsay's mouth tightened. "It wasn't that way at all."

"Frankly, Miss Raveneau, I don't care. Your total disregard for my thoughts and feelings can only make me reconsider the notion of marrying you." His eyes were like blue ice; his voice was without emotion. "If I had the time, I'd tie you up, take you back home, and lock you in your room! As it is, I need some food. I'm going downstairs to eat—and to think. You may do as you wish." Glancing back over one broad shoulder, his eyebrow curved upward sarcastically. "You always do."

*   *   *

The taproom was filled with villagers who were relaxing and conversing over mugs of ale, a dozen or so guests discharged from a stage, Ryan, and Lindsay. The stage passengers filled every settle and table except one. It was occupied by a distinctly unfriendly-looking Ryan Coleraine. He ate his pork stew, hot bread, and potatoes without lifting his eyes more than two or three times. Mrs. Craddock refilled his ale without being asked. Passing Lindsay, who sat on a stick-backed chair in the corner, plate on lap, the large old woman merely flicked her brows upward.

Lindsay pushed the aromatic pieces of pork and vegetables around her plate, but she felt far too upset to eat. Finally, she returned her dishes to the kitchen and went back to the room. She wished that she might douse the lights and pretend to be asleep before Ryan returned, but she wasn't certain he would even deign to share a bed with her.

After removing all her clothing except a thin linen shirt, Lindsay washed carefully with soap and water, scrubbed her teeth, then emptied the basin and poured fresh water for Ryan. She was sitting on the edge of the bed, bathed in the glow of one candle, when the door opened and he appeared.

Coleraine stared for a moment, then muttered, "Why aren't you asleep?"

"I wasn't sure you wanted me here," she whispered. Her palms were wet.

"I don't." Ryan stared out the window, moonlight silvering his chiseled profile, and added, "But then you haven't left me a choice, have you?"

"Ryan, I—"

"I'm too angry to discuss this any further. Go to sleep."

Tears filled her throat as she watched him strip off his jacket, shirt, and boots. Finally, she was able to say, "I could sleep somewhere else."

He let out a short bark of sarcastic laughter. "You've put yourself in enough danger as it is. I don't intend to let you out of my sight again!"

She stared at the play of muscles in his wide, tapering back as he washed, her stomach churning. When Coleraine approached the bed and bent to pull off his buckskin breeches, Lindsay said, sobbing, "Ryan, I'm sorry. I didn't realize—"

A muscle moved in his jaw as he blew out the candle and got into bed next to her. "Spare me your penitence, Lindsay. It's too late."

Pressing a hand to her mouth, she swallowed tears that tasted like acid and turned away from him, drawing her knees up. Ryan lay far away on the clean but lumpy bed. He might not have been there at all except that she could sense his anger.

Through the windows, the night sky was stunning. Clear and black, it made a perfect backdrop for a dazzling display of stars and a huge, luminous full moon. Lindsay's lower lip trembled as she found Cassiopeia, and then the North Star, the constellation of Cygnus, and the glowing light orange star called Arcturus.

The night on board *La Mouette* when Ryan had shown her the stars seemed months rather than weeks ago. How far they had come since then . . . until she undid it all with her folly. Wishing that she could go back to the moment when Ryan had asked her parents for her hand in marriage, Lindsay glimpsed the arc of a falling star. The voice of her grandmother returned to warn that shooting stars were the smoke of sin, and she felt more frightened than ever.

What if Ryan never forgave her?

The dawn sky was streaked with peach and rose when Ryan's eyes opened. The first thing he saw were curls that matched the sunrise spilling across his chest. Lindsay's delicate nose was pressed to the hard curve of his shoulder, and her fingers were splayed in the black hair on his chest. Instinctive tender emotions were cut off, however, when he remembered where they were and the fact that Lindsay had gone too far with her latest masquerade.

Still, the sight of the dark smudges under her eyes and the tearstreaks on her cheeks made him sigh inwardly, if only for an instant. Then he steeled himself.

"Wake up."

Lindsay nuzzled closer, then opened her eyes suddenly and rolled away from him almost as if she were frightened. "I'm sorry. I didn't mean—"

"To touch me? Never mind." His tone was caustic. "That's the least of your transgressions, Miss Raveneau. Get up now and get dressed. We have a very long day ahead of us. I mean to reach Exeter, at the very least, and I expect you to keep pace."

Coleraine continued to treat Lindsay with an icy courtesy that bordered on rudeness. Today, he did not ride ahead, leaving her to guess his route and catch up, but whenever her mare began to lag behind, he shot her a look of darkest rage. Each time they stopped, she stayed in the yard to water and rest the horses while he went into the inn. Ryan always saw to it that Lindsay had access to the facilities and enough food and water, but his stormy expression indicated that he was counting every minute she cost him, and Lindsay was too proud to allow that tally to grow beyond what was absolutely necessary. Besides, she only pretended to eat, stuffing the food into her pockets when he wasn't looking. The mere thought of food turned her stomach.

Over and over again, as her fatigue and despair mounted apace, she wondered what had possessed her to try Ryan's patience so sorely. He had forgiven her so many escapades and loved her so unreservedly that she had begun to think that his capitulation would be inevitable. She saw now that she had acted far too rashly. When she'd heard him speak to Able Barker about needing a groom, the smell of adventure had whetted her appetite almost irrationally. Lindsay couldn't bear the thought of being separated from Ryan, and this seemed like the perfect opportunity for them to share not only a fabulous adventure but also long hours alone, away from the prying eyes of her family and London society.

Only now did she realize, all too painfully, that her decision to proceed without consulting Ryan had been dangerously foolish. Every time she dared to glance at his proud, angry profile, tears stung her eyes. With his raven hair blowing in the wind and his buckskin-sheathed thighs flexing against Brady's sides, Ryan had never looked more splendid—or less attainable. As her own body weakened from sheer exhaustion, she began to believe that he was lost to her forever.

Lindsay's despair was such that she barely noticed the unseasonable chill in the air. By late afternoon, when they were a few miles outside of the village of Combe St. Nicholas, soot-colored clouds were racing across the sky. Pulling up his coat collar, Ryan instinctively looked back at Lindsay.

"Are you warm enough?" he called gruffly.

Although she felt chilled, Lindsay nodded, afraid to speak. Then, as the clouds overhead seemed to pause, swelling and darkening, a deafening clap of thunder sent both horses rearing back fearfully.

"Damn," muttered Ryan, "this is all I need." He looked over at Lindsay almost as if he assumed that she must be responsible. "We'll have to ride like hell for the village to beat the storm."

She nodded obediently and dug her knees into the mare's sides, and the horses and riders galloped over the darkening, hilly road. Raindrops began to spatter them, but Lindsay barely noticed. All she cared about was keeping pace with Ryan and Brady. Even when her hat blew off, freeing her hair, and the rain gradually soaked each strand, plastering them to her head and face, Lindsay refused to think of it. The rain intensified until it took all her concentration to keep Ryan and Brady in sight. Her clothes were soaked, the raindrops felt like needles against her face, and she was shivering from head to toe as she rode, yet Lindsay would have rather died than call out to Ryan.

Long minutes later, Ryan reined Brady in before a tiny alehouse called the Plough and Sail. Wiping his face with his fingers, he turned in the saddle to check on Lindsay. The mare was trotting up to them while her mistress rode with both arms wrapped around the horse's dappled neck. Rainwater streamed from Lindsay's hair and her half-closed eyes were glazed with fatigue and cold.

"Oh, God," Ryan uttered in stricken tones. In an instant, he vaulted from Brady's back to the muddy ground and reached up to catch Lindsay in his arms. To the approaching stableboy, he shouted, "Take care of these horses! We'll be staying the night. See to it that they're fed and kept warm and dry!"

Through a haze of cold, shivering misery, Lindsay was vaguely conscious of Ryan cradling her in his arms as he made his way toward the alehouse. If she had been able, she would have smiled.

"This is just an alehouse, not a proper inn!" cried the proprietor, a mountainous, red-faced man called Sedgwick. "We only let two rooms and they're both taken!"

Ryan was seated on a bench against one scarred stone wall and Lindsay occupied his lap. Her face was pressed to the curve where his neck and shoulder joined. "Look here, sir, I'll be happy to pay you handsomely if you can provide lodgings for my wife and me. Can't you see she's ill? I couldn't possibly take her back out into that storm."

"Don't see why you had her out on a horse rather

than in a closed stage, but then you didn't ask me, did you?''

Mrs. Sedgwick came scurrying across the taproom with two mugs of steaming tea laced with brandy and cinnamon. "Poor lass!" she cried over the noise of the storm. "Can you drink a little of this, Mrs. . . .''

"Coleraine," Ryan supplied.

A certain note of tenderness in his voice roused her. Still shivering in Ryan's arms, Lindsay reached for the mug and sipped tentatively. It seemed to be more brandy than tea, but it certainly warmed her. Slowly, as she drank, her shivering ceased.

"This little lass is going to have a hot bath and a warm bed tonight!" Mrs. Sedgwick declared, ignoring her husband. "My sister and her family have a nice, cozy cottage next door. They're away in Plymouth for the whole of June. You can stay there."

"That's very kind of you," Ryan said.

"The pair of you stay right there while I run over and put some supper on and some water to heat for a bath." She glanced at her husband. "You come along and light a fire."

By the time the Sedgwicks returned, Lindsay was feeling greatly restored. Ryan didn't talk to her, but he did keep one arm curved around her and the angry stiffness was gone from his body. For her part, she drank her "tea" and enjoyed the glow that spread over her. When Mrs. Sedgwick reappeared, her mobcap slightly askew, Lindsay was on the verge of dozing off.

"Everything's ready for you, and your horses are being looked after, too. Can you walk, Mrs. Coleraine?''

"I think so." She gave the old woman a slightly woozy smile. "You're very kind!"

Ryan helped her to her feet and kept one arm around her waist for support as they exited through the back door and followed the Sedgwicks' directions through the rain to a half-timbered cottage with golden light at each window.

*   *   *

"Feeling better?"

Lindsay looked up in the act of swallowing the last spoonful of oxtail soup to see Ryan pour another bucket of steaming water into the tub before the fireplace. "I was hungry."

He inclined his dark head toward her coat, which hung on a peg by the door. "I can see why after peeking inside those pockets. No wonder you were so weak."

Lowering her lashes under his regard, she murmured, "I wasn't feeling quite the thing today."

Ryan's eyes closed for a moment. "Well." His relieved tone was husky with emotion. "I'm glad that you're better. After a hot bath and a good night's sleep, you should be your old self tomorrow."

"An incurable termagant?"

"I'd settle for a brat," Ryan replied softly.

"Oh, oh . . ." Lindsay rose shakily and walked into his arms, weeping. "I thought I'd never hear you call me that again!"

"Shh, angel." He stroked her damp hair and found that his own hands were trembling. "I was a beast. Have you any idea how I felt when I saw you, soaking wet and faint, clinging to that mare's neck? I deserve to be shot for the way I treated you today!"

"No, you were absolutely right! I was very, very bad to ignore all that you said to me in London. It was terribly selfish and foolish of me, and I wouldn't blame you if you never spoke to me again!"

Suddenly, in the midst of their mutual apologies, their eyes met and they began to laugh, clinging to each other. Then Ryan was kissing Lindsay and stripping off her clothes.

"I think we've said enough for now. Let's have that bath before it gets cold."

Lindsay's eyes sparkled with delight. "You're coming in with me?" Then she blushed as his dark fingers opened her shirt, baring her creamy, rose-tipped breasts.

Ryan covered them with his palms. "You're so cold, angel. Come on." With that, he unfastened her breeches and stripped them away. Sensing Lindsay's shyness, he tried not to look but lifted her up and gently placed her in the tub.

"Oh, my!" She gasped. "It feels *wonderful*. Is there soap?" Accepting the bar he handed her, she concentrated on lathering her arms and tried not to stare as Ryan undressed.

Still, it was impossible to ignore the bronzed, sculpted beauty of his physique. His legs were long and solid with muscle, his chest hard, tapering, and covered with just the right amount of soft black hair. Lindsay tried not to see what was in between. Her face was burning as he eased into the bathtub opposite her, but Ryan held out his arms.

"Come here, angel."

Her embarrassment melted away under the heat of his love. Even the sensation of his manhood against her belly as she leaned against him felt endearing somehow. "Oh, Ryan, I've missed you so!" Suddenly, she began to cry.

"Oh, God, please don't!" he begged. "I feel guilty enough as it is." Lifting her face to his lips, he tasted salty tears. "Lindsay, my darling, you know that I would rather die than cause you distress, but—"

"I deserved to be taught a lesson," she replied firmly, gulping back her sobs. "You were absolutely right, Ryan! I thought about it a great deal today, when I feared that you didn't love me anymore, and I don't intend to forget it. If you had chuckled and forgiven me when I revealed myself to you last night, I don't doubt that I would have been completely incorrigible for the duration of our marriage!" Seeing Ryan's sudden white grin, she laughed herself and paused to kiss him. "It's true. Since meeting you in Pettipauge, I've come out of myself to a remarkable degree. I've always been very confident, but since my best friends were books, I was unschooled when it came to people. You've always known that, yet you learned to love me, anyway. That took a tremendous leap of faith on your part!''

"It wasn't conscious, I assure you. I simply fell in love with you, Lindsay." His strong, golden-brown arms slid around her back in the water, lifting her up so that their eyes met. For an instant, his dark head dipped and he kissed the wet curve of her breast, then came up to smile into her eyes. "Do you want me to be honest?"

She winced slightly. "Of course!"

"I love you more than my own life, angel, but that doesn't mean I love everything that you do. That's natural, isn't it? I'm certain there must be things that I do that rub you the wrong way, too."

She nodded with certainty while trying to remember even one of his flaws.

"When I realized that I loved you and then, later, that I wanted to spend my life with you, I also had to realize that I couldn't expect to change you—"

"Are there a *lot* of things I do that bother you?" Lindsay interrupted.

"Of course not!" He laughed. "I'm speaking of this contrary streak you have. You demanded to know that last night in London whether I intend to be your master, and I had to think about that today. It would be a crime to try to master a woman of your rare spirit, Lindsay, but at the same time we will have to work out a partnership that involves compromise and, above all, honesty. You can't rush off headlong into some dangerous adventure without discussing it with me any more than you would want me to do the same!"

She pressed her nose to his broad, wet shoulder. "I know. You're absolutely right! Today I learned my lesson."

"And I learned mine, darling. Now, let's have our bath." Ryan searched for the soap in the water, teasing her with his fingertips in the process.

Lindsay was nearly dizzy with happiness. Staring at

his splendid face, which had been so harsh and forbidding all day long, she felt overcome with love. "Can we hurry? I want to go to bed!"

His right brow curved upward suggestively. "Tired? Be patient. We'll tuck you up very soon."

Running slim hands over Ryan's shoulders and down the muscled contours of his chest, Lindsay smiled, cat-like, "Oh, good. I can't wait. . . ."

CHAPTER
33

June 27–29, 1814

Firelight burnished each strand of Lindsay's hair as Ryan brushed it; some were coppery, some gold, and some a soft shade of apricot. She sat in front of him, clad only in a clean, unbuttoned shirt, her head lolling in complete relaxation.

For Ryan's part, desire grew with each passing minute. Why did females have to wear their hair long, so impossibly long? It seemed to take hours for it to dry! Sliding his hand around the back of her neck, Ryan pushed upward with splayed fingers and was relieved to find that her beautiful curls at last felt dry to the touch.

Lindsay's head dropped back against his hand, completely limp. As he leaned forward to look at her face, she emitted a ladylike snore. His own eyes widening with frustration, Ryan cradled her against him and sighed. Lindsay responded by snuggling against his chest.

The perfect lover, he carried her off to bed and covered her with blankets, then stared down at her face with a sigh. Ryan told himself that she probably hadn't

slept much the night before and that the past two days
had been extremely tiring, yet he couldn't quite suppress the arousal that coursed through his body. How
beautiful she was! Asleep, Lindsay actually did look like
an angel; he'd thought it the first time he saw her thus,
after her fall on board *La Mouette*. Her thick lashes
swept finely delineated cheekbones that never quite lost
their rosy glow. Lindsay's nose was perfect and delicate, turning up just enough to hint at innocence, and
her mouth . . .

Leaning over, Ryan brushed it with the tip of his
forefinger. Its slightly pouting quality did hint at innocence, but he knew better. Those lips were the most
sensual and instinctive he'd ever kissed.

After tracing the fine line of her jaw, he shed his
breeches and climbed into bed beside her. Lindsay murmured contentedly and snuggled against him. Ryan's
own expression was pained yet amused as he gathered
her near and stroked her golden-rose tresses. In her
sleep, Lindsay puckered her lips and he kissed them.

"I love you, angel," he whispered.

"Mmmm." She smiled, burrowing against his chest.

The first tangerine-lavender rays of dawn were filter-
ing through the muslin bedhangings when Ryan awoke.
At first he thought a spider might be making its way up
his leg, but then he realized that it was Lindsay's hand.

"Are you awake?" she asked. "I've been staring at
you forever. Oh, Ryan, I love you so!"

"You do?" he inquired with sleepy amusement.
"Enough to let me clean my teeth?"

She stared in wonderment as he climbed naked from
the bed. "I've made tea if you want a cup."

Laughing, he glanced back at her with one black brow
arched and took in her bare shoulders above the blankets. "Don't be absurd. *Tea?* When I could have you?"

Lindsay felt faint with longing and happiness. It seemed

to her that if they had overcome this first huge quarrel so successfully, nothing could ever come between them again. When Ryan returned, still swishing water in his mouth, she took one look at his hard-muscled physique and held her arms open. He pulled back the covers to reveal her body and she scarcely flinched.

"Do you know what a beautiful woman you are?" he inquired huskily.

"I haven't had occasion to hear it before." Lindsay giggled.

"Shh." Ryan lowered his bronzed, powerful body until it barely touched her softer, cream-tinted form. "Oh, Jesus, Lindsay, you do try my powers of forbearance!"

"Why?" she inquired, all innocence. "There's no reason for it! All I want is for you to make love to me!"

For an instant, his blue eyes widened in astonishment, then he laughed aloud and kissed her. She tasted clean and sweet. Lindsay's arms twined around his broad shoulders, her fingers sinking into the black curls at the back of his neck. They kissed ravenously for long minutes, tasting and plundering each other's mouths. Then Ryan's hands slid from the sides of her face down to cup her breasts, then caressed the curves of her hips. Meanwhile, he kissed every inch of her face: brow, eyelids, cheekbones, nose, ears, and chin.

"Dear God, Lindsay, how I love you!"

"Why don't you show me?" she teased softly.

Ryan needed no further encouragement. His mouth blazed a fiery path down her throat, savoring every inch, then lingered over each breast. The sensations were still a surprise to Lindsay. She bit her lip in sheer ecstasy as he skillfully used his warm, wet, evocative mouth to tantalize her nipples. Strong currents of arousal traveled down to the place between Lindsay's legs until she ached for him.

The first time they made love had seemed almost a fantasy. The wine, the fire, the shadows, the subterfuge had all lent an air of unreality to their coupling on the sitting-room rug at Grimley Court. This time, though, the fantasy was different. Lindsay could almost pretend that they were married. Mellow shafts of sunlight bathed their naked forms and both of them were completely sober and aware of each touch and its meaning.

When Ryan finally lay back against the sheets, turning her body to go with him, then licked her nipples leisurely and smiled, Lindsay felt impossibly content. She moved away from him slightly and rose up on an elbow, studying his body. In turn, his dark blue eyes watched her face.

"I love the way you're made," she murmured, trailing slim fingers up his right thigh.

"Mmm. The feeling is mutual, Miss Raveneau." Ryan leaned forward to kiss her collarbone, but Lindsay eluded him.

"No, no. It's my turn now." Gracefully, she straddled his hips and smiled down into his eyes.

"Jesus!" He laughed, while his arousal reached near-excruciating proportions. "You amaze me!"

"Do you mind?" Her eyes were smokily seductive while luxuriant dawn-hued curls spilled around her shoulders.

Ryan focused on Lindsay's mouth, then shut his eyes. "Not in the least," he managed to groan.

"That's good." Her breath was warm as she spoke against his mouth. She traced its chiseled lines with the tip of her tongue, then moved upward to kiss his arching black brows, eyelids, cheekbones, thin, high-bridged nose, and strong jaw. Ryan was moaning by this time.

"You're asking for trouble," he muttered between clenched teeth.

"Exactly so!" She giggled softly, inching down to explore the hard lines of his neck and shoulders.

The male body was completely new to her, and it was a special delight to make this first investigation of Ryan's. He was everything she'd ever dreamed about: broad-shouldered, slim-hipped, flat-bellied, and well-muscled, with just the right amount of soft black hair on his chest and limbs. When she tasted his taut shoulder, it seemed delicious to her. Tentatively, Lindsay moved downward, touching lightly, drinking him in with her eyes, and kissing the contours of his chest, his flat nipples, and the muscled ridges of his belly. She liked to turn her cheek against the crisp black hair on his torso. In fact, she was fascinated and aroused by every difference between their two bodies.

Leaning back, Lindsay looked over her shoulder and studied his legs. She caressed each one in turn, then, blushing slightly, worked her hips backward so that she could see Ryan's manhood. It seemed to jerk slightly against her own warm woman's place when they touched, and Ryan let out a low groan.

Then she stared.

"What are you *doing,* brat?"

"I'm looking at you."

"That's not what it's for, you know." Deciding that she'd tortured him long enough, Ryan opened his eyes and reached down to clasp her hips in his strong hands. Lindsay squirmed with shocked excitement when she felt his maleness nudging her there.

"How did you do that?"

Ryan laughed deeply, infectiously. "Oh, angel, you are such a delight. You'd be surprised by the things I can do!"

She bent to stare at what seemed to be a huge weapon. "Isn't it awfully large?" Curiously, she caressed him.

Ryan groaned again. "I think that's the general idea, love. You'll like it."

"Don't I have to lie down, though?" Her brow was knit in consternation.

"God, but you're a wonder! Darling Lindsay, there are more ways to make love than you and I will probably ever care to explore. This is only one." He put his dark hands around hers and helped her connect their bodies. Sighing, Lindsay slowly eased herself down until her buttocks touched his hips. She felt completely filled by him. Ryan gritted his teeth and let out a moan of pure bliss.

"Are you all right?" she asked anxiously.

"Never better, angel," he replied, flashing a grin. "Come here." Putting a hand on each side of her face, he drew her toward him.

She felt more at ease lying over him, feeling his hands on her breasts and savoring his leisurely kiss. Ryan was a patient, happy man, helping her find a rhythm to aid in their lovemaking. Finally, sensing that she was still a bit nervous, he kissed her passionately, clasped her buttocks firmly, and rolled her over. Lindsay was more at ease knowing that he was in charge, though she found that the sensations weren't quite so intense in this position. Still, she loved the way their bodies arched together, harder and harder, and she wrapped her legs around his waist toward the end, glorying in his male strength. A hot, tingly feeling was building in her loins, cresting higher with each one of Ryan's powerful thrusts. Finally, it seemed as if an explosion of pleasure had started there and was spreading upward over her body, puckering her nipples and flushing her cheeks. Panting and astonished, Lindsay clung to Ryan's broad shoulders just as he let out a loud groan and thrust all the way into her. They lay gasping together, trying to kiss, then he drew back enough to meet her eyes.

"Lindsay . . ." Ryan exhaled.

Lindsay could only nod, her face damp and pink, and then they began to laugh breathlessly. He buried his face in her hair and hugged her so hard it hurt.

"I love you, Lindsay. I love you."

"I love you, too! How lucky we are."

Still joined to her, Ryan turned on his side, bringing her with him, and caressed the elegant line of her back and hip. "It's going to be a wonderful marriage."

"I promise to behave, too!"

He arched a black eyebrow, but his eyes were dancing. "Don't make promises you may not be able to keep, brat."

Tears made her blink, then spilled onto her cheeks. Ryan kissed them away. "You love me, anyway, don't you!" she whispered in wonderment. "You know me and still you love me!"

"I never could have loved anyone but you. I knew all about your headstrong, stubborn qualities long before I learned about the woman you kept hidden inside. The plain truth is that I began to fall in love with you that very first day, when you drove me nearly insane with your antics. I don't want you to change, Lindsay. If I get angry with you it's only because I'm terrified that you'll rush headlong into real danger. You must promise at least to keep me informed of your plans so that I can rescue you if the need arises!"

They kissed slowly, lingeringly, speaking to one another without words. Finally, Lindsay drew back and murmured soberly, "Truly, now I see the sense in what you say. Before, I swore to obey you because I was terrified of losing you, but this is different. We'll not only be husband and wife, and lovers, but dearest friends as well!"

"That's right, angel." Ryan smiled, inwardly sighing in relief. "Shall we make a pact to confide in each other always?"

"I think so." She nodded. "We're mates now, aren't we?"

"We are." His lips clung to hers. "In more ways than one . . ."

At seven o'clock, Ryan and Lindsay were in the taproom of the Plough and Sail, eating a hurried breakfast of cold partridge, boiled eggs, and grapes. He was rising to go settle the bill and get their horses when Mrs. Sedgwick approached the table.

"That black stallion is yours, isn't it?"

Noting her uneasy manner, Ryan replied, "Yes. He's all right, I hope!"

"The horse is fine. Something else has me befuddled. Two men came in from the rain after I sent you next door last night and we let them take shelter in the stable. They were up to leave before dawn, but while the blond young man washed up in the kitchen, the older one whispered to me, 'Please give this to the owner of that black stallion. It's a matter of life and death.' Well, I don't mind telling you that words like those frighten an old woman like me! I don't know what these goings-on mean, but there was something in that man's eyes that touched me. So I'm giving this to you on the condition that you ride out of here now and don't come back. We don't want people settling matters of life and death in Combe St. Nicholas!"

Her heart pounding, Lindsay watched as Ryan held out his hand and Mrs. Sedgwick pressed a tiny scrimshaw carving of a seagull into it.

"Oh, my Lord," she breathed fearfully. "Mama gave that to Papa when *La Mouette* was christened! Ryan, what does this mean?"

He looked up grimly. "I can only surmise that Harry has taken your father hostage for some unknown reason—and that they are en route for *La Mouette*. Come on, there's no time to lose. If they're only a few hours ahead of us, and Harry doesn't know we're in pursuit, we may be able to catch them before they set sail!"

Less than a quarter hour later, Ryan and Lindsay had bade the Sedgwicks good-bye and were riding out of Combe St. Nicholas. It was a glorious day, sunny and fresh-smelling, and the sky overhead was a deep vivid blue. They rode side by side, but this time it was Lindsay who was preoccupied. An expression of anguished

worry knit her soft brow, and Ryan felt her pain each
time he looked over at her.

Finally, a few miles outside of Yarcombe, he reined
Brady in opposite a hillside thick and fragrant with budding yellow tansy flowers, red campion, and lacy white
cow parsley. Dismounting, he swiftly gathered a bouquet
and came toward Lindsay with long, boyish strides.

Still seated on her mare, which had been christened
Emma, Lindsay watched him approach with a mixture
of consternation and tenderness. "What are you doing?
We haven't time to stop!"

Ryan caught her hand in his and kissed it. "Please,
don't worry so, angel. I can't bear to see you looking so
agonized! Your father will be fine. I give you my word."

She tried to smile and tears spilled onto her cheeks.
"I love you, Ryan."

"Trust me."

"I do." Lindsay took the bouquet and tucked it into
her saddlebag so that she might look at the tansy flowers
when her spirits began to flag.

All that day and evening, they rode hard, testing both
horses, only pausing when they had to for their sake and
that of the horses. Finally, they were forced to stop for
supper in Exeter because Brady halted as they rode past
the inn and glared back at his master. "I think my
faithful steed is registering a complaint," Ryan murmured dryly. "Perhaps it's time to rest for a bit."

After supper, they rode on until nearly midnight, and
Lindsay wasn't a bit tired. Her determination to reach
her father, Ryan's conversation, and the flash of his
smile in the darkness sustained her through the long
night's ride. In addition, she'd drunk a mug of ale with
supper that seemed much stronger than anything she'd
sampled in London. Galloping over the granite-capped
Bodmin moor, Lindsay eyed the stark moonlit landscape
and murmured, "Ryan, do you know that bit of poetry

by Shelley? About the moon and the moors? Papa was
reading it aloud one evening last week."

"Refresh my memory, angel," he replied gently.

She threw her head back, enjoying the wind in her
hair and the motion of the horse, and recited.

"Away! the moor is dark beneath the moon,
    Rapid clouds have drank the last pale beam of
      even:
Away! the gathering winds will call the darkness
    soon,
    And profoundest midnight shroud the serene lights
      of heaven."

Ryan smiled. "That was beautifully done considering
how tired you must be, sweetheart."

Her eyes gleamed in the moonlight as she imagined
that she could glimpse the distant sparkling ocean off the
Cornish coast. "I feel wide awake! Couldn't we just ride
all night?"

"I'm afraid not. No, don't argue with me. Brady and
Emma need their rest and you and I will need our wits
about us tomorrow. We'll stop in Bolventor for a few
hours' sleep."

Lindsay protested all the way to their room at a plain,
clean inn, then tumbled into bed without washing her
face. When Ryan joined her, kissing the side of her
neck, the only response he received was a muffled groan
as Lindsay buried her face in her pillow. Smiling, he
gathered her against the curve of his body and fell asleep
instantly.

Waking before Ryan in the predawn darkness, Lindsay hadn't the heart to disturb him. Instead, she arranged for a hot bath. There was no telling when she'd
have another if they went to sea. As she and a kitchen
maid hauled buckets to fill the wooden tub, the commo-

tion woke Ryan and he joined her in the bath. This time, however, they were careful not to touch each other beyond mutual backwashing.

By six o'clock, Ryan and Lindsay were accepting a bundle of hot muffins from the innkeeper's wife and emerging into the mild air. The village was bathed in aqua light as the sun peeked over thatched rooftops.

"How much farther is it to Falmouth?" Lindsay asked as she led Emma from the stable.

"With luck, we should arrive by midmorning." He gave her a leg up, then swung onto Brady's back. The horses cantered onto the road that would lead them south over the moor toward the rocky Cornish coast. Glancing over at Lindsay's determined, exquisite profile, Ryan said a silent prayer that Harry didn't know they were also bound for Falmouth. If Brandreth was unaware that he was being followed, he might still be abed and Ryan and Lindsay might reach *La Mouette* first.

CHAPTER
34

June 29–30, 1814

"I WANT YOU TO STAY HERE," RYAN ORDERED, SHADing his eyes against the sunlight as he scanned the ships lining the Falmouth pier. "If Brandreth and Chadwick are aboard, it could be dangerous."

"But I can't bear to wait! I must know if Papa is safe!" Lindsay's voice broke on a sob.

"I mean it!" His dark blue eyes were stern as they met hers. "I give you my word that I will signal to you as soon as I know it's safe. Now, don't move!"

With that, Ryan sprinted down the dock and took the gangplank with long strides. Most of the crew had been paid to remain in Falmouth, and Drew had agreed to supervise the maintenance of *La Mouette* and see to it that someone stood watch at all times during her months in port. When Ryan jumped to the gun deck, he spied a boatswain's mate he recognized.

"Higgins? Are you the watch?"

The seaman rushed over and saluted. "Yes, sir, Captain Coleraine! Are we going to set sail soon? Shall I alert the rest of the crew? Most of them are at the White Dog. When Captain Raveneau arrived this morning, I wanted to ask him, but—"

"Is Captain Raveneau on board?" Ryan cut in harshly.

"Yes, sir. He came a couple of hours ago with his son-in-law. They went below, then the other fellow came back up on deck and told me that the captain was tired from his journey and was going to sleep for a few hours. Said I shouldn't disturb him."

Struggling for control, Ryan pressed, "Higgins, do you know where Captain Raveneau's son-in-law went when he left here?"

"Yes, sir. I saw him rowing out to the *Lady Hester*, which was at anchor out in the harbor. I noticed that she set sail shortly after he came on board."

"Damn!" Coleraine raked a hand through his shining hair. "All right. Listen to me. It's imperative that we overtake that ship. I want you to go and tell Lindsay Raveneau to come aboard. Do you see her on the pier? Good. Then run to the White Dog and find Drew. The two of you gather as many of the crew as you can find and come straight back here. Understand?"

"Yes, sir!" His eyes agleam with excitement, Higgins scrambled to the rail and disappeared down the gangplank.

Dropping himself down through the hatch, Ryan's mind raced with confusion and concern. Why would Raveneau have stayed below after Harry's departure? As horrifying possibilities occurred to him, Ryan dashed down the gangway, praying that Lindsay took her time getting there.

The door to the captain's cabin was locked. When Coleraine's shouts brought no response, he kicked in the mahogany door. The cabin was in chaos: books and papers were everywhere. In the midst of the wreckage lay Raveneau, sprawled across his bunk at an awkward angle, his face drained of color. A large red stain spread over the front of his shirt.

"Oh, Jesus." Ryan groaned. "André, can you hear me?" He took the older man's face in his hands.

"Ryan." The word was barely audible, but Raveneau's eyes opened for a moment. "Help."

"You're damned right. You'll be fine, just fine." His strong fingers were busy as he spoke, ripping the linen shirt away from André's chest to expose the wound.

"Oh, my God!" Lindsay cried from the doorway. "What has he done to Papa?"

"Get me some water," Ryan instructed over his shoulder. "And soap. Hurry!"

Somehow, she gathered her wits and obeyed. As Ryan gently washed the blood away, Lindsay stared down at her father and swallowed hot, bitter tears. "Papa? Can you hear me?"

His fingers moved against her clutching hand. "Shh, *chérie*," he whispered.

"He's been stabbed, but fortunately the wound is near the shoulder," Ryan said. "Of course, if we hadn't arrived, he would have bled to death, which is doubtless exactly what Harry expected. We should remove him to an inn where a physician can look after him."

"No." Raveneau's voice was clearer. "I'm going . . . with you. Just need to heal."

Ryan finished cleaning the wound, then bandaged it with strips of linen. He and Lindsay removed André's boots, eased him onto the bunk, and then she sat on the edge, holding her father's hand.

"Papa, you cannot go to sea in this condition!"

Slowly, he opened his slate-gray eyes. "Surgeon—Treasel—will look after me."

"We don't even know if Treasel has remained in Falmouth with the crew," Ryan pointed out.

"Look, then," he advised evenly.

As it turned out, Treasel was among those who were boarding the ship, and after examining the captain, he agreed that the sea voyage would probably do him no harm as long as he stayed in his bunk. The wizened surgeon had served under Raveneau for thirty-five years and assured them that the captain had survived worse

crises than this. There was no time for Ryan to argue.
He left Lindsay to deal with her father and went above
to speed their departure along. This crime against
Raveneau intensified a hundredfold Ryan's determination to overtake Brandreth and Chadwick. He burned
inside with an outraged fury that surpassed any anger
he had ever felt before. Ryan wanted more than justice:
He hungered for revenge.

Lindsay came up behind Ryan on the quarterdeck as
he leaned against the rail. His hair was ruffled lightly in
the salty breeze, but the muscles of his thighs flexed
against his buckskin breeches, betraying Ryan's tension.

"The stars are beautiful tonight," Lindsay remarked,
resting her head against his shoulder.

"Are they? I hadn't noticed. I just keep hoping that if
I stare at the sea long enough, that damned ship will
materialize."

The rage in his voice made her uneasy. "Ryan, I
know how you feel. I'm angry, too. I could kill Harry
myself for what he's done to Papa." Pausing, Lindsay
covered one of his hands that clenched the rail. "However, I am *not* angry with you!"

Ryan's distraction was such that it took a few moments for her meaning to sink in. Then his body relaxed
suddenly as he exhaled and turned to take her in his
arms. "Oh, angel, I'm sorry. You've been through so
much yourself today. Forgive me."

"There's nothing to forgive. I understand." They shared
a bittersweet kiss, then Lindsay basked in the solid
comfort of his embrace for a long moment before she
spoke again. "Papa awoke a little while ago. I think
you'll feel better if you speak to him."

His eyes widened. "Let's go, then." They walked
toward the hatch together, arm in arm, stopping to speak
to Drew at the wheel. "I'm going below for a bit. Can
you manage?"

"Yes, sir, I'm fine." The young man bit his lip, then blurted out, "Why don't you steal a few hours' sleep, Captain? You could use it, I'll wager, and you can trust me to keep to the course you've charted."

"A very wise suggestion!" Lindsay exclaimed before Ryan could answer. "Come along, Captain Coleraine."

Below decks, Raveneau's cabin was bathed in the lantern's glow and he lay against snowy pillows on his wide bunk. Ryan went straight to his side, drew up a chair, and took André's hand.

"Are you feeling better, sir?"

"Some." He smiled weakly. "Treasel insists on giving me laudanum for the pain, but I wanted to speak to you beforehand. Might not wake again until we're in Galway Bay!" His eyes twinkled first at Ryan, then moved to Lindsay, who was perched near his feet. "Want to thank you both. So grateful."

Tears shone in Ryan's eyes as he nodded. "I'm going to take care of this for you, sir."

Raveneau studied the younger man for a moment, then murmured, "Harry's not worthy of your vengeance. Don't lower yourself."

"I don't want you to tire yourself, sir, but can you tell us briefly how all this came about? When I left the house, you were asleep, and I would have thought that Harry and Chadwick would have been far away from London by that time."

"They traveled separately. Harry waited until the house was dark. Came for my charts of ports. I interrupted him, said they were here, on ship. He couldn't leave me there to sound the alarm, so he brought me to show him where they were. I didn't give him trouble because I hoped to get Chadwick, too."

Lindsay fetched a cup of water and Ryan helped André sip it. "Can you go on, Papa?"

He nodded. "Harry meant to get the charts and sell them to the spy without telling Chadwick. Greedy fool. Chadwick never knew I was with Harry. We came on board, then down here. I pretended to show him where the charts were hidden, but meant to hit him over the head with a whiskey bottle. Turned, saw me."

"And he stabbed you?" Lindsay cried in outrage. "And left you to die? Vile, contemptible coward!"

Raveneau lifted his brows with a suggestion of amusement. "Very true. Last thing I remember before Ryan's voice was seeing Harry ripping things apart in search of the charts."

"Did he get them?" Ryan asked tersely.

"Look in sea chest. They were at the bottom."

"Never mind," Lindsay said sadly. "I cleaned the cabin while you slept, Papa, and put everything back in your sea chest. It was empty when we arrived. The charts are gone."

André's eyes met Ryan's. "Have to get them. I've made notations on them that could prove dangerously useful to that damned Cockburn and his British navy."

"We'll retrieve them, sir, I can promise you that. And I mean to make Brandreth—and Chadwick—pay for the suffering they've caused."

"How far ahead?" Raveneau asked, wincing with pain.

"Three, maybe four hours, I'd guess." A muscle moved in Ryan's jaw. "Not far enough, that much is certain!"

Lindsay had gone to fetch Treasel, who now appeared with a stoppered bottle of laudanum. Raveneau sighed in surrender, then glanced at his daughter. "You need sleep, too. Both of you. Good night."

The next day passed swiftly for Lindsay as she alternately sat with her father, whose laudanum-induced sleep continued, and dashed up on deck to talk to Ryan and take in the shipboard activity. To her surprise, she found that she felt invigorated by the ocean and the pervasive atmosphere of adventure. The sensation of *La Mouette* slicing through the sapphire waves as she was pushed onward by the wind that filled her sails excited Lindsay as it never had before.

Ryan continued to brood, though he was tender with her. In deference to her father's presence, they had slept apart in their former cabins and Lindsay missed him sorely. She missed the warm shelter of his arms during the night, but now that they were awake, she missed his laughter. Her father had been right when he spoke of vengeance. It was doing unpleasant things to Ryan.

At dusk, she took bread, cheese, and wine up to the quarterdeck, and they leaned against the carved rail together, eating and drinking slowly. When the food was gone, Ryan poured the rest of the wine into their mugs and gazed pensively out over the violet-tinted ocean.

"Would you care to see Ireland?" he asked quietly after several minutes of silence.

"Yes, of course!"

He picked up the brass telescope and handed it to Lindsay, who squinted next to the eyepiece, then cried, "I see land!"

"That's Toe Head. We're nearing the southwestern corner of Ireland, but there's still a long way to go. Galway is a good distance up the western coast."

"I've always wanted to see Ireland." She looked at him with shining eyes.

"This visit doesn't promise to be very enjoyable, angel."

Lindsay studied his rakish profile in the twilight, realizing that Ryan's mood had altered. He seemed almost melancholy now. Softly, she ventured, "You miss it, don't you?"

He closed his eyes and sighed. "I suppose I do. It's been so long that I haven't allowed myself to think much about Ireland. I supposed that it was behind me and that I had a new home in America, but—"

"We can never leave the past completely behind," Lindsay finished for him. "Ireland is in your blood, Ryan! I wish that you would tell me about it."

"Ireland?" He tasted the word rather tentatively. "Yes, I should tell you. It's time you knew." His eyes were far

away as he continued, "Ireland's rather a magical place.
I'm from an area known as Connemara, which stretches
across west Galway to the rocky edge of the Atlantic.
There, where the sea is wild, I lived until I went away to
Oxford." Ryan paused, remembering. "Connemara is
truly an ancient Gaelic kingdom—bogland, mountains,
and dramatic views of the ocean. It seems timeless, and
rather haunted and mystical. English has spread over
most of the rest of Ireland, but in Connemara everyone
still speaks Erse, the mother tongue, and the old ways
live on."

"It sounds wonderful!" Lindsay breathed.

"Ireland is different from America, or even England.
It's rugged and intense. You've never seen greener hill-
sides or bluer skies or steeper cliffs overlooking a more
violent ocean. It's beautiful, but not in a relaxing way.
Ireland makes one feel *alive*." He gave her a sidelong,
ironic smile. "Not a breeding ground for gentlemen, I
fear."

"Ryan, you *do* miss it! Why did you ever leave?"

"Part of me misses home, but it's always with me—in
my blood. I'm Irish, but I also have a restless streak. As
a child, I used to stand on those staggering cliffs above
the ocean and dream of going away to see the rest of the
world. I was never fit for a life in the same town, seeing
the same people all one's life. There's a great deal to be
said for settling in and being content with one's lot, but
it's simply not in my nature." Sensing the sudden whirl
of Lindsay's thoughts, Ryan laughed softly and slipped
an arm around her waist. "I think my wandering days
are over, angel. Right now, that's the least of our worries. There's something else I need to tell you now that
you've drawn me out this far."

"I'm glad. Remember our promise to confide in one
another?" When he looked down at her with concern in
his blue eyes, Lindsay knew a twinge of alarm. "Ryan,
whatever it is, I'll understand!"

"I hardly know where to begin." He glanced heavenward. "You know that I have always regarded my early years as part of a different life, one that I left behind when I sailed for America . . ."

"Ryan, if you're ashamed of your origins—"

"That's not quite it. I wasn't raised in a bog gnawing on raw potatoes. The truth is . . . my parents were the Marquess and Marchioness of Clifden." Seeing Lindsay's expression of astonishment, he hastened to add, "That doesn't mean quite so much as it might in England. Titled Irishmen are thought of as the bastards of British peerage, but it is a far cry from poverty. The first marquess, Hugh Coleraine, was given his title by Elizabeth. What he did to earn it remains a subject for debate, but it was whispered that his contribution was amorous rather than heroic. He built a rather modest castle overlooking the sea to the west and the village of Clifden to the south, and it was there that I was born. We had a large home in Galway, too, where my mother took me for months out of each year."

"Ryan, were you the only child?" Lindsay asked dazedly.

"No. I have a brother, Blake, fifteen years my elder. He had been groomed to become the marquess long before my birth, and when my father died when I was eight, the title passed to Blake. All I remember about my father is the sound of his raised voice. He and Mother argued, it seemed to me, all the time. After he died, we spent most of our time in the city of Galway. Blake loved Clifden Castle, loved Connemara, and was perfectly content to settle down there to raise his family. I, on the other hand, never quite felt welcome after Father's death and left for Oxford as soon as I was admitted. Mother died not long after, while I was in my first year at Christ Church." Ryan swallowed the rest of his wine, thinking back. "Blake was always very kind to me, the model brother, yet I never felt easy in his household. There were always undercurrents that I couldn't quite explain. . . ."

"Oh, Ryan!"

"For God's sake, don't pity me, Lindsay! My life has definitely turned out for the best. But, there's a part of me that wishes I'd been in Galway when Mother fell ill. No doubt she would have enlightened me and died happy. As it was . . ."

"What do you mean, enlightened you?"

"Hester told me the other night that Blake was illegitimate—and that he has known it since my father's last illness. Of course, by then, he'd married and begun a family believing that he'd inherit—and to be honest, he was better suited to the title and its responsibilities than I. I don't really blame him, and I think that fate was kind to me. What does bother me, however, was Hester's revelation that Blake conspired with Francis to force me to leave Britain. It was he who urged me not to see Hester again, to leave for America, and who gave me money, all because the Earl of Chadwick was blackmailing him, threatening to tell me that I was the legitimate heir to the title if I remained in England."

Lindsay's head was spinning as she tried to take it all in. "Ryan, are you saying that your brother is the Irishman who owes Chadwick a favor? Is he the person Harry and Francis intend to seek refuge with?"

"You're quite astute!" he teased gently. "*Now* do you understand why I wanted you to stay put in London? The explanation alone is too much trouble!"

She wasn't listening. "But what if we don't overtake them at sea and you are forced to follow them to Clifden Castle? That would mean that you would be confronted by all three of them: Chadwick, Harry, and your own brother! This sounds dreadfully dangerous! Wouldn't it be convenient for Blake if you were accidentally killed?"

Ryan kissed Lindsay's flushed cheeks and then her lips. His mood was much improved now that he had shared all of his secrets with her. He felt lighter. "If Blake were that sort, he'd have had me murdered by a footpad a decade ago. In truth, he always struck me as being a good man, if a trifle weak. And Hester told me one more thing that should reassure you. It seems that Blake is very ill and wants to make amends. His wife has left him and gone to France and his children have apparently grown into horrible adults. Hester believes that as Blake confronts the prospect of the title passing to his elder son, he's been having an attack of guilt. Perhaps he wants justice done. Perhaps he would take my side against Brandreth and Chadwick.''

Lindsay leaned against his chest, thinking. At length, she said, "It seems to me that it might be a good thing for you to visit Clifden Castle and talk to Blake even if we don't have to go there in search of Harry and Chadwick.''

To her amazement, Ryan kissed her golden-rose curls, smiled, and replied, "It seems to me that you may be right, sweetheart.'' Meanwhile, his hands strayed over the curves of her hips, drawing her against him. "Unburdening oneself is exhausting, I've discovered. I don't think I can speak another word for the moment.''

Lindsay wore an expression of mock perplexity. "What shall we do, then?''

Ryan put a finger over her mouth, then backed her up against the rail. Smiling roguishly, he arched a black brow, then bent to cover Lindsay's lips with his own.

CHAPTER
35

July 1, 1814

Eyes burning with fatigue, Ryan traversed the dimly lit gangway. It was three o'clock in the morning, and although he hated to give in to sleep, he knew he would need a nap in order to be alert when dawn broke. If the winds remained favorable, *La Mouette* would reach Galway by midday.

He paused in the doorway of Raveneau's cabin, rubbing his unshaven jaw. Silvery moonlight splashed through the transom, dappling André's slumbering form and that of his daughter, who sprawled in the chair beside his bunk. Lindsay's legs, clad in baggy breeches, were apart, her stockinged feet pointing upward. Her fingers were curled around the tails of her voluminous untucked shirt, while her head dropped toward one shoulder, curls tumbling over her cheek.

Ryan approached silently and paused, noting the shadowed sweep of Lindsay's lashes and the soft sound of her breathing through parted lips. He bent and tenderly gathered her into his arms. She curled against his chest, murmuring, as Ryan carried her into his cabin and laid her on the bunk. In the darkness, he drew off her clothing, then his own, and pulled the covers up over them both.

Still sleeping, Lindsay lifted her face, searching. Ryan cradled her in his arms, trying to ignore the soft, inviting warmth of her body, and kissed her gently.

"Mmm," she purred. Her lush mouth moved against his, then opened instinctively.

Ryan groaned, instantly and fully aroused. His senses drank in the taste of her, the scent of her hair, the smoothness of her neck as he kissed his way downward. Her breasts, warm with sleep, seemed more beautiful than ever to him. Ryan touched one wonderingly with parted lips, tracing the perfect swell until he reached the dusky, petal-soft nipple. Slowly, he circled it with his tongue, then took it into his mouth and suckled gently for long, relaxed minutes.

The cabin was completely dark. Lindsay and Ryan seemed to be floating, beyond reality, as her legs opened and his lean, tapering fingers slipped between them. His mouth moved lower, tasting and exploring until Lindsay's fingers tangled in Ryan's hair, drawing him up to drown in her kiss.

Their coupling was exquisitely slow, each of them savoring the keen, sweet jolts of pleasure. Eventually, they slept, arms and legs entwined.

"Captain Coleraine?" Drew pushed open the door to Ryan's cabin, took one startled look, then backed up and eased the door closed. For an instant, he wondered if he'd been seeing things. Before he could think what to do next, the door reopened and Coleraine's face appeared.

"What the devil is it, Drew?"

"Uh—uh—"

"If that's all, I have more important matters to attend to."

"No, wait!" Drew wondered if his face was as red as

it felt. "I think we've sighted the *Lady Hester*. She's on the horizon."

Coleraine's eyes sharpened. "What time is it?"

"Six o'clock, sir."

"Good God!"

The door slammed shut in Drew's face.

Ryan stared down at Lindsay, whose shapely limbs were twisted in the sheets while her apricot-hued curls splashed across his pillow. Willing himself to resist, he pulled on buff-colored breeches, stockings, boots, and a clean white shirt, then ran a hand through his crisp raven hair. Finally, armored against her potent charms, he leaned over and patted the curve of Lindsay's backside.

"Wake up, sweetheart."

Drowsily, she attempted to sit up. Ryan had gone over to the table to splash water on his face and to clean his teeth. Staring at him, Lindsay tried to get her bearings.

"Oh, my," she murmured at length, blushing. "I thought that was just a naughty dream."

"Don't you mean delicious?" He flashed a grin, then returned to drop a kiss on her brow. "We've been truant long enough. Drew thinks that Chadwick's ship is on the horizon. If that's true, she's less than ten miles away and the chase begins in earnest. You'd better get dressed quickly, my sweet, and take the news to your father."

Suddenly Lindsay was wide awake, inhaling air charged with excitement and danger. When Ryan tossed her clothes to her on his way to the door, she caught them neatly. Rested and well loved, Lindsay was ready to face the enemy!

As the sun rose higher in the cloudless, azure sky, *La Mouette* tenaciously shortened the distance between herself and her prey. Coleraine paced the quarterdeck like a caged panther, plotting his strategy with Drew and Hornbeam, the boatswain. Lindsay ran back and forth with bulletins for her father and offerings of food for Ryan.

Ryan's biggest concern was the relatively small crew on board. Too many men hadn't been at the White Dog when Higgins went to fetch them. When Lindsay heard Ryan worrying aloud about this handicap, she questioned her father about it.

Raveneau appeared to be much better. He sat up in bed, drinking ale and eating the muffins Lindsay pressed on him, eager for each bit of news. When his daughter mentioned Ryan's apparent concern, André waved her off.

"Don't be fooled by that. In here"—he pointed to his midsection—"Coleraine knows better."

"But, Papa, we're close enough that I can see the *Lady Hester* clearly through the telescope, and she looks bigger than *La Mouette*!"

"Slower," he amended firmly, brushing crumbs from his bandaged chest. "And I don't care if Chadwick has twice the crew, he's not a privateer captain. Ryan is expert at tactics that Chadwick's never dreamed of."

When Lindsay repeated this to Ryan, he laughed shortly and squeezed her arm. "I appreciate your father's vote of confidence. And he's right. Chadwick and Harry couldn't begin to prepare for me." He didn't mention that his only real worry was a proper boarding party. If it came to a man-to-man confrontation and they were greatly outnumbered, the outcome was less predictable. Narrowing his eyes at the ship that was a scant mile away, Coleraine added distractedly, "I think it's time that you went below—to stay. And get a pistol. I'll see if I can spare a man to stay with you and André."

Lindsay realized that he wouldn't appreciate an argument at that moment. She did go below, but remained on the ladder, peeking out of the hatch from time to time.

It was shortly after ten o'clock when Ryan told Drew that he was ready to close in for the kill. They were drawing near, sailing to the weather side of the *Lady Hester*, and Ryan was careful to keep *La Mouette*'s keel at an efficient angle to the wind. The gunner's mates were loading the cannon, while the gun watch armed themselves with cutlasses and pikes for boarding. Aloft, topmen were climbing the ratlines to oversee the action among the sails.

His jaw clenched and dark blue eyes narrowed, Ryan lifted the telescope. He scanned the familiar, craggy Irish shore, recognizing the Cliffs of Moher. They were just south of Galway Bay. Turning the glass, Coleraine then focused on the *Lady Hester* and smiled grimly at the sight of Harry Brandreth running back and forth on the quarterdeck in a state of obvious panic. "If he recognizes *La Mouette*, he must think it's Raveneau's ghost coming for revenge," Ryan murmured to Drew.

"That's not far off the truth, is it, sir?"

He didn't hear the first mate. "They're tacking to windward. Good! How fortunate that our fine Lord Chadwick hasn't any practice in sea warfare."

La Mouette, her speed being better to the weather side, was able to make a tight arc that brought her within shooting distance of the other ship's stern. Cannon volleys commenced from the *Lady Hester*, and Ryan gave the order to reply in kind.

Then, like a cat with a mouse, Ryan came abreast of his prey, then veered away as if yielding to her fire. Overconfident now, Chadwick gave the order to pursue and his ship veered toward *La Mouette*.

Laughing, Coleraine dodged a lit, cast-iron hand grenade thrown from the *Lady Hester*'s maintop. "That's right, you fools! Teach us a lesson!" he shouted.

Drew stared in joyous awe, awaiting the moment when his captain turned and said, "Tell Hornbeam to stand by to trim sails. The men in the maintop should be lighting the stinkpots." Ryan then signaled to the first gun watch, adding a wink for encouragement.

From then on, a well-organized sort of chaos prevailed. At the moment the *Lady Hester* veered into the position Coleraine was waiting for, he put his helm hard alee and the sails were quickly trimmed. In the next instant, grappling irons were thrown to the captured ship's lower yardarms, and the first gun watch stormed over the sides.

Drawing his sword, Ryan prepared to follow when he glimpsed André Raveneau leaning against the mainmast. The older man saluted, grinning, and called, "Well done, Captain! Now finish your work—but remember to save your vengeance for another day."

Coleraine felt a stab of raw emotion, but there was no time to indulge it. As he vaulted onto the *Lady Hester*'s main deck, dodging rifle fire, Lindsay peeked above the hatch. Terror for Ryan made her stomach churn. She longed to run after him and pull him to safety, but she could not. Her only alternative was prayer.

"Papa, come below before your wound opens or you're shot!" To her relief, he obeyed her, seeming to sense that he could do more good at his daughter's side.

Meanwhile, thanks to the flaming stinkpots thrown by Ryan's topmen, several fires had broken out on the *Lady Hester*'s battered decks. Chadwick's crew, untrained for battle, scattered in an effort to put out the flames or to repel Coleraine's boarding party. After more than a dozen bodies had fallen on the decks, the panic-stricken Chadwick surrendered.

He came down from the quarterdeck to face Ryan. Grimy with sweat and gunpowder, the Earl of Chadwick looked puny and frightened as he turned over his sword. Harry stood behind him, supremely incongruous in these surroundings. His golden curls were matted, his cravat untied, and his polished Hessians scarred. Fear, and dawning confusion, shone in Harry's eyes.

Ryan glanced at him and exclaimed, "Why, Harry, how fortuitous! I've been looking everywhere for you. Father will be so pleased. He's been worried sick about you!"

"You've beaten us, young Raveneau," Chadwick was muttering. "I don't know how you knew where to find us, how you knew your way along this treacherous coastline, or how you won this battle, but you did."

Ryan feigned solemnity. "One of life's great mysteries, hmm?" Glancing over to two solidly built gunners, he said, "For some reason, I don't trust these two. Stay close to them while Drew gets some handcuffs."

Harry stared at his erstwhile brother-in-law, noting the hard edge to his voice, the masculine way he stood and moved, the simplicity of his garb, and the keen intelligence in his eyes. "You don't act like the same Nathan I knew in London!" he accused.

Francis was leaning forward, peering more closely at Ryan. "If I didn't know better, I'd swear—"

Laughing in a way that sent chills down Harry's spine, Coleraine said, "You two would seem to be at odds on this score. Harry doesn't recognize me and Francis does!"

"It can't be," Chadwick muttered. "Coleraine?"

"Oh, yes, it can," he shot back caustically. "And it is. Just ask your wife, Francis. You thought you'd gotten rid of me for good ten years ago, didn't you? I'm afraid that you made your own luck today, my lord, and all of it bad."

"You mean you're not Raveneau?" Harry demanded. "Coleraine?" He nudged Francis. "Isn't that the name of that marquess you told me about near here?"

Chadwick paled as he considered his current situation. "Look, Coleraine, why don't you just kill me and have done with it?"

"I'm not that charitable."

Drew had arrived with the handcuffs, but when Ryan reached for them, Francis struck out at the gunner at his side and made a mad dash for the *Lady Hester*'s larboard rail. Ryan was just inches from gripping the earl's sleeve when Chadwick hurtled over the side. He struck his head against *La Mouette*'s hull on the way down and appeared to be already dead when he hit the ocean far below.

Ryan stared down at the body that floated for a few moments before being swallowed by the swelling waves. He turned back just in time to see Harry Brandreth grab a sword from the deck.

"Come on, Raveneau or Coleraine or whatever your name is! Why don't we just settle this score right now!" Without waiting for a reply, he charged with the sword.

Incredulous, Ryan drew his own sword and fended Harry off. He was tired, angry, and out of patience. Blades struck and flashed in the sunlight as Ryan fought with aggressive expertise. In minutes, after an ill-timed lunge by Harry, Ryan had knocked the weapon from his hand and pinned him to the deck with the sharpened point of his sword.

"I've been waiting to do this ever since I found André Raveneau alone, wounded, and bleeding in his cabin," he uttered in deadly tones. "You deserve to die—slowly—for what you did to him, and to Mouette, and to the country I love."

Harry was gasping for breath, sweat pouring down his face, as Coleraine increased the sword's pressure. Then, abruptly, it was removed. Ryan stepped away, while the two gunners rushed forward to handcuff the prisoner.

As they hauled him to his feet and led him off, Harry searched Coleraine's face, whimpering, "I don't know why you spared me, but—"

"Don't flatter yourself," Ryan broke in with cold contempt. "I wouldn't dirty my sword with your blood. Now get out of my sight."

When he stepped back onto *La Mouette*'s gun deck, Lindsay rushed forward and threw her arms around his neck, sobbing. Ryan held her securely and closed his eyes. Exhausted, drained, and relieved, he silently gave thanks to God that they had all emerged unscathed.

"Oh, Ryan"—Lindsay gulped through her tears—"I was so afraid that I would lose you!"

Over her head, he gave André Raveneau a tired wink. "I don't think that's a possibility, angel. I'm yours for life."

CHAPTER
36

July 2, 1814

T HE NEXT DAY AT NOON, RYAN AND LINDSAY RODE through the village of Clifden, not taking the time to stop. Gray stone cottages with thatched roofs lined the winding cobbled street that rose over the brow of a hill and seemed to disappear into the distant Atlantic Ocean. Lindsay was intrigued by the small Catholic church and its graveyard studded with ringed, ornamented high crosses. When she asked about them, Ryan told her that many were more than a thousand years old.

Men clustered outside the public house, chatting as if they had nothing better to do. Children and dogs scrambled over the cobbled street for a ball while their mothers gossiped. Everyone seemed to be dressed in shades of gray, except for an occasional bright blouse or waistcoat. The villagers almost blended with the stone houses and the stone street, Lindsay thought, but for their animated faces and voices. She only wished she could understand what they were saying! It fascinated her to think that this village was a part of Ryan.

Turning north, they followed the jagged cliffs that bordered the sea. The wind was invigorating and overhead seagulls cried and dipped against a vividly blue sky. Ryan was in his element. The sight of waves crashing against golden beaches and the choppy, sapphire Atlantic stretching to an impossibly distant horizon filled him with both nostalgia and longing. Somewhere inside of Ryan was the boy who had stood on these very cliffs and dreamed of other worlds. He'd had a great deal right here that had gone largely unappreciated, and now that he was a man and had seen so much, Ryan intended to concentrate on learning to enjoy all that he'd gained, not the least of which was the love of an extraordinary woman.

At length, Lindsay called, "I must say I'm surprised that you agreed to let me come with you without an argument!"

He laughed, his shining black hair blowing in the wind. "I may need you! If Blake comes at me with a weapon, I'm counting on you to rush to my defense. I'm far too fatigued after yesterday's exertions to fight again today!"

As they approached the crest of a hill, Ryan reined in his horse, knowing that Clifden Castle would come into view on the other side. How many times during childhood had he walked home this way with Donal, his wolfhound, trotting by his side? Now he paused at the top of the hill, gazing down at the gray stone castle that had been ravaged by the elements for more than two hundred years but remained unbeaten. Hugh Coleraine had built Clifden Castle in 1572, after the style of the older castles he'd admired in England. It was dramatic and imposing, with its crenellated towers and walls, yet was modified enough in size to possess some of the charm of a real home.

"Oh, my." Lindsay sighed admiringly. She looked at Ryan's thoughtful profile and left him to his reverie.

They rode in silence down the grassy hillside and into the courtyard of the castle. When Ryan lifted Lindsay down from her horse, she gazed at him with gray eyes filled with emotion.

"It will be all right, darling. I'm sure of it."

He managed a smile. "Well, we'll see."

The iron door knocker fell with an echoing thud, and they waited until at last the door was opened by a butler Ryan didn't recognize.

"We're here to see his lordship," he said.

"Lord Clifden is not taking visitors. He's very ill," the old man intoned.

"I'm afraid he'll have to see us. I am his brother, and I've come a long way."

"Well, I'll inquire. What names shall I give?"

Ryan told him, and they waited in the courtyard for several minutes while the butler disappeared on his errand. Ryan was too tense to talk. He paced back and forth, rubbing the back of his neck with one lean hand, while Lindsay watched him helplessly.

"His lordship will see you," came the voice from within.

They followed the butler through a labyrinth of vaulted stone corridors. The castle was eerily silent, apparently empty except for this solitary servant and his master. Finally, upon reaching a tower door, the butler knocked once and opened it, announcing, "Captain Ryan Coleraine and Miss Lindsay Raveneau, my lord."

They entered a tower room that appeared to be a library, its curved walls lined with rows of dusty books. Rays of sunlight pierced narrow windows, falling on a thin man who lay on a couch in the center of the room. He was covered by two quilts in spite of the warm weather, and the face he turned to Ryan and Lindsay was pinched with sadness.

Ryan didn't move or speak, but his keen gaze searched for the truth in his brother's eyes.

Blake extended a frail-looking hand. "My brother," he whispered.

Tears filled Lindsay's eyes as she watched Ryan walk

to the side of the couch, then bend to embrace Blake.
The older man began to weep.

"I have to tell you—" He choked.

"I know," Ryan murmured. "Hester has told me all of
it. And Chadwick is dead. He won't bother you again."

"I can't ask for your forgiveness. I've been repenting
my sins for years, but I'll never find peace in this lifetime. If I'd known how to find you, I'd have put it right
long ago."

"Blake, how ill are you?"

"I'm dying." He paused to cough. "I don't know how
to tell you how sorry I am for all I've done to you.
When I first learned the truth of my parentage, I couldn't
bear the thought of giving up my home, of doing that to
my family—"

"Never mind," Ryan said gently, patting his hand.
"It doesn't matter. I forgive you, if that's what you
want to hear. More than that, I'm glad that events
transpired as they did. You were much better suited to
being a lord of the land here in Ireland than I would
have been, especially at that age. I was always restless,
you know that, Blake, and I would have rebelled if you
had suddenly forced the title on me. You did the right thing
and I not only don't blame you, I'm grateful to you."

Blake Coleraine, Marquess of Clifden, gazed through
his tears at the strong dark hand that clasped his own
thin fingers. The last time he'd seen Ryan, he'd been
only a few years older than his brother was now; vital,
handsome, and determined. Yet deception and an unhappy marriage had taken their toll. As the years wore
on and his wife and children spent more and more time
abroad, he'd shut himself up in this study for days at a
time, drinking from breakfast until bedtime. Now, seeing
the spark of love in Ryan's eyes, he felt a pang for the
life he'd thrown away out of guilt and despair.

"I wish I had talked to you then, brother. If I'd
known how you felt—"

"It's all right. We can't reshape the past, only come
to terms with it."

"I can, however, set the future to rights!" Blake bent his gray head for a long minute of coughing, then resumed. "You should have been marquess since the instant of Father's death. That injustice must be corrected."

Ryan patted his hand again. "Look, Blake, I appreciate your sincerity, but why don't we leave matters as they stand for the time being? Let's just agree to right them if there's a question of your son inheriting the title."

"We may not have long to wait."

"I don't want to hear any more of that. What exactly is your ailment?"

Blake shrugged hopelessly. "It's difficult to say. This and that . . ."

"It sounds to me like an acute case of a broken will," Ryan said with a smile. "I think that's curable!" He looked over his shoulder at Lindsay, who nodded in agreement. "And I know just the place to start. We'll give you a healthy dose of Lindsay Raveneau. She can bring anyone out of the doldrums!"

"Mmph! The food here is excellent! Can't think why I didn't sample it sooner!" Chewing the last bite of salmon, Blake looked around the crowded taproom of Clifden's public house and beamed. He felt transformed. The day's excitement, coupled with this excursion out into the real world, had infused him with the kind of energy he hadn't experienced for a long, long time.

"Probably because you thought a marquess shouldn't mingle with the masses," Ryan suggested gently. "Let's toast to the abolishment of that myth!"

All three of them raised their tankards, then drank thirstily. Lindsay glowed as she watched the two brothers laugh together and noticed the way Blake turned back to finish his boiled cabbage and bacon, then took another piece of soda bread. In spite of his white hair and thin, craggy face, his cheeks were pink with happiness.

"Where did you find this little charmer?" Blake demanded, winking at Lindsay. "What a tonic she's been for me!"

Ryan laughed. "Yes, like all effective medicine, Lindsay's an acquired taste! And we met in Connecticut."

"I thought your brother was the rudest, most conceited man I'd ever laid eyes on!" she added.

Blake looked at the vibrant pair across from him and smiled rather wistfully. "I can't tell you how pleased I am for both of you. I suppose you'll be married the moment you return to London?"

"Just as soon as we can make the proper arrangements." Lindsay nodded. "I'd love to be married at Oxford."

Ryan's brows went up. "You *would*?"

She nodded dreamily. "Indeed. Have you ever been to Oxford, Blake?"

"I'm afraid not. I was educated at Trinity College in Dublin. I've scarcely left Ireland my whole life."

"Then you must come back with us! My parents have plenty of room, so you mustn't worry about that. There's so much to see in London, and, of course, Oxford is practically my favorite place in all the world! I'm hoping to persuade Ryan to settle down and teach there one day."

"Listen, my darling, I think you're getting a bit ahead of yourself—"

"My brother is right." Suddenly, Blake began to cough again. "I'm far too ill to leave here. Why, coming out tonight has been more than I've done in years!"

"Don't say that." Lindsay leaned forward and took his hand, her gray eyes huge and intent. "You must come with us, Blake. You've been feeling so much better during these past hours, and I'm convinced your health will improve with each day you spend in the fresh air among people. We'll go by carriage to Galway, and then you can relax in the sunshine during the voyage to England." She looked imploringly at Ryan. "Isn't that so, darling? Blake and Papa can regain their strength together!''

Perceiving the gleam of hopeful excitement in his brother's eyes, Coleraine made up his mind. ''As usual, Lindsay is right. Why don't you return to London with us? We'll pace ourselves on the road so that you don't become overtired.''

''Well, I suppose that it's possible . . .'' Blake allowed, sipping his ale.

''Anything's possible!'' Lindsay proclaimed. ''We'll be in London before you know it! I only wish we had a balloon here so that we could fly back. I've always dreamed of riding in a balloon—''

Laughing, Ryan put his hand over her mouth. ''Angel, I think that's enough dreaming for tonight. We'll all need a good night's sleep if we're to return to the ship tomorrow morning.''

''Pay no attention to him,'' Blake told Lindsay in a stage whisper. ''Keep dreaming. You're the kind of person who will turn them all into reality one way or another!''

She went over to hug him. ''I want to do the same for you, too, Blake.''

''It's settled, then? You're coming?'' Ryan's tone said that he assumed so. ''Good. Now I think we should return to the castle. I hope you don't mind houseguests!''

''No, no, of course not!'' As the two younger people helped him to his feet, Blake's expression was one of wonderment. ''My God, I'm embarking on an adventure—and just this morning all I had to look forward to was dying!''

Lindsay kissed his sunken cheek, her eyes wet with tears. ''From now on, I'm going to see to it that you're far too busy to even *think* that word, let alone say it!''

''Good God, but you're a cheeky little minx.'' Ryan laughed as he joined her in bed. ''Whatever happened to that toffee-nosed bluestocking who taught school in Pettipauge?''

"All *sorts* of things have happened to her." Snuggling against his hard-muscled body, Lindsay gazed up at Ryan's starlit profile, then turned to look out the window. "She met an arrogant, crude, uncivilized Irishman who eventually convinced her that there was more to life than leading an ordered, refined existence."

"*Much* more," he agreed, slipping one hand under the covers to caress the elegant curves of her breasts and belly.

"Look! There's the Big Dipper!" Lindsay pointed out the window at the glittering night sky. "Oh, Ryan, do you remember that last night on board *La Mouette* when you told me that in Ireland the Big Dipper is called the Plough? That was the first time we treated one another with tenderness."

"I suppose I should have known, certainly by that night, that we were fated," he mused, inhaling the fragrance of her hair. "I used to tell myself that just the opposite was true, that the stars were against us, but I couldn't have been more wrong."

Lindsay turned in his arms and caressed the tapering outline of Ryan's back. "I love you so."

"Ah, angel, I would gather the stars from the sky and spread them at your feet if it were possible."

Her heart began to race as he kissed his way slowly from her ear to the hollow at the base of her throat. "No, you must leave them in the heavens to light the way for the lovers who follow us. . . ."

Ryan's answer was a long, warm, heartfelt kiss that built to a fiery crescendo. When at last he spoke, gasping from her equally passionate response, it was to murmur, "Oxford, hmm?"

EPILOGUE

Oxford, England
July 21, 1814

ON THE AFTERNOON OF RYAN AND LINDSAY'S WEDDING, Christ Church meadow and the golden domes and spires of Oxford were awash with evanescent sunshine. Dean Jackson had succumbed to Lindsay's pleas and arranged for them to be married in the flower-drenched meadow, surrounded only by their loved ones and friends.

They stood together now before the minister, reciting their vows in the shade of misty-green pollard willows near the River Cherwell. Lindsay was an exquisite vision in a simple high-waisted gown of gossamer white muslin. Her strawberry-blond curls tumbled free over her shoulders, adorned only with a garland of buttercups, poppies, white campion, and violets. Against her bare throat sparkled diamonds in the shape of a small star; it was Ryan's wedding gift to her.

Standing in the front row of guests, Devon held fast to André's hand, her eyes swimming with tears as she listened to her daughter promise to love, honor, and obey. Ryan's eyebrow cocked slightly when he heard that last word, and the humor wasn't lost on his new mother-in-law either. How splendid he looked! she thought. How reminiscent the two of them were of her and André thirty-five years ago. . . .

Blake Coleraine, Marquess of Clifden, stepped forward to present the ring to his brother. It was one more sign of the transformation their lives had undergone since Ryan and Lindsay had returned from Ireland. Blake was with them now, still weak and ill but happy, and Ryan Coleraine was at last able to be himself. Gone were the quizzing glass, snuffbox, and his foppish demeanor. He was impeccably handsome on his wedding day, clad in snug champagne-colored trousers, a dark blue frock coat that nearly matched his eyes, an ivory silk waistcoat, a snowy shirt, and a skillfully tied cravat. His hair gleamed like a raven's wing, accentuating the rakish lines of Ryan's profile as he slipped the ring onto Lindsay's slim finger, then bent to kiss her. The radiant bride twined her arms about his broad shoulders, stood on tiptoe, and returned his kiss with unabashed rapture.

Then, arm in arm, they turned to greet their guests. The warm informality of the ceremony lent it the air of a true celebration. Silvery tears gleamed in Lindsay's eyes as she embraced her parents, and Ryan followed suit, careful not to press against André's tender shoulder. The one thing that *hadn't* changed was his love for the Raveneaus. He had felt like their son before, and though the charade had ended, reality was better.

"Oh, Mama," Lindsay whispered huskily, "I am so happy!"

"I know you are, darling, and we're happy for you. I'm so glad everything worked out. We were worried sick while you were away, but—"

"Now Ryan can do the worrying," Raveneau interjected wryly, grinning at his son-in-law.

"She's just taken a vow to obey me!" Ryan laughed. "Didn't you hear her?"

"I don't remember saying that," Lindsay teased. "I think you must have dreamed it, dear husband."

"Well, I can promise you one thing, son. You'll never be bored," André assured him. "Her mother continues to surprise me."

Dean Jackson came up then to offer his congratulations and to greet the Raveneaus. Embracing Lindsay, he caught the wink she sent him and smiled. Although the newlyweds planned to return to America when the war ended, Lindsay had confided to him that Ryan was talking about settling down at Oxford when they began to raise a family.

Servants appeared from Christ Church to serve champagne, and toasts were made by Blake, Raveneau, Dean Jackson, and, finally, Dudley Fanshawe, who was there in the company of Lady Emma Thorneycroft.

"I would like to propose a toast to the bride," he announced, smiling rather wistfully at Lindsay. "A most singular female! You're a fortunate man, Coleraine."

"I'm aware of that." Ryan nodded, trying not to smile. It wasn't fair of him to think back to all the times he'd played Fanshawe for a fool; after all, Dudley must have been humiliated himself once he learned the truth of Ryan's identity, and yet he'd had the courage to come to the wedding.

So had Hester. Clad in a simple gown trimmed with black mourning, she stood off to one side with her children. Although Amanda was blessed with raven curls and blue eyes, the effect was lessened by her inheritance of Chadwick's features. Six-year-old George was a replica of Francis in every respect. Only Maryann, at two, showed the promise of her mother's beauty. Mouette had drifted over to speak to Lady Chadwick. Watching them, Ryan felt a pang of sympathy. These women were the victims of their husbands' bad judgment. What would become of them?

"Would you excuse me for a moment?" he murmured

to Lindsay, who was engaged in an animated conversation with Beau Brummell and Lord Byron.

Following his gaze to Mouette and Hester, she nodded and kissed his cheek. Ryan procured two glasses of champagne from a passing steward and brought them over to the ladies.

At close range, he was struck by the melancholy in their eyes. "It was kind of both of you to come," Ryan said as they accepted the glasses and drank. "Lindsay and I both are grateful. And Hester, I must thank you again for the conversation we shared last month. It was very courageous of you."

"Well," she said with a sigh, "I had to do what was right. Mouette and I have seen quite a bit of each other these past weeks, and we agree that it was best that the situation was resolved before it went any further. I'm still numb when I think of Francis . . ."

"I'm sorry, Hester. But I know that you'll go on to build a new life for yourself and your children."

She gave him a sad smile. "At least you stopped Francis and Harry before they were able to turn over those charts."

Nodding, Ryan replied, "The war will be played out fairly, and I suspect that peace will come before long."

Charles and Anthony Brandreth had come to hold their mother's hands and Ryan bent to pat their heads. Harry was in prison for the attempted murder of André Raveneau and would likely be hanged. "Mouette, I am truly your brother now. What plans have you?"

"My marriage is over. The boys and I are going to stay at Grosvenor Square with Mama and Papa, and then we'll return to America with them. Mama tells me it will get easier." She began to weep. "Each time I remember that I explained about Papa's charts to Harry I am overcome with remorse. If Papa had died—"

"You must not blame yourself, Mouette," he said with conviction and embraced her. "You acted innocently and André is well. Who knows? Perhaps if Harry hadn't kidnapped your father, the adventure would have ended less successfully. Now we all must put it behind us and look to the future."

Coleraine kissed her cheek, then turned to meet Hester's emerald eyes. They were crowded with bittersweet emotions, but she blinked back the first threat of tears. "You know, my dear, that if you should need help—"

"I know," she whispered. "And Ryan, I wish you and Lindsay only the best. I mean that sincerely."

He touched golden-brown fingers to her cheek and smiled. Just then a voice spoke from behind him.

"Ryan, everything is ready." It was Blake.

"Where are you taking my sister for her wedding trip?" Mouette inquired.

"Paris—eventually," he replied, looking a trifle bemused. "Lindsay, who once declared that she never wanted to leave Pettipauge, Connecticut, now longs to travel everywhere!" Ryan looked back to find his brother staring at Hester, who had lowered her eyes shyly.

"Blake?" His mouth quirked in amusement. It began to look as if he wouldn't become marquess of Clifden for a very long time, and that was fine with him. "You were saying?"

The older man blinked. "Oh! Well, it's time. They're waiting on the south side of the meadow beyond those oak trees."

Together they walked back to join Lindsay, who was accepting congratulations from Lord Alvaney and several of the patronesses of Almack's. "You didn't have to do this, you know," Ryan murmured.

"Nonsense! I'd move heaven and earth if it would please Lindsay. She's brought me back to life, you know. Both of you have!"

"Well, we mustn't spoil her too outrageously." Coleraine laughed then and added, "Oh, what the hell. She's irresistible."

Joining Lindsay, he indulged himself in a delicious kiss. "How are you, Mrs. Coleraine?"

"Ecstatic!" She beamed at their guests.

Ryan greeted as many people as he was able to, while Mouette brought Hester over to speak to Lindsay; then, he finally whispered to his bride, "It's time for us to go."

"Now? You've been very secretive about this, you know. Where are we going?" Her eyes twinkled with excitement.

"It's a surprise. A present from Blake, as a matter of fact. Come along."

Taking her hand, Ryan led her across Christ Church meadow. Blake Coleraine, the Raveneau family, and the curious wedding guests followed. Through a screen of ancient oaks, Lindsay saw a huge, striped, swelling mass of color covering the grass beyond. It grew mysteriously as they drew nearer until it left the ground and was higher than the trees.

"Goodness . . ." Lindsay breathed in disbelief. "It can't be—but it must! Is that a . . . *balloon*?"

Ryan's eyes met Blake's over her head. "My wife possesses nimble powers of deduction, don't you think?"

The balloon was inside a roped-off area. Pulling Ryan along, Lindsay skirted it and saw that there were men on the other side, inflating the giant bag of silk with casks of hydrogen attached to hosepipes. The balloon was a gorgeous thing, its boat tethered to the ground. As it swelled to its full proportions, bright with vertical pink, white, and yellow stripes, Lindsay saw that they were bisected by a wide white sash that read, "Congratulations to Ryan and Lindsay Coleraine."

Blake put a hand on her shoulder. "I thought you might enjoy beginning your marriage this way. Ryan's learned to fly it and he's chosen a spot for you to land."

Lindsay was speechless as she looked from one man to the other. "We'll come down on the grounds of an estate near Mapledurham on the Berkshire border," Ryan explained. "It's not far and we need only follow the Thames south. Old friends of mine own the estate and are loaning us the house, and their servants, for tonight. Tomorrow we'll set out for Paris.''

"I must be dreaming!" she breathed.

"It's an honor for me to make one of your dreams a reality, my dear," Blake said with feeling. "My brother will have to see to the rest of them."

Lindsay embraced the older man and kissed his cheek. "How glad I am that we found you, Blake!"

"I'll second that, brother." Ryan smiled, shaking his hand.

"You two had better go now," Blake said. The balloon was fully inflated, cresting high above the treetops. The wedding guests stared in awe, then came forward to bid the newlyweds farewell.

Ryan had just lifted Lindsay into the blue-and-white boat and was stepping in himself when a man ran through the trees and called out, "Hey! Lindsay, is that you?" His voice was unmistakably American.

The crowd parted to let him through, and Ryan narrowed his eyes at a somewhat harried but unmistakably handsome young man. Devon and André Raveneau were embracing him, Mouette had begun to cry in apparent joy, and Lindsay was staring as if she didn't believe her eyes.

"Who's *that*?" Ryan demanded. "Not a spurned suitor from Pettipauge, I hope!"

The dark-haired man had turned from the Raveneaus and was walking toward the balloon, beaming. In wonderment, Lindsay exclaimed, "It's Nathan! My brother!"

"Wait, you can't get out, angel." Ryan put an arm around her. "They're ready to loose us from the moorings. Let him come to us."

Nathan Raveneau approached the boat, his blue eyes twinkling, and hugged his sister so hard she gasped, laughing. "Lindsay, what's going on?" he exclaimed. "I went to Grosvenor Square last night, not even knowing all of you were in London, and the Butters regaled me with a tale so incredible I was certain they were pulling my leg! Have you really gotten married? The sister I left in Connecticut last fall wouldn't even bat her eyelashes at a man!''

"Oh, Nathan, it's simply wonderful to see you! So much has happened since you left. This is Captain Ryan Coleraine, my husband!'' She beamed as the two men shook hands.

"It's good to see you again, Ryan," Nathan said with a grin. "Welcome to the family.''

"Thank you, Nathan." He looked down at Lindsay. "Your brother and I are already acquainted, angel, although we were rarely in Pettipauge at the same time.''

"How silly of me. Of course you must know each other. I never thought about it! Nathan, Ryan has been impersonating you these past few weeks. How fortuitous that you didn't appear before today! What would we have done?''

Coleraine smiled at the younger man. "I'm afraid that you may discover that you already have a reputation of sorts in London!''

Leaning forward, Lindsay gave her handsome brother another hug. "Mama and Papa will have to explain it all to you. I'll be back from Paris in a few weeks, but at the moment I'm afraid we must be off!''

"So I see . . .'' Nathan kissed her cheek, then returned to join the rest of his family outside the enclosure.

The balloon was released from its moorings as Ryan expertly operated the cord attached to the valve that controlled their ascent. Fearlessly, Lindsay laughed with delight and waved to the crowd as the balloon rose slowly into the sky.

Soon, their family and friends were dots against the green expanse of Christ Church meadow. The wind was with them as they sailed over the dreaming spires of Oxford and the surrounding countryside, following the River Thames as it wound southward.

Lindsay leaned back against Ryan, loving the feel of his strong arms around her waist. They looked down as they floated over softly rolling countryside dotted with sheep and stone farmhouses and roads winding throughout like golden ribbons.

"This is the happiest moment of my life," Lindsay announced.

Ryan leaned around to kiss her, touching her tongue with his, then drew back to smile and to arch a suggestive eyebrow. "So far, you mean!"

Lindsay's heart swelled as she tasted him on her lips and considered that prospect. "Oh, *my* . . ."

Author's Note

The town of Essex, Connecticut, one of the jewels of New England, was not called Essex until 1854. In 1814, it was still known by its Indian name, Pettipauge (or Potapaug or Patapoug). Today, visitors to Essex will find the village much the same as I have described it in the pages of this book. Although I have moved from Connecticut to California, I still long to return to Essex and spend a long, joyous evening at the Griswold Inn.

Another of my favorite places is the Turf Tavern in Oxford, England. When Ryan and Lindsay visited, it was known as the Spotted Cow. Visitors today can still reach this seven-hundred-year-old pub through a maze of twisting alleyways that seem to lead one back in time.

I hope that all of you enjoy reading *Surrender the Stars* as much as I enjoyed researching and writing it! These days, I'm spending time in San Francisco and the gold towns of California, soaking up the atmosphere in the company of Mark Twain's ghost. Places and times may change but, thankfully, the common theme of a man and a woman growing through love is universal.

All my best,

Cynthia Challed Wright
Sacramento, California

About the Author

Cynthia Wright lives in Sacramento, California, with her thirteen-year-old daughter, Jenna. They share their cheerful home across from the river with a food-oriented cat named Whitney and Eddie, an orange canary who sings while Cynthia works at her computer.

When she is not researching and writing her latest book, set in post-Goldrush California, Cynthia loves to spend time with her friends, both near and far. She enjoys cooking, photography, exploring museums, attending the ballet, and playing in the California sunshine with her daughter and their friends.

Cynthia invites all interested readers to write to her in care of her publisher, Ballantine Books, at 201 E. 50th Street, New York, New York, 10022.

One of the most beloved historical romance writers...
CYNTHIA WRIGHT
...casts her magic spell.